> **"How long are we going to pretend that we don't want to be in bed right now?"**

Ava gave a strangled laugh. "Clearly you don't understand the art of interviewing. It's all about finesse."

Unable to stop himself, Luc traced an index finger along the sharp line of her jaw. "Guess you shouldn't have flirted with a cop then, lady. No such thing as an interview in my line of work."

"No?"

"Nope." He moved in closer, shifting so that his upper body leaned into hers. "We start with interrogations."

"And then?" Her voice was flirty and light, but her eyes were pure heat.

His gaze dropped to his hand, which had found its way to her knee somehow. "Depends. If the cop's skilled at interrogation, things generally progress to handcuffs...and other things. If the cop's unsuccessful..."

Luc broke off and shrugged.

Ava looked at him over the top of her wineglass. "Which one are you? The skilled interrogator or the other?"

"Depends."

"On?"

He leaned in and pressed his lips to her ear. "Whether or not you like handcuffs."

ALSO BY LAUREN LAYNE

The Best Mistake Series
Only with You
Made for You

FRISK ME

LAUREN LAYNE

FOREVER

NEW YORK BOSTON

Copyright © 2015 by Lauren Layne
Excerpt from *Steal Me* copyright © 2015 by Lauren Layne

Forever
Hachette Book Group
1290 Avenue of the Americas
New York, NY 10104

www.HachetteBookGroup.com

Printed in the United States of America

First Edition: July 2015
10 9 8 7 6 5 4 3 2 1

OPM

Forever is an imprint of Grand Central Publishing.
The Forever name and logo are trademarks of Hachette Book Group, Inc.

The Hachette Speakers Bureau provides a wide range of authors for speaking events. To find out more, go to www.hachettespeakersbureau.com or call (866) 376-6591.

The publisher is not responsible for websites (or their content) that are not owned by the publisher.

ATTENTION CORPORATIONS AND ORGANIZATIONS:

Most Hachette Book Group books are available at quantity discounts with bulk purchase for educational, business, or sales promotional use. For information, please call or write:

Special Markets Department, Hachette Book Group
1290 Avenue of the Americas, New York, NY 10104
Telephone: 1-800-222-6747 Fax: 1-800-477-5925

*To the brave women and men of law
enforcement who put their lives on the line
on a daily basis. You're the true heroes.*

*And especially for Detective Larry
DePrimo, whose real-life acts of kindness
inspired the fictional ones of this book.*

ACKNOWLEDGMENTS

First, to the team at Grand Central—this series is absolutely yours as much as it is mine. Thanks for being there every step of the way, from conception to model photo shoots to final comma tweaks. To Lauren Plude, especially, for being the kind of skilled editor who knows exactly what this book needs. Ava and Luc thank you, as do I.

As always, to my agent, Nicole Resciniti, who single-handedly got me "un-stuck" when this book went off the rails right halfway through, and patiently brainstormed how to get it back on track.

For Jessica Lemmon and Kristi Yanta, my constant iMessage companions who were always there to talk me down from a panicked state of "This book will never get done! Ever!" You were right, of course. It got done, and it's extra fabulous thanks to your help in nudging me in the right direction.

For my family, especially my husband, for their unflagging patience when I drop off the face of the earth for days at a time when I get on a roll.

And lastly, a huge shout-out to my fabulous in-laws, Tony and Patty LeDonne, for your insight into the inner workings of an Italian family. From the typical Sunday family dinner to what's cooking on the stove, your input was invaluable. Your support of my career is much appreciated—so grateful to be Italian by marriage!

FRISK ME

CHAPTER ONE

Holy crap! You're like, *that* guy! You're *the* cop!"

Luc Moretti deliberately ignored the high-pitched squeal.

He took a slow sip of his much-needed coffee and threw up a silent prayer that for once, the women would be talking about some other cop.

"Tina, it *is* him! The cop from the YouTube video!"

Shit.

Pray as he might, it was *never* some other officer who was subjected to overenthusiastic hero worship. Not these days, anyway. It was always *Luc* who couldn't do so much as get on the A train without hearing some form of, *hey, aren't you that guy...?*

Yes. Yes he was that fucking guy. Unfortunately.

"Can we get a picture with you?" one of the women asked as they both closed in on him.

"Actually, I—"

Luc's ready protest was interrupted by the deep voice of his partner.

"Ladies, ladies, let's give Officer Moretti some space! The man likes to refresh his makeup before a photo op. Moretti, did you bring that special lip balm you like to use? The one you say makes your lips all rosy?"

Luc's eyes narrowed at his partner as he reached up and scratched his nose with his middle finger.

Both women had already pulled cell phones out of their purses, ready for a shot with New York's latest hero.

Luc shot another *fuck you* glare at his partner, but Sawyer Lopez was already reaching for the girls' phones, gesturing his hands in an "all-together-now" motion.

Two curvy blondes flanked Luc on either side. Their too-sweet perfume was ruining his caffeine buzz, but he smiled for the picture anyway. The grin was habit, if not exactly genuine.

Once, Luc's smiles for pretty women had been easy and authentic. Now they were reflexive, born out of a month's worth of misplaced hero worship.

Sawyer Lopez, on the other hand, had no such hang-ups, and was in full charm mode.

"So where you ladies visiting from?" Lopez asked, handing the girls back their phones.

Luc took another sip of his increasingly cold coffee and rolled his eyes. At least *someone* was profiting from Luc's brush with fame.

"Little Rock," the taller blonde said, her fingers moving rapidly over the screen of her phone.

Luc had no doubt that his face had just been plastered all over every possible social media site. Again.

"Ah, that explains the cute southern accent," Lopez told the woman with a wink.

Uh huh. It *also* explained what the women were doing wandering around Times Square—a place no New Yorker would be caught dead in unless someone paid them to be there.

In Luc and Lopez's case, that *someone* doing the paying was the NYPD.

Crowd control in midtown wasn't exactly the sexy part of being a New York cop, but it was a necessary one, especially on days where the latest teen pop star was giving a concert at 47th and Broadway.

Times Square was every cop's least favorite gig. But when there was a concert, parade, or holiday, it was all hands on deck.

"How long you here for?" Lopez asked, still trying to get the women to notice that he was giving them his best smile. They barely responded, still busy on their phones, and Luc nearly grinned at the irritation on his partner's face.

A month ago, Sawyer Lopez could have gotten the attention of just about any woman he wanted. With the dark skin and jet-black hair of his Latino father, and the pale blue eyes of a Norwegian mother, he was never short on female company.

Then Luc had become an overnight sensation, and now Lopez had to work twice as hard for his share of female attention. Luc would be gloating if the whole situation hadn't been so damned annoying.

"Excuse me, Officer, could you help us for a second? We're trying to find the Hilton—"

Luc turned to the tired-looking couple dragging around enormous suitcases and a cranky-looking toddler. Their expressions were more exhausted than star-struck, and he smiled when he realized they didn't recognize him.

He'd nearly forgotten how good it felt to be anonymous.

By the time Luc pointed the tourists to their hotel, his partner had finally managed to recapture the blondes' attention.

"Oh *God,* no," Lopez was saying. "Listen, you want *real* New York pizza, you're going to walk a bit. I'd recommend—"

Ah, shit. Once Lopez got started talking about pizza, he could go on for hours.

And since Lopez only shared his "pizza secrets" when he was trying to get laid, experience told Luc he was on the verge of being roped into a double date with a couple of Arkansas tourists.

"Lopez. Let's move out," Luc snapped.

The two women blinked in surprise at Luc's sharp tone, and he felt a sting of regret for being a complete and utter dick.

He used to be good around women. Back when women had liked him for *him*. Back when he'd been just regular Luc, not Super Cop Moretti.

But then everything had changed. Thanks to a couple of tourists with camera phones and impeccable timing, Luc's life had become a damned carnival.

Luc gave a slow smile to soften the blow of his irritation. "Sorry, ladies. Duty calls."

His partner grunted something that sounded like *horse-shit*.

Lopez had a point. Luc's excuse *was* a load of BS. The only duty they had at the moment was making sure Broadway didn't turn into a stampede.

But the women nodded in wide-eyed understanding at Luc. "New York's so lucky to have a cop like you."

Luc heard the words like a jab to the jugular, although he forced himself to smile through the wave of darkness that rushed over him. These women didn't have a clue just how undeserving of praise he was. Nobody did.

Pushing the haunting thoughts away before they could fully take hold, he gave the women a wide smile before dragging his partner away.

"I need a disguise," Luc muttered.

"Nah. Embrace it, man. Get yourself a cape. I'm thinking velvet," Lopez said. "I bet Clark Kent knows just the place to get that shit dry-cleaned."

"Hilarious. I haven't heard a million superhero jokes from my brothers, so please, bring it on."

Lopez grinned unabashedly. "I bet the Moretti cop clan is loving their little *bambino* being all famous and shit."

"You have no idea," Luc muttered.

Luc was the youngest in a family of cops. He couldn't even get in the door to Sunday dinner without his brothers bursting out of the bushes, pretending to be the paparazzi.

Generally speaking, his *bambino* status was hell, but he'd happily go back to taking shit about being the baby over this latest brush-with-fame crap.

Lopez skidded to a halt beside Luc, his eyes boring through the crowd as he slowly extended a warning finger. Luc followed his partner's glare to a sulky teen boy in saggy jeans and greasy hair parted down the middle. The kid was seconds away from attempting to ride his skateboard down a very busy midtown sidewalk.

Lopez said it all with one finger and look. *Not cool, kid. Don't make me come over there.*

Luckily the kid correctly interpreted the warning and had enough sense to keep his board tucked under his arm until he got to a less crowded part of the city. Or at least until he got out of sight of cops.

"Wish they were all that easy," Luc said as they resumed walking.

Lopez grunted before turning his attention back to Luc. "So how's your dad reacting to your newfound celebrity? I bet Big T's either disgusted at the circus or thrilled at the prestige."

"A little of both," Luc said, tossing his coffee cup in the trash. "He's always thought cops were supposed to be unsung heroes, but he's not above wanting the Department to look good."

"Even now?" Lopez asked. "He's retired. He's not supposed to care about anything other than sports and annoying your mom."

"*Especially* now," Luc replied.

"Ah," Lopez said, nodding in understanding. "He bored?"

Luc grunted as he surveyed the crowd out of habit. "Just last week he threatened to take up paint-by-numbers if one of us didn't go over there to watch the game with him."

"Can't be easy for the guy," Lopez replied. "One day you're head of the fucking NYPD, the next day, *bam*, you're looking at a future of mundane arts and crafts projects."

Lopez had a valid point. Just a year ago, Tony Moretti had stepped down as police commissioner. The adjustment to retirement had been a rough one, made easier only by the fact that four out of four sons were cops to carry on his legacy.

Or so Tony liked to claim.

What Luc was pretty sure his father *actually* meant was that Luc's three older brothers were carrying on the family legacy. But Luc...Luc suspected that deep down, his father didn't expect much out of Luc. Not since the Shayna Johnson case had gone to shit.

Luc's brothers may push the envelope on respect for authority, but none of them had had their partner die on the job.

No, *that* horror was Luc's private torture. Private, because nobody talked about it. Ever.

But at least the rest of the Moretti siblings were on a clear path toward securing the Moretti family name as NYPD royalty. Despite his brothers' penchant for bending the rules, all had made a name for themselves as some of the city's best.

Luc's oldest brother, Anthony, was next in line for captain in his zone.

Vincent was one of the city's best homicide DTs. *The* best, according to Vin. Modesty had never been his strong suit.

Marco had taken his fair share of crap for moving to California to follow his girlfriend, but he too was moving up the ranks of the LAPD at an obnoxious rate.

And then there was Luc. Luc was just lowly Officer Moretti. The one with a dead partner. The responding officer on the Shayna Johnson case.

Until now. Now Luc was *that* cop. The hero. The one who couldn't get a cup of coffee without the barista doing a double take and writing her phone number on the paper cup of his Americano.

For most cops, the attention would have been flattering at best, a nuisance at worst.

But for Luc, it was pure torture.

Because only he really understood that Luc Moretti was as far from *heroic* as it was possible to get.

CHAPTER TWO

Back at the precinct, Luc didn't even make it to his desk before Shitty Day, Part II, came roaring at him.

"Hey, Moretti, Cap wants to see you in his office," Officer Kerry said, clamping Luc on the shoulder. Luc set aside the coffee mug he'd been about to fill.

"You tell Lopez?" Luc called after him.

Kerry turned around and shrugged as he walked backward. "Cap said just you."

"Shit," Luc muttered.

Captain Brinker was a power-tripping prick, prone to sanctimonious lectures and unwarranted pep talks.

Luc, in particular, was a frequent victim of these little chats.

Brinker had gotten it into his head that Luc and his brothers were only in "the business" because their daddy had paved the way.

Never mind that the Moretti brothers had been top of their class at Academy and had flawless records.

Well, *flawless* if you discounted Anthony's ego problems and Vincent's penchant for going off-book.

But Luc? Luc had always played it straight.

It was an approach that worked 99 percent of the time. And as for that 1 percent of the time when going by the book could turn deadly...

Luc rapped a knuckle on the door of Brinker's office. "You wanted to see me, Cap?"

Brinker gave a jerk of his chin, gesturing for Luc to come in.

"How was Times Square?" his boss asked.

Total bullshit, Luc wanted to say. Instead he shrugged. "The same as usual."

Brinker gave him a dark look as though looking for sarcasm or something to reprimand Luc for, but Luc gave him a deliberately bland smile.

"You wanted to see me?" Luc asked again.

Brinker nodded once and gave a pointed look toward the back of his office, and Luc shifted his gaze, surprised to realize they weren't alone.

A woman stood in the back corner of the room, helping herself to coffee from the fancy coffee machine Brinker kept for his own personal use.

Her body was mostly hidden by one of the horrible potted plants that Brinker's wife insisted gave his office "homey character."

And then she stepped into plain view.

He couldn't help it; he checked her out. Everything about the woman demanded a second look, the legs in particular.

Luc had never really considered himself a legs-man, being more of an "equal opportunity" guy when it came to female body parts. (Although, if his mother ever asked, he'd swear up and down that he only ever noticed personality. Maybe the eyes.)

But the legs on this one were damn near perfect. For that matter, the high breasts and slim waist also earned high marks.

Her subdued black skirt and white blouse should have been boring, but they'd obviously been tailored to fit her trim frame perfectly.

Plus, the black high heels added an element of sexy to the otherwise demure attire.

Then he looked at her face, and for a second, Luc felt just a little bit dazed.

If anything, her features were even more appealing than the body. Her eyes were maybe just slightly too large for her otherwise petite features, but there was no doubt about it, the woman was stunning.

And yet, there was something else there too, just beyond the jolt of sexual awareness.

Recognition.

Luc might not have his brother Vincent's photographic memory, but he was pretty damn good with faces. And he was pretty sure he knew this one. His brain scrambled to place her, but he kept coming up blank.

Her eyes narrowed almost imperceptibly on Luc, and his narrowed right back. He *definitely* knew her from somewhere.

She came forward and shook his hand. "Fifth and Fortieth, three years ago."

He shook his head to indicate he didn't follow.

"You're trying to figure out how you know me. Three years ago, you gave my news van a parking ticket, and we exchanged…words. That's where you know me from. I'm Ava Sims."

"Well I'll be damned," Luc said quietly as the memory rolled over him. *Legs* had spotted Luc writing up her crew's media van and gone all crazy on him, apparently oblivious to the cuffs and *gun* he carried.

He'd issued countless parking tickets, but rarely was he caught in the act of actually *writing* one. And when you were caught in the act by someone who looked like her, you remembered it.

She had tried to pull her hand away, but Luc held fast, just to mess with her. She sniffed in annoyance, but he didn't miss that quick slip of her tongue over her lips.

He nearly grinned at her discomfort.

Yup. That zip of sexual chemistry was every bit as familiar as her legs.

Her eyes flicked to his mouth for a moment, and this time, he didn't bother to hide the grin. The physical appreciation between them hadn't faded.

But other things had. *Ava* had changed. She was still beautiful, but back then there'd been a sort of wildness about her. Hell, you *had* to be half-wild to get into it with a uniformed police officer on a crowded midtown sidewalk.

He had a fuzzy memory of her dark hair in one of those messy knots, with pieces falling down all over the place, her eyes sparkling with passion as she'd raged at him for obstructing her rights, or some hippie shit.

Somehow he couldn't imagine *this* version of Ava Sims losing her cool over anything, much less a parking ticket. Not only was the outfit completely buttoned up and tailored, but her hair, while still sexy as hell, had an almost stiff look about it. The lips too were full and tempting, but they had the shiny look of that goopy stuff women put on them. Gloss, or whatever.

Still stunning. But different.

Luc didn't break eye contact with the gorgeous brunette in front of him.

She was a couple inches shorter than his six-foot-one even with her high heels, but somehow she managed to give the impression that she was looking down at him.

Ava tugged again with her hand, and Luc tentatively released it, searching for the passionate woman he remembered. Instead, all he saw was icy reserve.

This wasn't the wild, *don't obstruct my rights* Ava. This was polished, TV-ready Ava.

He felt the loss more acutely than he should for a woman he didn't even know.

They continued to hold each other's gaze until Brinker broke up the moment. "Moretti, you were on traffic duty? I had no idea police royalty stooped that low. Were you grounded?"

Brinker laughed at his own joke, and Luc forced a smile, finally releasing Ava's hand.

"Well, *Officer*," Ava said with mocking respect, "it looks like you've come a long way from trying to impede on New York citizens' First Amendment rights."

Her voice was all sweetness and honey, but since Luc had a sister and a string of ex-girlfriends, he recognized her tone for what it really was: sugared venom.

He felt a strange surge of relief that she still had sharp edges beneath that tidy outfit and perfect makeup.

Luc moved a half step toward her, pleased that she didn't move back. "Tell me, Ms. Sims, where in the Bill of Rights does it permit citizens to park next to a Stop sign, in front of a No Parking sign, just three feet from a fire hydrant?"

She rolled her eyes, which up close, he could see were warm honey brown. "Yes, thank *God* you were there at that moment to keep the city safe. I mean, just where would we be if you hadn't been there to stop the local media from getting a shot of the mayor leaving a fund-raiser!"

He opened his mouth in anger. Maybe he wasn't so eager to see the passionate version of this woman after all. She may think the laws were frivolous, but they were there for good reason. He stood by every ticket he'd ever written. He stood by the laws behind them.

She held up a hand before he could respond, her expression all mock outrage. "Wait. Did you never get my thank-you note? I *so* wanted to express my gratitude for you putting a stop to my life of crime."

"Well here's your chance to thank me," Luc said, ignoring her sarcasm. "It would also be a good time to apologize for physically assaulting an officer of the law."

Okay, so assault was a strong word. But she'd touched him. He definitely remembered her touching him.

Her eyes narrowed. "Never happened. You're confused. Must be the sugar-high from too many doughnuts."

"You shoved me," he exaggerated. "And I seem to remember a threat..."

She cut her eyes over to Luc's boss. "Did Officer Moretti hit his head when he dove into the river to save that little girl? He seems to be disoriented."

Disappointment spiked through Luc at her reference to that damned river incident. She'd seen the damned YouTube video. And if she'd seen that one, she'd probably seen the other.

Luc froze as realization rolled over him.

That's why she was here.

The pieces fell into place slower than they should. Had he not had a half-mast boner he would have caught on earlier. She was here for *superhero* Moretti, not *parking-ticket* Moretti.

Three years ago, Ava had obviously been a hungry-for-the-story journalist, but if her prissy clothes were any indication, she'd moved up the ranks quite nicely. Luc was guessing that these days, Ava Sims spent a lot more time in hair and makeup than she did chasing after fund-raiser photo ops.

Brinker took a sip of his coffee before dropping the bomb that confirmed Luc's fears. "CBC wants to run a special on you."

Luc didn't even hesitate. "No."

Ava's eyebrows lifted. "It'll get national coverage. You'll go from being locally famous to being a household name across the country."

Her tone implied that Luc should be doing cartwheels at this development. She had no idea just how wrong she was.

"Oh well, in that case!" Luc said, letting his voice go excited before dropping back down to a monotone. "No fucking way."

Ava Sims didn't even flinch.

Captain Brinker broke in. "Listen, Moretti. You know that if it was up to me, you'd be doing the Bronx beat where maybe that pretty face of yours would see some action, not being paraded around like you're the best thing since Batman. But this directive is above me. The order's coming all the way from the top."

Pissed, Luc shook his head. "This isn't what the NYPD is about. We don't grandstand."

"You do when a cop with a Hollywood-heartthrob face can't resist putting himself in front of a camera," Ava said, checking out her manicure.

Luc resisted the urge to snap that he didn't *want* those fucking cameras capturing his every move. That if he could go back in time, some sort of dire accident would have happened to every one of those damned camera phones.

"We need the good publicity, Moretti." Captain Brinker's tone was serious now, and Luc knew why.

The NYPD wasn't exactly in good standing with the people recently.

Three months ago, an officer in uniform had shot an unarmed homeless man. The officer had claimed self-defense and mistaken identity of a weapon, but it wasn't enough to stave off the damage.

Trigger-happy cops made people nervous.

The officer had been suspended, and the NYPD had made promise after promise to implement additional training, but it hadn't done much good. Cops were getting a lot more boos than accolades these days.

Apparently, the higher-ups had just found the ultimate form of damage control.

And Luc was the sacrificial lamb.

"Shit," Luc muttered, realizing there was no way out of it.

Immediately on the heels of his irritation was just the slightest surge of fear.

Fear that Ava Sims would go digging back to November two years ago when Luc had learned, firsthand, the dark side of being a cop. A dark side where good officers died and little girls in pink dresses went missing.

Luc rubbed a hand over his face and forced the thought

back where it belonged. Far, far away from the prying eyes of Ava Sims.

Letting a journalist get to *him* was one thing. He'd be damned before he'd let her get to Shayna Johnson.

Correction: to the *memory* of Shayna Johnson. And he wasn't letting her get at Mike's memory either. He didn't know why he'd been spared the media attention when it had all gone down two years ago, but he was damned grateful. Luc wasn't about to let the legacy of two good people be tarnished now.

Ava Sims reached out and gave his arm a smug little pat, either oblivious or indifferent to Luc's inner turmoil.

"We start Monday. What time do you get to work?"

"Sorry?" he said.

"Your workday. When do you start?"

He shook his head. "Why does it matter? Don't you just tell me what day and time to show up at your studio?"

She rolled her eyes. "We can't just have three hours' worth of face-to-face interviews in cushy chairs. This is an inside look at America's Hero."

"Hold on now," Luc said, his irritation escalating to panic. "Three hours? And America's *what*?"

"*America's Hero*. It'll be the name of the series."

Oh sweet Jesus.

"Now hold the hell on," he said. "There's not going to be a *series*. Just ask me a few questions and be done with it."

Her grin had gone beyond smug to full out gloating. "It's already been approved. It'll be a three-hour special, divided up over three nights. Pretty standard."

"Standard, my ass," Luc snapped. "How the hell are you going to stretch four minutes of amateur video into three *hours*?"

Ava gave an expectant look at the captain, who cleared his throat nervously before explaining. "Ms. Sims and her team will be shadowing you for a while, Moretti. A day in the life of a New York's Finest, and all that."

"Just think, two whole months together!" she said with a mockingly bright smile meant to annoy him. "Won't that be *fun*? You can show me all the lives you've saved with those parking tickets."

Luc was too busy grinding his teeth to reply. Ava dug something out of her purse, slapping it against his chest before sweeping toward the door in her sexy high heels.

"See you on Monday, Officer."

Luc swallowed against the surge of panic. He couldn't do this. He *wouldn't* do this. It was one thing to be a local hero. Another thing entirely to become a "household name" as Ava had indicated. The last thing Luc needed was an even brighter spotlight on him, shining in places that should remain in the dark forever.

"I don't like it either," Brinker said gruffly, displaying a rare perceptiveness. "But I can tell you right now, there's no point in fighting it. Your father's replacement made it clear that this was an order. Not a request."

Fuck. *Fuck.* If he were Anthony, or even Vincent, he would have pushed back. Would have shoved his principles down Brinker's throat, superior or not.

But Luc wasn't his brothers. Luc wasn't a hotheaded hotshot. And he had far too much respect for the NYPD to pull a tantrum.

He would do his duty. He *always* did his duty. With pride.

Still, he couldn't stop the groan of dread in anticipation of what lay ahead. Luc glanced down at the crumpled piece of paper that Ava had thrust at him. There was a coffee stain in one corner, and something that looked like lipstick smeared across the front, but there was no mistaking what he was looking at.

It was a three-year-old parking ticket.

She'd never paid it.

CHAPTER THREE

Outside the precinct, Ava made it only a block and a half before necessity demanded that she stop.

With a quick glance to make sure *he* wasn't following, she ducked off into the alcove of an apartment building entry and made the exchange that nearly every New York career woman was well acquainted with:

The shoe swap.

Out of her roomy *I-can-fit-my-whole-life-in-here* handbag came the beat-up flip-flops from Target.

Into that same handbag went the black stilettos. Also from Target.

Ava inhaled gratefully as her toes wiggled in happy relief at being freed from the pinching patent leather nightmare.

She'd have happily sent her gritty contacts the same way of the high heels (far, *far* away), but she'd very deliberately left her glasses at home today to avoid such temptation.

Prime-time news anchors didn't wear glasses.

Of course, they didn't wear their hair in messy ponytails either, but that didn't stop Ava from pulling her hair—in which she'd spent half an hour creating loose, hair-sprayed curls—into a messy pony.

By the time she made it to the van, she looked a lot less *This is Ava Sims, reporting for CBC news* and a lot more, well, Ava *Nobody* Sims from Darrington, Oklahoma.

Luckily, the man waiting for her didn't care.

Mihail Petrov was leaning against the CBC van smoking a cigarette, his severe features schooled into their usual indifference even as sharp blue eyes took in every detail of Ava's appearance.

He blew out a long stream of smoke, and she stifled the urge to remind him—*again*—of the hazards of smoking. Mihail didn't *do* friendly advice. Unless he was the one giving it. And even then, it was rarely friendly.

But she loved him anyway.

"Knew you wouldn't make it," he said, gesturing with his cigarette from her bare toes to messy hair that was completely at odds with her prim pencil skirt and no-nonsense blouse.

"I made it long enough," she said, elbowing him aside so she could pull a bottled water out of the cooler they kept in the van.

"So they're going for it?" His slight Bulgarian accent made this sound more like a statement than an actual question.

"They didn't really have a choice." Ava tipped the bottle back and took three large gulps. "This meeting was a formality more than anything else. This BS story was handed down from the top on both sides, apparently."

"Huh," Mihail grunted. "So they weren't excited about it?"

"No," Ava mused, tapping her fingernails against the water bottle. "They weren't."

Which she found surprising. Ava had yet to encounter anyone who wasn't secretly thrilled to be at the center of attention, even when they threw up token protests.

And she would have thought a cop at the bottom of the NYPD food chain should have been a sure bet for delivering an, "aw shucks, I'm just a regular guy, but if you *really* think it's a good story…"

But Ava's reporter instincts told her Luc Moretti's hesitation had been real. And actually, *hesitation* was too soft a word. He'd been *pissed*. And something else too. She tapped her fingernails more slowly as she replayed the encounter.

For a split second Ava could have sworn that Luc Moretti looked…scared.

But of *what*? The man had gone above the call of duty and was getting recognized for it. She could see him being embarrassed. Maybe annoyed. But scared…

Something was off there.

Ava took another gulp of water.

But on the plus side, his reaction to her had been everything she'd secretly hoped for.

As much as Ava was dreading this bogus, fluff-piece of a story, she *had* been looking forward to seeing his face when he saw her again. She only wished she would have stayed behind to see his livid reaction to that unpaid parking ticket she'd thrust at him.

Ava grinned at the thought. She wasn't even sure what had prompted her to bring the ticket along in the first place. As much as she enjoyed pushing people's buttons to get at what made them tick, this move had been risky, even for her. But she'd done plenty of Googling to see just how bad an unpaid ticket was.

And in the end, she hadn't been able to resist needling

him. She too-well remembered all that righteous indignation three years ago. Getting under the skin of what had to be the most upstanding cop on the planet was a delicious prospect.

And he'd let her walk away, so she must have at least been *partially* right about being able to get away with it.

Then again, Luc probably didn't know that the unpaid ticket was no one-off fluke. Her eyes flitted to the back pocket of the passenger seat, which was bulging with small bits of paper. At least half of which were likely parking tickets for this very van.

Mihail watched the direction of her gaze before giving a little smirk, correctly reading her mind. "Freedom of the press, baby."

Welllll...

As Officer Moretti had so sanctimoniously informed her during their heated altercation three years ago, freedom of the press didn't *exactly* dignify breaking traffic laws... repeatedly.

But such explanations would go unheeded by Mihail. He'd been in the U.S. for almost twenty years, and a citizen for over half that thanks to a tumultuous marriage to a Queens-born bartender, but he was known to be a bit innovative with his interpretation of things like the Constitution and the law.

"Where to now, babe?" Mihail asked, flicking his cigarette to the pavement.

Ava put the cap back on her water bottle and rolled her shoulders. "Let's head back to the station."

Mihail's eyebrows lifted. "You never want to go back to the station."

Ava pulled down the visor and looked at the mirror there, checking for lipstick on her teeth. Yup. There it was. A rosy smear across her perfectly straight (thanks, orthodontics), perfectly white (thanks, network-sponsored whitening sessions) teeth.

She snapped the visor back up in irritation. She kept waiting for the day that looking perfectly put together became effortless. She'd been waiting a long-ass time.

"Yeah, well, it's not like I *want* to go back to the station," she griped to Mihail. "But this story is the big-time. I knew when they gave it to me that it would mean more face time with the higher-ups."

"So you think this is it?" he asked.

"Hmm?" she asked, distracted.

He lifted an eyebrow. "You know, it. *The* story."

"It better be," she muttered.

Mihail gave her a look, and she knew he was dying to start their usual argument. But for once he managed to bite his tongue, and instead of picking a fight, he pulled out one of his ever-present gummy worms from the bag in the middle console. He chewed grumpily.

Ava's relentless quest to be a CBC anchorwoman was the one area where she and Mihail didn't see eye to eye. It was cliché, and she knew it. The small-town Midwest girl dreaming of the bright lights and fame in the big city.

But she'd been chasing the dream since she'd moved to New York at twenty-two.

She wasn't going to stop now.

Even if a little part of her sometimes whispered that it wasn't *her* dream.

Ava started to bite her fingernail, then jerked her hand away when she realized it would chip the manicure she could never seem to keep looking fresh for more than twelve hours.

"Have you called your parents yet?" Mihail asked.

"Not yet. Tonight, maybe."

"I'm sure *they'll* be excited."

"Don't," she snapped, catching his emphasis and knowing what it implied. Mihail had only met her parents once (disaster), but he'd heard enough phone calls over the course of his and Ava's friendship to have formed a strong opinion on her family.

To his way of thinking, it wasn't *Ava's* dream that had her chasing the anchor chair. He thought it was her parents' dream. With maybe a *dash* of pressure from her talk-show-host sister and foreign-correspondent brother.

Maybe he was a little bit right. A *little* bit.

In the same way the Moretti family was NYPD royalty (she'd done her homework), the Sims clan was broadcast journalism royalty. Or so her father had declared.

Her parents had been co-anchors in Darlington back in the day, and apparently the popular husband-wife team had been slated for bigger things in New York.

Until Ava's mom had gotten pregnant with Ava's brother. Dreams dashed.

Or so the story went. Ava still didn't quite understand why they couldn't have pursued the NYC thing, even with her mom's pregnancy. *Plenty* of anchormen and -women had family.

But then, that wouldn't have given them something to complain about for thirty years.

It also wouldn't have given them an excuse over never making the big time.

So they'd done what any pushy, interfering parents would do. They'd transferred their dreams to their children.

Ava's brother and sister had fallen into line marvelously.

Miranda had her own current events talk show in Los Angeles, and Daniel was a foreign correspondent for a competing network, although never in a country that was actually relevant in current events. He didn't cover war or famine or natural disasters. No, Danny was well on his way to establishing a name for himself posing as an expert in art or food or wine, or whatever was popular in whichever country he was in. Emphasis on *posing*.

Her parents were proud of all their children. Their annual Christmas card was an embarrassing brag fest.

But Ava knew that *she* was their darling. The one who was really living the dream. The one who would do what they hadn't been able to:

National Anchorwoman.

And this story would get her there. Ava was sure of it.

"I can't believe we have to hang out with the fucking five-oh for two months," Mihail grumbled.

"I don't like it either," Ava admitted. "But this isn't your average cop."

Mihail glanced at her and wiggled his eyebrows.

She punched him. "I don't mean it like that."

"Sure you don't. I've seen pictures."

Ava pulled out her phone and pulled up her video player before shoving the phone in his face. "Yeah, but have you seen...?"

Mihail made a grunting sound and tried to push her hand away. "I know, I know, I've seen it."

Ava leaned toward him, holding the screen out so they could both watch it. For all of Mihail's fussing, he didn't look away.

"Are you seeing what I'm seeing, Mihail?"

"Grainy, shitty-ass movie recording?"

"Pretend for a second that you're not a damn cameraman." She pointed. "That is Luc Moretti, son of a previous police commissioner. Handsome huh? Oh, and what's that? He's running to the railing and jumping headfirst into the stank East River? Whatever could he be doing...oh look!"

Even though she'd seen the video dozens, if not hundreds, of times, both she and Mihail watched the grainy footage wobble as the tourist with the phone dashes to the railing where Luc had gone over, showing him swimming easily toward a small ladder.

A tiny pigtailed little girl is in tow.

But the story doesn't stop there. She and Mihail both watched as Luc easily hauls himself and the little girl out of the water.

Ava's eyes watered as they always do when it becomes apparent that the little girl wasn't breathing.

She'd seen the videos too often to count, but every damned time she felt her heart stop and then swell as Luc Moretti leans down and begins giving the little girl CPR.

Ava let out a gush of relieved air when the little girl turns her head and coughs up water, before being scooped up by her hysterical mother as Officer Moretti sits back on his heels.

The tourist holding the camera focuses mainly on the reunion between mother and daughter, but Ava always watched Luc in the corner of the screen. Watched as his chin dipped to his heaving chest, his palms resting against his thighs.

His face lifted, and he looked at the girl, and there was relief, obviously.

But there was something else in his expression too. Ava lifted her thumbnail and bit. *There was something else.*

She wanted to know what it was.

She *would* find out what it was.

"Yeah, yeah it's great," Mihail muttered, pushing her phone away from his face and interrupting her thoughts.

"Right?" Ava poked him in his bony side with a finger. "It couldn't be more perfect if it was a Spider-Man movie."

"Spider-Man? That's not wimpy Peter Parker; that guy is Clark Kent."

Ava ignored this. She didn't need Mihail's reminder that Luc was tall, broad shouldered, and gorgeously dark-haired. She was doing her best to forget that little fact.

"Okay, now look at this one…"

"I told you, I've seen the damned videos."

Ava pulled up the second video anyway. This one was shorter. Less than a minute, but it was every bit as poignant.

Taken a couple months ago in the middle of a late-winter cold snap, the frail figure of a homeless man sitting in the deserted Diamond District, his back against the wall of a long-closed jewelry shop, huddled against cold.

The now familiar figure of Officer Moretti approaches, his footsteps slowing as he spots the man. The video has no sound, but it's easy to see Luc crouching down, speaking to the man, his face kind, his smile easy.

The conversation apparently doesn't go the way Luc wants, because for a moment Luc's chin drops against his chest, as though in defeat. Then Luc moves, shrugging out of his winter coat.

Luc extends the jacket to the man, who doesn't reach for it. Then, incredibly, Luc creeps closer, gently maneuvering the man so that the warm coat is wrapped around him.

As though sensing the camera on him, the homeless man slowly turns his head, finds the camera before giving a heart-wrenching smile as he clenches the coat to his shoulders.

Officer Moretti stands, wearing nothing but his uniform as it starts to snow.

The camera jerks to the side before going to black, but the jarring end to the video doesn't ruin its impact.

If anything, it highlighted the spontaneity of the moment, giving the watcher the sense that he or she was a spectator to a private moment.

Not so private anymore, Ava thought.

The coat video had been taken a few weeks before the East River one, but the tourist behind the camera hadn't uploaded it until after the later video had been picked up by a small local news station.

From there, it had exploded.

And Ava had every intention of making it explode even more.

"Okay, you proved your point. It's good stuff," Mihail said, finally pushing her phone away and putting the key in the ignition. "I just don't see why we have to be the ones to cover it. Especially if this cop guy doesn't even want to be in the story."

Ava put her phone away, faking confidence she didn't entirely feel. "He'll come around. Once the advertising offers start rolling in, he'll be kissing my four-inch heels."

"Which are where, exactly?" Mihail looked pointedly at her flip-flops.

Ava pretended she didn't hear him.

"You know, I've never seen Gwen Garrison in anything other than five-inch spikes," Mihail said.

Ava inspected her manicure. Yup. Chipped. "Your point?"

He shrugged as he turned the ignition. "Just that Gwen's been anchor for a good many years now, and you've been chasing crap stories for how long? Maybe it's time to accept that you're destined for the gritty, in-the-trenches journalism and not the plastic talking head thing. And maybe you *like* it that way."

Ava dug out a gummy worm from Mihail's stash and ignored him. The guy was one of her best friends, nasty cigs and all, but she was tired of this conversation. It brought up unsettling thoughts she had no interest in dealing with.

She *did* want to be anchorwoman. She did. And Mihail was right in that Ava tended to choose the scrappy, real stories, no matter how small, over the more glamorous, attention-grabbing ones. That was about to change.

This was her break.

A gorgeous, big-city cop with a heart of gold was exactly what she needed. It was a huge story, with a big audience.

Even with NYPD being under a few shadows right now thanks to that unfortunate shooting a few months back, the Luc Moretti story appealed on every level, to every viewer.

Big city folk were partial to first responders, especially after 9/11. Small-town people liked cops, period.

And everyone liked a *hero*.

Especially a good-looking one.

As far as poster boys went, it didn't get more perfect than Luc Moretti in all of his tall, dark, good-guy handsomeness. No hot-blooded straight woman could look at that guy and not fantasize about what he looked like under that uniform.

Ava included.

She dug her nails into her palm, trying to forget about the way every part of her had seemed to tingle when they'd stood toe to toe in Captain Brinker's office.

"So how cooperative do you think Moretti will be?" Mihail asked, cutting off a taxi just because he could.

Ava went for another gummy worm. "Not at all."

Mihail glanced at her. "Yeah?"

She shrugged. "I dunno, something was up with him."

"Explain."

"I don't know yet," she said, tugging at the gummy worm.

"Maybe he just doesn't like being in the spotlight," Mihail said.

"Deep down, everyone wants to be in the spotlight," Ava muttered, staring out the window. "*Everyone* wants glory."

She felt Mihail cut her another look. "The cynical, storm-cloud thing is supposed to be my shtick."

"I'm not cynical!"

Mihail snorted.

"I'm not! I just don't buy for one second that Luc Moretti isn't secretly patting himself on the back for all of his recent good deeds."

Moretti had secrets all right, but they were more complicated than Mr. Too-Sexy-For-His-Own-Good wanting to keep his good deeds under wraps.

If he was reluctant, it was probably because he'd have to cooperate with *her*. Guys like him didn't like it when a woman didn't turn into a simpering mess in their presence.

She'd come close to simpering, though. Really close. Those deep blue eyes were a jolt to the system, more so because they were a surprise given his dark hair and Italian coloring.

But Ava hadn't kissed Moretti's ass during their run-in three years ago, and she wasn't about to start now.

"So what's he like then?" Mihail asked.

Ava jolted. "Hmm?"

"The cop. The hero one . . . what's he like?"

Gorgeous.

"He's perfect for the story," Ava said with a shrug. "The camera will love him."

Mihail tapped long fingers against the steering wheel. "So did he say why he did those things? Jumping into the river, giving his coat to the homeless guy?"

Ava groaned at the admiration in Mihail's voice. "Not you too."

"What?"

"You *actually* think he's a hero?"

"I mean we don't have to get fucking romantic about it, but the guy went above and beyond. He deserves a little credit."

Ava rolled her eyes and chomped grumpily on a green gummy worm.

She could grant that the guy had done a couple of good deeds. Okay, really good deeds.

But she couldn't stop thinking about that haunted look on his face after he'd saved the little girl.

Nor the panicked look when he'd learned that she was with CBC.

There was a story there. She was *sure* of it.

She just wasn't sure it was the feel-good story the network wanted her to tell.

CHAPTER FOUR

What do you mean CBC's doing a story on you?"

Luc took a grumpy sip of coffee before he met his father's dark gaze. "Is there a way I could rephrase to be more clear?"

Luc's sister leaned over to snag a piece of Luc's toast before pointing the toast triangle at their father. "It's true. Luc was *quite* clear with his word choice. And I'm a lawyer so I should know."

Tony Moretti scowled and propped a piece of bacon on top of a piece of biscuit. Then he dragged the whole thing through a puddle of gravy under the exasperated glare of Luc's mother. He took a bite and chewed as he glared at Luc and Elena. "Don't you two get smart with me. What I want to know is why are they doing a story *now*? You're old news."

Anthony leaned over and grabbed the remaining piece of Luc's toast. "It's nice when he builds us up like this, isn't it, bro?"

"So nice," Luc muttered, taking another sip of his coffee.

His mother caught his eye. "I think what your father is trying to ask, Luca, is why you're *agreeing* to a story when you've been unhappy with all the media coverage."

Luc set his coffee aside and reached for a piece of toast, only to realize that his family had pillaged everything.

"It's not like I have a choice." He immediately regretted the words. They felt...whiney. Small. And his father pounced.

"You always have a choice," Tony boomed. "How many times have I told you kids that we're in control—"

"Wait, wait," Vincent interrupted, leaning forward and snapping his fingers rapidly. "I've got this. We've heard it before, I think..."

"Like maybe once, or a million times?" Elena mused, tapping her lip.

"We are in control of our own destiny," Anthony said in a dramatic voice, or as dramatic as it could get around a piece of bacon. "Did I get that right?"

Tony Moretti turned to exchange a glance with his wife. "How is it I raised four smart asses?"

"Five, actually," Elena said. "Marco's missing all the fun."

"Probably on the beach somewhere," Luc's father said, his tone turning irritable the way it always did when he spoke of his West Coast offspring.

None of them had been thrilled when Marc moved to Los Angeles. Not only because it splintered the tight-knit Morettis into different time zones, but because the *reason* for his move was Mandy Breslin.

Mandy and Marc had been dating since high school, which should have made her like part of the family, but the truth was...the family couldn't stand her. She was manipulative, melodramatic, and seemed to think that an exceptionally pretty face made up for lack of other qualities. Say, like, being a decent person.

Still, what Mandy lacked in likability, she made up for in ambition. She'd gotten it in her head that she was destined for a Hollywood career. And Marc, being the epitome of loyal, had dutifully followed her.

They'd been in LA for over a year now, and as best as the rest of the Morettis could tell, the closest Mandy had come to her dream was watching TV all day while Marc worked his ass off in the LAPD.

The Morettis did their best to support Marco's decision, even as they secretly hated it…and missed him like crazy. But that didn't mean they didn't gripe about Marc's absence behind his back.

Because that's how the Morettis did things. They interfered with each other's business constantly, and unabashedly.

Take, like, *now*, for example.

Sundays meant two things to the Morettis.

Mass at St. Ignatius Loyola Church on the Upper East Side, and the follow-up brunch at the Darby Diner.

But it meant other things too. Like latching on to one person's personal life and taking it apart piece by piece.

Last week it had been Elena's new boyfriend. The guy was Irish, and with the way Tony and Maria had responded to this news, last week's breakfast was a scene out of *Gangs of New York*. Tony Moretti was born in New York, but from his fierce Italian upbringing, he might as well have been born in Italy. And Maria Moretti actually *had* been born there, which meant…well, an Irish boy for their only daughter had not gone over well, even though neither parent would admit their reasons were old biases.

The week before *that*, the fuss had been over Anthony's announcement that he was headed to Florida over Easter weekend to run a marathon and wouldn't be around for Easter. The week before *that*...well, Luc couldn't remember, but it was probably something to do with Vincent and the fact that the man had zero life outside of work and had turned down yet another of their mother's blind date attempts.

But this week? This week was all about Luc. Luc and the damned CBC nightmare that awaited him tomorrow morning.

The only possible silver lining in this whole mess was that Nonna had a stomach bug and had opted to skip the Sunday-morning histrionics. Luc loved his grandmother—desperately—but the woman had made it her life's mission to stir the Moretti family pot whenever possible. A tendency made even worse by the fact that, in a rather shortsighted move, the grandkids had bought her an iPhone for Christmas the previous year.

Now the woman didn't just stir the pot, she recorded the aftermath.

His grandma was a menace. A wonderful menace, but still...Luc was a *tiny* bit glad she wasn't here on his particular Sunday to shine.

"'Kay, seriously, though," Vin said, leaning back in his chair and fixing Luc with his usual serious gaze. "Dad's got a point. I would have thought all this hoopla with your heroics would be dying down."

"You and me both," Luc said.

His coffee cup was blessedly refilled, and he smiled thanks at Helen, the white-haired waitress who'd been serving the Darby Diner—and the Morettis—longer than Luc had been alive.

"Am I your favorite today, Helen?" Luc asked, intentionally turning his attention away from the too shrewd eyes of his brother.

"Depends, who's tipping?" she said with a wink.

Then she leaned down and whispered in Luc's ear as she refilled Anthony's cup. "'Course you're my favorite."

"Heard that," Anth said.

"Heard what, baby?" Helen said, blowing Anthony a kiss. "That you're my favorite?"

"That's not what you told me when I fixed your cell last week," Vin said.

"And by fixed her phone, you did what exactly?" Elena said, propping her chin up on her hand. "You hit the Power button? Turned if off and then back on?"

Vin lifted a shoulder. "Whatever works."

Helen refilled everyone's coffee and moved on to another table, having assured them individually that they were, in fact, her one and only favorite.

Luc reached for the bill Helen had dropped off, but as usual, Tony was too fast. "Your mother and I have this."

Luc lifted an eyebrow. "But you're retired."

"And I'm your father," Tony said in his usual no-room-for-argument tone.

Luc and Vincent exchanged a look across the table. Neither of them particularly liked their parents paying for their four grown siblings, but pride was an important element in the Morettis. And nobody had more of it than the patriarch.

"They're not going to put makeup on you, are they?" Anthony mused.

"What?" Luc asked.

"For this story. Do you have to get all dolled up?"

Luc rubbed a hand over the back of his neck, annoyed

that the conversation kept coming back to the damned CBC thing. "No. No makeup. It's just a reporter following me around for a few weeks..."

"Which reporter?" Elena asked.

Just as Tony broke in, "What do you mean a few weeks?"

"Oh my God," Luc muttered, taking a drink of his coffee. He looked across the table at his best shot at escape: his mother.

But Maria Moretti looked every bit as dismayed as his father, which was something Luc didn't fully understand. He knew why *he* was annoyed about the story, but he didn't get why his parents were all worked up about it. It didn't even have anything to do with them.

"Her name is Ava Sims," Luc said, glancing at his sister as he answered her question.

Elena nodded. "I think I know her. Brunette? Pretty?"

"A pretty brunette on TV?" Vin said. "I'm sure there's only one of those."

Elena made a face. "Seriously, I think I just saw one of her stories last week. She did some exposé on this supposed charity that was really a front for drug money, or something like that. Seriously, it was a big deal...she figured it out all on her own, and—"

"Because that's exactly what the city needs," Anthony broke in. "Amateurs that don't have a clue about law enforcement thinking they know the best way to keep order."

"Oh, come off it," Elena said in exasperation.

Luc was sitting between the two of them and held up a palm between their two angry faces, hoping to stifle the argument before it heated. Elena was not only the lone sister with four brothers, she was also the lone non-cop of the Moretti siblings.

But that wasn't the worst of it. Elena was an attorney... a *defense* attorney.

Her commitment to "the wrong side of the law," as Anthony liked to call it, was a frequent point of contention. And even though Luc was generally on Anthony's side, today he wasn't in the mood.

"Can we not do this?" he asked tiredly.

Both Anthony and Elena glanced at him, and then he saw them glimpse at each other, a surprised look on their faces. He knew why. His voice had been irritated, and Luc's voice was rarely anything other than easygoing.

He was the charming brother. The likable one.

But he didn't feel charming today. Hadn't felt charming in a long time.

And lately... lately he'd been tired of pretending.

"I still think you should say no to the story," Tony broke in.

Luc's head dropped forward at his father's stubbornness. "I can't, Dad. I don't like it any more than you do, but Captain Brinker made it clear that it wasn't up for discussion. After what happened with that shooting last month, they're desperate to get back in the public's good graces."

His father's jaw moved. "You're sure that's what this is about? Making amends for that trigger-happy cop who shot the homeless man?"

"Yeah, I'm pretty sure," Luc said, taking a sip of coffee as he tossed his napkin onto his plate. "Does it matter?"

His father nodded, looking thoughtful. And worried. Luc's mother set a hand on his father's arm, and Tony glanced at her. Luc's eyes narrowed as he watched something cross between them. A silent communication that he couldn't translate.

A temper that he very rarely felt started to creep up. "Look, I'll keep you all out of it, okay? Can we just…drop it?"

"Sure, bambino," Elena said, her voice easy as she ran a playful hand through his hair.

Vincent reached across the table with a pen and a paper napkin. "Another autograph. For my collection?"

Luc laughed and shoved his brother's hand aside. "Fu—screw you," he corrected, after a quick glance at his mother. "Can we go? My shift starts in an hour and I need to change into uniform."

Outside the restaurant, the family did the usual hugs and kisses exchange as his mother took an inventory of who, if any of them, would be coming to family dinner that evening. Church and Sunday breakfast were mandatory. Sunday dinner had become an "all is welcome, none are required" affair in recent years in deference to the unpredictable schedule of cops, and Elena's tendency to spend Sunday nights prepping for her Monday cases.

"Not me tonight, Ma," Luc said, wrapping his mother in a hug and kissing her cheek. "I'm working a double."

His mother pressed her palms to his cheeks and studied his face. "You'll be careful, won't you, Luca?"

He rolled his eyes. It was a common refrain in a family of cops. "Yes, ma'am. I always am."

Not that it always matters. Sometimes you could be as careful as can be, and you still…

"I mean be careful with this Sims woman," Maria said softly.

Luc frowned. "Ma. She's a little annoying, but she's not exactly a threat."

His mother opened her mouth, looking like she wanted to say more, but then she caught Tony's eye and fell silent.

Luc shifted his attention to his father, who was watching him with the same worried expression his mother had used.

Luc had the strangest sense that he was missing something. Missing something crucial.

But he didn't have a clue what it was.

CHAPTER FIVE

"Ava, your mom's calling."

Ava groaned as she stepped into her yoga pants and hopped repeatedly to wiggle them up over her hips. "Ignore it!" she called from the bedroom.

Scooping her hair into a messy bun, she headed out into her tiny living room just in time to watch her best friend hit the Decline button on Ava's phone.

Beth picked up her glass of wine and flopped back on Ava's couch, her bright orange hair bouncing around her shoulders. "Is it wrong, how much I enjoyed doing that?"

"Nah," Ava said, scooping her own wineglass off the coffee table and settling into the chair across from her friend, tucking her legs up beneath her. "It's acceptable for you to not like her. She's not *your* mother."

"Thank God for that," Beth muttered.

Ava grinned at her friend's honesty. Beth's no-BS policy

was one of the many reasons the two women had been nearly inseparable since their first meeting.

Ava had met Beth Salvers, a Brooklyn native, her first months in the city.

It had been Ava's twenty-third birthday, and she hadn't known a soul, but that didn't stop her from putting on a too-short sequin dress and hitting up one of the fancy bars a few blocks from her apartment.

She'd meant to treat herself to a drink or two before heading home for a thrilling night of *Friends* reruns.

The bartender had carded her, then insisted that the first drink was on him. The tiny blue-eyed redhead sitting next to Ava at the bar had insisted that the second drink was on *her*. Beth had just been stood up on a blind date and was looking for a man-bashing partner.

Ava didn't have a man to bash...but she *was* in desperate need of a friend. The rest was history.

But the only man-bashing Beth was doing these days was when her fiancé didn't sound properly enthused about thrilling topics like flower arrangements and venue and the weight of card stock for their save-the-date cards.

In a few months, Beth was marrying Christian Channing, and while Ava was wildly happy for her friend, she couldn't help feeling a little...ditched.

Their single-girl anthem had been her and Beth's jam for several years of friendship. All of that had changed when Beth met Christian at a charity event last year. And although the two women were closer than ever, Ava was also aware that she sometimes held back from Beth when it came to talking about men. Beth wasn't one of those annoying friends that expected everyone to be happily coupled up because she was, but talking about a bad date wasn't the same when you knew the other person had been cuddling the love of her life while *you'd* been stuck with a whopper of a dinner bill because the guy'd "forgotten" his wallet.

Still, there were some things Ava and Beth still had in common...

Griping over Ava's mother was one of them.

Ava didn't dislike her mom. Of course she didn't. She loved her. But Viv Sims could be...difficult. Something Beth had gotten a close-up look at whenever Ava's mom came to visit the city. Beth was a kindergarten teacher, which most people *melted* over, but Vivian Sims managed to find about a dozen different ways to belittle Beth's chosen profession.

There's not much challenge in that then, is there, dear?

Well I can see why you don't bother much with your clothes. They must get positively ruined with grubby handprints.

It's just as well. Having a face for the camera is as much a curse as it is a blessing, right, Ava?

Ava really couldn't blame her best friend for disliking her mother. Still, while Beth had no reason to feel guilty about screening Viv's calls, Ava did feel guilty. She tried to call her parents every Sunday, but she'd been avoiding them for two weeks now.

Ever since she found out about the *America's Hero* segment.

Her parents would be thrilled, which would have most daughters diving for the phone.

But her parents' excitement over the story was precisely the reason Ava *didn't* want to tell them. Strange as it sounded, some gut-level part of Ava rebelled at the idea of doing what her parents expected of her. Which made no sense. Their goals had always been Ava's goals. Sure, they were the ones who had nudged her toward the path of anchorwoman, but Ava had been the one to pursue it.

It was just...

She wasn't ready to tell them. Wasn't ready to listen to all of the "this is your big break!" enthusiasm until she was sure how she felt about it.

"Uh oh," Beth said, leaning forward to grab a handful of potato chips from the bag Ava'd set on the able. "You're biting your nail."

Ava dropped her hand to her lap. "Sorry."

Beth rolled her eyes. "Don't be sorry. Calls from my mom set me on edge sometimes too, and mine isn't, um..."

"A nightmare?" Ava said with a knowing smile.

"Yeah. That. But seriously, do you want to call your mom back? Reservations aren't until eight, so we have time."

"Definitely not," Ava said, taking a sip of her wine. "I'll call her tomorrow."

"To tell her about Officer McHotty?"

Ava lifted her eyebrows. "Is that what we're calling him now?"

"Oh, come on," Beth said, putting a hand over her chest and sighing dramatically. "I've seen the videos. And did you see that story in the *Times*? The one where they caught a picture of him laughing with his brothers? That whole family can frisk me any old time."

Ava threw a chip at her. "Pull yourself together."

"But he's hot, right? In person?"

Ava pursed her lips and glanced at her wine. "He's good-looking."

Beth snorted. "From anyone else, that would be an epic understatement. But coming from you, it's... something."

"What do you mean, *coming from me*?"

"I mean," Beth said around a chip, "that you're overdue. Past ripe."

Ava groaned. "That is *terrible*."

"It's true! I mean this with absolutely unabashed love, but I've started to wonder if your lady parts weren't expiring from lack of use."

"My lady parts are just fine, thank you very much."

"So you admit it. Officer Moretti is hot."

Ava laughed at her friend's relentlessness. "Yes, okay, fine, I admit it. He's hot."

Beth's eyes narrowed and she leaned forward. "You gave in way too easily. What's the catch. Is he secretly a prick? Gay? Super short?"

"No, no, and no. He…" Ava broke off as she considered. "He seems like a nice guy."

Beth flopped back with a groan. "Oh *no*."

"What?"

"You're writing him off before you've even started the story."

"Okay, let's hold it right there. I'm glad you realize that he is in fact a *story*, not a potential suitor."

"Suitor? Easy there, your Oklahoma's coming out."

"You know what I mean. Quit pretending that Luc is a romantic prospect."

"*Luc*, huh?" Beth's eyebrows wiggled.

Whoops.

Ava leaned forward and grabbed the wine bottle, topping her glass off. "I'm just saying…your upcoming trot down the aisle's got you all match-makery, and I don't want to have to spend the next two months having to explain that Officer Moretti is a part of my professional life, not my personal one."

Even if he is the best-looking guy I've seen in a long time.

"Good," Beth said, holding out her hands and wiggling her fingers for the wine bottle.

Ava handed it over. "Good?"

That was so not the response she'd been expecting. Ava hadn't been joking when she'd said that Beth's upcoming marriage had gotten her in a matchmaking mind-set. They couldn't so much as go out for happy hour without Beth trying to set Ava up with the bus boy.

"Yup! Now that I know that dark-haired, blue-eyed cops with broad shoulders and a rugged jaw line aren't your type, you have no reason to say no when I invite you out to dinner with me and Christian next weekend...and one of Christian's co-workers, who's blond, brown-eyed, and lanky."

Ava groaned as she realized she'd walked right into Beth's trap.

"*Please?* Gabe is really sweet. One of the good ones, I *swear*, and if it doesn't work out, I won't push, and you never have to see him again—"

Ava took a swallow of wine. A big one. "No."

Beth stopped mid-rant, her blue eyes blinking in confusion. "No? That's it?"

"I'm saying no, but saying it kindly. And not because I don't trust you, but because I'm just not in a place to fall in love right now. Work is crazy."

And actually, falling in love seems to be one thing I don't seem capable of. Ever.

Beth sulked. "How about after you finish this big story?"

Ava sighed. Her best friend was like a dog with a bone. "Maybe. Maybe then."

Beth grinned happily. "Yay!"

"Yeah," Ava mumbled. "Yay."

She didn't have the heart to tell her friend, but Ava would bet serious money on the fact that she wouldn't be falling for any of these guys that Beth seemed determined to set her up with. Not because they wouldn't be perfectly nice.

In fact, sometimes *nice* was the problem. The nice ones never said it out loud on a first date, but they were the ones who were angling toward marriage and babies and things that Ava just wasn't at all sure she was ready for. Or would *ever* be ready for.

Ava knew there was supposed to be some deep, dark secret…some festering *reason* why she didn't want to get married, didn't want to commit…but the truth was, it just didn't appeal. It had never appealed. Maybe it was her parents' stable, but symbiotic, relationship that had turned her off, or just one too many boring boyfriends over the years, but lately Ava had been finding the prospect of marriage more and more unappealing.

And the more she thought she was supposed to want it, the less she did.

She leaned forward and grabbed a handful of chips. "Beth, do you think I'm completely screwed up?"

"Well, if you are, nobody can blame you," Beth said without hesitation. "Your family's a piece of work."

"So true," Ava agreed as she munched on the chips.

"But," Beth said, pointing a finger. "You are fabulous. You have to forget the crazy fam. Do what *you* want to do."

Ava ran a finger around the rim of her glass. "Yeah, that's kind of the problem."

"Meaning?"

Meaning, what if I don't know *what I want to do?*

But she wasn't ready to say it. Not out loud. Not even to Beth.

So instead she changed the subject to the one and only thing that could deter Beth from her fix-Ava campaign... "Hey, what did you find out about that band Christian liked for the reception? Are they still available?"

As expected, Beth was only too happy to have the chance to talk wedding, and for the next hour, Ava was able to let herself forget, just for a little while, that despite her life looking pretty perfect on paper, she felt utterly and totally *lost*.

CHAPTER SIX

Luc crossed his arms over his chest and glared.

Ava Sims glared right back.

"No cameras," Luc said. "That's nonnegotiable."

She narrowed her eyes as though to say *everything's negotiable*.

And for a woman who looked like Ava, everything probably was.

She was wearing a pantsuit today. It was light gray and should have been dull as hell, but the way it hugged her slim body was anything but subdued. And the strawberry-red of her high heels was distracting as all get-out.

"Perhaps we should get your supervisor." Her snooty tone made it clear that she expected to out-gun him, but this was one area where Luc knew that Captain Brinker, power-tripping as he was, would have his back.

"By all means," Luc replied with an easy smile and a

sweeping of his arm toward Brinker's office. "May I show you the way?"

Ava moved forward, as did her sulky-looking camera-man, and Luc held up a hand to stop the lanky blond from getting in the front doors.

"Not you. Her."

Ava rolled her eyes. "Wait here, Mihail. I'm sure Captain Brinker will clear this up."

Five minutes later, Luc didn't even bother to hide the smug grin as Ava regretfully told her cameraman that while the NYPD had every intention of cooperating as best they could, they simply couldn't allow a camera inside a building where sensitive documents were piled high on every desk.

As it was, Ava herself had a mound of confidentiality-agreement paperwork to get through, and Brinker set her up in one of the conference rooms.

Luc decided to take his last few moments of peace to catch up on his own paperwork.

His partner had other ideas.

"Dude. You never said she was hot."

"Who's hot?" Luc asked.

Lopez threw a paperclip at Luc, hitting him squarely in the chest. "Don't insult our friendship."

Luc grunted. It was bad enough that he had to put up with Ava Sims for the next few weeks; he drew the line at dis-cussing her almost painfully good looks with Sawyer.

Lopez was a damned good partner, but it was times like this that Luc missed Mike most acutely.

Luc had never had to worry about these sorts of things with his former partner. Mike Jensen had been happily mar-ried to a school nurse. They'd had a six-year-old son who'd had a *serious* case of hero worship for his dad...

Luc's fingers clenched around his pen. The last thing he needed on his mind right now was his former partner. Not with the fucking paparazzi sitting twenty feet away with an all-sanctioned pass to pry into his life and share his secrets with the world.

Not that he had any intentions of sharing his secrets with a reporter. Especially the one currently sitting down the hall.

But Ava Sims was smart and driven as hell. His instincts told him that if she wanted to find the story—the real story—she would.

Fuck.

Luc considered himself a *don't-stress-about-it* kind of guy, but from the second he'd heard the words *America's Hero* and *TV series*, he felt like he had a ball of tension permanently lodged in his chest.

Luc's eyes fell on his partner who was not-so-subtly doing the occasional 360 spin in his chair in hopes of catching sight of Ava when she finished up with her paperwork.

Inspiration struck, and Luc leaned back in his chair, trying to look at Lopez from Ava's point of view. His partner was good with women. Luc already knew that. But Sawyer tended toward the bubbly cheerful kind.

Not smooth-talking career women with just a substantial layer of *chill*.

Still...it was worth a shot.

Luc stifled the smile, letting his former scowl resettle on his face. If Lopez thought he was being played, there was no way he'd go for it.

"Hey, so Cap said the hot reporter would be doing ride-alongs with us. That'll be cool," Lopez said.

"Seriously? You hate ride-alongs," Luc said.

Lopez held up a finger. "No, I hate the dippy, *I-wanna-*

be-a-cop-someday type of ride-alongs. Those stupid kids are always offering advice when they don't know shit about shit. But Ms. Sims will be a nice kind of ride-along. Just sitting, observing... looking fine..."

Luc withheld the snort. If Lopez thought Ava wouldn't be offering *plenty* of unsolicited advice, he had an unpleasant surprise. He doubted *mind your own business* was in her DNA, not to mention it was a blatant contradiction of her job description.

"Hot or not, same rules apply," Luc said, just to set the record straight. "She can come on the *tame* ride-alongs. That's it."

"Shit, and here I was planning to bring her to a shoot-out," Lopez mused.

Luc flung the paperclip back at his partner, nailing him in the forehead. "Hey. So, I need you to be my wingman."

Lopez rubbed the red spot to the right of his temple with a knowing grin. "Ah, so you *do* want a piece of Miss Media."

Yes.

No!

Damn it.

"Let me rephrase," Luc said, sitting back in his chair. "I need you to be my *reverse* wingman. Do whatever you need to keep that plastic, nosy diva away from me."

There was a light tap on his shoulder before a female voice spoke up. "Gonna be hard when this nosy diva is hell-bent on getting *all* up in your business."

Whoops.

"Nice job, *Wingman*," Luc said with a glare at Lopez, whose grin indicated that he'd definitely seen Ava approaching and had opted not to mention it.

Luc pivoted around in his chair so he faced Ava. Only he

was sitting, and she was standing, which put him exactly at eye level with Ava's slim hips.

Generally speaking, Luc liked a little more curve to his women, but apparently his preferences were shifting, because he couldn't help his sex-starved brain from thinking that Ava Sims's hips were the perfect size for his hands to wrap around, his fingers holding her still as he prepared to plunge into her...

The fantasy dissolved into a million pieces when she opened her sassy mouth again.

"You know..." her voice was considering, her finger tapping idly against her lips. "I'd always heard that the whole man-in-uniform thing was supposed to be a turn-on. Guess it's an acquired taste."

Luc's eyes narrowed just slightly. "See, here I am having a similar revelation. Always thought you TV people were supposed to be likable. Guess that's subjective too."

Lopez snickered behind them. "Doesn't look like you need that reverse-wingman, Moretti. This one's not exactly throwing herself at you, now is she?"

Just like that, Ava's bourbon-colored eyes left Luc's and landed on his partner. She apparently liked what she saw, because the tension around her mouth eased and she actually smiled. Not one of those forced shark smiles either. A real one.

Apparently she wasn't so immune to the man-in-uniform thing after all.

She was just immune to *Luc*. Exactly as he wanted it.

Riiiiight.

Luc watched as Ava moved around Luc's desk to Lopez's. "Ava Sims. You're a colleague of Luc's?"

"Give the woman a medal," Luc muttered. "What was it that gave it away, the uniform or the badge?"

Ava didn't bother to turn around, but her right arm curled around behind her small waist to present him with a lone middle finger.

Nice.

Luc tried not to pay attention as Lopez and Ava chatted it up like old friends.

Just like he tried to ignore the fact that her new position meant he was free from looking at her hips, but now had her perfect ass in view.

Once again, this woman's body sent his mind directly to the gutter, and even as he wanted her to stop yapping, he also wanted to bend her over this very desk, inch those nice-girl slacks down her thighs to reveal naughty-girl panties.

Jesus. Luc rubbed a hand over his face. *Get it together, Moretti.*

It didn't help that her perfume exuded spicy and sweet at the same time.

The spice he could see. But the sweet...*ha*. Talk about a fucking red herring.

"Yo, Lopez, Moretti!"

Thank God. An interruption. He hoped it was something bloody and gritty as hell to free him from Ava Sims–inspired fantasies.

Both he and Lopez looked up to see Sergeant Anders standing up to get their attention. "Ten-fifty over at Chelsea Pier. You want?"

"On it," Luc said, standing up so quickly his chair nearly tipped backward.

Lopez grumbled but stood as well.

"What's a ten-fifty?" Ava asked.

Lopez met Luc's eyes. "We taking her?"

"Yes," Ava said, just as Luc said *hell no*.

She'd already whipped out one of those annoying little reporter notebooks with the spiral on top—really, they actually used those?—and looked up at him defiantly.

And a little bit smugly too, because she knew what he knew:

He was *supposed* to take her with him. The only reason she was here sending him into a daytime wet dream was because she wanted to shadow his every move and then blast his every secret to the entire country.

Luc longed to put an end to it here and now. To tell Ava Sims he wasn't going to sell out as some sort of hero because he did the same job that thousands of first-responders did every day.

He wanted to tell her to go harass one of those officers who *hadn't* been unlucky enough to get caught on camera.

Anders ambled over glancing at his notes. "Mid-thirties, white male. Witness reports range from hefty to huge. Last seen at Pier thirty-one, although seems to be roaming."

"What's a ten-fifty?" Ava asked again.

"Disorderly conduct," Luc said, already moving toward the door.

"Intoxicated?" Lopez asked Anders, following Luc.

Anders shrugged. "Undetermined."

Ava was hitching her bag over her shoulder, trotting along beside them. "I'm coming."

Luc halted and turned, putting a hand against her chest to stop her forward movement.

A mistake.

His hand was high enough to keep his fingers out of reach from her more interesting parts, but he could still feel her heart hammering against his palm all the same.

It was . . .

Shit, she *really* couldn't come with them. He couldn't be near her and think straight.

Luc jerked his hand back. "You. Stay."

"Which would defeat the purpose of me being here, wouldn't it? I'm your shadow." She pushed his wrist aside. "Learn how to deal with it."

"I need to do my job, Sims," he said as she moved past him to follow.

Her spine straighter. "And I need to do mine."

"Luc, we need to move," Lopez called from the door. "She can wait in the car if the guy's out of hand."

Luc opened his mouth to protest, when Anders broke in with one more detail. "There are also reports of ID."

Luc and Lopez groaned at the same time, both heading toward the door.

Ava followed, and this time Luc let her. Maybe he could use her nosiness against her.

It was time to let Sims see just how unsexy this job could be.

CHAPTER SEVEN

So, apparently, there was a naked man running up and down Chelsea Pier.

Well, not a *totally* naked man. Ava had overheard Lopez questioning an elderly couple, and according to them, the perp still wore his too-small white tank top and beat-up leather sandals.

But the crucial, um, *bits* of him were apparently flopping out there for all to see.

And judging by the old lady's hand motions, *flopping* was unfortunately literal.

Ava stood near the car where Luc had curtly told her to stay put. She didn't see what the big deal was. Not like she hadn't seen a naked man before.

Well okay, it had been a while.

Her eyes found Officer Moretti as he interviewed a couple of runners, her eyes taking in wide shoulders and tapered waist.

He was taller than average, but there was nothing lanky or gangly about him. His standard-issue uniform did little to disguise the clench and release of muscles when he moved, and her mouth went dry as she imagined her fingers unbuttoning his shirt, sliding it off sculpted shoulders to reveal what she was about 90 percent sure would be a flawless six-pack...

Ava shook her head to clear it.

Okay, so maybe it had been a *long* while since she'd seen a naked man.

But she hated it was Moretti who made her remember that her last date had been...

When exactly?

Three months? Six?

Why couldn't it be Officer Lopez who made her a little crazy? Luc's partner was drop-dead gorgeous, and a hell of a lot more charming than Moretti.

So why did it have to be *Luc* who reminded her that she'd been celibate for way longer than she'd like?

It's not like Ava was one of those hyper-independent women who was determined to remain single at all costs.

Ava loved to date. Or at least she liked the idea of dating. That giddy anticipation of whether she'd feel *it*—that spark of, *yes, maybe this could work!*

Okay, so, admittedly, as far as expectations went, the bar was pretty low.

But Ava was no naive twenty-two-year-old college grad who thought the right guy was just around the corner. She'd kissed a lot of toads.

A *lot*.

She wasn't at *all* sure her happily ever after was out there, so when it came to first dates, Ava was just fine settling for a *maybe* and decent conversation.

But even the *maybes* had been few and far between. For a city with several million people you'd think there'd be at least one guy she found attractive who didn't bore her silly.

Ava sighed and readjusted her pony.

After this story, she'd put more effort into the dating scene. She loved her career—sometimes—but she didn't want to be married to it.

Actually, she didn't want to be *married* at all. Ever. To anyone.

As though sensing her gaze on his back—okay, his butt—Luc whipped his head around and his eyes clamped on hers.

Embarrassed to be caught staring, Ava jerked her gaze away. This was so not the time to be playing sexy-eyes with a grumpy cop.

Part of Ava's job was knowing when people were at their limits, and Luc Moretti had been at his when they'd first arrived at the pier and he caught her taking notes while he interviewed a witness.

Whoopsie.

She'd been banished to the car.

But hey, bright side...at least now she knew what an ID was in cop-speak:

Indecent exposure.

It *also* explained why Luc Moretti had changed his mind about letting her tag along. He thought she'd be scared off.

Please. It would take a hell of a lot more than a flaccid penis on a disorderly drunk to scare her off the story.

She would, however, be omitting this particular cop-experience from her prime-time coverage.

And the story *would* be prime time. That had been the only reason Ava had agreed to do something so...scripted.

The network had been hard up for the type of feel-good

story for the summer evenings after the featured farm in their farm-to-table, organic food series had gotten nailed on animal cruelty charges.

The higher-ups had been in a panic, and Ava had (stupidly, in hindsight) mentioned the local coverage of a hero cop video gone viral. Her boss had gone crazy for the story.

And as a reward, Ava had gotten first shot at it. This was it. Her make-or-break story. She knew it, Mihail knew it, her bosses knew it…

But Luc Moretti didn't know it. Or perhaps more accurately, Luc Moretti didn't *care*.

Ava slumped back against the car for a second before realizing it would probably get dirt all over her suit, and she jumped back before turning around and frantically trying to check out her own ass for smudges. Anchorwomen were supposed to care about these things.

Thank God Mihail wasn't here. He'd be armed with another comment about how Gwen Garrison could wear a white gown at rush hour on the J train and walk away without so much as a speck of dirt on her.

Well Ava Sims wasn't Gwen Garrison, and this whole fancy, polished thing was *hard*.

But she was determined to get used to it.

After confirming that she didn't have brown streaks on her butt from the patrol car, Ava turned back around to see if Luc and his quick-with-a-line partner were wrapping up their 10-50-whatever so she could get in a few interview questions.

She wondered how long Lopez and Luc had been working together. She made a note in her spiral to find out.

Sawyer Lopez shared Luc's same dramatic coloring, with

dark hair and blue eyes, and she imagined the pair of them were like heartbreak on a plate for those women who liked the men in uniform thing.

Which Ava didn't. So she kept telling herself.

She bit her nail, then jerked her hand away as she tried not to get impatient. Sitting still and waiting were so not her favorite activities. Ava pulled out her cell phone. A missed call from her sister, several Instagram updates from her brother in what looked like Vienna, and a text from Beth beginning with SOS.

Ava scanned the text from Beth. As expected, it was wedding related. *All* of Beth's texts were wedding related these days, and at least half of them were SOS. Not that Ava minded. What were best friends for if not to make the appropriate soothing noises when the videographer you'd been hoping for was already booked.

Dutifully, Ava responded that the videographer was mediocre anyway, they'd find a *way* better one, and why don't they meet up for happy hour tonight to discuss it?

Beth was definitely toeing the line on Bridezilla territory, but luckily Ava had found the cure: wine.

Maid of honor duty done for the time being, she put her phone away, and to prevent herself from staring—and drooling—over the way Luc Moretti looked in his uniform, Ava began running through the structure of the *America's Hero* footage.

It would probably take hours of following Luc around to get even five minutes of footage. That's how it was with stuff like this. Nobody wanted to see that cops sometimes got stuck in traffic too, so they'd resort to a montage.

Likely with a voice-over about "the side of a cop's day-to-day you never see in the movies."

Which was really just reporter talk for *boring stuff*.

Her fingernail crept up to the corner of her mouth, and she nibbled at the edge of her ring-finger nail.

It was a horrible habit. One she was determined to break. Eventually. Mihail was a champ about always batting her hand away when she got the nervous nail-biting urge, but he was nowhere to be seen today.

Ava groaned and dropped her hand as she remembered her friend. *Mihail*. Why hadn't she thought to call him? How was she going to get even five minutes of footage when she'd gone and forgotten her cameraman?

It was Luc Moretti's fault. Those damn blue eyes were distracting.

Her eyes searched for Lopez, but she didn't see him anywhere. Then she looked for Luc and found him almost immediately. It was like he was a damned beacon for her gaze.

Her eyes narrowed just slightly. What made him tick? What caused that compelling combination of easy charm, effortless competence, and guarded mystery?

Because regardless of how boring her opening voice-over was, the real grit of the story would come from interviews.

She needed to get Luc Moretti to talk to her.

Which wasn't likely considering she couldn't seem to go five minutes without pissing him off, but honestly, the man was almost painfully easy to goad.

At least when it came to her.

"Hello, pretty lady."

It was only pure shock that prevented Ava from jumping out of her skin. That, and Ava hadn't grown up with two annoying siblings and not been in for a few nasty surprises.

Of course, her siblings hadn't usually been, um, nude.

And they weren't mid-forties and balding.

Mr. Indecent Exposure had found her.

And he was still very much *indecent*.

With her heels on, Ava was almost eye level with the half-naked guy, and she kept her eyes very, very carefully locked on his.

She'd been sort of assuming they were dealing with someone who was mentally ill, or perhaps under the influence. But up close, this guy seemed merely mischievous and perhaps not too bright.

His blue eyes were round and twinkling. This man was very aware of what he was doing, even if he was a little clueless about the consequences.

"Sir, I don't want to embarrass you," she said, keeping her voice mellow and easy, "but you seem to have forgotten a couple of important items of clothing."

"Damn straight. Wouldn't you, to win a bet?"

Oh yikes. That's what this was about? A bet?

Still, Ava was nothing if not a skilled conversationalist when need be. *Where was Luc?*

She needed to keep Mr. Almost-Naked here, and touching the man was out of the question. Obviously. Somewhere along the way, the white tank top he'd supposedly been wearing must have gone the way of his pants.

She gave him an easy smile, never letting her gaze stray below his eyes. *Reel him in, Ava.* "Truth be told, I find it a bit hard to turn down a dare myself," she said, her voice low and confidential.

Do not look down. Do not look down.

"Yeah!" He brightened, moving as though to sit down on the curb for a nice long chat. "See, *you* get it. I've been trying to explain, but—"

"Sir. No." Ava held up a solitary finger. "Put your pants on."

"But you said—"

"I said it was *hard* to turn down a bet, not impossible. Have some dignity, man."

"But I have to stay this way until noon or I don't win."

She heaved out a sigh, resisting the urge to ask what prize could possibly be worth this humiliation. She looked around for Luc and his partner. Maybe *this* was why they'd wanted her to stay in the car.

Oh, wait, the *car*...

Ava hitched a thumb over her shoulder. "You do see the vehicle I'm standing next to, right?"

The man followed the direction of her point and for the first time, his impish smile slipped. "Shit. Are you..."

"A plainclothes police officer? Maybe." She folded her arms across her chest.

He began to back away, and Ava shifted her eyes to the sky to avoid nightmares for a week.

"Sorry, sir. Ma'am. Sir. Officer. Um, I won't bother you..."

"I'll tell ya what," she says, snapping her fingers. "I won't turn you in, *if* you agree to put on some clothes and then knock some sense into your moron friends who put you up to this."

But Naked Man wasn't paying attention to her rather excellent advice. His gaze was locked behind her shoulder, his eyes wide and terrified.

Uh oh.

"Sims, Sims, Sims," came the low, horribly familiar voice. "Did I just hear you impersonate a police officer, bargain with a known suspect, and then propose that he commit battery?"

"I like to think of it as a Good Samaritan thing," she said, turning around to face one very pissed Officer Moretti.

"Or...citizen's arrest?" she asked cheerfully when he didn't respond.

Behind her, she heard Lopez's slightly accented voice mingled in with the loud protests of the guy who was now being cuffed. Luc still hadn't said a word.

"Is um...Lopez putting handcuffs on a butt-ass-naked dude?" she asked, pointing over her shoulder. "Because *that's* gotta be an interesting visual."

Luc continued to study her with dark blue eyes.

Ava heaved out a sigh. "Look, *he* found *me*. What was I supposed to do? Run away screaming?"

"Well you sure as hell aren't to engage him in a conversation!"

"Well I wouldn't have had to if you'd actually done your job."

Luc's eyes flared and he took an angry step toward her.

Interesting, Ava thought, eyes narrowing. Officer Moretti takes his job very seriously.

Behind her, she heard Mr. Naked explaining the virtues of following through on a dare to a very unsympathetic Lopez. The car door slammed and Lopez came around to interrupt Luc and Ava's staring contest.

"We are going to need *serious* disinfectant in the backseat," he said, gesturing toward the car.

Eeew.

Luc pinched the bridge of his nose. "Great. Fucking great. Okay, let's take him in."

Lopez set a hand on the small of Ava's back, and Ava didn't think she imagined the way that Luc's eyes traced the motion.

"Sweetheart, this is where we part ways," Lopez said. "Can't let you ride along with the perp. Not that you'd want to."

Ava gave a regretful glance at the backseat of the cop car where Mr. Naked had his face pressed to the window and was shouting something she couldn't hear. "Do you think I could get his phone number? I think we really connected."

Lopez arched an eyebrow and leaned in a little, his white teeth flashing sexily against his dark skin. "So you're single, huh? Because I think I can give this perp a run for his money, if you know what I mean."

"Jesus," Luc muttered, shooting his partner a look. "I thought we agreed to try and get rid of Sims, not ask her out."

Ava frowned, a little stung, even though he hadn't made it a secret that he didn't want her around. "You *do* see me standing here, yes?"

His eye skimmed over her, hot and angry. "Yes, Sims, I see you. I've *been* seeing you. But don't think for one second that just because the NYPD decided to bend over for your network means I have to like the fact that you're interfering with my job. Got it?"

Loud and clear.

But instead of responding, she ignored his outburst completely and turned to Sawyer as though Luc had never spoken.

"I'll take a cab back to the precinct," she said. "What do you say I take you to lunch, and you can tell me all about what it's like to be the partner of this sweetheart of a super-hero here."

Lopez winked. "Love to."

Luc growled.

Ava turned on her heel, pausing only to kiss the tip of her index finger before pressing it against the backseat window where Mr. Naked was continuing to holler.

She very deliberately did not turn around to see if Luc Moretti watched her walk away. And she definitely didn't put a little extra wiggle in her hips just in case he was.

Okay, maybe she did that last part. Just a little.

Her eyes began scanning for a taxi as she began mentally compiling her story notes for the day:

Luc Moretti: a good cop? Probably. An ass? Definitely.

Simply following him around wasn't going to cut it. Luc Moretti the *officer* was the cover of the story, but Luc Moretti the *man* was the heart of it.

This would only work if she could get at the man beneath the uniform. Figure out what made him tick. What he loved. Whom he dated...

Did he have a girlfriend?

She needed to know.

For research's sake, obviously.

"Watch your back, Moretti," she muttered to herself as she raised her hand to hail an approaching cab. "I'm about to get *all* up in your personal life."

"What was that?"

Ava spun around and found herself toe to toe with one very annoyed, very attractive police officer. Over his shoulders she spotted their squad car pull into traffic.

"Did Sawyer just leave you here?"

"I told him to."

"Ah ha, so you left him to handle naked guy on his own."

"He can handle it."

"Why didn't you go with him?"

"Thought you and I need to have a little chat," he said.

Ava glared. "Thought we just did that when you berated me back there."

"You were interfering with police business."

"You sure you want to power-trip me this early in the game, Moretti? We're going to be spending lots of time together. You might want to save your lectures for the important moments."

Luc inhaled deeply. "You're a pain in the ass."

"And you're an absolute *delight*."

Ava was pretty sure that neither one of them actually moved, but somehow they were closer than ever now, and she didn't think it was her imagination that both were breathing harder than necessary.

And despite the cloudy skies, Ava was definitely feeling warmer than the weather warranted.

Confused by the unfamiliar onslaught of want, totally inappropriate given their circumstances and the fact that she didn't even know the guy, her eyes helplessly found his.

Ava was both gratified and alarmed to see the same frustration and confusion in Luc's expression.

Whatever was between them—this odd mix of attraction and distrust—he felt it too.

His forehead wrinkled in irritation before his head dropped toward her, bringing their mouths infinitesimally closer.

Suddenly, attraction was definitely winning out over distrust, because Ava knew if he kissed her...

She would kiss him back. Damn it. *Damn it,* that was so not what she needed to be feeling right now.

His eyes left hers to drop to her mouth and Ava felt her lips part, just slightly. It was an unbidden invitation, and from the flare of heat in his eyes he knew it. His mouth lowered, closer, and then—

"Excuse me, Officer?"

Ava jumped back so quickly she teetered on her high heels, and only Luc's quick reflexes as he grabbed her elbows to steady her kept her upright. The warmth of his palms branded her arms, but he released her just as quickly to turn to the young woman who'd interrupted her.

The girl was early twenties, wearing too tight jeans and a too tight shirt that definitely worked for her toned curves.

She grinned as she caught the full impact of Luc Moretti in uniform. "It *is* you. Oh my gosh, can I get a picture with you? My uncle's a cop, and he says you've done wonders to restore the department's prestige."

"Um." Luc looked pained, and Ava was surprised to feel a surge of sympathy. She still had her suspicions that he secretly relished the attention, but it was clear he was embarrassed at the moment.

It was exactly the moment she needed to shake off the sexual tension.

Ava reached forward and plucked the cute brunette's phone out of her hand. "Here, I'll take it."

"Thanks," the girl said, her eyes never leaving Luc's profile as he turned with a grimace toward the camera.

"Okay, I'll count to three," Ava said pointedly to the girl whose hand rested on Luc's abs as she moved in close, apparently oblivious to the camera and Ava.

But the girl knew what she was doing. As Ava got to three, the girl turned her head toward the camera with a well-timed hair flip, and the result was a picture-perfect moment between a stoic cop and an adorable groupie.

Ava handed the phone back to the girl, who took it back reluctantly, likely because the motion meant letting go of Luc.

"So, Officer…" The girl's eyelashes fluttered. As in actually *fluttered*.

Ava stuck her tongue in her cheek to hide her smirk. This should be good.

"Can I buy you a drink?"

"I'm on duty," he said, gesturing down at his gun.

The girl all but salivated and pressed on. "Oh, I know. I was thinking whenever you got off. Or another day, if that would be better."

Luc's smile never wavered, but Ava was surprised to see that the polite grin seemed almost pasted on his face, as though he'd rather be anywhere else. Which didn't make sense. The guy was gorgeous.

"Actually, I'm sort of seeing someone."

He was?

Luc's announcement caused more of a tug than it should, but when she looked at him more closely, she noticed the way he wouldn't meet the girl's eye.

Officer Moretti was lying. And from the guilty look on his face, he didn't lie easily.

Ava all but shook her head. As far as excuses went, it was merely *okay*. Not a good enough explanation for a girl who looked like a lingerie model and had confidence radiating off her in waves. Girls like this one would take *I'm seeing someone* as more of a challenge than a rejection.

"Lucky lady," the brunette said, wiggling closer to Luc. "But look, if it doesn't work out between you two, I can give you my—"

"Hear that, sweetie? At least *someone* thinks you're a lucky lady."

It took Ava several seconds to realize that Luc was talking to her.

Oh no. No freaking way...

But he merely grinned, reaching out a hand and pulling her closer. She opened her mouth to tell him off, but there was something in his gaze—desperation, maybe?—that had her hesitating. Ava let herself be pulled to his side, even sliding her arm around his waist, but the pinch she delivered to his side said he'd pay for the lie later. At least she *tried* to pinch. The man had, like, zero body fat.

The way their bodies pressed together caused a shiver of awareness to come over Ava. A shiver she ignored.

At least until he slid his hand over the small of her back, down over her waist until his fingers splayed over her hip as though they belonged there. And damn it, it felt like they *did* belong there.

Like she belonged *here*. With him.

Oh, this was so not good.

"Oh my god," the girl said, her hand flattening against her chest. To her credit, she looked genuinely dismayed. "I'm so sorry. When I saw you guys standing here I thought you were arguing—"

"We were," Ava said.

"Foreplay," Luc interrupted huskily, as his gaze raked down Ava's body. "It really revs her motors."

"Revs my motors?" Ava asked, pushing against him in annoyance. Because annoyance was safer than arousal. "Are you kidding me right now with the woman-as-car metaphors?"

"You like it," he said, looping his arm casually around her neck while giving the girl a boyish grin.

"You know what else I'd like?" Ava hissed. "If you took your police baton, or whatever it's called, and shoved it up your—"

His mouth was on her before she could finish the sentence.

It was a quick kiss.

Just a hard stamp of *shut-the-hell-up*. There was no tongue, just the press of his mouth against hers, lingering only slightly, but the kiss rocked Ava all the same.

Luc, on the other hand, seemed completely unaffected, and as soon as his mouth left hers, his eyes sought his admirer who was already walking away.

With a look of relief, he released Ava, who was still feeling a little unsteady from the feel of his lips on hers, however meaningless and quick it had been.

"What the hell was that?" she asked to his retreating back since he was already walking away.

He stopped and turned back. "What was that?" He turned around, but didn't stop moving as he walked backward. "That, Sims, was a test."

She started after him. "Yeah? What did it prove?"

"That I like your mouth a hell of a lot better when it's not yapping. Now, you coming or what?"

Ava glared at his retreating back.

Yup, it was official. America's Hero *was* a total ass.

But the man could kiss.

CHAPTER EIGHT

Luc had become a creature of habit.

Which shocked the hell out of him, because as a kid, he'd been all over the place. As a teen, he'd stopped just shy of being unmanageable.

But as an adult?

He was like clockwork.

Not because he was the uptight, rigid type. He wasn't. But when your career was such that an average week involved transitions between life-threatening situations one day and mind-numbing boredom, it helped to fill everything in between with routine.

Coffee at the same place.

Grilled cheese from the same food cart every Friday.

Somehow, this structured lifestyle had seeped into Luc's days off as well, because it was no longer a conscious decision to head to his favorite hole-in-the-wall diner for a late breakfast when he was off duty. It was simply what he *did*.

Luc had never been one of those introverted, solitary types. He loved filling most of his spare time with friends, family... women.

But these morning breakfasts?

These mornings were Luc's time. To reflect. Think. Try to forget.

Which was why on a sunny spring Saturday, nearly a week after the indecent exposure incident at Chelsea Pier, Luc's feet suddenly seemed incapable of moving when he walked into the Darby Diner and saw *her*.

Ava Sims.

Luc's reaction to seeing Ava, not just at his favorite restaurant but at his favorite table, was too jumbled to sort out. Anger at her gall. Annoyance at having his solitude ripped away. Panic at what she might find out about him when he didn't have his uniform to protect him.

Arousal. Definitely arousal.

Luc settled on clinging to the anger, and he let his scowl show it. The line between classy television reporter and stalker-paparazzi was proving very murky indeed.

Luc intended to ignore her. To walk right past her to a different table, to pretend she hadn't just crossed a very serious boundary of harassing him outside of work.

And he started to do just that.

Right up until the moment he found himself sliding into the seat across from her.

"Sims."

"Officer."

Her eyes dropped briefly to his chest, and she blinked a little in surprise. "You're not in uniform."

"If you had a uniform, you wouldn't wear it on your day off either."

She tilted her head. "What makes you think I don't have a uniform?"

There was something in her voice that made Luc give her a second look, taking his eyes off her only long enough to give Helen a smile and a wink in exchange for the coffee she poured him without asking.

Helen winked back, sliding two menus on the table, more for Ava's sake than his.

Luc didn't order the same thing every time (he wasn't *that* OCD), but he *did* know the menu by heart.

Ava smiled in thanks as Helen refilled her coffee mug as well, and Luc noted that this was one of her *real* smiles.

The type of smile that made her eyes light and nose crinkle just a little. It was a smile he'd seen her give to about everyone but him.

Damn it. He wanted that smile.

"One of your groupies?" Ava asked, nodding in the direction of Helen after she'd moved on to another table.

"Something like that," Luc said.

Helen was special to the Morettis. Was special to Luc, especially these days. The elderly waitress was one of the only people who'd always treated Luc like a person. Not a cop. He suspected Helen was the biggest reason the Darby Diner continued to be the Morettis' favorite Sunday brunch place. Not because the food was outstanding, or the décor was comfortable, or even because it was habit.

But because Helen Carter understood that despite the legacy, the Morettis were a family first. Cops second.

"So your uniform," Luc continued, not wanting to explain any of this to Sims. "Is this it?"

Luc used his eyes to gesture rather than his hand.

She was wearing another button-down blouse, this one a lime green that made her eyes look almost hazel.

Don't notice her eyes, dude.

He couldn't see her bottom half, but considering her makeup was flawless, her hair perfectly styled, he figured it was the same tailored dress pants she'd been wearing for the past week.

High heels, almost for sure.

Damn it, now he was hungry. And not for breakfast.

"Let's just say it's not *my* day off," she said, her eyes dropping to her coffee mug.

In spite of himself, Luc was intrigued. "What do you wear on your days off? Be descriptive."

Right down to the bra. Or tell me you're wearing no bra.

Yeah, actually, make that *definitely* on the no bra.

Ava cupped her hands around her mug, leaning toward him. "Hey, here's an idea. How about *you* become a reporter, then *you* get to ask the questions."

He leaned forward. "And by become a reporter, I assume you mean put on a lot of makeup and ask prying questions?"

Her head snapped back a little, and although her eyes moved down to her coffee before he could read her expression, he felt an instant surge of regret.

Just because he was frustrated didn't mean he needed to be an ass. She was just doing her job. It occurred to him that maybe he was every bit as much in *her* way as she was in his.

For a second, the old Luc—the one that was good with people—returned, and he touched her hand.

"Hey," he said softly.

Her eyes lifted, but the wariness remained.

Damn it.

"Sorry," he said bluntly. "I may not love your career, but belittling it's a dick move."

To Luc's surprise, she merely nodded in acceptance, not making a huffy drama out of it. Instead she reached for one of the vinyl-covered menus.

"What's good here?"

"Don't you have my favorites memorized?" he teased.

Her lips twisted into a small smile and she glanced up. "You want to know how I found out about this place, don't you?"

"I do."

She tapped her nails against the table, and he noticed that at least two of them were dramatically chipped. It was the only part of her incongruent with an otherwise perfectly manicured persona.

"Sawyer told me. Said your family comes here every Sunday, but that on your days off, you come alone."

"Figures you got Lopez to talk," Luc said, taking a sip of coffee. "How'd you get it out of him, agree to go on a date?"

"He tried. I dodged."

Luc grunted, oddly relieved by this revelation.

"I opted for a lap dance instead," she deadpanned.

Luc choked on his coffee.

"He even got change for a twenty," she continued. "And let me tell you, there's something oddly gratifying about having all those one-dollar bills slide against your skin when he tucks them into your G-string, you know?"

Luc coughed up the coffee that he'd aspirated. "That's just...no words. I have no words."

Helen returned to take their order.

Luc got a bacon, spinach, Swiss omelet with fruit instead

of potatoes. Ava ordered the same, with the addition of mushrooms.

"Fruit, huh?" she asked when Helen had walked away.

"I like it," Luc said with a shrug. "Not manly enough for you?"

"Yeah, because that's what *all* women look for in a man. The right breakfast side-order."

They both sipped their coffee, and Luc finally asked the crucial question. "What are you doing here, Sims?"

Ava took a deep breath, but to her credit, she met his gaze dead-on. "I wanted to get to know you."

Well that was...blunt. And interesting.

He leaned in a little. "For the sake of the story? Or for *you*?"

"The story," she said, the words coming out too quickly, despite the fact that his tone had been deliberately teasing.

Luc sat back and considered.

"Sims, we've spent every day of the past week together. You're practically my second partner on the job, even if you're in the way more often than not."

"Hey!"

He held up a hand to stop the protest. "No. You are, and you know it."

She huffed. "I just wanted to turn on the siren once. Just to try it."

"Uh huh. You're telling me it had nothing to do with the fact that it was rush hour and you had to pee?"

She waved this away. "Look, I know that I've been... annoying. But I'm just trying to do my job."

He groaned. "Enough with that. We both want to do our jobs without the other getting in our way, but that's not going to happen, is it? In order for me to do my job well, I need you to go away. For *you* to do your job well, you need me to kiss your ass."

She leaned forward, her eyes as intense as he'd seen them. "You don't have to kiss my ass, Moretti. Truly. I just need you to talk to me."

"I do talk to you."

"No, you grunt, growl, and lecture."

Luc took a sip of coffee to hide his surprise at the accusation.

Luc was not the grunting, growling type.

Not to toot his own horn or anything, but truth be told, Luc had always thought of himself as being fairly, well... likable.

Of all the Moretti clan, Luc was the quickest to smile and according to his mother, the easiest to talk to.

That last one, of course, could have been due to his mother buttering him up so he'd come over and help her move her recipes from ragged index cards to "the cloud" on the new laptop his dad had bought.

But with or without his mother's praise, Luc was sure of one thing:

This was the first time a woman had ever accused him of being an irritable prick.

And although he was tempted to snap back that it was only *her* that drew out this grumpy, unlikable version of himself, the truth was he felt a little ashamed of himself.

Like those assholes who disdained all law enforcement for life because of one "undeserved" speeding ticket when they were seventeen, Luc had been making similar stereotypes about the media based on his own desire for privacy.

Ava was right. She was just doing her job.

And he may not like it, but that didn't authorize being a complete dick.

After Helen had delivered their breakfast, Luc picked up his fork and made a decision. He wasn't going to bend over backward for her.

He still thought this story was bullshit.

But...

"All right, Sims. I'll talk."

She was about to take a bite of egg, but her fork paused halfway to her mouth. "Seriously?"

"Today only," he said, liberally adding pepper to his dish. "Don't be expecting the welcome mat at the precinct on Monday, and this isn't a free pass to turn on the siren whenever you get hungry, and you still have to pay that parking ticket. But I respect that you have three hours of stupid television to put together. So for today...shoot."

He half expected her to go all rabid on him, pulling out a notebook or worse, a recorder, and firing question after question, but she merely chewed her omelet and looked thoughtful.

"Thank you," she said finally.

"You're welcome."

She smiled. "We're having a moment, aren't we?"

"Sims, if this is your idea of a moment, your social life must be seriously up a creek."

"Speaking of social life," she said, plopping a piece of cantaloupe in her mouth.

Here we go...

"Do you have a girlfriend?"

The question was more direct than he'd expected, and Luc had to remind himself she was asking as a reporter, not as an interested party.

"Nope."

"Ex?"

"I'm twenty-eight. I should *hope* I had a couple exes under my belt by now."

"But anyone serious?" She took a sip of coffee.

"I don't do serious, Sims."

She cocked her head to the side. "Ever?"

Luc shrugged. "Lots of cops don't."

"Because of the frequent brush-with-death thing?"

He was silent for a moment as he pictured Mike. And Mike's funeral. Then he remembered Mike's widow and son sobbing silently in the front row of the church...

His fingers clenched into a fist beneath the table, and he forced himself to take a long, slow breath. *This* was why Ava Sims was dangerous to him. It would only take a few well-placed questions, and the entire world would know that their hero-cop was so far from a hero it wasn't even funny.

"Let's just say I know a few too many cop widows—and widowers, for that matter—to ever put a woman I cared about through that."

"But your entire family is cops. Surely they don't all feel that way."

"No," he granted. "My parents have been happily married for over three decades. And my brother Marco is halfway to the altar already. The other two...hell, I doubt they could *pay* a woman to put up with them for life, so it doesn't really matter."

She opened her mouth as though to argue, but Luc beat her to it.

"Cops don't make good husbands, Sims." He softened the statement with a smile.

It was hardly the first time he'd had this conversation with a woman. Luc was always careful to set expectations upfront, but some women seemed to think they were the exception to the rule.

But Luc's commitment to non-marriage was one rule he had no intention of breaking.

Ava surprised him. "No judgment here. Marriage is..." she paused, as though searching for the right word. "Crap," she finished.

Luc washed a bite of bacon down with a sip of water, surprised by her succinct dismissal of marriage.

It wasn't that he thought all women were secretly trying on wedding dresses in their spare time, but in his experience it was rare to run into a woman who was so openly *anti*.

And though he was tempted to ask why...to know what made her tick, he took the easy path instead.

"Sims." He let his eyes go wide in bafflement. "Did we just have something in common?"

She smiled, and it was a pretty thing, this genuine smile instead of the knee-jerk smile he was used to seeing from her. "I won't tell if you won't."

"Deal. So what else do you have for me? You've got until I clean my plate to pick my brain, because once I'm on duty, chitchat is off-limits."

"Hold on there, cowboy, we're not done with the prior topic just yet," she said, nipping a corner of her toast with her perfect white teeth. "So you're not looking to march down the aisle. I get it. But what *does* a bachelor cop's love life look like?"

"What's it look like? Lots of curvy blondes, mostly. Often naked," he replied.

"Sounds very Beverly Hills brothel."

He smiled at her tart tongue as he took his last bite of omelet. "Probably could make room for a skinny brunette who talks too much though."

Ava pulled her napkin off her lap and began fanning herself. "Wow. With moves like these, how do you ever find time to sleep?"

"Seriously though, Sims, leave my love life out of the story, would ya?"

"But—"

"Look, I get it," he said, his voice gentle. "People want to see that stuff. They want to know I'm half-smitten with a childhood sweetheart or 'waiting for the right one,' but I can't give you that."

She threw up her hands. "Well I can't just say you're a bed-hopping commitment-phobe."

He frowned. "Why not? It's the truth."

"Which usually is what I'm after, but—"

His head snapped up at that little slip. "What do you mean that's *usually* what you're after? What's different about this story?"

She lifted her hand and nibbled on her thumbnail before tucking it into her fist and putting her hand back in her lap. "I just mean that this is a big story. A lot of people will be looking at it."

"Isn't that the point of network television? Lots of people looking at it?"

"No, I mean, a lot of *network* people will be looking at it. My bosses."

He searched her face, surprised to see the conflict there, even though he didn't understand it. "And they're expecting to hear about my love life?"

She chewed her lip, the nervous gesture at odds with her polished appearance. "Let's just say a little romance wouldn't hurt the story. They want something that'll make the audience melt, you know?"

Too damn bad. The only secrets Luc had were the kind to make the audience hate him.

He reached across the table to pat her arm. "You're a good reporter, Sims. You'll find a way to romance it."

"Maybe I'll stick with the 'currently married to his job' thing. They don't need to know that *currently* is actually *indefinitely.*"

"There you go. What else?" He held up his last piece of toast. My plate is nearly clean."

"Tell me about college."

"What about it?"

"Cops don't have to go, and yet you and all of your brothers did. Sister too."

Luc paused in his chewing, torn between admiration and annoyance. "You know, your tenacity is bordering on creepy."

"Are you deflecting?"

He shrugged. "Of course not. There's just not much to say. It was college. Dorms. Dorm food. Professors. Exams. Finals. Cute girls. I mean, I'd tell you that I was a decent student, but you've probably already tracked down and memorized my transcript."

"Three point nine two; major in Econ. Not bad, Officer."

He smiled in thanks at Helen as she cleared their plates. "But you want to know why I'd go if I didn't have to."

Her lips tilted. "Sort of."

Luc leaned back in the booth. "Well, I'd like to tell you I was an incredibly driven eighteen-year-old, desperate to pursue my education, but the truth is it was all my mom."

"She made you go?"

"Sort of. I mean, being the youngest, I sort of knew it was coming, and it never occurred to me to resist. But even as she was my dad's biggest supporter as he climbed the ranks, Mom never wanted her children to think they *had* to follow in his footsteps. College was her way of giving us a chance to know something other than the cop life."

"But you're all cops."

"The guys, yeah. My sister, no." Luc pulled out his wallet as Helen dropped off the check, but Ava was too quick. "I've got it."

He considered for a second and then put his wallet away. "Because you ruined my solitude on my only day off this week, sure."

Luc was a little surprised at the flash of guilt on her face. Ava might be tenacious but she wasn't without a conscience.

That little flash of humanity bothered him.

He couldn't afford to like her. Not when there was so much to lose.

"One more question?" she said as he moved to the edge of his booth.

"No guarantee there'll be an answer, but sure."

"When you did those things . . . jumped into the river and gave the homeless guy a jacket. Did you know there was a camera on you?"

All friendly thoughts he'd had toward her dried up.

Instead of replying, he lifted his coffee mug, draining the last sip before standing.

He met her eyes with a silent *fuck off* before he walked away.

There were some idiotic questions just not worth answering.

CHAPTER NINE

For the last time, the dress does not make your butt look big," Ava said.

"I look bottom heavy. I know I do."

Ava slowly rotated around her best friend, taking a sip of champagne as she did. "Okay, you're right. The dress doesn't work. You're too tiny, the ballroom gown style overwhelms you."

Beth scowled down at her from the podium in the center of the shop's dressing room. "How dare you. I look like a princess."

Ava chewed on the inside of her cheek. "You *just* said you looked bottom heavy. Now you're a princess?"

Beth's scowl grew. "Princesses can be bottom heavy."

Ava wordlessly plucked Beth's champagne flute off a side table and handed it to her. "So get the dress then."

"But I don't *like* this one." Beth took a sip of her drink

before handing it back and holding out a hand to be helped down from the podium.

"You've got to pick one soon, sweetie," Ava said as Beth moved back toward her dressing room, barely fitting through the door in her huge dress. "You're five one and negative twenty pounds, so whatever you pick is likely going to need to be tailored."

The door opened, a pair of blue cat eyes and a cloud of orange curls glaring back at Ava. "Are you *trying* to give me a heart attack?"

An arm shot out and Ava handed her the champagne glass before the door closed again.

"You pick the next dress," Beth grumbled from inside the room. "That way when it makes me look like a church bell I can blame you."

"Try this one," Ava said, picking up a mermaid gown that she'd spotted earlier. She set it over the dressing room door and waited for the protest she knew was coming.

"It's mermaid style."

"Which will look fabulous on you."

The door opened again, and her tiny friend stood unabashed in green bikini panties and the nude-colored strapless bra she'd dubbed her "Saturday uniform" for the past few weeks.

"I said no mermaid style. I'll look like Ariel."

"There are worse things than resembling an adorable Disney princess."

Beth scowled and pointed at another puffy-skirted dress on a mannequin. "I'll try on that one. I like the pearls on the hem."

"Sure. *After* the mermaid one," Ava pressed.

"But—"

Ava reached into the dressing room and snatched the yellow sundress that Beth had worn into the shop. "Fine then. You can walk out of here naked."

With an exasperated sound her friend shut the door. "I knew I should have asked my cousin to be maid of honor."

"Tonya's a pushover and a total girly-girl. You want to *not* look like a cupcake on your wedding day, you've gotta stick with me."

"How's she doing?" asked the saleswoman who'd wisely given them some privacy after Beth had thrown a tantrum over her tenth dress. And that was eight dresses ago.

"Really getting somewhere," Ava said with a smile. "Nearly there, I think."

"If by nearly there you mean I'm going to look like a sea creature!" Beth called over the door.

Ava caught the salesperson's eye and held up her empty champagne class, and the woman nodded in understanding.

Sitting on one of the aqua-cushioned benches meant for enthusiastic mothers and exhausted bridesmaids, Ava waited for her friend to emerge with her umpteenth dress of the day.

Ava didn't need any reason to doubt the appeal of marriage, but if she did, the proof was right here. Beth Salvers's impending wedding had turned Ava's best friend into a temperamental stress ball.

Granted Beth had always been a little high strung, but since being engaged, she was about one bad cake tasting away from an aneurysm. Lucky for Beth, her fiancé Christian found her short-lived tantrums adorable.

So did Ava…with the help of a glass of champagne. Or three.

Still, Beth could turn into the worst sort of Bridezilla imaginable, and Ava would give up all her Saturdays to help her find the perfect dress. It was what best friends did. Especially when it was the gold standard of best friends, which Beth Salvers definitely was.

The salesgirl returned with the champagne bottle, topping off Ava's glass before offering to leave the bottle for Beth, should she also need a refill.

Judging from the prolonged silence inside the dressing room, Beth was definitely going to need it.

"Hon, you okay?" Ava asked, standing and going to the door.

There was a beat of silence, before her friend opened the door a tiny crack. "If I come out, you can't say one word."

"Oh, come on, if you don't like it, you don't have to come out." She handed her friend's sundress back. "Here, I won't even hold your clothes hostage."

And then the door opened and Ava understood exactly what words she wasn't supposed to say.

I told you so.

Beth held up a finger. "Remember. Not one word."

Ava pressed her lips together. But oh, she had been *so* right it was almost painful not to point it out.

The dress was perfect.

It was *the* dress.

Rare was the woman who could pull off a mermaid dress, but Beth's tiny curves absolutely could.

But it was more than the exact right fit and the perfect shade of ecru to complement Beth's coloring that made the gown perfect.

It was all about the enraptured look on Beth's face when she saw herself in the mirror. All of the other dresses hadn't worked, because they hadn't been Beth. But this dress—the *right* dress—made Beth look like the best version of herself.

Ava was a little surprised to feel wetness gathering in the corner of her eyes. Ava wasn't much of a crier, and she *certainly* wasn't prone to happy tears, but there was no other way to explain how she felt, sharing this moment with her best friend.

Happy.

But there was something else warring with the happiness, just below the surface. Something that felt like the tiniest seed of doubt.

That morning at the diner, Ava had meant it when she'd told Luc Moretti that she didn't want to get married.

But every now and then, a moment slipped past her defenses. Moments like this one.

And sometimes, only sometimes, she thought *maybe*.

CHAPTER TEN

No. No damn makeup," Luc said, wrenching his head away from the black-haired woman who kept trying to come at him with a variety of weird brushes.

The makeup artist, Carly something or other, merely chomped her pink bubble gum and shot a look over her shoulder in a way that signaled she'd dealt with this kind of resistance before, and it wasn't her problem to solve.

Ava was talking with the photographer, but she held up a finger to halt the conversation when she saw Carly's look.

"Hey, Luc!" she said, coming closer to where he sat perched awkwardly on a stool.

He rolled his eyes at her tone.

He *knew* that tone.

When Luc had been a kid, before Anthony was old enough to babysit the rest of them, a high school girl who'd lived next door to the Morettis had sometimes come over to babysit.

His parents had thought it was *hilarious* to tell poor Kimmy that the kids *had* to eat their vegetables.

The poor girl had spent hours trying everything from choo-choo train with broccoli to trying to sneak a green bean in with a Cheetos.

Ava's voice right now had the exact same tone as Kimmy when she thought she could get him to eat a steamed Brussels sprout just by using her "nice voice."

"Don't even, Sims," he said.

"Don't what?"

"Try to sweet-talk me into wearing makeup."

"Now, I know it's not manly," she said, quietly taking a bottle of some beige-covered fluid and one of the brushes from Carly. "But look, *all* the guys that come in here wear it. And nobody who looks at the picture will ever know."

"Let me get this straight. You want me to wear makeup, even though nobody will *know* I'm wearing makeup?"

"Look, Moretti," she said, her voice turning bossy. "You're gorgeous as you are, you really, *really* are, but when it comes to headshots you'll notice every shadow, every dark spot, and—"

She'd lifted her hand to dab something under his eyes but he grabbed her wrist. "No flattery, Sims."

Kimmy had tried flattery too.

Oh my gosh, you're turning into such a strong handsome boy. You know what would make you look even better…

Please. He saw right through that shit.

Ava's eyes went big and limpid as she met his gaze, and her voice went low and imploring. "I know it sucks, but it's just for a few minutes, and then we'll get you out of here."

Yup. Kimmy had tried pleading too.

Hadn't worked then, wouldn't work now.

"Will I get an ice cream cone?" he asked, his voice full of fake excitement.

Ava frowned in confusion. "Well sure, if you want—"

His fingers tightened meaningfully on her wrist. "No makeup, Sims. That's final."

She huffed, throwing her hands in the air with such exasperation he was forced to release her wrist. Ava shoved the makeup back at Carly before turning to scowl at him.

She was wearing a dress today, a knee-length blue number that seemed to somehow wrap around her, belting at her waist. The shoes were matching, and almost lethal in their height.

Even as he kept one eye on Carly and her evil makeup weapons, the other was on Ava. Things had been easier between them since that day at the diner, friendly even, when she wasn't getting in his way.

But that didn't mean he didn't have some very pesky thoughts about how to undo that wrap-dress...

"All right, Carly, let's back off," she said, stepping back and folding her arms across her chest. "Guess we'll have to go with *haggard* cop for the photos."

"I thought you said I was gorgeous," he said, shifting his weight on the stool.

"Oh, she says that to everyone," Carly said, moving toward her black box of doom and putting the makeup away.

Luc caught himself before he could frown, but it annoyed him, just a little, that Ava didn't seem to find him as attractive as he found her.

Sometimes, when their eyes caught, it was like fireworks.

But other times—*most* times—she seemed to prefer Lopez to him. Hell, she seemed to like *everyone* better.

And Ava actually *touched* Lopez. A teasing brush of the shoulder there, a slap on the arm here.

She never touched Luc. Not if she could help it.

But then, as though reading his thoughts, Ava proved him wrong. She moved before Luc could react, stepping forward so she was directly in front of him, her fingers lifting upward to rustle through his hair.

He let out a growl of protest, but she leaped back before he could grab her and darted across the room behind the photographer.

"It looks better mussed," she called to Luc before gesturing at the photographer to do his thing.

That was *not* what he'd had in mind when he'd thought about Ava Sims's hands on him.

Luc started to lift a hand to smooth his now tousled hair, but then the photographer was all up in his face, clicking an enormous camera as he turned it this way and that, and Luc could do little more than sit there and silently bemoan that this was what his life had become.

Up until this point, most of CBC's interference in his life had come in the form of Ava following him around, and when it was NYPD sanctioned, having her cameraman tag along as well. He'd almost gotten used to them. Almost.

But this short bald man wasn't Mihail, and Luc was really not enjoying the way the guy looked at him like he was a bowl of fruit in a still life.

The photographer—Bob? Ben? Bill?—paused his rapid-fire clicking so that he and Ava could have a quick pow-wow in the corner, talking in hushed tones as they reviewed the pictures they had so far.

Ava chewed on her bottom lip.

Not a good sign.

Whatever was in those pictures, she didn't like.

Well *tough shit*. Luc was a cop, not a model, and he wasn't about to preen.

"Officer, can I be blunt?" Ava asked, moving toward him.

He put a hand over his heart. "What I wouldn't give to go back in time and have you ask that three years ago when you were chewing my balls out for that parking ticket."

She ignored this. He liked that about her; she was damned good at not getting sucked into conversations and situations she didn't want to be.

Ava was always in control, and the more he watched her boss her way through life, the more he wanted to find her trigger of self-control.

He wanted to unravel Ava Sims, just like he wanted to unwind that curve-hugging dress.

"Moretti, are you listening to me?"

"Not really."

She sighed. "The pictures are fine, but quite honestly, you look pissed. Like you don't want to be here."

"What?" He faked a scandalized look. "I've been dreaming about this moment for years!"

She pressed her lips together as though she wanted to smile but couldn't bear to give him the satisfaction.

Instead, she went to her purse and came back with her phone, poking around the touch screen until she found what she wanted, and turned the screen to him.

It was a picture of the Moretti males on Luc's graduation from the police academy.

There'd been a minor story about them in the paper that week.

Something about New York's "police royalty" completing their reign, or some shit like that.

But he didn't recognize the picture she showed him.

If memory served him correctly, the one that had been printed in the paper was a posed, forced-smile shot.

But this was a candid one.

Vincent appeared to be about to sock Luc in the gut, and they were all laughing, even Police Commissioner Moretti. As always, Luc's father had that perfect combination of authority-figure and paternal-approachability.

Despite his bad mood, Luc smiled. Moments like the one in the picture were part of the reason he became a cop. That sense of belonging to something...belonging to something decent and good.

"Where'd you get this?" he asked.

"Sources, Moretti. Sources. But my point is, *this* is the Luc I want people to see."

"The twenty-three-year-old version?"

"The *happy* version. Where do I find him?"

Luc rubbed his chin with his palm as he pretended to consider. "I think he bailed right about the time he saw you in Brinker's office."

She stepped closer, getting in his face, and his hands lifted instinctively to reach for her hips, but he clenched them into fists instead.

It wasn't the urge to touch her that bothered him; it was the *naturalness* of the urge. As though Ava Sims were his to touch whenever he wanted.

"If you cooperate...just the tiniest smile, I'll buy you a drink after," she said.

"You're bribing an officer of the law? Or just really desperate to spend time with me, Sims?"

Ava sighed. "Two questions, Moretti. What *exactly* is up your ass? And how the hell do we remove it?"

He ran a hand through his hair, answering honestly, because honesty was what Morettis did best. "Sexual frustration. As far as how to fix it…"

His eyes fell on her mouth.

Her eyes narrowed before she took a tiny step backward.

She huffed in frustration and Luc grinned, because the only thing better than getting into Sims's pants was getting under her skin.

"Coward," he said, leaning forward and grinning.

"Ass," she shot back.

Click.

Click.

There were three more rapid-fire clicks before Luc finally tore his gaze away from Ava to realize that the cameraman had been dancing around them, taking pictures as they'd argued.

"I think we've got something, Ava," the photographer said, looking at the most recent shots.

Ava shot Luc one last warning glare before she walked to the photographer and looked at the camera. In seconds, her face transformed from frustrated to elated.

She shot him a cheeky grin as she moved closer. "Well whadya know, Moretti. I make you smile."

He grunted in irritation, and she twirled her hair around a finger flirtatiously before winking.

"Okay, that's enough with the seated headshots. Let's get a few with him standing."

Luc groaned.

"Don't worry, baby," she said in a sugary voice, "you can scowl for these ones."

"Much as I'd love to be your boy toy for all day, I've got things to do—"

"I know, I know, puppies to save, tickets to write, et cetera, et cetera. But really, Moretti, is this so different from your regular life? You're just posing for a big camera now, instead of a tourist's iPhone."

He didn't realize he'd moved until his fingers were wrapped around her bicep, pulling her around to face him before she could move away.

Her look of surprise turned to one of nervousness, and Luc knew exactly what she was seeing in his face.

Anger.

"You want to hold on to your jaded little fantasy that I've intentionally brought all of this on myself, go right ahead, but you damn well better keep it to yourself. I'm doing this because it's my orders, and that means something to me. And I jumped into that river because it's my *job*, and that means something to me too. All the cameras in the world could self-destruct, and I'll do it all over again. You got that?"

The formerly bustling room had grown dead quiet, and though Luc hadn't raised his voice, it was immediately clear that everyone had overheard everything. Or at least caught the gist.

Ava's cheeks were pink, and at first he thought it was embarrassment, but then her fingers found his where they gripped her hand, the cool pads of her fingertips lightly touching his knuckles. "Luc—Officer—"

He jerked his hand back, releasing her as suddenly as he'd grabbed her, annoyed with himself for losing his cool.

"Forget it, Sims."

"No, wait, I—"

"Ava?"

Ava froze, her entire body seeming to stiffen before turning toward the sound of the voice.

Luc, too, turned, watching in interest as an attractive brunette in black slacks and a striped top walked toward Ava, arms outstretched.

"Miranda."

The woman's arms went around Ava, although there was a definite pause before Ava returned the hug.

The woman—Miranda—pulled back slightly to look Ava over. "Sweetie, you look adorable."

Luc's eyes narrowed slightly. The words were complimentary. The tone was just subtly condescending.

"What are you doing here?" Ava asked.

Luc's eyes narrowed even further. Ava's voice was all excitement, but there was a false-note too. Whatever the relationship between the women, there was an edge there.

"Some way to greet your sister," the woman said with a husky laugh. "I came to see you."

"You flew from Los Angeles to New York to see me?"

"Well yeah, it's your birthday week!" Again with that low laugh. Rather villainous, actually.

"My birthday's been the same day for years, and usually I only get a text. Generally a day or ten late."

There was no real ire or irritation in Ava's voice, only befuddlement at her sister's presence, and for some reason that made Luc's chest squeeze. Her own family didn't remember her birthday?

"Sweetie." Her sister's hands found Ava's shoulder. Squeezed. "You know how busy I am. And Danny too. And Mom and Dad—"

"I know," Ava said, her voice just the slightest bit sharp. "You're all very busy and important."

But her sister had already moved on, looking around the room with an expression half-curious, half-disdainful.

Miranda's eyes locked on Luc, giving him an impressively subtle once-over.

"So...this looks fun," she said.

Ava sighed before forcing a smile and raising her voice slightly. "Everyone, this is my sister Miranda Sims, here from Los Angeles."

Although it wasn't really his place, as the mere subject of Ava's story, the mood in the room had turned definitely awkward and he decided to throw Sims a bone. He moved toward Miranda, extending a hand. "Hey there. I'm Luc."

Miranda met his hand with a firm handshake. "Miranda Sims. Ava's little sister."

Miranda was a good four inches taller than Ava, so "little" was a misnomer, and there was a harshness around her eyes that made her look older than Ava. But even still, she was a gorgeous woman, and the cocky tilt of her chin said that she knew it.

"Nice of you to come up for Ava's birthday," he said.

"Oh well." Miranda gave a little dismissive wave of her hand. "It's also for business."

"Mmm," Luc said, his eyes flitting to Ava to see if the real reason for her sister's visit had any impact on her. But her face was carefully blank.

"What business is that?" Luc said, feigning interest. Ava still hadn't moved.

Miranda gave an incredulous little laugh. "Um, the *Miranda Sims* show?"

Luc shrugged and shook his head. *Never heard of it.* And even if he had heard of it, he wouldn't give Ava's sister the satisfaction of showing it. The woman had self-absorption coming off her in waves. He'd known the woman for all of forty seconds, but it was long enough for him to know that he didn't like her.

"I have my own talk show," Miranda said with a self-deprecating laugh, even though nobody had asked.

"Well it's nice to meet you," Luc said, deliberately skipping over her announcement. "Didn't realize Sims here had any siblings."

Miranda's brown eyes narrowed just the tiniest fraction to show she'd caught the unspoken jab:

Ava's never mentioned you. I've never heard of your stupid show.

"Our Ava's a busy girl. What are you working on this time, sis? Fluff piece on cops?"

Ava's bottom teeth dug just briefly into her upper lip in what might have been a grimace, but she recovered quickly with a huge fake smile. "Yup. Totally fluffy. Sort of an unsung hero type of thing, you know?"

"Oh well that's great, sweetie!" Miranda said with another of those condescending little laughs. "Not bad at all for the local news, you know? Mom and Dad must be over the moon. And look, if they start to get on your case about not being anchorwoman yet, just call me, 'kay? I'm happy to run interference."

"Right," Ava said, plastic smile still stuck in place.

Luc's eyes narrowed. Something was going on here. For starters, Ava's story was national, not local. Luc didn't know shit about broadcast journalism, and even he knew that was an important distinction. A distinction that most of the time pissed him off. He didn't want to be a local hero, much less America's Hero.

But that didn't mean he liked the way Ava was letting her sister belittle her. *Deliberately* belittle her, if Luc had to put money on it.

"So can I steal you away?" Miranda was asking Ava.

"I'm sure they can handle taking a few pictures of a cute cop without you," Miranda said, linking her arm through Ava's and pulling her toward the door. "I'll take you to lunch."

"Um, sure." Ava shot an apologetic look at the photographer. "You good getting those last few shots we talked about?"

"You got it," the photographer said distractedly, apparently unaware of the sibling drama playing out before him.

Luc, however, wasn't unaware. And he didn't like it one bit.

"I love your outfit, Avie," Miranda gushed as they headed toward the door. "I feel like I don't even get to pick my own clothes anymore. Now that it's my name on the show, they're extra careful about which labels I wear, you know?"

Ava murmured something in agreement, and Luc's eyes narrowed as the two sisters finally exited. Ava hadn't looked at him once. Hell, she hadn't even seemed the same person. Five minutes in the presence of her domineering sister had brought out a meek, self-deprecating version of Ava. He felt her lack of sass acutely.

"Poor Ava," Carly muttered beside him. "I bet her sister totally keeps old trophies on her mantel and thinks she deserves a gold medal just for being alive."

Luc nodded in agreement, but his mind was still putting the pieces together. Ava's sister had her own talk show. And based on what Miranda had said about their parents, it would seem Mr. and Mrs. Sims were putting pressure on Ava as well.

An uncomfortable realization settled over Luc:

What if all of Ava's exhausting ambition wasn't even *hers*? What if Ava did what she did because it was *expected* of her?

If anyone understood the power of family pressure, it was Luc, although lucky for him, his own ambitions had lined up with his family's desire to see him join the force.

But there had been something on Ava's face when she'd let her sister belittle her career. If Ava had been passionate about this *America's Hero* story, wouldn't she have jumped at the chance to tell her sister it was getting national coverage?

And she hadn't. Instead she'd looked...

Tired. And maybe a little lost.

Luc frowned.

"Good," the photographer said, circling around Luc with the damn camera clicking. "That pensive, thoughtful look is exactly what Ava's looking for."

Luc barely heard him, still lost in thought.

If the polished, perfectly dressed anchorwoman-wannabe wasn't the *real* Ava, then who was?

And even more annoying...

Just why the hell should Luc care?

CHAPTER ELEVEN

Wait, I thought your sister came into town for your birthday."

This from Mihail who stared at her over the edge of the cubicle wall separating their desks at the station.

"That's what my sister *wanted* people to think," Ava said, not bothering to pause in the e-mail she was writing.

"But she flew home. *On* your birthday."

"Correct."

Mihail scratched his long nose with a finger. "That's messed up."

Ava sighed and looked up. "Honestly? Her leaving was the best present ever."

And she meant it. Three days with her little sister had been...hell.

Even though Miranda had spent the majority of it with her oh-so-important *contacts*, she'd made a token effort of making time for Ava.

Nightmare.

Miranda's idea of "making time" for her sister was Ava dashing over to Miranda's hotel every time Miranda had a five-minute break, only to wait awkwardly on the sidelines while Miranda "networked" in the lobby.

But the *real* icing on the cake was Ava's "birthday dinner" the night before. It had, of course, turned into a dinner with three other producers in which Miranda had run through the gamut of the Sims family achievements.

Miranda herself, of course, was one of the youngest talk-show hosts in the history of the network.

Danny was the leading authority in international relations.

(It had taken all of Ava's self-control and good manners to keep from pointing out that expertise on various types of *wine* did not an international relations expert make.)

Their parents, of course, were Oklahoma royalty and would have been household names had it not been for the unexpected conception of Ava's brother…

And Ava—how had Miranda put it?

Oh yes. *Poor Ava has all the makings of a great anchor-woman; she just needs her big break.*

It would have been the perfect time to point out that she had gotten her big break, in the form of Officer Luc Moretti.

But Ava hadn't said a word, even though it would have been slightly fabulous to watch her sister's smug smile disappear.

It was bad enough Ava was using Luc Moretti to get ahead in her career, even though it was becoming increasingly apparent that he legitimately didn't want to be in the limelight. Ava hadn't been able to bring herself to use Luc's goodness as ammunition against her family.

She wanted to get her family off *her* back her way.

So she'd endured the hell of all hellish pre-birthday dinners. As such, Ava hadn't even been the *tiniest* bit fazed when her sister's flight was scheduled for the morning of her actual birthday. In fact, watching her sister get driven away in her fancy town car was the best Ava had felt in days.

Mihail dangled a red and yellow gummy worm in front of her face. She raised an eyebrow, because it was his favorite flavor.

"Your birthday present," he said.

She accepted the gummy with a smile. "You spoil me."

"Someone has to," he muttered.

"Hey!" she said around the gummy. "Quit making me feel like a loser just because my sister didn't stick around for my birthday. I'll have you know I have plans tonight!"

Since Ava's birthday was their "friendship anniversary," Beth always went all out for the celebration.

In their early twenties it had been all about clubs. Mid-twenties, it was fancy cocktail lounges.

And now that they were officially in their *late* twenties, and had more respect for things like bedtime, tonight was girls' night at a fancy wine bar.

And after three straight days of her sister's crafty belittling, Ava fully intended to drink a bottle to herself.

Her phone rang, and Ava waved Mihail away as she picked it up. "Sims."

There was a pause on the other end. "Sims? Is that how they answer their phone in New York?"

The remainder of the gummy worm nearly got stuck in her throat, and she took a gulp of water to wash it down. "Mom."

"Happy birthday, sweetheart."

"Thanks. How come you're calling at my desk phone instead of my cell?"

Her mom let out one of her tinkling, practiced laughs. "You don't raise three children and not have a sixth sense about when they're screening your calls."

Ava sucked in her cheeks to stave off the feeling of guilt. She didn't *always* screen her mom's calls…only when she knew they'd be served up with a healthy dose of *you're not achieving your potential.*

"Sorry, Mom. Things have been kind of crazy lately."

"Yes, Miranda mentioned you were doing some feel-good documentary on traffic officers?"

Ava pinched the bridge of her nose. It was a real gift her family had—make everything Ava did sound insignificant.

"Something like that."

"Hmm. Well, I guess they can't all be make-or-break stories. Your father heard from some of his connections that Gwen Garrison is eyeing retirement."

Ava nibbled her nail. "Yeah, that's the rumor."

"Well that's great, sweetie! This could be it! Your big chance. I mean, not as long as you're doing traffic stories, but you only have so many windows, and at your age, this might be your last one."

"I'm only twenty-seven," Ava ground out.

"Twenty-eight today!" her mother said cheerfully.

"Right. Twenty-eight today. Thanks for that."

"Anyway, sweetie," her mother continued. "I won't keep you. I'm just about to head out to my Junior League meeting. Did I mention I was reappointed president?"

How absolutely earth shattering.

"Miranda told me all about it," Ava said, hoping to avoid a play-by-play about how her mother was overqualified and overbooked, but still managed to make time for her "old friends in the Junior League."

"Did she? That's sweet," her mom said fondly.

As sugar.

"Well I just wanted to say happy birthday, honey. I'm sure your dad will try to give you a call later if he doesn't get too busy. He's had his hands full trying to get a stop sign put in on Rhodes Street. You know, right there by the bowling alley that's a hit and run waiting to happen?"

"Uh huh," Ava said, already resuming the e-mail she was writing. "Good for him."

Her mom missed the sarcasm. Her family always did.

It's not that Ava didn't respect her family's actions. Everyone did really great things. It was just that they did them all for the wrong reasons. It was hard to describe unless you'd grown up attending family dinners in which conversation centered around not only what "good deed" you'd done that day, but whether or not your teacher had seen you do it.

They weren't bad people, not really. But there was a lack of genuineness among the Simses that had always left the straight-shooting Ava feeling like she was on the outside.

"Okay, Mom, my boss is giving me the signal," she lied as her mom rambled on. "Have fun at Junior League. Thanks for calling."

Hanging up the phone she huffed out a sigh and slumped back in her chair. Mihail reappeared, and the red and yellow gummy worm he offered said that he'd heard it all.

Ava didn't talk about her family much, but friends like Mihail and Beth had been around long enough to figure out what was going on.

Beth in particular knew just how bad it could be.

She'd been dragged to a few Sims family dinners in which she'd blown their little Oklahoma minds with her "indulgent" teaching job.

They didn't award Nobel Prizes for teaching kids to finger-paint, after all.

"Did Mommy save a life today?" Mihail asked.

"Dozens, I'm sure," Ava said with a halfhearted smile.

He jabbed a finger at her. "No pity parties. It's your birthday. Come on, let's go get drunk."

"It's two p.m."

"Perfect," he said, grabbing her purse off the desk. "I'm holding this hostage in the van until you come join me."

"Mihail!"

But it was no use. He was already gone, swinging the Coach bag she'd bought as a birthday gift for herself over his head.

"Fine," she muttered. A beer wouldn't kill her. And she needed to shake off the ick that dealing with her family always caused.

She was just shutting down her computer when one of the runners who worked the main reception area downstairs approached with a gorgeous bouquet of flowers.

"Ava Sims?"

"Yep!" she said, greedy hands already reaching for the flowers.

She felt her bad mood start to slip away. She loved flowers on principle, but she loved getting flowers at work even more.

Joey Chavers whistled as he walked by. "White roses, nice. Who they from?"

"My best friend," Ava said with a smile, loving Beth all the more for thinking of her on her birthday when Beth was knee-deep in bridal crap.

Ava pulled the tiny card out of its envelope, and her smile slipped.

The flowers weren't from Beth.

Joey, ingrained with reporter nosiness, craned his neck to read the card.

"Who's Luc?"

Ava couldn't stop the smile that burst over her face any more than she could the happy dance taking place in her stomach.

Luc Moretti had remembered her birthday.

CHAPTER TWELVE

If I let you live here, the least you can do is pick up your stupid bells."

"Dumbbells, Nonna," Luc said, not taking his eyes off the Yankees game. "They're called dumbbells. And they're Anthony's, not mine."

"Well they don't belong in my living room," his grandmother muttered. "I need room for my yoga mat."

That got his attention.

He turned to see his eighty-two-year-old grandmother unsuccessfully try to lift his older brother's makeshift gym out of the way. Luc set his beer aside and went to help, depositing the free weights and jump rope in his brother's room.

Retrieving his beer, he watched as his tall, thin-as-a-rail grandmother very carefully unrolled a pink yoga mat on the floor.

This was new.

"Um, what's goin' on?" he asked as she pulled her chin-length white hair into a stubby ponytail.

"Gotta get my chi on."

"Sorry?"

"Maybe that's not right," she mused. "Zen? Going to get my Zen on?"

But instead of actually moving onto the mat, she scowled down at it. "Maybe I should make some carbonara."

"Thought you just ate with your latest boy toy."

"Don't you sass me, Luca Moretti. We're Italian. Celebrating food's a part of the culture."

Luc smiled. It said a lot about his nonna that she scolded him for daring to question food, not for the boy toy comment. When it came to her love life and metabolism, she was eighty-two going on seventeen.

Plus, she wasn't even Italian. Not by blood. But she insisted that fifty years of marriage made her Italian and dared anyone to say otherwise.

Nobody ever tried.

Carbonara wasn't even a classic Italian dish, as Luc's mother pointed out every chance she got. It was Nonna's favorite only because she'd discovered it at one of the trendy new Italian restaurants that opened on the Upper West Side. Luc's mom had a conniption fit every time Nonna tried to sneak it onto the family dinner menu. Though Luc would never take sides against his mother, when his mother wasn't around, Luc *really* liked his grandma's carbonara.

"We've missed you this past week," he said, meaning it.

She sniffed as she went to the fridge and pulled out eggs and pancetta, apparently planning to make good on her carbonara threats. No complaints on his end.

"Sure you did. You and your brother love when I go

babysit your parents. Allows you to bring hookers round here without me knowing."

"Too true," he said, taking the huge pasta pot out of her hands and filling it with water before putting it on the stove. "We actually have the system down pat by now. The second you're out the door is the second this joint turns into a brothel. Hope you don't mind we rent out your room."

"Shameful way to speak to your *nonna*," she said, taking a swat at him.

Luc grinned knowing that she didn't mind one bit. With two cops as sons and four cops as grandsons, she was well used to their salty sense of humor. Which was a damn good thing, because it was the only way the living arrangement worked without the three of them killing each other.

It wasn't quite a typical arrangement.

While it was standard for Italian elders to live with their children or grandchildren, things were a little bit backward when said elder had a rent-controlled apartment on the Upper West Side of Manhattan.

It was an address that neither Luc nor Anthony could dream of having on a cop's salary, but Nonna had lived in the gorgeous three-bedroom apartment since the 1950s, back before rent for an address in the upper seventies on the West Side went sky-high.

God bless rent control.

Of course, more and more lately, Nonna had been spending time at Luc's parents' house on Staten Island. She liked to say it was because she wished to keep an eye on her daughter-in-law's cooking and her son's waistline, but Luc was pretty sure she did it to give Anthony and Luc their privacy.

Which Luc appreciated. There was something uncomfortable about bringing female company around for *night-time activities* when your grandma was in the next room, just waiting to offer the woman biscotti the next morning.

Come to think of it, Luc should probably text his older brother and let him know that Nonna was in the house. It wasn't unusual for Anthony to finish up his shift and come home with a female "friend" in tow.

Not long ago, it hadn't been unusual for Luc either.

But recently he'd been in a bit of a rut. The whole "hero cop" thing had made him suspect all interested females of being groupies, and it had been too long since he'd felt genuinely intrigued by a woman.

Luc tipped back his beer bottle and tried very, very hard not to think of Ava Sims.

Nonna watched him out of the corner of her eye as she added salt to the pasta water, and then she turned and pointed a long finger at him. "I know that look."

"What look?"

"You think I raised two sons and four grandsons and don't recognize when they've got a woman on the brain? Who is she?"

"Nobody."

Nonna sighed. "Just because you're the baby of the family doesn't mean I'll let you get away with fibbing like your mother does."

Luc lowered himself into the ancient wood chair at the tiny kitchen table. If having his grandmother for a roommate for the past three years had taught him anything, it was that the woman wouldn't let up until she had her answers.

Neither would he get any of that carbonara until he'd thrown her at least a nugget to fret over.

Luc sighed and set his beer aside before leaning forward,

resting his head briefly in his hands. She patted him on the head before settling into the chair across from him.

"Is she a looker?" Nonna asked.

Luc snorted and lifted his head. "It's not quite what you think. There's nothing even close to romantic going on, but...you know that godforsaken CBC story?"

"Don't you go blaming the Lord because you're a good guy and some tourist happened to catch that on camera and put it up on that Yoo-hooTube."

"Well I'm more than happy to let God off the hook, because it just so happens there's a very real-life person I can blame for the fact that I'm not able to put this circus behind me."

"Ah, now we're getting right down to it," Nonna said, rubbing her hands together. "The Woman."

"Ava Sims," Luc said, his voice getting more irritable just by saying her name out loud. "She's the main reporter assigned to the story, and she's been following me around like the fu—freaking paparazzi for the past couple weeks."

Nonna laughed and patted his hand. "So it's like that then."

"No, it's just...I wish this whole thing would blow over."
Even though I bought her flowers.

Her smile slipped a little. "Is it so bad then? Being rewarded for being an exceptional cop?"

Luc gritted his teeth to stop the instant denial. He *wasn't* an exceptional cop.

If he were, Shayna and Mike would still be alive. But he didn't talk about that. Not even with Nonna.

"Did I mention that Miss Sims and I have a history?" he said, knowing it would be exactly the kind of topic change that she would latch on to.

Nonna's gray eyebrows lifted. "Did you fornicate?"

Luc choked on his beer. "Jesus, no. And there should be a ban against that word."

"Don't be prudish, Luca. So if you didn't fornicate with this girl, how did you know her? Did she fornicate with one of your brothers? Anthony gets around."

"I'll tell him you said so," Luc muttered. "And no, she hasn't fornicated with any Moretti."

At least he hoped not.

"Three years ago, I gave her a parking ticket."

Nonna's eyes went big. "No! Not a parking ticket!"

He gave her a look. "Are grandmothers allowed to be this sarcastic? Aren't you supposed to be doting with baked goods?"

She pointed toward the kitchen. "I've got pancetta from Ottomanelli's sizzling in the pan. You don't think that's doting?"

Nonna had a point. He'd take the salty Italian bacon over a cup of hot tea any day.

"So if you haven't bagged her, what's the story with this Sims girl?"

"Bagged her, Nonna? Really? But it's like I said . . . I gave her a parking ticket a couple years ago. We had words. Sparks, I guess," he said, feeling awkward.

And I bought her flowers.

Nonna cackled.

"She didn't pay the ticket," Luc muttered. "Presented it to me on the same day she dropped the bomb about this damn *America's Hero* story."

"I hope you cuffed her. Can't be letting a criminal like that roam the streets."

Luc closed his eyes. "How is it possible that you gave

birth to the former Police Commissioner of New York City?"

"Posh. You think your father hasn't waved away a few parking tickets back when I had a car for a hot minute in eighty-four?"

Luc leaned forward. "Has he?"

Nonna ignored him, getting up to baby her pancetta. "This girl bothers you."

Hell yes she bothers me.

Luc took another sip of beer. "Mostly she worries me. She has a lot of power over my life; she can portray me however she wants, to God knows how many people. I should be trying to get on her good side."

"Oh *passerotto*. You've looked in the mirror. You don't have to try to get on any woman's good side, you just give a little wink."

"So I'm your favorite then?" Luc gave her his best smile.

"Depends. You going to do my yoga with me later?"

"God. No. Never."

"Then Elena's still my favorite. We're doing hot yoga next week."

"Sounds...awful," Luc said, standing and going toward the cheese that she put purposefully on the counter for him to grate.

They worked in companionable silence for several minutes before Nonna spoke again. "You know, if you want to get on the good side of this girl without shagging her silly—"

"Try to be appropriate. Just try."

"She needs the Moretti treatment," Nonna pressed on.

"Another euphemism for sex?"

"Better."

Better than sex?

"Invite her to family dinner. Show her that the hero thing runs in the genes."

Luc pauses in grating the cheese. "You want me to invite Ava Sims to Sunday dinner."

Nonna patted his cheek. "How bad could it be?"

CHAPTER THIRTEEN

Once again, Mihail had been banished. Only this time, it wasn't for any official NYPD media ban.

This time it was about common decency. Because even the pushiest of reporters didn't bring a camera to a family dinner.

Especially when the family wasn't yours.

When Luc had suggested she accompany him to the weekly Moretti Sunday dinner, Ava thought he'd been joking.

They couldn't seem to go five minutes in the same building without fighting, and now he wanted her to meet his parents? His siblings?

It was a disaster waiting to happen.

Tonight there would be none of Sawyer Lopez's easy charm to help ease the tension, and no cop business to distract them from whatever animosity always seemed to be simmering beneath the surface.

Still, there'd been no way to say no.

Every journalistic instinct told her that the only thing the public would love more than a cop with a hero complex was a cop who ate Sunday dinner with his cop family.

And of course there was the not-so-minor fact that he'd bought her flowers.

Which they hadn't talked about.

Ava had said thank you, of course, in an awkward, *I'm not sure what's going on here* kind of way.

And Luc had said *you're welcome.* Equally awkward. And if something important had passed between them in that second, it was gone before she could identify it.

She wasn't even sure she wanted to.

Because deep down, she was worried that the flowers had been pity flowers. He'd seen the way things were with Miranda. Had he gotten her the birthday flowers because he'd been worried that nobody would remember?

The thought chafed.

When a man like Officer Luc Moretti bought you flowers you wanted it to be because he couldn't stop thinking about you.

Not because he felt bad for you.

Ava pushed the annoying thought aside and focused on the evening ahead.

She needed to be on her A game.

Ava would have preferred to simply meet Luc at his parents' house, but since his parents lived on Staten Island, which she wasn't at all familiar with, they'd agreed to meet at the ferry dock.

A quick glance at her phone showed she was fifteen minutes early, and she took advantage of the time to clear her head.

Or at least try to.

She wandered toward the railing of the harbor, leaning over as far as she could, staring into the murky water. There was a floating water bottle. A clump of hair or something nasty. A condom.

"Nice," she muttered.

"You know, most people kill time waiting for the ferry by ogling the Statue of Liberty, not taking in the trash."

Ava stiffened slightly at the sound of Luc's voice, although it was blissfully free of its usual agitation. Pulling back from the railing, she turned to face him, seeing that his expression was also easier than usual. He even gave her a half smile when their eyes met, and Ava's stomach flipped.

It was only then she registered that she was seeing him out of uniform. She'd seen him in jeans before, once, at the diner, but this time felt different.

It was intimate, probably because this time she'd been *invited* to see him like this, rather than crashing his free time.

It was as though she were seeing Luc Moretti the *man*, not Luc Moretti the cop.

And Ava the woman responded.

Alarm bells sounded. She ignored them.

He was wearing jeans, brown boots, and a long-sleeve gray T-shirt that made his blue eyes seem lighter than usual. The wind coming off the harbor messed his dark brown hair slightly, making him look completely approachable and harmless.

Ha.

Luc stuck his hands into his back pockets, rocking back on his heels as he studied her right back.

She'd agonized over what to wear, not wanting to go too casual for fear they were a dress-for-dinner family, but neither wanting to go with one of her usual dress-to-impress ensembles for fear she'd come off as trying too hard.

She'd opted for a cream-colored sundress and blue cardigan with strappy platform sandals. Her hair was pulled back into a high ponytail in an effort to look like the approachable girl next door, instead of *hungry reporter after your family's darkest secrets.*

Ava hated herself for watching his face for a reaction to her appearance. Not that it mattered. Other than a brief glance-over, his eyes didn't so much as flicker before he joined her at the railing, leaning over so that his weight braced on his forearms.

He inhaled deeply. "You know, I've been making this trek about every other Sunday for years now, and I haven't once gotten sick of this."

Luc gestured with his chin, and Ava followed his gaze to the far-off Statue of Liberty.

"I know some people think it's a tourist trap," he continued. "That *real* New Yorkers don't care about stuff like that, or the Brooklyn Bridge. But I like to think it's us locals that can appreciate it the most, you know? To have this sort of history in our own backyard."

"Pretty romantic for a guy who spent the better part of yesterday patrolling Times Square," she said, mimicking his posture at the railing.

He made a disgusted noise. "Times Square isn't in the same category as the Statue of Liberty. Both are tourist magnets, but one is history. The other is..."

"Hell?" she supplied.

The corner of his mouth lifted upward. "Pretty much."

"You said every other Sunday," Ava said, glancing at him. "You don't do this every week?"

He shook his head. "Nah. Church is every week. Breakfast after church is every week. But Sunday nights are sort of a standing invitation, if it works out sort of thing. My parents are old-fashioned, but they're just modern enough to respect their adult children's busy schedules."

They fell silent for a moment, although not in the awkward way, just the peaceful kind. "Is your brother meeting us here?" she asked finally.

"Not sure. They might have caught the earlier one."

"They. They're both coming? Anthony and Vincent?"

"You've done your homework."

She shrugged. "It's easy when they're all cops. Public record and all that. The details on who they are to *you* is a bit fuzzier though."

He gave her a look that said he knew she was on a fishing expedition, but to her surprise, he humored her.

"Short version? Anthony's the oldest, and is likely a shoo-in for captain over in the nineteenth precinct. Vincent's a homicide detective. They're both cocky, arrogant pains in my ass, but damn good cops."

"And the third brother?"

"Marco. Marc." Luc glanced down at his hands. "He's with the LAPD."

She caught the change in tone. "You miss him."

He glanced at her sharply, likely assessing to see whether she was prying as a reporter, or as a woman.

She held up her hands. "Off the record."

He rolled his shoulders and stood up straighter. "He moved to California a couple years ago because his high school girlfriend got it in her head that she wanted to do the Hollywood thing."

"Are they still together?"

He grunted.

"I'll take that as a yes, but I don't like it?"

Luc turned around so that his back was to the railing, crossing his feet at the ankles. "Marco's a good guy. We all miss him."

It wasn't exactly a spill-your-guts kind of answer, but neither was it a fuck-off, so she supposed she'd take it as progress.

"You guys are all close?"

His eyes narrowed slightly, and Ava's patience tweaked. "Look, you can't invite me over to family dinner under the guise of cooperating with my story and then not expect me to ask questions. I just want to make sure I don't misrepresent you guys."

"Uh huh. And if I told you that my parents were assholes, my siblings and I fought constantly, and that we only did family dinners out of some sort of warped Italian guilt, you're telling me you wouldn't sugarcoat it when it comes down to actually shooting video? You wouldn't ask us to *pretend*?"

She crossed her arms over her chest, mimicking his posture. "No. I know all about families that pretend, and I wouldn't wish it on anyone."

His dark blue eyes found hers. "Tell me."

Just like that, he'd turned the tables. Giving her a chance to talk about *her*.

And even more incredibly, she wanted to.

"Well…" she said, taking a long breath. "You've already met my sister. I'd like to say you just caught her at an off time, but the truth is, she's always like that. Miranda's always been really good at the *put others down to prop yourself up* thing. The others aren't much better. My brother's a condescending ass, and my parents...well, let's just say there's no way on God's green earth that we'd be caught dead having Sunday dinner together."

He looked away. "Let me ask you something, Sims..."

"Yeah?"

When he turned back, his gaze was fierce. "Given all of that, what would *you* do, if your boss told you that you had no choice but to let a pushy reporter come inspect every area of your life, all because you were just trying to do your job and got unlucky, hmm? Would you become an open book? Would you become BFFs? Or would you watch your back because your private life is supposed to be *private*?"

Ava's stomach twisted with an unfamiliar sensation. *Guilt.*

Ambition was the name of the game in her career, but never before had she been so conscious that she might be coming very, very close to crossing a line. If the anger on his face was any indication, she may have already crossed it.

But beneath the guilt there was also confusion. She'd thought—*hoped*—that they'd gotten past this, but sometimes it felt like they'd never gone anywhere at all. That he hadn't bought her flowers on her birthday.

She searched for words. "I—"

He turned away, swearing. "Sorry." The apology was gruff. "I shouldn't throw your family issues in your face like that."

But he shouldn't be the one apologizing, and they both knew it. "Luc—"

He turned around quickly, his gaze sharp, and Ava realized he was responding to her use of his first name. She'd used it before. But this time felt different.

Because *this* time, she was thinking about him as a person

instead of the story subject that could make or break her career.

She moved closer, and taking a risk, put her hand on his arm. "I'm not here to sell you out. Or your family."

His eyes flitted briefly to her fingers against his arm, and she swore she wasn't imagining that the air around them grew hot, even in the cool spring breeze.

A loud horn noise made her jump, and Luc took a quick step back, killing the moment. "Ferry's here," he said gruffly. "And it looks like Anthony's on the same boat as us."

She followed his gaze to the tall, gorgeous guy who watched them approach with a scowl. Good looks definitely ran in the family. So did the *go-fuck-yourself* scowl.

"Anthony can be irritable; try not to piss him off," he said out of the corner of his mouth.

"Sure, I'll just tape my mouth shut," she snapped, all warm feelings of before evaporating.

For a second, he looked hopeful. "That's an option?"

She gave him a withering look before pasting a smile on her face for Luc's older brother. Up close, the family resemblance was startling. Anthony's eyes were brown instead of Luc's deep blue, and he was taller by a couple of inches. But there was the same strong jawline, the same broad shoulders and sculpted torso.

Anthony Moretti was gorgeous.

"You're staring," Luc whispered in her ear.

Ava jumped, holding out a hand to Anthony.

He glanced down at it in amusement before giving his brother a look she couldn't decipher. Only then did he shake her hand. "You're the Sims woman."

Luc rolled his eyes. "Nice, bro."

Anthony shrugged, looking her over. "You know, I was

trying to figure out how the hell you finagled an invitation to family dinner, but I think I get it now."

The look Luc gave his brother was lethal. "Seriously."

Ava smiled. "It's all right. I came prepared. I've seen you in action. It makes sense that your brothers share your same...*charm*."

Anthony's eyebrows crept up. "Luca, do my ears deceive me? Is there actually a woman alive who hasn't fallen all over herself in love with you?"

"Trust me," Ava said before Luc could respond. "That is *definitely* not the case."

Anthony smiled then, slow and sexy. And practiced, if Ava was reading it right. He offered her his arm. "Well then, Ms. Sims. Come. Walk with me. I think I like you already."

"That makes one of us," Luc muttered from behind them.

But when Ava glanced over her shoulder at Luc, he didn't look as irritated as his words implied.

Instead he looked thoughtful.

CHAPTER FOURTEEN

It was a weird thing, watching your sexy enemy join forces with the people most dear to you.

Ava had all but charmed the pants off Anthony on the ferry ride over to Staten Island. Anthony, whose condescending, big-brother routine practically seeped out of his pores. Anthony, whose volatile temper and legendary glare had sent more than a handful of rookies to therapy.

Anthony who distrusted all women, everywhere.

Except, apparently, Ava Sims.

By the time they'd gotten to his parents' house, Luc was grinding his teeth, and Anthony was in all-out charm mode (which Luc hadn't even known was a thing), and Ava was practically simpering.

To punish her, he'd nearly left her in Anthony's oh-so-doting care for the evening. *That* would show her.

But then Luc had seen it. He'd seen *her*, with the sassy layers stripped away.

It happened when Anthony opened the front door, and just as Luc was inhaling the familiar aromas of his mother's cooking, he caught Ava's expression out of the corner of his eye.

She hesitated, her bright, ever-present smile slipping, and she'd looked lost and completely unsure of herself.

Her description of her family flitted through his mind. After meeting Miranda, Luc had been hoping the bad vibes with her sister had been a fluke.

But the tension in her shoulders when she'd talked about her family looked decades old.

In other words, the Sunday dinner that had always felt like coming home to him was completely foreign to her.

Luc mentally sighed. He wanted to leave her to the sharks.

To let her sink or swim as she went about interviewing his family, sticking her nose where it didn't belong, stalking his baby pictures to see if he fixed the wings of baby birds, or something she could use for her stupid hero story.

Her finger fiddled with the sleeve of her cardigan, as a loud burst of laughter came from the kitchen. White teeth nibbled nervously on the corner of her bottom lip, and Luc broke.

Before he realized what he was doing, he reached out a hand to her.

Ava blinked in surprise, staring in confusion at his outstretched hand. When her eyes lifted to his, they were confused and wary.

"Come on, Sims, it's just a bit of kindness," he said, intentionally keeping his voice light. "You're about to be sucked into the Moretti vortex."

"Is the rest of your family as cranky as you?"

Luc frowned. "You still think I'm cranky?"

"I think if there was a boarding school for personality makeovers, you'd probably get a scholarship."

He let out a little laugh before wiggling his fingers. "Sweetheart, I'll have you know that I'm the charming one of my family."

She frowned. "Anthony was lovely."

"I assure you. He's not. Vincent's worse, my sister's a pain in the ass, my mom will probably ask to measure your hips and utter the word *womb* at some point during the evening, and my father was the New York Police Commissioner for twenty-seven years, which pretty much says it all."

"And what are you?"

"Your savior for the evening."

"Well all right then." She slipped her hand in his, and the sensation of her fingers against his was oddly calming.

He ignored it, tugging her down the hall toward the kitchen, which had always been the heart of his parents' household.

Luc meant to release Ava's hand before entering the kitchen. No need to give anyone—especially Ava—the wrong impression.

But somehow his fingers didn't release when he meant them to, and when they walked into the kitchen, the usual fighting, laughing, and yelling tapered off so there was only Nonna at the counter muttering about how her daughter-in-law "still couldn't cut tomatoes for the life of her."

Ava quickly tugged her hand away, but not before his entire family had seen exactly what was going on. It was times like this that being part of a family of cops sucked. They missed nothing.

And while his mother's experience in law enforcement

had been as a dispatcher, she was a mom. Her observation skills put her cop husband and sons to shame.

At least when it came to her flock.

"*Bambino*," his mom said, giving him a beaming smile before holding her arms to the sides.

"Ma." He moved toward her, kissing both cheeks.

"Bambino?" Ava asked.

"Baby," Vincent translated from the corner of the room where he stood with his back leaned against the wall. His serious face as unreadable as ever as he studied the newcomer.

"Luca's the youngest of the family," Elena explained, moving toward Ava and swooping her into a hug.

"Oh!" Ava said in surprise before giving his sister an awkward pat on the back. Luc almost grinned at her discomfort. Ava apparently wasn't a hugger, which Luc didn't find all that surprising. For all her bright smiles and talk-to-me! expressions, the woman had a veritable force field around her.

"Yeah, we do that," his mother said, explaining the hug, even as she followed up her daughter's hug with one of her own. "We like to blame it on the Italian, but mostly we're just pushy."

"You guys, um, know me, right? Know what I'm doing here?" Ava said, shooting Luc a nervous glance.

He responded by going to the sideboard and pouring them both a liberal dose of wine. They were going to need it.

"That you're showing the world just what kind of man my son is? Of course we know. We couldn't be more thrilled." This from Tony Moretti.

Luc closed his eyes briefly, jarring only slightly when a big hand clamped down on his shoulder. "Hi, Dad."

"Son."

His father's fingers squeezed on his shoulders, and although Luc knew the gesture was fatherly...protective...it was also a warning. Not to say too much. Not in front of *her*.

Then his dad moved away from him, descending on Ava with a broad, genuine smile before he, too, kissed both of her cheeks.

Good God, was the woman *blushing*?

What was it with her and the Moretti men?

Was she enamored with all of them except him?

Luc hadn't been kidding when he'd said he was the charming one. Well, he and Marco.

But Marc was in another time zone, and his two Moretti brothers that *were* here had the gruff, growly kind of vibe that didn't appeal to vivacious, straightforward women like Ava.

Unless he was wrong.

Too late, he realized that his mom was threatening her with a tour of the house and an invitation to come stay with them any time.

Jesus.

"Ma, how about some introductions before you start monogramming her a towel?"

He moved beside Ava to hand her the wine he'd poured. She accepted it with a murmured thanks, and the normal thing to do would have been to step back.

He stayed where he was.

"Ava, these women who ambushed you are my mother, Maria, and my sister Elena. The grump in the corner with the social skills of an eggplant is my brother Vincent. Then there's my dad, Tony, his namesake, Anthony, whom you've already met."

"Forgetting someone, *bambino*?"

"Just saving the best for last, Nonna. That old crone cutting tomatoes is my grandmother. Her name's Teresa, but I'm pretty sure she'll insist you call her—"

"Nonna," his grandmother proclaimed, pointing the knife in Ava's direction for emphasis. "And it was *my* idea to invite you. Remember that when you're deciding who to give the most screen time to in your little TV special."

"Wait, is you inviting me supposed to be a good thing?" Ava asked. "Because jury's still out on all of this."

Nonna snickered. "I like this one. She doesn't smooch my butt like half the girls you bring round here."

Ava lifted her eyebrows. "Other girls, hmm?"

His eyes locked on hers.

Her tone had been joking, but the way she'd phrased it had seemed distinctly couple-minded. If the hand-holding hadn't set his family into a tizzy, *this* would.

And they didn't even know about a certain two dozen white roses.

"Nonna, what are you doing to the tomatoes?" his mother demanded, pressing her palm heels to her temples. "You're mangling them."

"Posh. You never do a good job of releasing the juices."

"Those 'juices' are all over my floor."

"So I'll clean it."

"You're eighty-two."

"But I do yoga, which is more than I can say about some people—"

The Moretti siblings exchanged an exacerbated glance. Their argument over tomatoes was pretty standard.

And if it wasn't tomatoes it was the brand of ricotta Ma bought, or that Nonna oversalted the pasta water, et cetera, et cetera.

Luc's mom had been born in Italy and, although she'd only lived there until she was two, considered herself *real* Italian.

Unlike Nonna who only had a long-lasting marriage to the late Rico Moretti.

Still, Nonna didn't let a little thing like genetics undermine her authority.

And when it came to cooking methods, the animosity between his mother and grandmother was mighty.

"What's going on?" Ava whispered.

"If you're wondering if they're going to kill each other... maybe..." Luc's father said, not looking the least bit perturbed by the escalating argument between his wife and mother.

"I'm so glad you're here," Elena said, wiggling her way between Ava and Luc and linking arms with Ava. "I *never* get any girl company. Except when Jill joins us."

"There are more of you?" Ava looked ready to pass out, although no doubt she was just peeved that there was a player that her research hadn't uncovered.

"Jill is Vincent's partner," Elena said with a nod toward Vin. "She joins us for dinner whenever she and Vin aren't fighting."

"Which is never," Vincent said, finally pushing away from the wall and snagging an olive from the charcuterie board. "The woman's a menace."

"Ah, so *all* of the Moretti men are good with the ladies then," Ava said with a pointed look at Luc.

"Oh God, no," Elena said, missing Ava's sarcasm. "Vincent's lucky to get through a first date without a woman breaking into tears. Not even kidding. And Anthony's got that tall, brooding thing happening that women *think* they want, but then he remembers that he's married to the job, and he forgets his girlfriends' names at inopportune moments—"

"That happened *once*," Anthony broke in with a warning finger pointed at Elena. "And you know I was in the middle of that Weedleton case."

"Yawn," Elena shot back. "No cop talk at dinner, remember?"

"Is that even possible?" Ava murmured.

No, Luc thought to himself.

"No," Elena said with a sigh.

"So you were never tempted to go into the family business?" Ava asked, taking a sip of wine.

Luc nearly smiled. The reporter was definitely still there under all her pretty manners.

"Hell no," Elena said. "For starters, Dad wouldn't let me, because he lives in the Middle Ages—"

"Because he loves his only daughter," Tony corrected.

"But it's never been my dream job anyway," she continued.

"What is?" Ava asked politely.

Elena shot a cheeky grin at the men of her family. "I'm an attorney. Defense."

Luc watched as Ava's lips pursed. Her research already had revealed Elena's career, but he could tell she was just now putting together the pieces of what Elena's job meant for family dynamics:

Four brothers and a father on one side of the law. A lone sister on the other.

This was why they didn't talk shop at family dinners.

"Anyway," Elena said. "Vincent and Anthony are terrible with women. It's Luc that's always been the ladies' man."

Luc groaned. For the first time ever, he actually wished his sister would keep going on about her career.

"Oh, *do* tell," Ava said, giving Elena her full-on attention.

Luc plucked the wineglass from Ava's hand.

"Wait, I wasn't done," she said, her voice just a tiny bit desperate.

"I'm getting you a refill. Trust me," he said, heading back toward the side bar, "you're going to need a big-girl pour tonight."

CHAPTER FIFTEEN

As far as Moretti family dinners went, everyone was on their best behavior. Mostly. Sure, Elena checked her phone under the table, and Vincent was short on smiles, and his mom and grandma dropped a few too many hints about wishing Luca *had a nice girl like you*.

But all in all, it was as good as Luc could have expected.

And yet still, Ava was nervous. Not that she showed it outright. She was perfectly pleasant, smiling at all the right things, making all the appropriate small talk. But more than once he'd caught her fingernail sneaking up to her mouth where she nibbled it lightly before catching herself and taking a sip of wine.

It broke his heart a little. This confident, successful woman who was so clearly out of her element in a family setting. After meeting Miranda, he'd definitely suspected that they weren't exactly one big, loving family, but seeing how uncomfortable Ava was around hugs and compliments and laughter confirmed it.

Luc sincerely hoped he never met the Sims family, because he'd be hard-pressed not to give them a piece of his mind.

Ava was sitting to his right and fidgeting so much that Luc longed to reach under the table and touch her...just to calm her. But he wasn't sure that wouldn't make her more jumpy.

There was a rare silent moment at the table as everyone devoured the food, and Ava jumped to fill it. "Mrs. Moretti, this roast is *amazing*. And the pasta—"

Nonna broke in. "You like this, you should come to my place for some good cooking. I don't dry out my meat."

Maria Moretti ignored her mother-in-law and smiled warmly at Ava. "I'm glad you like it, dear. And please, call me Maria."

"Okay," Ava said, her smile quick and shy. "I'd like that."

His mom caught his eye and winked.

"Ava, you said you're from Ohio?" Luc's father asked.

"Oklahoma."

"Okay no offense," Vincent broke in, "but aren't those like the same thing?"

Elena made no efforts at subtle as she kicked her brother under the table. "Seriously? Don't be a douche bag."

"Yeah, don't be a douche bag," Nonna chimed in.

"We all remember how we feel about name calling at my dinner table, yes?" Maria asked quietly, taking a sip of her water.

Elena gave her mother an exasperated look. "But—"

"So, Ava, you're from Oklahoma," Tony Moretti interrupted.

She smiled. "Yes. Darrington. And don't feel bad if you've never heard of it. Most people haven't."

"Trust me, I don't feel bad," Vincent griped.

Elena tried to kick him again, but he dodged this time.

Tony quieted his squabbling offspring with a single look before he continued his talking. "So Darrington's a small town?"

"Very," Ava said.

"New York's a big change. Did you come specifically for your career?"

Luc's chewing slowed as he caught the too-casual note in his father's voice. Warning bells went off in Luc's head. He knew that tone. It meant his father was after something. And what Tony Moretti wanted, he usually got.

Ava seemed to sense the danger, because she set her fork aside. "Yes, I came for my professional development. New York is definitely the hub of broadcast journalism."

"Hmm," Tony said. "It's the hub of a lot of things. Why this profession?"

"Dad, you're making her sound like she chose prostitution," Elena said, giving her father a scolding look.

Tony merely lifted a shoulder and took a bite of pasta, and Luc glared.

"You don't like reporters, Mr. Moretti," Ava said, picking up her fork and resuming eating. It wasn't a question.

"Well now, I don't know that I'd say that," Tony said with a quick grin. "I'm just not convinced of their purpose."

"*Dad!*" Elena said at the same time Maria exclaimed, "Tony!"

Luc remained silent, but the glare he shot his father was lethal. A glare his father ignored.

"No, it's okay," Ava said, dabbing her mouth with her napkin. "Plenty of people feel that way about reporters."

"That may be so," Luc's mother said quietly, "but you're a guest in our home."

"I'm a guest in your home because I'm doing a story on your son," Ava said, her voice kind but firm. "It's fair that you all would have some concerns. And I'm more than happy to answer any questions you might have."

"Okay, I've got one," Anthony said, jumping in for the first time. "I think we all know why Luca got chosen for this article over any other cop. The face. The smile. The jumping into rivers to save kids. But what I want to know is how you're going to stretch Luca's good deeds into three hours' worth of television."

"Well," Ava said slowly, "it won't just be about Luc. He'll be the focus, certainly, but we'll be talking about the NYPD and law enforcement in general. And when we do focus on Luc, we'll of course cover his recent good deeds, and the fallout of that, but we'll look into the complete picture as well. Who is Luc Moretti *off* camera? What's his journey been like from youngest son of the police commissioner to officer?"

The silence in the dining room was deafening.

Luc knew that Ava thought she'd be putting the family at ease, but her words had done anything but.

"So you're planning to dig into his past," Tony said.

"Well, not dig, exactly," Ava said, shooting a confused look at Luc. "I mean, we want to tell a complete story, but if there's something you want us to avoid…"

"No," Luc broke in before his family could interject. "We have nothing to hide."

He looked around the table as though to say *right*?

Not a single family member met his eye. Not even Nonna. His eyes narrowed. What the hell was going on here? It's not like Luc *wanted* Ava to start digging into Mike's death...or Shayna Johnson's...but the way his family was skulking around like there was some sort of deep dark secret was bound to arouse Ava's suspicions.

He glanced at her, and sure enough, her eyes had sharpened, and he could all but hear the wheels turning in her head.

She shifted her gaze toward him, and he forced himself not to look away. Not to look as ridiculously guilty as the rest of his family.

Which made no sense. Luc knew why he felt guilty. He'd been the one to watch Mike die. The one to find Shayna's body. The one who could have stopped both deaths.

But from the NYPD's perspective, Luc was clean. He'd followed process. He'd done exactly what he'd been trained to do.

Which didn't ease Luc's guilt. At all. But it did mean that if Ava Sims went digging into Luc's past, she'd come up empty. On a professional level, at least.

On a personal level, Ava Sims could destroy him.

But somehow, Luc didn't think that was what his family was worried about. At least not *all* they were worried about.

When the silence had stretched too long, Nonna jumped in with a too-detailed description of her adventures in Bikram yoga, and Luc allowed himself to relax slightly.

At least until he found his father watching him with an unreadable expression.

And that wasn't the worst part. The worst part was that *Ava* was watching Tony.

And Luc didn't like the speculative look. Not one bit.

CHAPTER SIXTEEN

Luc's family was lovely. *Really* lovely.

As in...Ava hadn't even known families could be like that. She hadn't been exaggerating when she told him that the Simses were not the Sunday family dinner types. She doubted they would be even if they lived in the same state.

But the Morettis? The Morettis were everything family should be. The bustling mother. The mouthy grandma. The overbearing yet warm patriarch. The squabbling yet protective siblings. Granted, there'd been that tense moment when it had become rather abundantly clear that Tony Moretti wasn't keen on the press. And Ava was almost positive the family was keeping something from Luc.

Still, by the time she'd left, stuffed with delicious tiramisu, Ava hadn't been thinking of them as a reporter thinks of a story subject. Even Tony had hugged her. Insisted she come back.

It had been...nice.

"So," Luc said, raising his voice just slightly to be heard over the roar of the ferry motor. They were at the back of the boat, Staten Island behind them, as they headed back to Manhattan.

Back to reality.

"So," she repeated, shivering slightly. The day had been gorgeous and warm, but it wasn't summer yet. Without the sun, there was a definite nip in the air.

Luc noticed. "I wish I had a coat."

"I'm glad you don't. I'd have to start thinking of you as a nice guy."

He turned, leaning his side against the rail as he faced her. "Still not convinced, huh?"

"Jury's still out. Half the time you're buying me flowers and holding my hand, the other you're jumping down my throat."

His mouth quirked in the corner. "What can I say, Sims? You've got a way about you."

"Meaning?"

He glanced out at the water. "Meaning I don't know quite whether to kiss you or strangle you."

The first one.

The thought popped unbidden into her mind, and she tried to shove it away. Kissing Luc would be a bad idea. A wonderful idea. But also, really, really bad.

The tension seemed to crackle between them in the night air, and Ava racked her brain for a way to diffuse whatever was between them.

Not that whatever between them even had a name. Or if it *did* have a name, it seemed to change every two minutes.

"So, your grandma's a hoot," she said, steering them toward safer territory.

Luc smiled. "She likes you. Be flattered, because the last girl that one of us brought around to dinner ended up getting an inquisition about her rather obvious boob job. Nonna wanted to know if the implants could double as a flotation device in the case of a water landing."

Ava snorted. "I think I'm safe there. When I was helping her clear the dessert plates, she informed me that she knew some excellent push-up bra brands to recommend."

Ava realized her mistake when Luc's gaze dropped, and her nipples tightened in response. She didn't think he could notice...she had her cardigan wrapped across her chest to block out the cold, but from the way his gaze heated, it was clear she wasn't the only one affected.

"Sorry about Nonna," he said. Was it her imagination, or was his voice a little more gruff than before? "Her sense of boundaries is nonexistent."

"I liked her," Ava said, meaning it. "I mean, she's not exactly the warm, maternal figure I associate with Italian families. That's more your mom's thing, and I love her too. But Nonna beats to her own drum. I only hope I can be that spunky when I'm her age."

Luc snorted. "Somehow I doubt that will be a problem. I can't picture you as sweet and docile at *any* age."

Ava gave a little smile as she rubbed her hands over her upper arms. "Sweet's never really part of my job description, but luckily we journalist types tend to get a free pass."

"Yeah?"

She nodded. "See, when journalists are pushy, we get labeled as tenacious. Which is a good thing. If *non*-journalists do the same thing, they're merely obnoxious."

"Oh, I dunno. I think the 'obnoxious' label fits just fine."

Ava pressed her lips together and glanced down at her sandals.

It stung a little.

It shouldn't; Luc Moretti had every reason to think that she was obnoxious.

It was just...she'd hoped—*thought*—maybe things were changing. The way he'd reached out his hand when she'd faltered there in the hallway at his parents' home; it had been sweet.

And then he'd stuck close by her side all night, even sitting next to her at dinner, carefully steering his family away from topics that he could tell made her uncomfortable.

And actually, that instinct he seemed to have for sensing when Ava was nervous or uncomfortable was the weirdest part of the entire evening. The man seemed to read her better than anyone; even Beth and Mihail.

Which was why it burned a little that he still thought she was annoying. It told her that his kindness at dinner was a fluke. Just a generic, nice-guy gesture. It hadn't been about *her*.

Why was she surprised? Ava had never been the kind of girl that brought out the tender side of guys.

Ava turned her head slightly so she wouldn't have to look at him, her ponytail whipping against her cheek as she took in the beauty of the Statue of Liberty at night.

She took a deep breath, reminded herself that she didn't need a man like Officer Moretti to validate her existence. She was smart and successful, and was well on her way to achieving career heights that other people only dreamed of...

Only that thought process didn't feel quite right, so she focused instead on the looming Statue of Liberty as they passed it. Luc had been right when he'd said that it never got old, living in the backyard of national monuments like this one.

Hell, *nothing* about New York was old to Ava. And not just because of what it represented. She knew her family thought she was here because it was the very center of the broadcast journalism world, but it was more than that to Ava. This city was about self-discovery and making something of one's self.

Ava's parents only saw one side of New York—the one that represented fame and Park Avenue penthouses and glossy galas. But there was another side of New York too. With its honking cabdrivers and pushy pedestrians, and filthy subways and occasional rats, New York could be dirty and gritty and mean.

But at least it was honest. New Yorkers liked their dirty side. Relished it, even.

In New York, nobody pretended to be a hero.

Well, nobody except the man standing beside her.

"Why'd you do it?" she asked, turning her head to find him watching her.

"Do what?"

"Jump in the river after that little girl . . . give your coat to a homeless guy."

He ran a hand over his face, and she was surprised to see that he looked . . . tired.

"Who's asking?" he asked.

"Sorry?"

"Ava the reporter?" He turned to face her again. "Or Ava the human being?"

"Would you stop with that?" she snapped. "I'm tired of this hot and cold crap. You don't get to say asshole things and then apologize, only to repeat the whole thing all over again. Either you're a nice guy or a jerk. Pick one."

Their gazes clashed for several seconds before he finally looked away.

Ava huffed out a sigh. "You know, I'm finding it increasingly hard to believe your family's claim that you're a regular heartthrob."

"They exaggerate."

"So you don't…how did your grandmother put it…go through women faster than she goes through her hemorrhoid medicine?"

Luc gave a small smile. "No."

"That day at the diner, you made it sound like you didn't date much. Your family made it seem differently."

"Why so interested, Sims?"

"Why so reluctant, Moretti?"

"Maybe I don't want my relationship history showing up on the six o'clock news."

"Don't be ridiculous," she said with a wave. "The *America's Hero* special will likely air at eight. Gotta make sure everyone's home from work and the dishes are put away so the housewives can swoon over your handsome face."

At some point in their conversation, he'd inched closer, and now he nudged her shoulder with his. "It *is* handsome, huh?"

"It's okay," she said grudgingly. "You're not nearly as good looking as your brothers."

"Considering that we grew up with people assuming that there had to be twins or triplets somewhere in the mix, I'll take that as a compliment."

"But you're the only one with blue eyes."

He winked. "Noticed that, did ya?"

Crap.

"It's just unusual for such a solidly Italian family. Or am I stereotyping?"

"Blue eyes aren't as common as brown, but it happens. And I'm not the only one to have them. Elena's are blue too."

Oh. *Whoops.*

While Ava had liked Elena very much, Ava couldn't say she'd noticed her eye color. It was hard to pay attention to the women in the room when there was so much male eye candy.

And the Morettis really were an exceptionally attractive family.

But Luc, with his strong jaw, sparkling blue eyes, and lean strength?

He belonged on a movie poster.

The crowning jewel of the family.

Orrrrr . . . maybe she was biased.

"It's a pain, huh?" he said, interrupting her thoughts.

"What's a pain?"

"Being attracted to someone you're determined to dislike."

Her mouth went dry at his husky tone. "You speaking from experience, Officer?"

His answer was to drop his gaze to her mouth, and Ava swore she felt butterflies. Ava Sims did not *do* butterflies.

"You didn't answer my question," she blurted out. "About why you jumped into the river."

Luc tipped his head back and laughed, and Ava went all fluttery at the sight of his Adam's apple.

Get a grip, Sims.

"You and I do a lot of that, have you noticed? Dodging each other's questions? Answering with other questions?"

"Part of the reporter thing, I guess."

"Answer my question, Sims. You attracted to me?"

He moved in, then, not quite touching her, but somehow

pinning her against the railing using body heat alone. Ava kept her eyes locked on his chin even as her pulse flipped into overdrive.

Luc touched a knuckle to her cheek. "I think the woman behind the reporter is pulled to me. Just like the man behind the cop is drawn to you."

He was going to kiss her. She could tell by the firm command of his voice, the positioning of his body.

She wanted it.

Oh, how she wanted it.

She wanted to wind her arms around him, arch her back into him, wanted to absorb all of his heat and goodness.

But it was that last part that gave her pause.

People weren't good.

This man may have the wool pulled over the eyes of his family and half of New York City, but Ava wasn't about to get pulled into his vortex.

At least until she saw the side of him that *wasn't* so shiny.

Most women *liked* the early stages of a relationship because the men hid their dirty laundry.

Ava hated it.

She wouldn't be kissing Luc Moretti any time soon. Not until he showed her the real Luc.

Ava sidestepped; she patted his arm. "The Statue of Liberty really does get you all sappy and romantic, doesn't it?"

The light went out of his eyes, his head tipping back just slightly as he watched her with a narrowed gaze. And the slight twist of his lips told her he wasn't done with her yet.

Fine.

She wasn't done with him either.

CHAPTER SEVENTEEN

Avie, how's the story coming along?"

Ava glanced up to see her boss, Brent Davis, taking an uninvited seat on the edge of her desk where she'd been solidly in the zone while Googling the Morettis.

She moved her coffee mug out of the way of his leg, careful not to let her hand touch his leg, even though she was fairly certain he'd placed himself too close on purpose.

It was so grossly cliché, the aging media boss chasing after the young skirts in the office, but Davis seemed all too happy to play his part.

"Earth to Avie." His knee bumped her arm.

Okay, that was another thing. Wasn't the point of nicknames to shorten the original name? Ava and Avie were the same number of syllables, which meant her boss only utilized Avie to breed a familiarity that wasn't there.

Still. He was the boss. And like him or not (she absolutely did not), he was a key part in her path to anchorwoman. Not that he was high enough on the food chain to make the final decision, but he was certainly a gatekeeper.

So even though she itched to tell him to get his bulging thigh out of her personal space, she smiled.

"Sorry, this story's taking up all of my mental capacity."

He smirked. "It should be. A three-hour prime-time special is no fluff piece. It's the real deal. The rest of the girls are yapping behind your back."

"Good to know," she muttered. Though she wasn't all that surprised. There was no such thing as real friendship at CBC. Mostly it ranged from two-faced, to backstabbing, to cutthroat.

"Hey, are you familiar with the name Shayna Johnson?" she asked, tapping her pencil against her notepad.

Brent Davis may be a lecher, but he was a good newsman. His memory for stories, no matter how small, was legendary.

He folded his arms across his beefy chest, blue eyes scrunching as he went into what she thought of as his thinking mode.

"Kidnapping case gone wrong?" he said.

"If by wrong, you mean she died, yeah," Ava said, glancing at her notes. "And sadly, not all that unusual, especially in the rougher area of Harlem."

He frowned. "Wasn't that a couple years ago? What are you doing looking at a story that's stale *and* common? You're not chasing a cold case, are you?"

"No, they caught the bastard," she said distractedly, her pencil tapping more quickly against the notepad. "He's rotting in prison."

"Ah. So no recent escape then." He sounded disappointed and Ava game him a disgusted look.

Davis had the decency to look ashamed. "Right, right.

Glad the perp's still behind bars. Still not getting why we're talking about this then. What am I missing?"

"Maybe nothing," Ava said. But her pencil was moving at warp speed now. Her reporter instincts were buzzing.

Something wasn't right.

She opened her mouth.

Shut it.

Opened it again.

"It's just…something's strange about it. The case was high profile for the entire week she was missing. The little girl was the daughter of a city councilman. But her death barely registered a blip on the local media scene. The story just said that the suspect had been apprehended, but sadly, authorities were too late to save Shayna."

"And this is related to the Moretti story how?"

"I'm not sure yet," she mused. "Give me time."

Davis rolled his eyes, pushing off her desk. "Thanks for leading me down the rabbit hole for nothing."

"Anytime," she said sweetly, giving him a little finger wave as he waddled away.

After Davis was out of earshot, a permanently scowled forehead appeared over the wall, followed by shrewd blue eyes, then a long nose and sulky mouth with a red and yellow gummy worm hanging out the side.

"I'm dismayed you weren't forthcoming with our boss," Mihail said, wiggling his eyebrows. "Absolutely appalled."

"How do you know I wasn't telling the truth?"

His expression didn't change as he chewed his gummy worm, watching her.

"Okay fine," she said on a sigh, lowering her voice. "I *may* know more than I said."

"And?"

Ava hesitated, then immediately felt guilty. She told Mihail *everything*. He was her sounding board, her partner, her ball-and-chain when she chased a story that simply wasn't there.

The fact that she was hesitating showing him *this* meant that she might have deeper feelings for Luc Moretti than she thought.

And since that scared the crap out of her, she quickly unlocked her computer screen and gestured Mihail to come around to her side before she could change her mind.

Mihail grunted when he saw the masthead on the website she'd pulled up. "That website is trash. Beyond trash. It's paparazzi bullshit."

"I know, I know, but look," she said, scrolling down to a post from two years ago.

"What am I looking at?"

She pointed at a police officer on the right.

"Recognize him?"

Mihail leaned in and squinted. "That Moretti? Sure. So he was there when shit went down. So what?"

Right. *So what?*

Luc Moretti was a cop. There was nothing unusual about him being on the scene when a kidnapper in a high-profile case was arrested.

It was nothing, and yet...

Why was there so little about the resolution to this story?

Ava suddenly remembered her first reaction upon meeting Luc that day in his captain's office. She'd thought then that something had been off, but then she'd gotten so wrapped up in, well, him, that she'd gone and forgotten all about it.

But her reporter instincts were buzzing now, and they'd never led her astray before. And Ava loved the thrill of a good story. Particularly one people didn't want told.

CHAPTER EIGHTEEN

Finally, *finally* Luc typed up the last sentence on the last report for the week, putting one fist in the air.

Victory.

"You know, for some reason, it never really occurred to me that cops could take sick days," Ava mused, never looking up from the magazine she'd been flipping through for the past half hour.

Luc dropped his arm. He'd almost forgotten he wasn't alone. The operative word being *almost*, because it seemed his subconscious was *always* aware of Ava Sims.

He reached for his Coke. "Well here's something to know about Lopez; his 'sick' days tend to come on heavy paperwork days. Write that down."

She scrunched her nose. "You think he's faking it? He sounded pretty stuffed up on speakerphone earlier."

"That's because he thinks he's allergic to paperwork. It's psychosomatic."

"So we're all done?" she asked, finally flipping her magazine closed.

"*I'm* done," he said, giving her a pointed look.

"Hey, I've been here too. You think hanging around until eight o'clock in a deserted precinct is my idea of a good time?"

Luc snorted and stood. "Don't even. I wasted thirty minutes trying to get rid of you. I think we can both agree that the 'American public' you're so anxious to impress isn't going to give a shit about all the filing we cops have to do."

"No," she admitted. "They want the sexy, jumping into rivers, saving babies stuff."

"So why are you still here?"

She stood as well, putting her hands on the small of her back to stretch. "I need to understand the full picture of Luc Moretti the cop. Even if the boring stuff doesn't make it into production, our interview will be richer if I'm informed."

"Interview?"

"Don't worry, the camera will love you," she said, patting his forearm before reaching for her handbag.

"I never agreed to that. You said the reason you had to follow me around was because people didn't want to see a boring interview. Now you're changing it up on me?"

Ava huffed out an exasperated breath. "No, I said they didn't want *just* an interview. Honestly, Luc, what did you think this news special entailed? Of course there'll be an interview. It'll be a huge component of the story."

Christ. He should have seen it coming, he supposed.

Showing the brief video clips of his "good deeds" over and over wouldn't fill up three hours.

Luc rubbed a hand over his face before leaning to shut down his computer. "You're going to turn my life into a spectacle. You know that, right?"

"I'm afraid it already is, Officer Moretti. A woman asked you to sign her bra the other day. I think you've passed the point of no return."

He studied her. "Is that why you're able to do what you do without guilt? You figure my anonymity's shot with or without you, so I'm fair game."

She tilted her head. "You really don't trust me, do you?"

"Should I? Seems to be our relationship's a lot about you taking, and not much giving."

And a lot of you running hot and cold, he nearly added, remembering that almost kiss on the ferry when she'd freaked out.

"Relationship, huh?" She smirked.

Shit.

Relationship had not been the word he'd meant to use.

He also hadn't meant to infer that he expected—or wanted—her to give anything back. He didn't need to know Ava Sims.

Didn't need to know what made her tick.

Other than her career ambition, but he suspected even *that* came from a deeper, dark place. Probably having to do with her messed-up family.

But beyond that?

He didn't know Ava Sims at all.

And it bothered him more than he liked to admit.

Ava slung her purse over her shoulder. "Okay then."

Luc gave her a wary look. "Okay what?"

"I'm buying you dinner."

Luc shook his head as he followed her out. "Not exactly what I meant."

Ava spun around and put a hand against his chest to stop him. "Maybe I wasn't clear. I'm taking you to dinner...and you get to ask whatever questions you want. About me. My company is asking you to be an open book, with essentially no choice in the matter. I can't give you that choice back. But I can, at least, make this a two-way street."

Luc studied her. It was an unexpected move. Every vibe he'd gotten from Ava so far was that she was fiercely private. Sure, she could have a conversation with anyone, flirt with anyone, wrap anyone around her finger, and yet he'd have sworn that the real Ava was on lockdown.

And here she was practically volunteering transparency? There had to be a catch.

But he could handle the catch.

Luc shrugged. "You're on."

Ava blinked. "Really? You'll have dinner with me?"

He maneuvered them so that his hand was on the small of her back as he ushered her toward the door. "Sure. Hey, does your cell have a camera built in?"

"Um, sure?"

"Good." He ushered her out into the night air. "Get it ready in case I just happen to catch any babies falling from burning buildings, or throw myself in front of an elderly person to protect them from a runaway cab. Gotta document that shit."

"*Crap*," Ava said, skidding to a halt. "We forgot your cape. I was up all night sewing sequins onto it."

"There goes your whole story," Luc said with a shake of his head. "I don't suppose this means we can call the whole thing off?"

"No, although now you know why Clark Kent had multiple Superman outfits on hand," she said, linking her arm in his and pulling him toward the curb to hail a cab.

"I hardly think he called them *outfits*," Luc said as he followed her into the taxi.

"West Village?" he asked skeptically after hearing the address she gave the cabbie. "That's your neighborhood?"

"Nah, I don't make enough to live there. Yet," she added with the sort of firmness that told him she fully expected to make enough someday to live in one of Manhattan's trendier neighborhoods.

"So where do you live?"

"A tiny box in the Financial District," she said. "When I first moved to the city, I didn't know what the hell I was doing, and the broker assured me it was the best I could do while still living in Manhattan, which at the time, I was hell-bent on. You're in Upper West, yeah?"

He turned to see her watching him in the shadows. "Dying to know how I can afford it, huh?"

"Nope, your grandma filled me in. Roomies! That must be fun."

Luc grunted. "This morning I woke up to her shouting at the window washers across the street asking them to, and I quote, 'shake it.'"

She laughed softly. "You love her."

"I love my whole family."

Ava's smile faded a little. "As you should. They're great."

The restaurant Ava picked was tiny, trendy, and crowded, even on a Wednesday night, and definitely not a typical NYPD hangout.

"Don't worry," she said, catching his expression as they claimed a spot at the bar to wait for a table. "I've got this handy thing called a corporate credit card and a hefty spending limit. So what can CBC get you from the bar?"

The restaurant was noisy, so Luc dropped his head slightly so his lips could get close to her ear. "I'll have what you're having."

"You like wine?"

He gave her a look. "I'm Italian."

"Does that mean I should limit it to Chianti, or are you up for a little adventure?"

Luc's brain went in a sideways direction. He wanted to take an adventure with Ava all right. And not with wine.

"Surprise me," he said, turning to face the bar more fully in hopes that nobody noticed that his response to this woman was immediate and potent. At least he wasn't in uniform tonight. Boners and cop uniforms didn't go well together.

Out of habit, Luc surveyed the restaurant while Ava chatted up the bartender about the wine list. He didn't eat out much, beyond the odd late-night cheeseburger run, and he had to admit that while he wasn't much of a "scene" guy, there was something sort of nice about being out for a late dinner with a beautiful woman.

It made him feel his actual age.

Despite the fact that his family frequently reminded him of his status as the baby, the truth was, Luc generally felt a good deal older than his twenty-eight years.

The job had aged him. The things he'd seen, the long hours...Mike.

Shayna.

He closed his eyes briefly to block out the haunting image of her tiny body. *Not now*, he pleaded his subconscious. *Not when I'm having dinner with a reporter.*

But Ava would never connect him with the case.

Somehow, Luc had gotten lucky, and none of the follow-up news reports of the kidnapping gone sideways had gotten into the specifics of the first responders.

As far as the world knew, this was just the sad case of a sick fuck-wad killing little kids.

Of course, everyone wished that it would have worked out differently; that the cops could have gotten in front of it. But the public was sadly accepting that sometimes it didn't work that way. There was an assumption that the cops had tried their hardest, but sometimes it wasn't good enough.

It was a mistaken assumption.

But nobody knew it.

Except Luc.

"Here," Ava said, turning around to face him. Luc grasped at the oversized red wineglass like it was a lifeline.

Her head tilted a little, her brown eyes worried. "You okay?"

Luc clinked his glass to hers. "Never better. Now what are we drinking?"

"Pinot Noir from Oregon. The good ones are expensive, but hey. We're worth it."

Luc didn't buy into the whole swirl and sniff routine with wine—any wine—but he did appreciate the good stuff, and his taste buds told him right away that this was good. Very good.

"So," Ava said, slipping onto a recently vacated bar stool and crossing her legs. The motion made her pencil skirt ride up just a little, exposing smooth knee and long calf. His fingers itched to run from her ankle all the way up to her knee, to her inner thigh and beyond...

She snapped her fingers against his upper arm. "Do not look at me like that," she said, her voice husky. "When I suggested a get-to-know-Ava evening, I didn't mean *little* Ava."

Luc choked on his wine. "Is that what you call your—"

She laid a finger over his lips, although she looked as surprised by the gesture as he felt. Very slowly she removed her hand, shaking her head slightly as though to erase it.

"Let the questions commence," she said, taking a sip of her wine. "And keep it clean, Moretti."

She licked a little speck of red wine from her bottom lip, and it took every ounce of self-control not to crush his mouth to hers.

Clean. Right.

"All right," he said, clearing his throat. "Let's start with the basics. How long are we going to pretend that we don't want to be in bed right now? Or against the wall? Or on a kitchen counter?"

She gave a strangled laugh. "Clearly you don't understand the art of interviewing. It's all about finesse."

Unable to stop himself, Luc traced an index finger along the sharp line of her jaw, dragging the pad of his finger down to her stubborn chin. "Guess you shouldn't have flirted with a cop then, lady. No such thing as an interview in my line of work."

"No?"

"Nope." He moved in closer, shifting so that his upper body leaned into hers. "We start with interrogations."

"And then?" Her voice was flirty and light, but her eyes were pure heat.

His gaze dropped to his hand, which had found its way to her knee somehow. "Depends. If the cop's skilled at interrogation, things generally progress to handcuffs...and other things. If the cop's unsuccessful..."

Luc broke off and shrugged.

Ava looked at him over the top of her wineglass. "Which one are you? The skilled interrogator or the other?"

"Depends."

"On."

He leaned in and pressed his lips to her ear. "Whether or not you like handcuffs."

CHAPTER NINETEEN

The hostess at La Printemps either had very good timing, or very bad timing, depending on how you looked at it.

Considering that sex with Luc Moretti was a *terrible* idea, Ava was inclined to think she should tip the hostess for interrupting.

Her humming body said otherwise.

And although the sexual tension eased *slightly* as they were seated at their table, the evening continued to feel like a date.

The best date she'd had in a long, long time.

Luc leaned back as the server cleared their appetizer plates. "I just can't picture you as a small-town, Midwest girl."

"Believe it," she said, looking down as she swirled her wineglass. "My graduating high school class had under a hundred people. I passed cornfields on my way to cheerleading practice."

"Cheerleader. That's hot," he said, taking out a piece of bread after offering the basket to her.

She rolled her eyes. "What is it with men and cheerleaders?"

Luc chewed his bread thoughtfully before leaning toward her. "What is it with women and men in uniforms?"

"Nuh uh," she said, holding up a finger, even as she enjoyed his blatant cockiness. "We already established that I'm not going to be one of your groupies."

"Is that why you kept that parking ticket as a love souvenir of our first meeting?"

Ava giggled. *Giggled*. What was wrong with her? "Believe me, that is *so* not what it was."

"No? Because it had lipstick on it, Sims."

"So that's your theory? You think I kissed it good night for three years?"

He wiggled his eyebrows. "You tell me."

"All right," she said, giving a little shake of her head. "I get it."

"Get what?"

"Why you're the family charmer. You're pretty good at it when you're not being an uptight bore."

"Such sweet love words coming out of that pretty mouth." He gave her that lady-killer smile that she was pretty sure had caused many a damp panty.

Not Ava's though.

Well *maybe* hers. Just a little.

Ava inhaled, trying to remember all the reasons she hadn't kissed him on the ferry the other night.

She couldn't remember a damned one.

"Stop flirting," she said, desperate to get them to safer ground. "You've been whining for two weeks about how

I'm prying into your life. Here's your chance to pry into mine."

He dunked another piece of bread in the flavored oil as he considered. "Okay then. I do have a question that's a little bit...prying."

"Bring it," she said, hoping he didn't notice the way her shoulders hunched. She didn't have any intention of letting him get too personal. She was much too skilled at evasions. But that didn't mean she wasn't a little worried about him getting beneath her skin.

"Well I'm just wondering...how short was that cheerleading skirt?"

Ava blinked a little in...disappointment?

Obviously Luc had every intention of keeping the evening flirty and superficial.

She should be grateful. Hell, hadn't the thought just crossed her mind that she didn't want him to get too close?

But if she was honest with herself—*really* good and honest with her apparently fickle brain—a little part of her wanted Luc to ask the hard questions.

To know more about the real Ava, not Ava Sims, journalist.

But it wasn't her *brain* that wanted that.

And no way was she going to put her heart out there when the guy couldn't even bother to *ask*.

Instead of letting on to her disappointment, she gave him a saucy wink. "It was as short as you're hoping it was."

"I knew it. You were my high school fantasy."

But not your adult fantasy?

Ava was saved from having to follow that thought by the arrival of their entrées.

"A piece of your duck for a bite of my steak?" he said after gesturing for the server to bring them another round of wine.

She didn't stop him.

Superficial conversation or not, having a long, lingering meal with a guy who was straight-up decent was too nice to pass up.

They exchanged bites of their entrées, and Ava didn't protest when he snagged another bite of her truffled mashed potatoes as though it were his right. He didn't even blink when she helped herself to a Brussels sprout on his plate that tasted way better than any cabbage had a right to taste.

They ate in companionable silence for a few moments until Ava felt his gaze on her. She looked up at him. "What?"

"Do you do this often?" he asked.

"Eat dinner?"

He smiled his slow, dangerous smile. "Don't be a smart ass. I mean eat dinner with a *man*. Go on dates."

Ava took a tiny sip of wine, trying to ignore the thrill that went through her. So maybe he *did* care about getting to know her after all. He hardly sounded jealous, but he did sound...interested.

"Not much recently," she said. "I used to try a little harder to date. It's what single twenty-something women in New York are supposed to do, but..."

"But?"

She gave him a toothy smile. "Men are shits."

He laid a hand over his chest. "You wound me."

"I didn't say *you* were a shit."

"But you sometimes think so. Admit it."

"I may or may not be revising my opinion," she said after taking a sip of wine.

"I knew it. You *did* keep that ticket as a memento of your feelings for me. How did your boyfriend feel about that?"

This time Ava's smile was wide and genuine. "I give you a free pass to dig into my *entire* personal life, and you seem to be focusing only on my romantic endeavors, Officer Moretti. Why is that?"

She awaited the flirtatious banter that rolled off him so easily, but to her surprise, his expression went serious.

"I can venture into other topics if you want, but somehow I don't think you're going to like them."

Ava's smile slipped. "Meaning?"

He leaned forward, his expression more intense than before. "That first day in Captain Brinker's office...I didn't bother to hide the fact that I wanted no part in this damn news special. But my cop instincts were telling me that you didn't want any part in it either. Explain that."

The bite of duck Ava had just put in her mouth suddenly seemed to dry and swell up on her, and she forced herself to chew slowly and methodically as she reached for her water.

Finally the piece of meat went down, and she was able to respond.

Only to realize she had nothing to say.

Journalists were good at evasive bullshitting. Ava in particular was great at it; it was the only way to explain away why you were somewhere you shouldn't be when researching a story, and the occasional white lie here and there wasn't unheard of to get interview subjects to open up and spill their guts.

But she and Luc seemed past that somehow. And so she didn't quite lie.

She did, however, evade.

"Maybe your cop instincts were wrong," she said, forcing herself to meet his gaze with a steady, bland look of her own.

"They haven't been yet."

She leaned forward. "Oh, come on. You're telling me you've never made a mistake."

His eyes shadowed before he looked away and picked up his wine. "I didn't say that. I said that my instincts were never wrong."

Ava studied him. It was an interesting and precise evasion. If he admitted to mistakes but also stood by his claim that his instincts were never wrong, it meant that his mistakes must center around not *acting* on his instincts.

"You mean like—"

Ava broke off, suddenly unsure she wanted to go in this direction. Not when he'd just finally started to relax around her.

"Do I mean like what?" he asked, his voice sharp.

You mean like the Shayna Johnson case. The one where a little girl ended up dead. Where were your instincts then?

But she couldn't ask him that. Not only because she wasn't at all sure she'd get a straight answer, but because she knew very well what her bosses would say to that little development in her story: *cut it.*

There was no room for pesky things like kidnapping and police error and the truth in her line of work.

"Never mind," she said, forcing a smile.

Luc had set his fork aside and continued to study her. "You're hiding something, Sims. Holding back on me."

"I am," she said honestly. "Just like you're holding back on me."

He lifted his glass as though to toast her. "To secrets."

She rolled her eyes, even as she mimicked his motion. "To secrets you get to keep *for now.*"

He was silent for a few moments longer before he seemed to shake off whatever dark cloud had hovered around him. "Okay, but at least tell me this, Sims."

"What?" She was curious.

"This story wasn't your idea, was it?"

She grimaced. "No. What gave me away?"

He shrugged. "It seemed too tame for you. Your clothes and plastic smile all said that you were merely a network lackey following through on your assignment," he replied. "But your eyes said otherwise."

Ava groaned. "Oh, come on, Moretti. I'm going to have to retract my statement about you being good with the ladies if you feed me some garbage about being able to 'read my eyes.'"

"Ah, Sims. Such a cynic."

"Realist," she said, tapping a fingernail on the table. "Facial expressions and tone might give things away, but eyes are eyes. They're blue, they're brown, they blink, but they don't tell stories."

"You're wrong," he said, so confidently that she almost believed him. Almost.

"So tell me, then, Officer. What was it you saw in my eyes that day?" She fluttered her eyelashes dramatically.

He cut a tidy piece of steak and surprised the hell out of her by offering her the bite on his fork as he held her gaze, and God help her, Ava actually found herself leaning forward and nipping the juicy piece of meat between her teeth.

Luc gave her a slow smile.

"Hunger."

"I'm sorry?"

"*Hunger* was what I saw that day," he said, helping himself to another bite of her mashed potatoes. "I couldn't place it at first—"

"Because it wasn't there shining in my *eyes*," she interrupted.

"—But after you walked away I realized…you're not the type of woman who wants a story that's handed to her. You're the type of woman who wants the story she has to chase."

Ava blinked. The observation was so shrewd, so dead-on, that she nearly gave him a round of applause.

"You're wrong," she lied, sitting back and studying him.

He grinned. "Am I?"

Ava sucked the inside of her cheek between her teeth and considered her best move.

The woman in her was dying to tell him the truth…to tell him everything about her, the way she would if they were just Ava and Luc.

But they weren't Ava and Luc. They were Ava Sims, reporting for CBC, and Officer Luc Moretti.

If she told him the truth—that she really *did* like a story she had to chase after—he'd run.

Because Ava would bet serious money that Luc was that story. And not in the way her bosses expected.

Still, she had to give him something. Wasn't the entire point of this dinner to earn his trust?

To let him into her life a little so he'd let her into his?

The more she scraped beneath the gorgeous surface of Officer Moretti, the more she realized that he wasn't the open book he pretended to be.

And if she wanted to find out what *really* happened to Shayna Johnson, she was going to have to put a little skin in the game.

"Okay," she said, allowing only the smallest sigh. "You caught me. The truth is, these fluffy, shiny pieces…the three-hour scripted specials…I don't love them."

He sipped his wine and watched her. "Then why did you agree to it?"

She fiddled with her fork. "It's a no-brainer. When your boss's boss offers you a prime-time slot, you take it. Especially when..."

"Especially when...?" he prompted when she broke off.

"Especially when Gwen Garrison is getting ready to retire. And that's confidential," she said, jabbing a finger in his direction. "Don't tell a soul."

"Believe me, I won't," he said with a little laugh. "I don't even know who Gwen Garrison is."

A laugh bubbled out of Ava. A genuine one. He didn't know who Gwen Garrison was. The most famous anchorwoman on television, and he didn't know her.

It figured. Figured that she'd fall for the one guy who couldn't care less how close she was to the big time. Didn't even know what the big time was.

And she *was* falling for Luc. She couldn't deny that now.

She idly scratched her temple. "Let's just say that if all goes according to plan, I'll *be* the next Gwen Garrison."

"And that's a good thing?"

"It's a huge thing," she replied.

Luc's blue eyes held hers. "That's not what I asked. I asked if it was a *good* thing."

"Yeah," she said, her voice tripping over the lie. "Of course."

His eyes flickered with some emotion she didn't yet recognize from him...disappointment?

But instead of pressing her, he merely picked up his fork and resumed eating. "Say what you want, Sims. I think we both know this whole thing is all because you've been pining for me for three long years since the parking ticket incident."

"Yes, that's definitely it," she said, knowing he was letting her off the hook. "I spent three years in the prime of my life lusting after a traffic patrol officer who gave my news van a parking ticket, and decided that rather than just call him up and ask him out on a date, I'd mastermind a national television series on him."

Luc nodded. "I like a woman that goes after what she wants. As long as she's gorgeous and what she wants is me."

Ava refused to let herself blush because he called her gorgeous. It was just a line. She *knew* it was a line. And yet…

"I never said I want you," she said.

"You didn't have to, Sims." He winked. "It's all right there in your eyes, baby. All in the eyes."

Ava took a bite of duck and shook her head. "You're a piece of work, Officer."

And I like you, she added silently. *Very much.*

After dinner, Ava let him walk her home. And by *let*, she actually crossed her fingers in hopes that he would offer.

He did.

"I still can't believe you paid for dinner," Ava said, giving him a chiding look as they strolled in the general direction of her apartment.

He glanced down at her. "Let a woman pay on the first date? Never."

"I told you, the station would pay," she said. "And the fact that my employer would foot the bill should make it rather clear that it wasn't a *date*."

He smiled and held her elbow as they crossed an uneven part of the sidewalk so she wouldn't teeter in her high heels. "You keep telling yourself that, Sims."

She huffed out a breath.

He really was cocky as all hell. He'd slipped the server

his credit card while she was checking her phone. It wouldn't have bothered her if she hadn't known that his cop salary likely didn't have room for trendy dinners. Especially when it had been her idea.

But he was right about one thing...

It *had* felt a bit like a date. Even more so now that he was walking her home on a warm spring evening.

"So you never answered my question," Luc said as they wove around a group of drunken businessmen. "Why did you trick us into this story?"

She glanced up at him, making her eyes go wide. "It isn't all written right here, in my eyes?"

He gave a half smile. "That only gives me the highlights. I want the full version. The what-makes-Ava-tick account."

She looked away. "I don't know how to explain it without sounding...driven. Ambitious. Aggressive."

"Well good news, Sims, the cat's already out of the bag on all those traits."

His tone was teasing, but her smile slipped a little all the same.

It was true...she *was* driven in her desire to succeed in her career. And that trait had never bothered her before.

If anything, she'd been proud of being a modern woman, or whatever.

But tonight, she was seeing herself through Luc Moretti's eyes. And Ava wasn't entirely sure she liked what she saw.

Still, she had promised him the truth, so...

"I want to be anchorwoman," she said, stopping when she realized they were outside her apartment building.

He stopped and turned to face her. "Sounds like a reasonable goal for a TV reporter."

Ava shrugged, feeling oddly restless. "Yeah. But it's competitive and political, and I'm worried by the time something opens up, I'll be too old."

Luc's eyebrows lifted. "Old? You're what, twenty-five?"

"Twenty-eight. And don't start in on me about how I'm a spring chicken with my whole life ahead of me, because time and age work differently in TV."

"If I look like the type of guy that would use the phrase 'spring chicken,' I need to do some serious reevaluating of my manliness."

Trust me. Your manliness is just fine.

Two women came out of Ava's apartment building, and she gave them a little smile and wave. Like most New Yorkers, she wasn't necessarily buddy-buddy with her neighbors, but you never knew when you'd need someone to pick up your mail or loan you coffee.

One of them gave Ava a little wave, but the other was too busy checking out Luc, and curse the man, he wasn't exactly oblivious to the attention. He stuck his hands in the back pocket of his jeans and smiled, looking very much like a gorgeous single guy and less like the superstar cop.

"Did you just wink at that girl?" Ava asked incredulously after the two women were out of earshot.

"What's it to you if I did, Sims?"

"Nothing." She pursed her lips. "For a self-proclaimed ladies' man, I thought you'd have smoother moves."

"Could be that my moves are *so* smooth you don't even know they're moves."

"Doubtful, Lothario. Most women over the age of fourteen know when a guy's into them."

He gave her a crooked smile. "Do they?"

For a second her breath caught, and she might as well be back in tenth grade because she really, really wanted to ask if

he was implying what she thought he might be implying...
that he was into *her*.

But before she could get up the courage to ask, he poured
ice water all over the moment. "So you never really answered the question...am I your ticket to the anchor seat?"

Right. *Right.* Because ultimately this evening wasn't
about winning over Luc, it was about gaining Officer
Moretti's trust. And to do that, she needed to lay all her cards
on the table.

Almost all her cards.

"Yes," she said succinctly. "I heard about your hero an-
tics, saw the videos, and followed my instincts that it could
make for a career-changing story."

Luc studied her as he rocked back a little on his heels.
"The thing is, Sims, I'm not sure you're right about that. At
the end of the day, I'm just a man in a uniform, you know?"

His expression was so open and honest that her heart
melted.

Just a little.

Sometimes Ava felt like she had a little wall of ice around
her emotions. Not because of any traumatic breakup, or
angsty romantic past, but just like she was sort of born without that softness that most of her girlfriends seemed to have.

But now...now it was occurring to her that maybe she
just hadn't met the right man. Hadn't met the person who
cared enough to look beneath the surface.

And *this* man had. He'd asked about Ava the person. Not
Ava the talking head on TV.

Ava's emotions felt anything but frozen at the moment.

"The man beneath the uniform is exactly what I want to
show people," she said, keeping her voice soft. It's that human
element that made you pseudo-famous in the first place."

Luc's eyes went warm, and he took a half step closer. "Now who's putting on the moves?"

She hadn't realized how close they were standing before, and now there were only inches separating them. The world around them seemed to go quiet, and her gaze dropped to his mouth.

It would be so easy to lean into him.

So easy to take this simmering attraction between them to the next level.

And yet...

He was a *story*. *Her* story. *The* story.

And if this thing between them went south...

Ava took a quick step back, then another. Luc gave her a small smile that said he knew exactly what she was up to, but he didn't fight her on it.

He pulled his hands out of his pockets and gestured toward the door as though the heat of the previous moment had never happened. "Come on, Sims. Let's get you home."

"I am home."

"You've met Nonna. What do you think she'll do to me when she finds out I didn't walk a lady to her door?"

"All right, Moretti. But let it be known that I will be calling you old-fashioned at some point in my story."

"Bring it on. The kind of girls I like *love* old-fashioned."

It was on the tip of her tongue to ask what kind of girls he liked, but instead, she rolled her eyes and headed toward the front door of her building.

She looked at him expectantly when he reached out to hold the door for her, and he shook his head. "No way, Sims. All the way to your door."

"Said the stalker," she muttered.

"Said the cop," he corrected.

"Fine," she said, oddly charmed by his old-school ways. It had been a long time since anyone had walked her to a door. "But the elevator only works about half the time, so stairs it is."

Stepping into the stairwell, Ava had already reached into her purse and was pulling out her flip-flops before she remembered that she wasn't alone.

She halted in the process of pulling off her stiletto heel and gave a curious Luc a sheepish smile. "Sorry, habit."

He waved a hand. "Don't change routine on my account."

Since it was too late to reverse the process without looking like an idiot, Ava quickly slipped her feet into her flip-flops before scooping up her stilettos and carrying them by their heels in one hand.

She eyed him testily. "What, no lecture on how we women shouldn't wear uncomfortable shoes if they make us miserable?"

He held up his hands. "I said nothing of the kind. I'm not going to stand here and tell you that I don't think the four-inch heels are dead sexy."

Ava huffed and headed up the stairs. "Then *you* wear them up three flights of stairs!"

"A well-fed Sims is an ornery Sims," she heard him mutter, as he followed her up the stairs and down the hallway to her third-floor apartment.

Ava dug her keys out of her bag and turned to face him. If this were a date—a *real* date—this would be the moment of truth.

The kiss-or-no-kiss moment, which if ended in the *kiss* option would have turned into the nightcap or no nightcap, which would turn into sex or no sex...

Not a date, Ava. He's just a job.

"Thanks again, for dinner," she said, giving him a bland smile. "You really didn't have to pay, but I appreciate it."

He nodded, but didn't respond.

Huh. Charming Luc was apparently gone. She didn't know if she was disappointed or relieved.

"Well, good night, Officer. It's been nice talking to you when you're not carrying a gun around your belt."

His smile tipped up a little at that. "Good night, Sims."

Always *Sims*.

She'd never really noticed before, but the man hadn't used her first name. Not once.

Strange.

Maybe she wasn't the only one with boundaries. Maybe he was protecting himself too.

Ava clenched her fingers around the sharp edges of her key to keep her from throwing herself at this generous, kind man who would be so easy to care for.

Instead she turned and slid the key into the lock, giving him one last half smile before slipping into the safety of her apartment.

And damn her hormones, because she closed the door as slowly as possible, giving him the chance to make a move.

He didn't.

When the door finally shut between them, Ava told herself she was relieved. Glad, even, that a night that had had distinct moments of *sexy* had ended so harmlessly platonic.

It was a good thing. Really.

Her lady parts, on the other hand, were screaming *moron*.

Dropping her heels by the door, Ava went to the table and set down her keys and purse before making the cooing noise she always used to summon her cat.

As far as cuddly, supportive pets went, Honky Tonk was a dud.

She'd rescued him a couple of years ago thinking he'd be great company, but mostly he did his own thing.

The only time he really let her pet him was when she got sushi.

Smart cat.

Ungrateful. But smart.

"Here Honky Tonky Tonky," she said in her cat-call voice.

An orange head peeked out from under the couch, gave her a sleepy blink before promptly disappearing again.

"Okay then," she muttered. "Good talk."

Ava put her hands on the small of her back, stretching and debating whether a long, hot shower would help ease her restlessness, or make it worse.

Then the image of Luc in the shower with her, pinning her to the wall as his hands skimmed over her wet, soapy body, his mouth...

Damn it. So that was a no on the shower then.

Ava made it only two steps toward the fridge for a much needed glass of water when she heard the knock.

Luc.

It had to be him. The only people who ever knocked on her door were the sushi delivery guys that she saw way more than she probably should.

She opened the door, and he was there.

One hand was braced on the door frame, and the other...

His other hand reached for her.

Luc's palm slipped around the small of her back, barely giving her a chance to gasp her surprise before he tugged her to him.

And then he kissed her.

His lips were firm and smooth as they moved against hers with just the right amount of roughness as his other hand slipped around the back of her head to hold her still.

It was the kiss of a man who knew what he wanted. And if the way his lips pulled at hers was any indication, right now he wanted Ava.

And Ava wanted him right back.

It took her only seconds to adjust to the feel of his mouth on hers before her arms found his waist, clutching at the soft fabric of his shirt.

Luc tilted his head just enough to take the kiss deeper, and Ava was right there with him, reaching for his tongue with hers. Luc let out a raspy groan as the fingers in her hair tightened and Ava was forced to face a rather disturbing reality:

It was without a doubt the hottest, most perfect kiss she'd ever had.

It was the rightness of it that finally had her coming to her senses, although it took her several moments before she could force herself to break away from his lips.

She was slow to open her eyes, and when she did, she was braced to see triumphant male ego on his face. But although he was watching her, the only things she saw on her face were the very same things she was feeling: heat and confusion.

"Well," he said, his voice raspier than she'd ever heard it. "That's . . . inconvenient."

She nodded slowly, touching her fingers to her swollen lips. "It probably shouldn't happen again. Conflict of interest and all that."

He shook his head just as slowly as though also convincing himself. "Right. Shouldn't happen again. Our lives are incompatible. I want to be left alone to do my job; you want to push me into the limelight."

Right. *That* whole thing.

She didn't blame him for wanting to keep his distance, and he didn't know the extent of research she was doing on him *behind* the scenes.

"So this is good night, then," she said. "For real this time."

"Night. And Sims?"

"Hmm?"

"I'll see you tomorrow."

He winked and was gone, and it wasn't until after she'd closed the door and opted to take a hot shower after all that she realized this was the most she'd looked forward to *tomorrow* in a long, long time.

CHAPTER TWENTY

The nightmares didn't come often, but when they did, they were real pissers.

It took Luc several minutes after wrenching his eyes open to orient himself—to let the panicked part of his brain recognize the agony for what it was:

A memory.

Luc sat upright in bed, leaning forward and digging the heels of his hands into his eyes, trying to push out the memory of Jensen's shocked eyes as the bullet ripped through his chest. The mental image of Shayna Johnson's tiny, unmoving body on the bedroom floor.

Fuck.

He knew from experience that going back to sleep now would risk him falling back into the dream, so he rolled out of bed and headed into the kitchen for water and something—anything—to distract him.

He was halfway through his second glass of water when

Anthony's bedroom door opened. Luc caught a glimpse of long blond hair spread out on his brother's pillow and the rustle of sheets before his brother stepped out into the darkened kitchen.

Luc jerked his chin toward the bedroom door that his brother had just closed. "Is that the same woman from last week? Kelsey?"

"Kelly. And no," Anthony said, loosely tying the string on his pajama pants before opening the fridge. He pulled out a Tupperware of pasta leftovers and held it up to Luc with raised eyebrows, but Luc shook his head.

The shitty nightmare had killed any semblance of an appetite.

Anthony shrugged and popped the leftovers into the microwave before pouring himself a glass of water. Luc waited and watched.

Anthony drank the entire glass in three gulps, refilled it, and then turned to stare at Luc.

There it was.

The big-brother-inquisition. It was a silent inquisition. Most things were silent with Anthony. But the question was there.

Scratch that.

The *demand* was there. The one that said *talk*.

As always, the desire to talk about what happened warred with the desire to bury it deep inside him in hopes that the memories would die a quiet death.

But Luc had heard about too many cops going off the deep end because they didn't deal with the shit they'd seen head on.

"Another dream," he said finally, setting his glass on the counter and folding his arms over his chest.

Anthony said nothing as he retrieved his pasta, stirred it up a bit, and placed it back in the microwave. "Same shit?"

"Same shit."

"Tell me."

Luc gritted his teeth. "I just told you it was the same shit. The definition of *same* meaning that it's identical to every other Goddamn time that I've told you about it."

Anthony pulled his pasta out of the microwave again, popped a piece of penne in his mouth to test the temperature, and deeming it hot enough, dug in with his fork.

All the while, he stared at Luc.

That damned silent inquisition.

Shit. Luc caved.

"It's like a movie reel," Luc said, arms still crossed over his chest, fingers clenching his arms. "Except I never see the beginning. I never see the part where we get to the house of the suspected perp and sit outside, awaiting orders. I never relive those agonizing moments where we sit with our thumbs up our ass outside that house waiting to see if the lead is good."

Anthony pauses in his chewing, looking like he wants to interrupt but instead nods at Luc to continue.

Luc runs a hand over his neck. "I never see any of the early stuff. It's like my subconscious wants to utter the ultimate *fuck you* by dropping me into the dream right at the moment that the front door opens and there's a Goddamn thirty-nine barrel pointed at Jensen. Two pops, and . . ."

Luc paused. This was the hard part. No, *one* of the hard parts.

"I see Jensen's face. The walk, the front door, even the gun, they're all kind of a quick blur, like they're just details, and then the dream sequence hits slo-mo when I turn and watch Jensen go down. His eyes . . ."

Anthony sets his pasta aside unfinished, and Luc knew he'd just killed his brother's appetite. Mike Jensen had been Luc's partner, but he'd been Anthony's friend too.

"What else?" Anthony asks, breaking his silence.

Luc stared down at his bare feet. "The girl. I see her every time, lying there, still. That's the only part of the dream that deviates from memory . . . the way it actually went down; when I first saw her body, I knew she was dead, but didn't know just how recently."

Luc tensed his jaw, once, twice, before continuing. "But in the dream, I know. In the dream I've got the shitty benefit of hindsight, and I know that she's been dead only minutes. Dead because Jonas Black saw our fucking car parked out front like a couple of rookies and panicked."

Anthony's gaze was steady. "Black was going to kill her anyway, Luca. You know that. He killed three other girls before that, without any cop intervention."

"I could have saved her. I fucking knew it was him, and I sat there waiting for orders."

"Luc—"

"I knew it was him!" His shout echoed, and both men glanced toward Anthony's bedroom door, but it stayed shut. His sleepover buddy was apparently a deep sleeper.

Luc took a deep breath. Calmed himself. "I knew it was him in my gut, Anth. I *knew* it. But I was too scared of getting reprimanded for disobeying orders."

Anthony shook his head. "Your captain tells you to hold off, you hold off."

"Is that what you would have done?"

It wasn't a casual question. It was a *challenge*, and Luc could tell from the narrowing of his brother's eyes that Anthony knew it.

"Following orders is the *job*."

It wasn't a straight answer. Luc wasn't sure he wanted a straight answer, although he was afraid he already knew.

Anthony would have gone in there without permission if his cop instinct was buzzing.

If Anthony had been called to the scene instead of Luc, Jensen and Shayna would still be alive.

But even chewed up as he was over the nightmare, Luc knew that going down the path of hypothetic wasn't healthy. It wouldn't happen. Except…

It had been *Luc* who had been called to the scene.

It had been *Luc's* partner who had gotten shot.

It had been *Luc* who had to touch the angry marks on Shayna's neck to check for a pulse that wasn't there.

"Hey," Anthony said, his voice gentler than its usual gruff bark. "Whatever you're thinking…stop."

Luc met his brother's eyes, and then with every burst of willpower did what the cop therapist had suggested he try whenever the memories threatened to take over.

He took a deep breath. Counted to three. Another breath. Three again.

One…

Two…

Very slowly the pressure in his chest started to ease. He gave his brother a nod. *I'm okay.*

Then he reached for Anthony's discarded leftovers, not bothering to get a fresh fork, because…*brothers.*

"Guess I should be thankful the paparazzi and tourists weren't around for that part of my career, huh?" Luc asked with a wan smile, trying to lighten the mood.

Luc stopped chewing and narrowed his eyes on Anthony's face. His brother had suddenly stopped making eye contact and was making a big deal out of washing his water glass.

Not having Anthony's power of silent inquisition, he went for the regular, verbal kind. "What's up?"

"Huh?"

Luc speared the last remaining piece of penne and studied his brother. "Don't *huh* me. You got all weird when I mentioned the media."

Luc's fork dropped loudly to the counter as he stood up straighter. "You didn't. Tell me you didn't tell Ava Sims about Shayna Taylor."

"No!" His brother looked uncharacteristically expressive, and the expression was pissed. "Fuck you."

Luc relaxed only slightly. "Nonna? Did she tell Ava?"

"Christ, Luca... We're your family. We're here to protect you, not throw your most painful memories out to a hot reporter."

"Then why'd you go weird?"

"I *didn't*," Anthony said, shoving past and using his shoulder to jar Luc's. "You're the one being weird. I'm going to bed."

Luc watched his brother head to the bedroom. "Hey, Anth."

His brother paused, turned his chin almost to his shoulder, although he didn't look back all the way.

"Thanks. For listening."

Anthony held up his hand in a silent *you're welcome*, before slipping back into his bedroom to spoon his overnight guest.

Luc stood for a long while in the dark, the sharpness of his dream fading into the usual shadows of his mind, even as his instincts hummed that that episode in his life wasn't over yet.

Not by a long shot.

CHAPTER TWENTY-ONE

This is bullshit," Luc said, running two hands through his hair. "You've already seen the video. *Everyone's* seen the video. What's the point of reenacting something when you can watch the real deal?"

Ava's chest expanded slightly in what Luc now knew was her *don't lose your shit* internal pep talk to herself. "So we can have dinner together, but we can't just walk and talk along the river's edge in Battery Park?"

Sawyer turned and gave Luc an incredulous look. "Sharing meals? Like, you guys split a candy bar from the candy machine, or…"

"It wasn't like that," Ava snapped.

Only because you won't let it be, he wanted to snap back. Still, keeping things platonic had been his idea too. Sort of.

But *fuck*. That kiss.

"Can't you have a stand-in go through the motions?" he asked. "You know, a body double, or some shit like that."

"Great idea, Officer, that'll make for really compelling television. Here, folks, we have a random person off the street *pretending* to be a—"

She broke off suddenly and gave him a look. "You know why I stopped just then? That's a million people changing the channel."

He shrugged. "Not my problem."

Ava rolled her eyes to the sky as though dealing with a petulant child. He knew he was being difficult, but that was tough shit.

Just because he had some seriously raunchy fantasies about this woman didn't mean he was going to become her lackey.

As a woman, he wanted her. As a news reporter, she was more a pain in his ass than ever.

If he went through with this, it would make his "heroic" actions seem manufactured and calculating, and the last thing he needed was people thinking that he was the type of cop that over-thought things.

Overthinking led to tragic circumstances.

He knew that better than anyone, and no way was he going to sell himself out on national television.

"It's not like I'm asking you to jump into the river, Luc," Ava said, her voice slightly softer. "Just talk us through what happened that day."

"You mean talk to a couple thousand viewers who I don't even know."

"No, talk to *me*. Ava. Ignore Mihail, ignore the camera, ignore the shit that Lopez will be flinging your way before and after."

"Who says I'll be flinging shit?" Luc's partner asked.

They both looked at him, and Lopez lifted a shoulder. "Okay, maybe. Probably."

"Look, Luc, what the hell did you think was going to happen when you agreed to this?" Ava asked.

"I *didn't* agree to this!"

"Well it's happening," she shot back. "And it'll happen a lot faster, and a lot less painfully for everybody, if you'd cooperate."

Luc stuck this thumbs into his belt and remained resolutely silent. He knew he was on the verge of being out of line, and he didn't blame her for being confused. He was all over the place with her. Amiable one minute, prissy the next.

Kissing her one day.

Yelling at her the next.

A match made in heaven, they were not.

Still, in the grand scheme of things, her request should have been harmless.

But with last night's nightmare fresh on his mind, he felt…threatened. Being asked to perform like a trick pony was bad enough on most days, but on a day when he was running on hardly any sleep and a couple years' worth of bad memories?

Let's just say Ava didn't have a clue.

You could tell her.

He pushed the thought away almost as quickly as it had popped into his head. Tell a woman he hardly knew his deepest, darkest pain? Bad idea.

Telling a reporter his deepest darkest pain?

Really bad idea.

Nobody wanted to see a cop *pretending* to be a hero. But wasn't that exactly what he was doing every damned day?

"Dude," Lopez said under his breath. "You okay? I know you're not the biggest fan of all this but you're being kind of a dick."

Luc almost smiled. Sawyer Lopez was completely different from Mike Jensen in almost every way ... Mike had been quiet and focused, whereas Lopez was outspoken and spontaneous. Mike short and broad, Sawyer lean and lithe. Mike fair, Lopez dark.

But his former partner and current partner had one very crucial characteristic in common: they were both damned good at calling Luc on his bullshit.

"Christ," he muttered. "Fine. Sims, let's get this over with."

He half expected her to continue to give him crap, but at the end of the day, Ava Sims was a professional and she gestured over to her camera crew as though there had never been a delay.

Ava spent a few minutes explaining the shot she wanted to Mihail and some other guy whose name Luc had already forgotten. Then Ava turned to Luc. "Okay, Moretti, you're up. Nothing to it. We'll just walk nice and slow along the river talking. I ask you questions about that day, you answer, taking me through what happened as best you can. 'Kay?"

Luc gave a curt nod.

"What about me?" Lopez asked, surreptitiously checking out a well-endowed brunette who was trying to ascertain what the camera was for.

"Watch for bad guys," Ava said. Then she followed his line of sight. "Or go get that girl's number."

Luc followed Ava over to the start of the shot.

"Take a deep breath," she said quietly.

"I'm not nervous," he said irritably, just annoyed.

"Yeah, I got that," she said, her mouth curving into a smile. "But it's just me, Luc."

It was her use of his first name that got him. He would do well to remember that they weren't friends.

But sometimes it felt like they were.

She touched his arm briefly to indicate that they were about to start, and her fingers seemed to linger.

Sometimes it felt like they were more than friends. Definitely.

"So, Officer Moretti," she said in her reporter voice.

Shit. Here we go.

"How many times would you say you'd walked along this very riverbank before the fateful events of February twenty-first?"

Fateful events? It wasn't like there was a second coming.

She looked at him patiently and he realized he had to speak, or else risk looking like a mute on national television.

Fine.

"It's not my usual beat," he said as they moved slowly forward, the camera in their faces but more or less ignored. "My precinct is in midtown, but I'd come down to the Battery for another call...false alarm, as it would turn out."

"What was the other call?" she interrupted.

"Cop business," he said with a little wink.

It had been another charming indecent exposure call, but the perp was long gone by the time Luc had arrived.

Luc figured the fewer details the better.

The entire country didn't need to know *quite* how often New York dealt with naked weirdos.

"So you were just strolling along..."

"Can't say we on-duty cops do a lot of strolling," he corrected, although he added a smile to soften it.

She laughed softly, and in an instant he knew why she was so good at her job. Her voice called people in. Her laughter made them want to stay.

"Okay, so you were walking. With purpose," she said, making a jokingly macho move forward with her hands.

"I was," he said, playing the game.

They came to a stop, and both of their smiles faltered a little.

"It was here?"

Luc pointed a few feet to the right. "She was there. Wearing a red dress and singing the chorus of some terrible pop song, but she was messing up all the words."

"And it was cute," Ava said with a smile.

He smiled back. "It was cute."

"Tell us what happened next. Because in that YouTube video, all we see is you diving headfirst over the railing and coming up with a little girl soaked, wearing a red dress."

Almost done, Luc told himself.

"Well she had, like this . . . doll," he said. "A little one."

Ava's brow furrowed. "A little doll?"

"Like a . . . Barbie. Or something."

"The NYPD cop knows what a Barbie is, folks. Do you have daughters, Officer Moretti?"

She knew that he didn't, obviously, but the audience didn't, so he played along. "I do not."

"Nieces?"

"No nieces, although I think my brother Marco might be working on that."

Marco absolutely was *not* working on that, but it served the bastard right for moving to Los Angeles.

Ava leaned forward slightly, her mouth in a teasing smile. "Then pray tell, Officer, how do you know what a Barbie is?"

"I'm a man of the world, Miss Sims," he said mysteriously. "A man of the world. Anyway, the little girl had her

Barbie dancing along the railing, and I'm still really only half paying attention, but then I hear her cry of distress, and the doll is gone."

"She dropped her Barbie into the water."

"Yes. And she's full on crying by this point, because, I mean, who *doesn't* hate to lose a Barbie, and I look around for her parents, but before I can figure out who she belongs to, she's managed to get herself on top of the railing."

Ava walked to the railing and put her hand exactly in the spot the little girl had gone over. "Here?"

Luc nodded.

"And then she went over," Ava said.

"And then she went over."

"How soon after her going in did you follow?"

Luc shrugged. "Instantly, I guess. I don't remember."

"Do you remember making the choice? Thinking, do I really want to throw myself into the river for a little girl I don't know?"

Good Lord, she was milking this. He gave her a slightly withering look he hoped the camera would miss before continuing.

"When a child's life is in danger—*any* life is in danger—you don't stop to think."

"Because you're a police officer. Because it's your sworn duty."

Fuck no was on the tip of his tongue but he bit it back. "Because I'm human."

Ava tilted her head. "So you're saying anyone would do this."

Luc gave a little shrug. *Anyone decent.* "I would hope so."

Ava let that sink in a moment before she turned and looked over the railing. "So this brings us up to the moment that the tourist started filming you. Right as you kick off your shoes. Were you aware of the tourist?"

"I was not."

"So you didn't know there was a camera."

"Absolutely not."

For a second, just a split second, Ava looked skeptical, but she smiled to cover it.

"Was the water cold?"

"You have no idea," he said with a little smile. "Although I don't think I really registered that until long after I'd pulled her out of the water."

Ava's face sobered at that. "And when you pulled her out...she wasn't breathing."

Luc's eyes squeezed shut at the memory. Not just of this little girl, but of another one who'd also been too still, too cold, when he'd gotten to her. Only that one hadn't had a happy ending.

He shook his head and forced himself to meet Ava's eyes. "No, she wasn't."

Ava paused, as though to let his statement sink in. "You gave her CPR."

Luc swallowed. Nodded.

"What were you thinking?" she asked quietly. "You jumped in on instinct, but when you pulled her out, and realization set in that this little girl might not make it, what were you thinking?"

Luc ran a hand over his face and answered the only way he could. Honestly.

"I was thinking *please*. *Please* let this little girl be okay."

Ava's smile was gentle. "And she was. Because of you."

Luc lifted a shoulder and scratched the back of his neck, feeling almost unbearably embarrassed.

Luc answered the rest of Ava's questions as briefly as possible while still being polite.

Yes, he'd known to swim her around to the side of the boardwalk where there was a tiny ladder built in.

Yes, he'd given CPR before.

Yes, the mother was grateful. Beyond grateful.

"And just one last question, Officer Moretti."

"Shoot."

Ava leaned in with a conspiratorial smile. "Were you able to save Barbie too?"

Luc laughed, mostly because he knew it was expected. "Sadly, Barbie met her demise that day."

"Aww, well that's too bad. Perhaps I'll talk to the station manager about replacing her myself."

Luc opened his mouth to respond, but closed it just as quickly, catching himself.

But he wasn't fast enough. Ava's brown eyes missed nothing, and she pointed a friendly finger at him. "Officer Moretti, is there something else you'd like to add?"

"Nothing comes to mind."

Ava moved closer with a laugh. "Officer Moretti, you replaced that little girl's Barbie doll, didn't you?"

Luc pressed his lips together, but it was all the answer she needed.

"Out of your own pocket?"

He said nothing, but he couldn't lie either, so he gave only a curt nod.

She turned and for the first time, looked straight into the camera, giving it a secret smile.

"And that, ladies and gentlemen, is what we call a *true* American hero."

CHAPTER TWENTY-TWO

Laid it on a bit thick, didn't you, Sims?"

"Luc, you bought a little girl a *Barbie*. Clark Kent wouldn't have done that," Ava replied.

Sawyer dropped his mug to the table with a clank. "Hey, I just thought of something."

"I knew I smelled smoke," Luc said, gesturing in the vicinity of his partner's brain.

"So if Baby Moretti here is Superman," Lopez pressed on, "and if *you're* a reporter…" He pointed at Ava.

Ava laughed, choking a little on her swallow of beer. "No. Don't even say it."

Sawyer sat back, looking thoroughly pleased with himself. "We have our very own Lois Lane."

Luc rotated in his chair to smirk down at her. "Well I'll be damned. If I wear glasses, will you suddenly not recognize me?"

"I am *not* Lois Lane, all running willy-nilly all over the

city, throwing myself into danger," Ava said, taking another sip of beer. Slower this time.

After they'd wrapped up the interview, she'd insisted on buying them a round of drinks since they were off duty, loading them all into the network van and driving both Sawyer and Luc to their respective homes to change out of uniform.

She was a little surprised that they'd both accepted, but as Lopez had pointed out, cops get a lot of free coffee. Free beer, not so much.

Mihail had come too, although they'd lost him after he'd gone up to fetch the first round of drinks and discovered that the bartender was Bulgarian. He'd grabbed a stool and was chatting happily—or as happily as Mihail could manage—about the motherland, while the three of them had grabbed a table in the back.

"So, Sawyer, if you're free next week, I was thinking we could do a quick on-camera recount of your version of that day," Ava said, taking advantage of the mellow mood.

Lopez leaned forward, wiggling his eyebrows. "I knew you'd see it eventually."

"See what?" Luc asked, leaning back in his chair and casually dropping his arm around the back of Ava's chair.

She was reasonably sure he hadn't realized he'd made the gesture.

But Ava was aware. Very aware.

"That I'm a natural," Lopez said, flexing his fingers. "Get calls from Hollywood agents all the time."

"Weird, I've never seen that," Luc muttered. "*Ever.*"

Sawyer ignored him, pointing at his own face. "See this chiseled jaw? The camera loves it."

Ava turned slightly toward Luc. "Are you paying attention? *This* is what a willing and cooperative interview subject looks like."

"Great!" Luc said, taking a sip of beer. "Then you can shift the focus of your *America's Hero* thing to Lopez."

"She probably would have," Lopez broke in. "But then you had to go and buy a Barbie."

Luc closed his eyes and groaned, and Ava reached out to poke a joking finger at his stomach.

His eyes flew open and met hers, and her hand faltered, just long enough to register that the man had very, very nice abs.

"I think it's cute," she said, yanking her hand back. "Did you pick it out yourself?"

"I bought it online," he growled. "Free shipping. It was no big deal."

Ava pressed her lips together. It wasn't a big deal, not really. A few bucks.

But the gesture spoke volumes.

She knew it, Lopez knew it, and everyone who watched that segment would know it.

Hell, her female viewers would positively *melt*.

Scratch that. Her female viewers will be a puddle the first time they see the man smile.

But right now, Ava didn't care about Lopez or her viewers.

She was thinking about Luc. And herself.

The man had surprised her.

She'd been clinging to the probability that on some level, Luc *must* have known that his dramatic dive-in-the-water routine would get him accolades.

He'd wanted to save that little girl, of course.

But did he really regret that the entire world was fawning over him? She hadn't been sure.

But the Barbie... the *Barbie*, Ava couldn't explain away.

"Does your family know?" she asked abruptly.

He broke off the argument he was having with Lopez about whether he had to turn in his man card because he bought a doll.

"Does my family know what?"

"About the Barbie," she said.

"Well they sure as hell will when they see your stupid show," he said grumpily.

"But you didn't tell them before. Any of them. Not even Elena who could have helped pick out the Barbie?"

"Are you kidding me? Elena would have taken a simple task and turned it into a shopping expedition."

"What about your brothers?"

Luc gave her a look. "Yeah, that's what every younger brother yearns for. That moment when he can tell three big brothers that he bought a Barbie with his weekly beer money."

Oh God he was cute.

Luc jabbed a finger in the direction of his partner. "You see how Lopez is responding? Multiply that by a thousand, and you'd have Vincent's reaction."

"Well aren't you all, big strong men, being all manly," she said in a mocking macho voice, making a Popeye-like gesture.

"We are, aren't we?" Sawyer said. "Do you want to see me flex?"

Luc groaned. "Go home, Lopez."

"And leave you two to wallow in all this sexual tension? Never."

Ava froze, her eyes flying to Sawyer's, but he merely gave her a friendly wink.

Then she turned to Luc and glared. "Don't look at me. I didn't tell him shit."

Sawyer pounced. "There's something to tell?"

Just a kiss that forever ruined all future kisses with its sheer perfection.

"No," Ava said, turning back around to face Sawyer, her face composed. "There is nothing to tell."

Luc laughed. "You are a terrible liar."

"I am an excellent liar," she shot back.

"Not really," Sawyer said, giving her an apologetic pat on the hand. "So. Who wants to tell me? Are we talking accidental boob brush?"

Ava gave him a glare.

Sawyer's eyebrow lifted. "Full-on cop-a-feel? *Duuude*." He reached over to fist-bump Luc, who batted his hand out of the way.

Luc's partner grinned and drained his beer. "This is nice. Me, Superman, Lois Lane, and unfulfilled lust."

"It's not…" Ava made a huffing noise and did what any skilled conversationalist knew how to do.

She changed the subject.

"So, I can't believe I haven't asked this before, but how long have you two fine officers been involved in your bromance here?"

"'Bout a year," Lopez said. "I was doing the Brooklyn thing for a while, but got sick of looking at all the hipsters. There was a spot in Luc's precinct, so…"

"Only a year?" Ava asked, genuinely surprised. She'd assumed that they'd been together since the police academy, not only because of their easy relationship, but because Luc had never mentioned having any other partner.

"Who was your partner before this?" she asked Luc.

If she thought she'd seen Luc Moretti's emotional shutters slam down before, it was nothing like the ice-cold shutdown she was witnessing now. His eyes went cold and dead before he pushed his chair back. "I'll get us another round."

"Oh God," Ava said, horror flooding her as she put the pieces together.

She turned to Sawyer.

"When you said a spot in Luc's precinct opened up, you meant that…"

"Mike Jensen," Lopez said, his face uncharacteristically somber. "I didn't know him, but he and Luc were solid partners, you know? Luc knew his wife and kid and everything."

For a second, Ava's mind caught on the name, because Mike Jensen sounded familiar for some reason, but that thought was flooded by the horribleness of the reality as she put the pieces together.

Luc's former partner had *died*.

"What happened?" she asked quietly.

Sawyer opened his mouth but hesitated, his eyes searching her face as though looking for something and finding her lacking. "You'll have to ask him."

"He doesn't exactly look like he wants to talk about it," she said, her eyes finding Luc's broad back at the bar as he waited to get the bartender's attention.

Only after Luc had returned to the table and let Sawyer coax him into a good-natured argument on Mets (Sawyer) vs. Yankees (Luc) did Ava realize why the name Mike Jensen was so familiar.

It was the name of the officer killed in the Shayna Johnson case.

The one whose death had gotten the barest mention in the media coverage, as though the newsperson on duty had been reporting the weather instead of an officer who'd died in the line of fire.

There was no doubt that Luc Moretti was very, very wrapped up in the Shayna Johnson case, and she couldn't blame him for not wanting to talk about it.

But the question was...

Why was it nobody *else* seemed to have talked about it either?

CHAPTER TWENTY-THREE

I still don't understand how the hell you got her phone number," Luc said, pushing his fingers to his temples and trying to assess whether the urge to yell at his own grandmother was a first-class ticket to hell or not.

"You're scowling, Luca," Nonna said, patting his shoulder before starting to unroll her yoga mat.

"Damn straight I'm scowling!"

"Here, why don't we do some nice yoga together; it will improve your demeanor," she said.

"You know what else would improve my demeanor? You *undoing* your handiwork."

"I know not to what you refer," she said before standing on one leg and crossing her other foot over her knee with rather remarkable balance for an eighty-something woman.

"You know damn well to what I refer. The fact that Sims just texted me and said they were running thirty minutes late but should be here within the hour."

"Sims?" his grandmother said, her dark brown eyes all cloudy confusion.

"*Ava*," he ground out.

Nonna's responding smirk told him she'd known all along what Ava's last name was and had just wanted to call the wily reporter by her first name.

She dropped into a yoga pose and Luc growled before going to the fridge for a beer. It was only two o'clock, but he had the day off and he was sure as hell going to need it when the cavalry arrived with cameras to his house.

"I thought the home was supposed to be a sacred thing, Nonna," he said, leaning against the counter. "Isn't that like an old Italian proverb or something?"

"If it is, I've never heard of that damn-fool nonsense. But you know what is an Italian proverb? A good lay with a pretty brunette will make you less irritable."

"That's not a fucking proverb," he muttered.

It was true though.

Very true.

It had been over a week since he'd kissed Ava at her apartment, and although things between them had been friendly enough, it was harder than ever to be around her without touching her.

Even Lopez had noticed.

Not only had he sent Luc a variety of links on cures for blue balls, but he had also backed off his own flirting with Ava, along with a solemn "dicks before chicks" proclamation, which had just sounded plain wrong.

His grandmother rolled out of an awkward crab-like position and looked him over. "You should change."

Luc glanced down at his jeans and white T-shirt. "Into what?"

"Your uniform."

"Hell no. It's my day off. The only day where I don't have to let polyester anywhere near my skin."

"Well at least wear your badge."

"Nope."

"But you're carrying, right? Let her see your bulge."

He gave her a look. "Nonna."

She heaved out a sigh and glanced at the clock behind his head. "Fine. Doesn't matter anyway. Anthony should be here any minute, and he'll be in uniform. Your Ava can fawn over *him*."

"She's not my Ava," he said, tipping the beer bottle back.

He sure wanted her to be, though.

As though he'd heard his name, Luc's older brother trudged through the front door, taking in the yoga mat and the beer in Luc's hand before nodding his chin toward the fridge.

Luc was one step ahead of him, already pulling the cap off the beer as Anthony went to the safe where they locked their weapons when off duty.

"You may want to stay armed," Luc said, handing his brother the beer. "Your grandmother has invited the CBC sharks into our home to film how cops live, or some shit."

"I heard," Anthony said, taking a long pull on the beer.

"And you still came home?"

His brother grunted. "Turns out the family interference? Not limited to our lovely grandmother. Also, Nonna, please stop... I'm not taking you to urgent care for a pulled groin again. Anyway, Nonna got the parents in on this. Dad called in some favors, got me the afternoon off so I could be here for the, quote, *family affair*."

"Jesus," Luc muttered. "Do you think we should get matching sweaters and pose in front of the mantel?"

Nonna clamped her hands together in delight. "Oh, that's wonderful. I wish I would have known, I used to knit..."

"Oh, that's right. You finished a coaster once, didn't you?"

His grandmother was already rolling up her yoga mat. "What color lipstick do you think I should wear? Classic red or shocking orange. I'm thinking orange. Also, have either of you seen my push-up bra? I'm worried I left it at Ned's house."

Neither brother responded, and Anthony very slowly turned his head to look at Luc. "She belongs in a home. One with bars on the window."

"I'm beginning to think the Manhattan zip code isn't worth this," Luc muttered.

"*Nothing* is worth this," Anthony said, watching in horror as Nonna made a puckering motion in the mirror and applied coral lipstick before trying to plump her nonexistent cleavage.

A knock at the door ended Nonna's primping, but it launched Luc into a whole other kind of hell. One where the woman he wanted so much it hurt would be in his bedroom.

And not in the kind of way that would end with her on her back on the bed. Or on her knees. Or, hell, he'd take Ava Sims just about any way he could get her.

The sight on the other side of the door reminded him of every reason why he couldn't back her against the wall and inch up her tight skirt.

It wasn't *just* Ava.

It was Ava and two men with hefty cameras on their shoulders.

Luc nodded at Mihail. The other guy wasn't familiar, but he stuck out a hand with a curt, "Tom."

Finally Luc let himself look at Ava, but she'd already scooted past him and was laughing like crazy at something his brother had said.

Damn it.

Maybe Nonna was right; he should have put on his uniform.

For all of Ava's posturing about how men in uniform didn't do it for her, she was certainly doing an awful lot of simpering over his older brother.

As though reading his thoughts, Nonna caught his eye and made a pistol gesture with her fingers, mouthing *get your gun*, before doing some Wild West twirl thing and tucking it into her belt.

He closed his eyes and took a deep breath.

"Thanks so much for inviting us to your home, Mrs. Moretti," Ava was saying to a gloating Nonna.

"It was Luca's idea," his grandmother said, eyes all wide and innocent. "I just asked since he's so shy."

Anthony snorted and Ava arched a dark eyebrow. "Shy?"

"Luca, why don't you show Ava your bedroom?"

"Sure. Nonna. Did you leave the condoms on the nightstand like I asked?"

"Luc!" Ava looked scandalized, but his grandmother hooted.

"I can show you *my* bedroom," Anthony said, giving Ava a wink.

A wink.

Anthony was fucking winking now.

Luc dropped his chin to his chest in defeat. "Hey, Mihail?"

"Yeah?" The spindly cameraman paused in the process of setting up his equipment, looking surprised to be addressed.

"If I tell you where my gun is and how to get to it, do you

think we could have a safe word, and if this keeps up, you put me out of my misery?"

Mihail reached into his pocket, fished out a yellow gummy worm, and chewed thoughtfully. The man actually looked serious.

"No guns," Ava said in her bossy voice. "Anthony, stop flirting, Nonna quit interfering, Luc, remove stick from ass—"

"I don't—"

Ava charged again, refusing to be interrupted. "For the next thirty minutes, I'm in charge, and you're all going to be damn glad for that because I can get us out of this quickly. Okay?"

She looked expectedly around the room, waiting for someone to argue, but nobody did.

Luc *wanted* to argue, but he'd gotten kind of distracted by wondering if she was that bossy in bed, and how he would feel about it if she were.

Her eyes collided with his, and Luc decided. He would feel good about it. Very good.

She gave him a narrow-eyed look before clapping her hands together and starting to point every which way and shouting out orders.

Luc dimly listened as she began barking out commands, some of which were probably to him, but mostly he just watched her.

Her hair was pulled back into another of those high pony-tails she seemed to favor, and her skirt was a bright poppy red that made her butt look pert and perfect. The white blouse would have been demure had it not hugged her small waist perfectly.

The shoes, though…those shoes just about undid him.

Tall and the same color as her skirt, the high heels practically screamed at him to bend her over the counter and take her from behind.

Luc ran a hand over his face. Had he really thought the worst part of this whole CBC story was going to be having his privacy destroyed?

Because the sexual frustration was much, much worse.

Ava shooed all of the Morettis into the kitchen. "We'll do a couple off-the-cuff interviews next, sort of let people see you in your natural habitat, but first I want to just get the home. It has a great old-school charm, and viewers will love that there've been three generations of cops to come out of here."

She and the camera guys started talking techy, and once again Luc resumed watching her, noticing for the first time how tiny her earlobes were. Cute. The woman had cute earlobes.

"Told ya," he heard Nonna stage-whisper to Anthony.

"I'm appalled to admit it, but I think you're right." Anthony's voice was thoughtful.

Luc cut them a look. "Do I even want to know what you're talking about?"

"Just that I can't wait to be an uncle," Anthony said.

"It doesn't even matter that she's not Italian," Nonna said in a hushed voice. "She has dark hair and dark eyes so we'll just lie. We can change her last name. I know someone."

Luc tipped his head back and looked at the ceiling.

"Try to talk her into it tonight, Luca. Oh, and find out if she's Catholic, would you? I suppose we could lie about that too, although I don't know how Jesus would feel about that..."

"He'll probably feel okay about it, but you should light a

few extra candles just in case. As soon as possible," Anthony said, patting his grandmother on the shoulder.

Ava was positioning herself in the doorway, and Luc could tell by the straight set of her shoulders that they were about to start filming.

Luc held up a finger and lowered his voice to a whisper. "Hold on. Nonna, what did you mean talk her into it *tonight*? Our place isn't that big. This should take an hour, tops."

For the first time, his grandmother looked guilty, and if Nonna looked guilty, it meant she'd pushed waaaay past the limits of appropriate.

"I may have suggested that she join us for a family get-together at Lombardi's," Nonna said.

Anthony frowned. "This is the first I'm hearing of it. Why does nobody tell me anything?"

Luc gave his brother a withering look, and Anthony's mouth dropped open for a second before giving an understanding nod. "There is no family dinner, is there?"

Nonna held up her hands in an innocent gesture. "Everyone else was busy."

"Oh, so if I text Vincent and Mom and Dad and Elena, they'll all confirm they knew about this?" Luc asked innocently, pulling his cell phone out of his back pocket.

Nonna snatched the phone away. "Take the girl to dinner, Luca. I need her uterus for grandbabies."

"Not at all creepy," Anthony said, quietly opening the fridge and grabbing another beer.

Luc shifted slightly, his gaze finding Ava just as she finished up her opening monologue about a "home in the heart of Manhattan."

As though sensing his gaze, she turned and met his eyes with a private smile.

"What did Ava say when you mentioned the dinner?" Luc asked his grandmother.

"She asked if you knew about it. If it was your idea."

"What did you say?"

"I lied, of course. Told her that it was all your doing. I also might have mentioned that I thought I heard you say her name when you were napping on the couch the other day."

Luc frowned. "I haven't napped on the couch in months."

His grandmother shrugged. "Might have lied about that too."

Luc watched as Ava gestured the cameramen into his bedroom for God only knows what kind of assessment, only to see her emerge several seconds later looking confused.

Luc nearly choked when he saw what was in her hand.

It was a framed picture of Ava. A publicity shot, if the posed, wide smile was any indication. He'd never seen it before, and yet the picture had come from *his* bedroom.

Very slowly he turned to look at his grandma. "Nonna…"

"I know," his grandmother said on a heavy sigh. "I should light *all* the candles when I stop by church."

CHAPTER TWENTY-FOUR

Taking her stilettos off when she got home every evening was the highlight of Ava's day.

Taking her stilettos off at the end of a *Friday*, signaling the start of two whole days of flip-flops, sweatpants, and damp ponytails, makeup optional?

That was the highlight of her *week*.

Ava had this routine down pat.

The high heels were off before she even made it through the door.

She stopped in the kitchen just long enough to drop her bag on the counter, pour herself a hefty glass of wine, and then head to the closet for a moment that was *almost* as good as kicking her work shoes...

Yoga pants.

It was always tempting to leave her work clothes in a messy pile on the bedroom floor. Maybe to teach them a lesson about being binding and damned uncomfortable.

But since dry-cleaning bills were expensive as heck in the city, for the most part she tried to keep things looking nice for as long as possible.

"Look at you, being all boring and shit," she said to her charcoal wool pants as she carefully folded them along the crease and looped them over the hanger. "I bet you have no friends."

She picked the sleeveless white blouse off the floor and pulled another hanger off the rack. "Well, I guess *this* guy could be your friend. Just look at all these stupid ruffles."

She didn't even bother speaking to her bra as she undid the front clasp. It deserved the silent treatment.

Left in only her panties, Ava sighed in relief as she pulled on gray, cropped yoga pants and a pink sleeveless tank that she'd gotten at a Las Vegas gift shop after she'd forgotten her pajamas on a bachelorette party trip.

Then it was to the bathroom to swap out her contacts for her black-rimmed glasses, before piling her hair into a messy ponytail.

Life was good.

Plucking her wineglass off the dresser she padded back into the kitchen to survey the contents of her fridge.

She closed it two seconds later.

Sushi takeout it was.

When Ava had first moved to the city and was learning her way around the world of tiny Manhattan kitchens and a reliance on takeout, she'd had her favorite places on speed dial.

But nowadays there was something more magical:

A website and phone app that had an ungodly number of takeout options just a Checkout button away. There were the standards, of course. Chinese. Pizza. Thai.

But this was New York, and food options didn't stop

there. You could also get Ethiopian and bagels and Philly cheese steak sandwiches delivered within half an hour.

It. Was. *Glorious.*

Sushi was her Friday-night go-to, though. It drove Beth and her other friends crazy, but unless it was a special occasion, Ava kept her Friday nights pretty sacred. Saturday she could go dancing, have a martini or four, maybe go on a date (although not so much these days), but Friday nights were Ava nights.

Just her, her comfy clothes, and whatever TV show she was currently binging on. Lately, it had been *Lost.* She'd completely dismissed it when it first aired, but at Beth's insistence she was finally giving it a shot.

It was weird as hell.

And she couldn't get enough.

"What are we feeling today, Honky Tonk?" she asked as her fat orange cat chased his toy mouse around the floor. "Spicy tuna or dragon roll?"

The cat pounced. "Right. Both it is."

But a knock at the door delayed her sushi purchase. Honky Tonk went shooting under the couch, and she wished she could join him.

It was probably her creepy landlord who'd left, like, a half dozen "notice of entry" letters over the past week. Something about checking the screens on the windows. Naturally he would wait until seven o'clock on a Friday night.

"Better make it quick, Don," she said, setting her phone aside and checking the peephole.

It wasn't her landlord.

Luc.

Ava's stomach gave a little flip as she remembered the last time he'd stood on the other side of her door.

She didn't want a repeat of that kiss.

Did she?

"Sims, as a cop, I commend your safety precaution, but think you could open up now that you know it's me?" he said to the peephole.

Right.

She opened the door.

He gave a little blink of surprise as he looked her over. "This is a new look."

Too late, she remembered that she was in Friday Frumpy mode. Luc, on the other hand, looked delicious. His cargo shorts were a nod to the unseasonably hot day, and the white T-shirt stretched perfectly across his shoulders.

"I wasn't expecting visitors," she said, resisting the urge to smooth her lumpy ponytail.

He held up his right hand, which was holding a small red binder.

"Ah!" she said in delight. "My planner. I've been looking everywhere for it! Why do you have it?"

"Found it on my coffee table," he said, handing it to her.

She frowned. "But I didn't take it out of my bag when we were filming at your place yesterday."

He tilted his head slightly and gave her a look.

"Ah," she said with a smile. "Nonna."

"Yup. Gotta give her credit for matchmaking balls, if not originality."

"You didn't have to bring it all the way over here," she said, leaning against the door. "I could have gotten it at the precinct on Monday."

He shrugged. "Gave me a chance to get out of the house. Anthony has female company. This one's lasted a whole week, and she's um, noisy."

"Ah, gotcha."

It was on the tip of her tongue to invite him in but he was already taking a step backward, and she doubted a night of sushi and TV appealed to him.

"Well thanks again for bringing it by," she said, setting the planner on the console table by the door.

"Any time, Sims."

Neither of them moved.

Common sense was demanding that she close the door. Hormones were demanding something very different.

"You know, the last time we were in this position, things were a lot more interesting," she said.

Common sense: 0.

Hormones: 1.

The flare of heat in his eyes showed he didn't mistake her meaning, but instead of a repeat performance of The Kiss, he tensed up, his face losing its easy expression.

Oh. *Shit.*

He was about to reject her. Not that she could blame him. She wasn't exactly in sex-kitten getup, and the man had to spend most of his workdays with her.

Why would he want to spend his days off with her as well?

"Sorry," she said, rushing to give him an easy out. "You don't have to say anything, I just—"

"Sims."

She broke off at the gruffness in his voice. "Yeah?"

Wordlessly he reached out a hand, grabbing a fistful of her tank top and yanking her forward. Hard.

Then his mouth was on hers, and her body responded instantly, arching against him as her hands fisted in his hair.

She sought his tongue with her own, smiling in gratification when he groaned and tightened his grip on her shirt. He held her still for long moments as his mouth explored hers, both of them oblivious to the fact that they were standing in her apartment hallway.

Ava lifted to her toes to get closer, and his other hand moved to her back, pressing her against him as their lips melded, their tongues exploring.

When they were both out of breath, he pulled back slightly as he stared at her mouth. "Damn."

She kissed him again, but instead of holding her still, this time he backed her up until they were in her apartment, kicking the door shut behind him.

Ava launched herself at him, using her body weight to push him back against the door, her mouth fused to his. He let her control the kiss for about ten seconds before he spun around, pinning her to the door.

His hands found her butt, lifting her legs around his waist as her arms wound more firmly around his neck.

Yes.

Luc's mouth trailed over her cheek before nudging her chin up to get at her neck. Ava's head fell back as he ran hot kisses down the column of her throat, and she gasped as his teeth nipped softly at her shoulder.

His fingers dug into her ass possessively before he slowly released her, sliding her down his body, supporting her ribs with his big hands as he placed her back on her feet.

For one heart-stopping moment she thought he was going to suggest they stop, but he merely smiled and righted her glasses, which had gone askew. "Much as I'm tempted to take you against this door, this has been a long time coming. I want to see you."

She swallowed.

"All of you," he said, brushing his knuckles against her collarbone.

"And I want to touch you," he said, his lips finding hers again. "And taste—"

Ava groaned, pulling him in for a tongue-tangling kiss before pushing him back and grabbing his hand.

Wordlessly she led him to the bedroom, although once there she felt strangely awkward.

How long had it been since a man occupied her bed?

Months, definitely. A year? God, did her parts even still work?

Seeming to sense her uneasiness, Luc moved slowly, coming toward her until there was no space between them. No room to think about anyone or anything but him.

His hands cupped her face, his thumbs skimming beneath the rim of her glasses.

"I like this Ava," he whispered.

She looked at him skeptically.

"These"—he touched the outside corner of her glasses with one finger—"are sexy as hell. And these pants"—his hands slid down to her yoga-pants butt—"make your ass look amazing."

"It's my Friday Frumpy," she whispered, her voice catching a little as his lips nuzzled her neck.

He smiled against her throat. "I like it. Very much. It's like my own private Ava. The one nobody gets to see but me."

Her eyes closed at the sweet possessiveness in his tone, and she felt him slide off the glasses and set them carefully on top of the dresser.

"Much as I love the sexy librarian look, things are going to get a little bit rough," he said in a low growl.

Her eyes flew open.

Rough?

And then she was on her back on the bed, her hands pinned above her head with one of his hands as he used the weight of his body to hold the rest of her in place.

He devoured her mouth with urgent kisses as his other hand roamed along her sides, over her hips, never quite touching where she needed.

Finally she was able to maneuver her lower body so that he was between her thighs, and when she arched up to him he groaned, relaxing just enough for her to free her hands to explore.

His body was hard and perfect. Just like she'd imagined.

Longed for.

Luc let her touch for several moments, but when her greedy fingers found the hem of his shirt, he gently recaptured her hands, placing them once more above her head and holding them immobile.

His eyes skimmed her face as though to see if she was okay with the lack of control. She answered his silent question with the only words that came to mind.

"Touch me."

His lips tilted in a smile as the hand not holding hers slowly slid up her side, his fingers sliding against each rib, one by one.

His eyes followed the motion of his hands, but Ava never took her gaze off his face.

She loved the way he looked at her.

His eyes came back to hers, their usual bright blue had gone the color of midnight, and when he slid his hand over her breast she called his name.

"No bra," he said huskily as his fingers explored the shape of her over the thin fabric of her tank top.

"No," she said helplessly as his fingers plucked her nipple into aching response.

"I like," he said. She moaned when his hand left her, only to purr in satisfaction when his hand snaked under her shirt, touching bare skin before his hand claimed her breast once more.

The man knew his way around. He refused to hurry even as he teased her to an almost breathless state, alternating between using the palm of his hand to grind against her before trailing torturous fingers along the undersides of her breast. He switched to the other, then did it all over again.

And when she thought she couldn't stand it anymore, he took her to the next level, his lips closing around a nipple, his tongue lapping gently at the tight peak until she was helplessly whimpering his name, unsure of what she was even asking for.

But Luc knew. His free hand had been roaming careless circles along her bare stomach, but they inched downward now, his palm finding her over the top of her pants, the heel of his hand grinding against her as she bucked, wanting more.

Always more.

She wanted everything from him.

Then his hand was gone, his fingers back to tracing lazy patterns over her belly.

"Luc."

"Sims," he said, his tongue wickedly stabbing at her nipple.

"Please."

"Please what?"

"You know what."

He glanced up at her. "Ask for it."

She wanted to be stubborn. She wanted to be in control. But when he pulled her nipple into his mouth once more and suckled, hard, she gave up.

"Touch me."

"Here?"

His hand slid up to her breast.

It was good. But not enough. She squirmed, wrapping her fingers around his wrist and moving his hand downward.

"Ah, *here*," he said, his fingers dipping just slightly under the waistband, touching the edge of her thong but not going any farther.

She moaned a little laugh as his thumb brushed her just lightly over the fabric of her thong. "I'm very close to hating you right now, Moretti."

"Yeah?" he asked, his voice husky as he lifted himself just enough to watch his hand as it teased between her legs. "So I should stop this?"

"Don't you dare." She gasped as a finger slipped under the elastic.

"You're a liar, Sims," he said on a groan as he found her silky wetness. "You don't hate me at all."

Her thighs fell open on a gasp. It was almost painfully erotic, the sight of his hand moving beneath the tight fabric of her yoga pants as he fingered her.

Luc slid a finger deep inside her and she arched her back, even as he pulled out and circled her clit in idle, circular motions.

She would be embarrassed about how fast she approached the brink, but she was too busy reveling in the sensations of his teasing fingers, his flicking tongue on her nipple.

Luc pulled away seconds before she went crashing

into blissful oblivion, and she all but shrieked in outrage. "You—"

His mouth crushed onto hers, and she felt his smile.

"I like you like this, Sims."

"What, half-naked?" she muttered even as she hungrily returned his kiss.

He pulled back, glanced down at her. "You're not even close to half-naked." His hands went for the hem of her tank bunched around her ribs. "We should fix that."

Ava let him tug her up, pulling the shirt over her head, and his eyes turned even more smoldering as they roamed over her.

"Uh uh," she said when he was about to push her back down. Her hands found his T-shirt, inching it upward. He quirked an eyebrow at her before reaching behind his head to grab a fistful of fabric and yank the shirt up and off in that effortless way that guys could.

Okay. Wow.

Luc chuckled, and Ava realized that she'd whispered her awe-induced admiration out loud.

She ran her fingers over his chiseled abs. She knew the guy looked good, but this…the guy belonged on a men's fitness magazine. "I see you've been letting yourself go," she said with sham dismay.

He grinned and hooked a hand behind her neck, smiling into her eyes before his lips captured hers in a playful, toying kiss.

Somewhere in the back of her sex-dazed mind, Ava registered that sex had never been like this. It was hotter than hell, yes, but it was also…fun.

Sex with Luc Moretti was fun.

Her hands found his face, her palms rubbing over his

lightly stubbled jaw before her fingers sank into his hair as she took control of the kiss.

Ava used her body weight to push him backward and he let her, his palm on his spine as she leaned over him, her lips exploring his mouth, his jaw, moving down his neck until she got to his beautiful chest.

She scraped her nails lightly downward and he hissed. Ava watched him as she experimentally licked at a nipple, and his eyes closed as his hand stroked over her hair. Ava moved farther south, her lips and mouth exploring his torso as he'd explored hers.

He made no protest when her fingers unsnapped the button of his shorts, nor when she slowly slid down the zipper.

She traced the hard outline of him with one finger through his boxer briefs, watching his face as she did so. His eyes were at half-mast, his jaw tight as she explored him, and when her fingers moved to tug down the waistband, he put up no resistance.

When Ava's palm found his warm shaft, he said her name, and the sound of her name on his lips, her hand on his cock, only increased the restless throb between her legs.

He said her name again, a prayer, a plea, and Ava answered with sure, confident strokes. He let her play only for a couple of minutes, before grabbing her wrist and pulling her hand away.

"You're dangerous to me," he said gruffly.

"Payback," she said, planting a quick kiss on his shoulder before she found herself rolled beneath him.

The time for teasing was apparently over, because this time when Luc's fingers found the waistband of her pants, it was to yank them roughly over her hips, along with her panties, so she was naked beneath him.

He chucked her pants to the side, sitting back on his heels, totally confident of his own nakedness.

"Beautiful," he said.

His eyes were on her face, not her body, and Ava mentally added another descriptor to sex with Luc Moretti.

Hot. Fun. And sweet...

That last one was more than a little alarming, considering that she knew this was just sex, but the way he looked at her did something treacherous to her heart.

His hand slid up her side. "Uh uh. You're overthinking, Sims."

Caught. "No, I just—"

His lips were on hers as he pinned her all the way beneath him, his hands cupping her face as he kissed her long and deep.

"Sims." His voice was gruff when he pulled back. "I told myself when this happened—if it happened—I'd make it last all night, but—"

"I know," she interrupted, giving him a quick kiss as her hands slid over his muscled back. "Now, Moretti."

He rested his forehead against hers, his breath hot and frustrated. "Trust me I'm right there with you, but..."

"Got it," she said, pushing at his shoulders. "I'm on the pill, but since we're smart adults..."

She quickly wiggled out of the tangled sheets, going over to the dresser and digging through her underwear drawer.

She came up with a box of condoms, to see a naked Luc watching her with an amused smile. "That's why nightstands exist, Sims."

Ava chucked a condom at his chest. "This is Manhattan. I'm lucky I can fit a bed in here, much less a nightstand."

"Actually, your plan is a good one. Gives the guy quite a tantalizing view of your ass."

She moved back toward the bed, and he caught her around the waist with one arm before she could lie back down. He kissed a warm, wet kiss against her stomach, and her hands found his hair.

"You like your fingers in my hair," he said. She felt his smile against her flesh.

"Maybe."

She did.

His mouth inched lower, his tongue teasing just below her belly button. "Gives a woman lots of control, doesn't it? She could have his mouth wherever she wanted..."

Ava's nails dug ever so slightly into his scalp, as his palm slid up between her thighs before he ran one finger lightly over her slit. "Anywhere, Ava."

Oh God.

And as much as she wanted his mouth between her legs, there was something she craved even more.

She leaned down slightly, picking up the condom near his hip before holding it up meaningfully.

"Greedy girl," he said as she tore open the wrapper.

She glanced down. "Very."

Luc's eyes glazed over before he snatched the condom out of her hand and rolled it on in one smooth motion.

He slid his hands over the backs of her thighs, pulling her forward even as she lifted her legs so that her knees were on either side of his hips, as she knelt over him on the bed.

They both watched as she reached down, stroking him twice before guiding him to her entrance. Their eyes locked for a crucial moment before she lowered, sinking onto him inch by exquisite inch.

When he was all the way buried inside her, they both stayed very still, her face buried against his neck as his arms wrapped around her, pulling her as close as they could get.

"Damn, Sims."

She smiled against his shoulder. Damn indeed.

His hands moved to her hips, lifting her slightly before pulling her back down again, and that was all she needed. She sat back slightly, letting him support her weight as she began to ride him in a rhythm that started slow and silky, but quickly escalated to furious and frantic. The room filled with the sounds of their quickened breathing, the smooth slap of her body against his.

Luc made a harsh noise that told her he was close, holding back for her, and she rode him harder, determined to drive him over the edge. But then his hand moved around to her front, sliding between their writhing bodies to find her damp center. His thumb found her clit, pressing against her in delicious circles.

The pace had been fast before, but it turned furious, and Ava never wanted it to end, even as she was desperate for the release that was right around the corner.

Then his teeth found her shoulder, nipping hard, the rough pad of his finger pressing against her, and Ava was lost.

She went over the edge with a gasp, riding him in urgent, graceless motions, letting his hands hold her hips to him, and only as the last shudders racked her body did he let himself go.

His hips bucked up, one arm wrapped around her body as his other hand clenched into her sheets as though needing to ground himself as he came with an earthy groan in her ear.

The aftershocks seemed to go on forever, until finally,

they slowed to a stop, her damp body draped over his, her head on his shoulder as arms crossed over her back, hands resting possessively on her shoulder blades.

Ava could have fallen asleep there, slumped over the firm, male body of Luc Moretti, but dimly she became aware that it was probably a lot less comfortable for him, having to hold them both upright, and she pulled off him, standing on shaky legs as her hands went to her hair, thinking to straighten it before she realized the futileness of the effort.

Luc stood and then, cocky bastard that he was, gave her a wink and a smack on the ass before heading out of the bedroom toward the bathroom.

Ava started to tell him where it was, but instead flopped onto the bed in a boneless mess. Her apartment was small. He'd find it.

A lady would probably find her panties and put them on.

No, a lady would find *fresh* panties, and would have some sort of classy silk robe, but the only robe Ava had was a neon pink terrycloth number from college, and even if she knew where it was, she didn't have the energy.

Luc reappeared in the doorway, taking in her naked body with a smile. "I like that you don't rush to cover up. You're a confident woman, Sims. I like that."

Ava grunted, her brain still at half-functionality. "You there, boy. A cigarette."

"You don't smoke."

"No, but I feel as though an orgasm like that calls for it, does it not?"

He moved to the bed, picking up his boxers and putting them on before stretching out beside her.

She scowled. "If I don't cover up, why do you get to?"

He kissed the spot where he'd bit her shoulder earlier, and

she shivered at the memory. "Well, let's just say you don't have an unflattering flop immediately after."

She rolled toward him. "How long until the flop goes away?"

He played with a strand of her hair. "Usually? Ten minutes. With you? Two."

She smiled, flattered, even though she knew it was a line. "Betcha say that to all the girls."

His eyes narrowed just slightly. "Do I?"

She bit her lip briefly before taking a chance. "That mean you're staying?"

His lips tilted on one side. "You asking me to stay the night, Sims?"

She rolled her eyes. "Relax, it's not exactly a wedding band."

Luc watched his fingers play with her hair. "Right. Because you don't do that."

"And neither do you," she said, running a hand over his abs.

Neither made eye contact just then. It was better that way.

Luc rolled onto his back with a self-satisfied sigh. "All right. I'll stay. Under one condition."

"You're totally about to start negotiating with blow jobs, aren't you?"

Luc barked out a startled laugh. "I wasn't, but damn if you didn't just put the thought into my mind."

"What was your original condition?"

"Who cares? BJs trump all."

"Offer revoked," she said with a teasing smile as she pulled herself into a sitting position. "I have more pressing issues on my mind."

"What the hell is more pressing than oral sex?"

She slapped his roaming hand away as she went to her dresser and pulled out a pair of yellow boy shorts with a blue and white bow on the front. "Food."

He got a thoughtful expression, but she held up a finger to stop his dirty thoughts. "*Real* food."

Luc sighed. "Admittedly that was going to be my original suggestion before you distracted me with sins of the flesh."

"Sins of the flesh?" She picked up his shirt and chucked it at him. "Say that again, and you'll be out on your ass with no food, and definitely no blow job."

He laughed and pulled the shirt over his head before reaching for his shorts.

Ava retrieved her tank top and yoga pants, and once they were both clothed it was slightly easier to not think about sex.

Slightly.

"You like sushi?" she asked.

He lifted an eyebrow. "Is that a euphemism for...you know?"

She rolled her eyes, retrieving her glasses and headed back toward her computer to finish the takeout order that had become derailed by the best sex of her life.

"I'm ordering without asking for your input," she said as he followed her into the kitchen. "I don't think I can handle any spicy tuna jokes right now."

"I would never."

She gestured toward the fridge as she doubled her previous order, then remembering that Luc had several inches and a six-pack on her, tripled it. "Wine."

He poured them both a glass of the sauvignon blanc as she placed the order.

"Forty-five minutes," she said on a groan, leaning back

in her chair and patting her stomach forlornly as she took a healthy swallow of wine.

"What?" she asked, noticing that he'd paused mid-sip to watch her with a funny expression on his face.

"Nothing," he said, recovering and taking a sip of the wine. "You're just different than I thought you were."

"Good different?" she asked, hating herself for asking, but needing to know.

His eyes were still warm, but they'd lost that mysterious look of before. "Depends."

"On?"

"How about that blow job?"

She laughed and gave him the finger.

Just like that, they were back to normal. Which was a good thing.

Right?

CHAPTER TWENTY-FIVE

"It's not exactly a fishing trip," Tony Moretti said as Luc came back to the table carrying four beers.

"Well that's the thing about having three cops for sons," Vincent said, snagging one of the bottles and tipping back in his chair. "Harder than shit to get overlapping time off for an entire weekend."

"We did it last year," Tony grumbled.

"Well last year, we had an in with the police commissioner," Anthony pointed out.

Their father's expression turned downright brooding, and Luc resisted the urge to slap both brothers upside the head.

Just what their dad needed on Father's Day: a reminder that he was retired and that instead of floating on Seneca Lake with a growing pile of trout, he was settling for father/sons drinking time in a Lower East Side dive bar.

Tony's eyes narrowed on Anthony. "Has Dempsy announced his retirement yet?"

Anthony's scowl deepened as he idly peeled at the label on his bottle. "You don't know?"

"I'm not commissioner anymore, as you've just reminded me," Tony snapped.

Luc opened his mouth to interfere but thought better of it. The Moretti men always relaxed after a beer or two, and after they'd gotten their shop talk out of the way. In twenty minutes, they'd move on to cracking jokes and playing pool, but first there was the inevitable career talk.

"Nope," Anthony said finally. "I'm beginning to think talk about his retirement was premature."

"Maybe," Tony said, tapping his fingers against the bottle. "You still think you're next in line?"

"Hell yes."

But Luc noted the defiant tilt of his oldest brother's chin. It was a big show of confidence, but Anthony was the cockiest guy Luc knew.

When he was *really* confident, it didn't occur to him to show it. He simply was.

If Anthony was posturing—which he was—it meant he was unsure.

He'd have to ask Anthony about it later, when their dad wasn't around.

Tony Moretti loved his sons more than anything, save for maybe Elena, the family favorite. But they were also his legacy. Their successes were *his* successes.

And their failures were his failures.

So far, Luc had only been the one to fail. Not that anyone ever talked about it.

Anthony rolled his shoulders. "I told you, Pops, I'd let you know as soon as there was a change, 'kay?"

Vincent made a big show of checking his shirt pocket before leaning forward and patting his back jean pockets as well.

"What?" Anth snapped.

"Just looking for my Midol," Vin said with a fake-puzzled voice.

Anthony flung a peanut at their middle brother. "At least *one* of us is moving up the chain."

"Hey, I don't give a fuck about rank, so don't pull that shit on me," Vin said, chucking a peanut right back.

Anthony sipped his beer and declined a comeback, probably because he knew Vincent spoke the truth.

Vin had been angling for the homicide detective gig from the moment he entered the police academy. It was often a thankless job; not half as sexy as the TV shows made it, and they were outranked more easily than the public assumed. But Vin had always wanted it, regardless of pay, regardless of the fact that Anthony was several ranks ahead of him and likely always would be.

So was Marco, who, despite being younger than Vin, had just been promoted to sergeant over in LA.

Only Luc, as a lowly officer, was lower on the totem pole than Vin, although that was mostly due to his junior status and lack of experience. Luc had no intention of remaining an officer forever.

Not that he was power hungry. And not that there was anything wrong with officer.

Luc just wanted...*more*.

He wanted to be the best. Or at least not to be the worst.

Luc grunted to himself as he drank three rapid swallows of beer.

His father noticed. "Something on your mind, *bambino*? A woman?"

Ava's face immediately came to mind, and because it was

easier to picture her slight curves naked beneath him than it was to remember Jensen's dead eyes, Shayna Johnson's limp body, he let his father take the conversation there.

"Maybe."

Anthony and Vincent both turned their attention to him, argument forgotten.

"He's banging the reporter," Anthony said, gesturing at Luc with his beer bottle.

"I'm not *banging* her."

Well okay, he *was* banging her. But it wasn't like that. It was...he didn't know what the fuck it was, but it was damn good.

So good that he'd broken one of his own rules and stayed the night with a woman.

And then he'd done it all over again on Saturday night.

Hell, they'd spent the whole fucking weekend exploring each other's bodies, and leaving her apartment for his own had been disturbingly difficult.

"What?" Tony's bottle hit the table with more force than necessary. "Tell me your brother has it wrong."

Luc met his father's gaze stonily. He knew his dad was wary about this Ava Sims thing, but his father wouldn't even tell him why. And his dad had been plenty friendly to her when she'd come over to dinner. The whole family was.

So if there was a problem—and it was evident from Tony's irate face that there was—then he'd just have to explain to Luc what the hell that problem was.

Luc gave a careful shrug, shooting his dad an easy grin. "She's a gorgeous woman. We're enjoying each other."

Tony's lips rolled inward and he wrapped his fist gently against the table. "Nobody's arguing that she's gorgeous. We all liked her well enough at dinner, but what the fuck you thinking, getting your cock tangled up in her reporter's world? I thought you hated this story shit, and now you're yakking it up via pillow talk."

Luc's own temper went off. "Okay that's enough," he snapped. "I can understand your concern, but you don't get a vote in who I sleep with."

"I do when you're screwing the *press*."

Luc plowed his fingers through his hair. "Look, Pops, you know how I feel about all this hero crap, but that's got nothing to do with what Ava and I do in our time off."

"So no cameras in the bedroom, huh?" Vincent asked, sounding genuinely curious. "Because if there's a way to crop you out of it so it's just her tight—"

Luc gave his brother a warning finger, his eyes never wavering from his father.

"Seriously, what is the big deal?" Luc asked his dad.

Tony leaned forward and there was anger in his eyes, but there was something else too. Fear.

"Playing nice with her for the sake of the department is one thing. We were all set to get her on your good side. But for the sake of her story, not your pecker!"

"What difference does it make?" Luc asked, his own voice rising. "I'm allowed to talk to her about myself while in uniform, or as long as the entire Moretti family's around to chaperone, but not in bed?"

"Well I can't keep you from saying something damned stupid in bed!"

Luc threw his arms up. "What is it you think I'm going to say? It's not like there's some cliché mob connection that we're trying to bury behind the badge."

"That'd be cool, though," Vin said to himself. "Very bad-ass."

Luc dimly registered what was happening. His hotheaded brothers were trying desperately to diffuse the mood and prevent a fight. A feat that normally was Luc's duty.

The change in roles irritated him all the more. He didn't need to be protected, not by them, not by his father.

"I've got nothing to hide," Luc said, leaning forward and meeting his father's dark brown gaze.

Luc nearly winced as he heard the police therapist's words coming out of his own mouth. How many times had Dr. Kaperski leaned forward in that very way, looking into Luc's eyes and telling him he had nothing to hide?

That it wasn't his fault.

"Of course not," Tony said, looking away.

A quick glance around the table showed that Anthony and Vin weren't meeting his eyes either, and Luc very slowly set his beer on the table, instincts buzzing in a bad way.

"What am I missing here?"

For a second, nobody responded, but then Vin gave him a not-so-gentle kick in the shin, brother-to-brother. "Just that you should be careful. Who knows what her motives are, you know?"

"Her motives are to get in my pants," Luc said crassly. Ava wouldn't appreciate the sentiment, but she'd like it a hell of a lot better than what his family was implying.

"So she doesn't ask about your career?"

"Sure, I guess," he said, feeling more agitated than ever. "I mean, you guys know that. You fucking told her all about it when she was at our house for dinner."

His message clear: they couldn't have it both ways. They couldn't welcome her to the Moretti fold while telling him not to let it get personal.

It had been personal for weeks.

So what had crawled up their respective asses?

"Just be careful is all we're saying," Tony said. "We don't want her asking about Mike."

The table fell silent, and Luc waited for either brother to give their dad shit for breaking the unspoken code.

We don't talk about fallen cops around family.

Certainly not around *Luc.*

But to his surprise, Anthony and Vincent exchanged a look that Luc was left out of.

A *worried* look.

"She hasn't asked, has she, bro?" Anthony asked. His older brother had a smile pasted on his face, and since Anthony didn't smile, the humming Luc had been feeling escalated to a full-on siren.

He pointed around the table. "Someone tell me what *exactly* I'm not supposed to tell her about Mike. It's all public record if she wants to see it."

There. There it was on his dad's face. Guilt.

Luc's eyes narrowed. "It's public record. The Shayna Johnson case, Mike's death."

"There are police records, of course," Tony muttered.

It was an odd distinction. A crucial one.

"Police records, but not media records?"

Again. The flash of guilt.

Luc ran a hand over his face, hoping to God he was misunderstanding their silence.

"Pops." His voice was rough. "What the *hell* did you do?"

CHAPTER TWENTY-SIX

Can you come over?

Ava was about to head down the steps into the subway station when she got Luc's text. She'd had a rather epic shopping day with Beth, and was fully intending to head home, unpack her merchandise, and try desperately to forget the major damage she'd just done to her credit card.

When, exactly, had bra and panty sets gotten so expensive?

And why had she let Beth talk her into a half dozen sets of ridiculously unpractical lacy, strappy numbers?

Luc texted again: *Please.*

Ah, *that's* why. Because after months of indifferent celibacy, she was finally getting some.

Getting the best she ever had, actually.

Still, instinct told her that Luc's message was no ordinary booty call. For starters, it was Father's Day, and he'd told her that he and his brothers were taking their dad out for a day at the pub to watch the US Open.

And second, there was something wrong with the tone of this message. It lacked the flirty coyness of their usual exchanges.

Ava started to respond, telling him she'd be there after she swung by her place to drop off her shopping bags.

But instead she found herself crossing the street to get on a northbound train to Luc's place as she replied, *be right there*.

Fifteen minutes later, she was at his front door. For a half second she was paranoid about the fact that Nonna might open the door while Ava held two huge, magenta Victoria's Secret bags. Then she remembered that this was the eighty-something-year-old woman who'd told Ava in excruciating detail how to use bronzer to "fake" cleavage.

If anything, Nonna would likely try to borrow the new purchases.

It wasn't Luc's feisty grandmother who opened the door.

But neither was it the relaxed, quick-to-smile Luc who just yesterday she'd watched charm the pants off an irritable cabdriver, even as Luc wrote him a hefty ticket for blowing through a red light *and* blocking the intersection.

This was a Luc she hadn't seen before, even when he'd been good and pissed about being trapped into being the NYPD's golden boy.

Tension radiated off him in taut waves, and his usually friendly eyes were guarded and pained.

This Luc was hurting.

Wordlessly she stepped inside.

"Is Anthony or Nonna here?"

He shook his head, closing the door before turning to face her. She itched to touch him, but instinct held her back. Instead she set her purse and shopping bags by the door and moved into the kitchen, giving him plenty of space. Plenty of room to talk about it, if he wanted.

It was pretty clear from the way he stalked toward her that he didn't want to talk, and the way his hands possessively found her hips as he pinned her against the kitchen counter made it plenty clear that he had called her here for a very different reason.

His kiss was hard and angry, his lips slanting over hers with a fierceness that went beyond sexual hunger.

Luc was mad.

At her?

Her hands found his shoulders, and she started to push him back...to figure out what the hell was going on, but his hands moved up her back, tangling in her hair.

He tipped her hair back, his tormented eyes locking on hers. "I need you."

Ava felt something unfamiliar unfold in her chest. Luc Moretti needed her.

Nobody had ever needed her.

She'd never let herself be needed.

But tonight...tonight she wanted to be here for this complex man with hidden secrets.

Ava responded the only way she knew how. She lifted to her toes, wrapped her arms around his neck, and returned his hot, angry kiss.

He groaned, lifting her roughly to the counter, his hands finding her ass and scooting her forward until he was nestled between her thighs.

Wrapping her legs around his waist was the most natural thing in the world, and his hips tilted forward, and even with his jeans and her shorts separating them, the contact was electric.

Luc's hands ran up her sides, moving over her breasts, lifting their small weight in his hands as his tongue flicked at her upper lip.

There was no slow, patient seduction this time. He yanked the sleeveless blue sweater up and over her head, leaving her only in her pale pink demi-cup bra.

"Pretty," he said, running this thumbs along the upper slopes of her breasts.

"I bought some prettier things today," she said, catching his lower lip between her teeth.

His hands stilled. "Show me."

She laughed a little. "You want me to take off one bra to put on another."

His lips followed the path of his fingers, his tongue tracking the edge of her bra. "Did you buy them for me?"

She sucked in a breath. It was a crucial moment—buying lingerie was hardly the equivalent of his and hers towels, but telling him that she'd bought it with him in mind would give away the fact that she'd made plans when they'd promised each other they'd had none.

His teeth rasped gently against her skin. "Sims. You bought them for me."

She let out a little laugh at his familiar cocky arrogance. "Yeah. I bought them for you."

His fingers ran lightly over her ribs as he pulled back. "Show me."

She bit her lip. "But your grandma..."

"At my parents'."

"Anthony...?"

"Not here." His hands grasped her hips, this time pulling her forward so he could set her back on the ground. "Model for me, baby."

And that's when she heard it. The meaning hidden beneath his teasing plea.

Distract me.

Whatever he was dealing with, he didn't want to deal with right now.

She understood all too well what that was like.

"Okay," she said, putting a hand on his chest to move him backward. "But you're waiting in the bedroom."

"I want to watch."

She laughed. "Trust me. Watching a woman put on a bra will not be nearly as sexy as watching her take one off."

"Point taken," he said, pulling her close for a kiss before backing toward his bedroom. "But be fast. There are things I want to do to you."

She knew firsthand just how her body responded to the things he did to her, and she was all but buzzing with anticipation.

Heading to her shopping bag as he backed into the bedroom, Ava quickly rummaged through the pink tissue paper until she found what she was looking for.

Of all her new purchases it was the most daring, the most blatantly sexy. She slipped into the bathroom to avoid any awkward "why is there a half-naked woman in my foyer" should Nonna or Anthony show up unexpectedly.

She ditched the pale pink T-shirt bra, and her mismatched panties quickly followed.

Next up: black lace. Not original, but as Beth had pointed out...why mess with the classics?

The bra was low cut and nearly sheer, but gave her just enough lift to be interesting. The panties were equally tiny, little more than a black triangle and a few straps held together with a naughty pink bow on the back.

But it was the garter belt that made things really interesting. Ava pulled on the new knee-high black stockings and attached the black garter, with the pink bow that matched the thong.

For once, Ava was glad that she'd opted to go with sexy heels for her shopping expedition, and she slipped the black patent leather stilettos back on.

Luc wanted a distraction?

He was about to get one.

She grabbed her discarded clothes, putting them in a tidy pile on top of the toilet seat, and hoped like hell he was right about his grandmother and Anthony being long-gone for a while.

He hadn't shut the door all the way and he was lying on his back, hand locked behind his head when she pushed it open.

Luc turned his head when she entered, and so blank was his expression, that for a horrible moment she thought he'd gotten so lost in thought that he'd forgotten all about her.

And then he saw her. Really saw her.

The dazed, slack-jawed expression told her that her extravagant lingerie purchase was worth every penny.

He slowly sat up, swinging his legs around the side of the bed. Luc opened his mouth as though to say something, but instead swallowed, as though his mouth was too dry to speak.

Gaining confidence Ava turned in a slow circle, feeling just the tiniest bit slutty, and getting all the more turned on by it.

"God *damn*, Sims."

He started to stand, but she held up a hand, pinning him with a fierce look. Stay.

Eyes locked on his, she flicked the door all the way

closed, slowly walking the short distance to the bed as her hands ran up her thighs, her stomach, teasing her breasts, sliding up to pull her hair back and up before releasing it and letting it tumble around her shoulders once more.

She stopped in front of him, and his hands reached out, but once more, she held up a hand, really getting into her bossy femme fatale routine.

Slowly, Ava traced her index finger over the thin strap of the bra, down along its edge, which was just mere centimeters from her nipple.

"I chose well?" she asked, her voice flirty as both hands now trailed across her nearly exposed breasts.

"You've damn near blown my mind," he said. Again he lifted her hands, and this time she stopped him with merely a look.

"You touch when I say you can touch."

He met her eyes. Swallowed. And though she knew it pained him, he lowered his hands back to the bed, gripping the edge so tightly his knuckles turned white.

Ava let one finger slip beneath the edge of the bra, brushing against her nipple as it immediately hardened and Luc groaned. "Sims."

Emboldened by his reaction, she repeated the motion on the other breast, until both nipples were hardened points beneath the thin lace.

Ava had never been shy in the bedroom, but this unabashed sex kitten routine was new to her, and she loved it.

Loved that it was only Luc who'd been able to bring out this side of her.

She toyed with her nipples for several moments, her breath quickly turning to little pants before she moved her hands downward, across her stomach, over her thighs to the thin strap of the garter as she inched closer, continuing to tantalize him with the look-don't-touch torture.

"Touch yourself," he said hoarsely.

"Here?" she asked, her finger skimming along the top of the knee-high stocking.

"Higher."

His eyes were glued to the motion of her hands.

"Here?" Her hand slid up, gently stroking the soft skin beneath her belly button.

"Or here?" Her hand slid down, covering the tiny V of the front of her thong.

"Sims." It was a tortured moan, and Ava gave him a naughty smile as she touched herself through the panties.

"Uh oh," she said, pulling her hand away and lifting it to his lips. "All wet."

He licked her fingers, moving his hands.

"Not yet."

"You're killing me."

"Am I?"

This time when she touched herself, her fingers slipped under the lace, and Luc's breath hitched as she touched herself in tiny, torturous circles.

She could come just like this. Standing before him in sexy lingerie while his eyes devoured her.

But this wasn't about her.

Slowly, she removed her fingers, moved closer to him, and lifted one foot to the bed, placing the heel of her shoe carefully near his thigh.

"Your turn to touch."

Luc swore softly, and he wasted no time getting his hand on her, although it wasn't with the rough urgency that she expected.

Instead, his hand slid along her exposed inner thigh, his eyes watching hers as the edge of his fingers reached her center.

His other hand joined the first, pulling the black lace aside so she was completely exposed to him.

Luc ran one finger over her, tracing her from clit down to her damp opening and then back again.

This time, it was Ava's turn to moan. Ava's turn to be tortured.

He smiled evilly as he repeated the light, teasing motion. Ava knew he wanted her to beg, but this was her game, and she refused to give in.

His finger moved again, this time lingering on her clit, circling once before moving downward.

Ava bit her lip. Do not beg. Do. Not. Beg.

He slid a long finger inside her, and her breath hitched as she leaned forward, her hair covering both of them. A second finger joined the first, sliding in and out of her with perfect friction.

"Like this, Sims?"

She nodded, and he thrust his fingers again, a little harder this time. Her nails dug into his shoulders.

He dipped his head, his lips finding the smooth skin on the inside of her thigh.

He nipped her gently as his fingers continued their slow in-and-out torture.

He turned his head slightly, moving his mouth ever closer to her center, and her fingers slid from shoulders to his hair as he traced his tongue along her thigh.

His hand disappeared then, and Ava nearly wailed at the loss, glaring down at his smirking face.

"You played with fire, Sims. You don't tease a man like that and not pay the price."

"What price—"

He licked her. One silky lap of his tongue over her slit.

Ava's knees buckled, but the hand that wasn't holding her panties to the side grabbed her ass, holding her to him as he licked her again, longer this time, letting his tongue explore.

Luc ate her with gentle laps, seeming to know when to tease and when to suck, and she could do little more than fist his hair and hold on as he took her to the edge in record time.

"Wait," she said on a gasp, trying to tug him away. "I—"

His palm moved her closer, pinning her to his mouth as he caught her clit in his mouth, circling with his tongue once, twice—

She was gone.

She came in harsh, breathy pants against his mouth, hips bucking wantonly against him.

When the aftershocks subsided, he gently slid her panties back into place, leaning back slightly to look up at her face. She was expecting male triumph, but saw only a fierce want that matched her own. Whatever they had, it wasn't typical sexual attraction.

It was something deeper.

Darker.

She touched her fingers briefly to his glistening mouth before moving her stiletto-ed foot back to the ground.

Ava dropped to her knees, making room for herself between his legs as she inched forward.

Her fingers made quick work of the buttons of his jeans.

"Sims, you don't have—"

He broke off as her quick maneuvering of his boxers freed his erection. Her hand fisted over him, and he swore.

She meant to tease him like he'd teased her, but then

she remembered his expression when she'd first come in the door.

This was a man who wanted to get lost.

Needed it.

So without preamble or teasing, she leaned forward, taking him in her mouth.

Luc gasped, his hands pulling her long hair back so that he could watch her mouth on him. Ava let his responses guide her, looking to make it last for him. She slowed down when his fingers tightened, teased when his breathing grew faster.

When she lifted her eyes to his, watched him watching her as she gave him head, he whispered her name in reverent want.

When he was close to the brink, he pulled her hair firmly back, and she let him. He scooped her up onto the bed with him, pushing her flat on her back as he shoved his jeans and boxers down to mid-thigh.

They couldn't wait. Not to remove his pants, not to discard her panties.

He pulled the black triangle of her thong aside once more, but this time it was to make room for his cock, still damp from her mouth.

This first thrust was hard, and she gasped. The second was harder, and she moved her hands above her head to hang on to the headboard.

"Fuck, Sims."

Fuck was exactly what they did, his body pounding hers in rough, deliberate strokes. The fabric of his jeans chafed at the inside of her thighs, the buttons of his shirt rasping against her bare stomach, but it was perfect.

All of it was wanton and perfect and apparently exactly

what she needed because she was on the brink again before she could even register the impending orgasm.

"Condom?" she gasped, digging her nails into his back.

He paused, swearing before he rolled them to the side to dig through his nightstand drawer.

Luc withdrew just long enough to roll the condom on, and then he was inside her again, his hands splaying her thighs wide as he watched his cock move in and out.

"Sims."

She lifted her hips for him before reaching down to touch herself, and he groaned. Ava had always thought of simultaneous orgasms as an overrated unicorn of sorts, best in theory, if they even existed, but she was dead wrong.

Because when the first shudder racked her body, he was right there with her, bucking against her even as she clenched around him.

Somehow it went on forever and not nearly long enough, but when Luc collapsed on top of her, Ava knew only one thing:

She was exactly where she was supposed to be.

CHAPTER TWENTY-SEVEN

Ava didn't push him to talk about it. Luc liked that about her.

Hell, Luc liked a lot of things about her. Maybe too many.

He lost count of how long he lay collapsed on top of her like a post-rut frat boy, but for the life of him, he couldn't bring himself to move after the orgasm to top all orgasms.

Sexual distraction was exactly what he'd been looking for when he'd booty-called her over there, but what he got was in a whole other universe.

When he did finally move, it was only to roll to the side, one arm still draped heavily against her waist.

She wiggled slightly into a more comfortable position before lightly running her nails over his forearm.

It was then that he braced for the inevitable questions. He'd seen on her face that she'd known something was wrong when he'd opened the door to her, and Luc figured at some point he'd have to answer for the fact that he'd just used her to forget his problems.

Just one problem, actually. A big one.

Like the fact that his father had paid off the media to not make a scandal out of the Shayna Johnson case.

His arm tightened against her stomach, but she didn't stop the soothing motion of her fingers.

Incredibly, he wanted to talk to her about it. Not for advice, or sympathy, or absolution. But just to let someone in.

To let Ava in.

But he couldn't.

Because at the end of the day, Ava Sims was a reporter.

Even worse, she was a reporter focused on him.

The irony didn't escape Luc. No wonder his dad and brothers had flipped their shit when they'd learned that he'd found himself in Ava's bed. His father had risked his own career to protect Luc from the very type of person who was currently cuddled against his side in outrageously sexy lingerie.

It also explained why they'd all been on suspiciously good behavior as they'd welcomed Ava into their little family fold.

The more information the Morettis spoon-fed her, the less she'd have to go digging.

And it was very, very important that Ava didn't go digging.

It was bad enough that Lopez had let it slip about Mike being Luc's former partner.

About Mike dying.

About Shayna dying...

He buried his face in her shoulder, and her fingers paused briefly before slowly moving upward so that her palm cupped his cheek.

He kissed it, and she gave a little sigh of contentment.

It wasn't supposed to be like this. Hot, raunchy sex was

supposed to be followed up with a shower and a beer and a good-bye.

Not cuddling and soft kisses and the urge to share his deepest, darkest secrets.

She turned her head slightly toward his. "Um, Luc. I have to pee."

Sims.

Her unembarrassed announcement was his out, but damned if it didn't make him feel oddly tender. He smiled against her hair, lifting his arm just enough so she could wiggle out from beneath it.

His cock was totally spent, but that didn't stop him from watching her taut, tiny ass exit his bedroom.

He'd had plenty of gorgeous women, but none did it for him quite like Ava.

And not just physically.

Mentally.

Emotionally.

No.

He pushed the thought aside. She was not for him.

He was not for anyone.

Luc swore softly, punching a pillow out of frustration for thoughts he couldn't yet sort out. He was tugging his jeans back up and buttoning them as Ava came back in.

Gone were the thigh-highs and garter belt. Back were the short shorts and blue top. The high heels were still on too, which was admittedly sexy as hell, and already his cock twitched at the memory of her standing in stilettos as he ate her out...

But Ava hated stilettos.

She only wore them for show.

And walking.

And since the show was over...

"You're leaving?" His voice came out rougher than he meant it to.

Her brows snapped together in surprise. "Well, yeah? I thought...?"

Luc's eyes narrowed. "You thought what? That I called you over here for a blow job and Victoria's Secret fashion show, and then wanted you to walk-of-shame yourself home at six p.m. on a Sunday?"

Her confusion turned to irritation. "Hey, quit making it seem like I'm the tawdry one here. We've both agreed we're not looking for a relationship. We both know that the sex is awesome. But you have to spend enough time with me at work, I don't expect—"

"You hungry?" he asked, pushing past her toward the kitchen.

She followed him, and he expected some snappy comeback, but she remained silent.

Silent and Ava. Not a common combo. Probably not a good one either.

Their eyes locked and held, and she studied him as though looking for something. He didn't know what the fuck it was, but apparently she found it.

She lowered primly to a bar stool. "I could eat."

She was staying.

The relief that went through him was as potent as it was alarming, and Luc inhaled a deep breath. He started to open the fridge, but there was something he needed to do first. Something he needed to say.

He advanced on her, noting the way her brown eyes went both wary and aroused as he neared. He nearly smiled. Good to know that strange push-pull effect was mutual.

Luc moved around her, pivoting the spinning seat of the bar stool so she was facing him. He started to put both hands on the counter to pin her against him, but at the last second his hands seemed to have other ideas and he gently cupped her face.

"Sims."

"Moretti."

He smiled at her tart response. Damn, he liked her.

"I like you."

Her eyes went a little wide. "I like you—"

"Uh uh, let me finish." His thumbs stroked over her cheekbones. "And I like your body a *hell* of a lot, but when I asked you to come over...it wasn't about that."

She arched an eyebrow.

He laughed. "Okay it wasn't *just* about that. Just because I'm not looking for the whole long-term, love and marriage thing doesn't mean I can't enjoy the company of a female. A particular female," he added.

"So you're using me for sex and companionship," she said, her voice wonderfully free of feminine outrage.

"Are you okay with that?"

"Depends." Her fingers wrapped around his wrists, her eyes affectionate. "Do I get to use *you* for sex and companionship?"

He leaned down to nuzzle her neck. "I sure as fuck hope so."

"Then it's a deal," she said, pushing him backward playfully.

"You should also use me for my cooking skills," Luc said, resuming his quest to make them something to eat.

"That whole Italian thing rubbed off on you, huh?"

"It did. As long as you like pasta."

"I do."

He held up two boxes. "Linguini or rigatoni?"

"Surprise me," she said, leaning forward and resting her chin on her hands.

He set the linguine back on the shelf, then set the rigatoni next to the stove. Without missing a beat, he pulled a recently opened bottle of Chianti off the counter and poured them each a glass.

Ava lifted her glass to his. "To using each other."

Luc grinned. Yes. He liked this one. He clinked his glass lightly against hers. "To using each other."

Their eyes locked as they took a sip, and a tiny sliver of unease ran along his spine as he acknowledged the one not so minor detail that neither would address.

Using each other...

For how long?

CHAPTER TWENTY-EIGHT

Avie, baby. What the hell, where you been?"

Ava sighed around the straw of her iced coffee. She'd been unusually lucky these past couple weeks; her times at the studio had conveniently not overlapped with Davis's time in the office.

It would seem her luck was out.

She plastered a smile on her face, spinning around in her chair to face him. Unnecessary. He was already in his usual position on her desk, crowding her space with chunky thighs and a leering grin.

"I've been working," she said, carefully keeping the edge out of her voice. Davis had this annoying way of thinking that his female reporters should be both drumming up prime stories while simultaneously being in the studio where he could see—ogle—them. Not so much with the male reporters who had all sorts of leeway in their schedules.

"So tell me about the cop thing," he said, picking up her drink and taking a long slurp.

There went $4.72 down the drain. No way was she touching it now.

"It's going well. I have all the footage for the first and second hours. Lots of interviews with the NYPD, more than enough for my day-in-the-life section, following around Luc and Sawyer."

Davis's bushy eyebrows crept up, and out of the corner of her eye she saw Mihail's head pop above the cube wall, gummy worm hanging from his mouth as he blatantly eavesdropped.

"*Luc* and *Sawyer*?" her boss asked.

"Officers Moretti and Lopez," she clarified irritably.

"You're on a first-name basis, huh?"

"Well yeah, that happens when you spend nearly every day together for a month," Ava snapped.

It also happens when you spend every night in one of their beds for the past week, but she didn't go there. Obviously.

Mihail wiggled his eyebrows at her, but she ignored him. The Monday morning after her and Luc's Weekend of Amazing Sex, it had taken Mihail all of two minutes to figure out what had happened. He'd claimed that they'd steamed up the lens of his camera every time they made eye contact.

It had taken Sawyer only a bit longer; he'd made it to lunch before asking when they'd decided to "do it."

Their friends knowing was one thing…Ava's boss finding out that she'd blurred the lines?

No.

She kept her face carefully blank as she not-so-subtly checked her watch.

Davis either missed or ignored the gesture. He crossed his arms over his chest and settled back on her desk, getting comfortable. "So what are you thinking for the last hour? That's the denouement, Avie; it's gotta be great if you want to convince everyone you're anchor-ready. We need something that will have the housewives swooning and young'uns dashing off to be a cop, and the men puffing up their chests and saying *that's what it means to be a man in this country.*"

"Absolutely, that's exactly the response we're going to get," Ava said with confidence she didn't feel.

Because the truth was, Ava wasn't at all sure she could tell the story of Luc Moretti without also telling the story of what had happened to his partner. Mike Jensen had died on duty while on the scene of a kidnapping gone wrong.

And Luc had been there.

But that wasn't where the story was. A cop had died, and that was awful. Shayna Johnson died, and that was awful.

But the really awful part was that neither of those had made even the tiniest blip in the news circuit. At first Ava thought maybe there had been another story that might have overshadowed it. A natural disaster or political scandal that had allowed for two deaths to go nearly unnoticed.

Her search had come up empty. November two years ago had been a slow news month. And the week of Shayna Johnson's death? The top local story had been a *flower* show.

No, the story here wasn't that two people had died violent deaths. The story was that there *was no story.*

And Ava would bet her right eye this was no fluke. She bet this had to do with Luc's father, and whatever they'd fought about the other day when Luc had been so upset.

There had to be some perks to having a police commissioner father. Say, like his dad deflecting attention away from a messy situation. This was a cover-up, good and simple.

And a police cover-up made for a damn good story. Just not *this* story.

Professional Ava knew exactly what she should do. Blow this thing wide open. Find out exactly what happened that day, and find out exactly why it was all hush-hush.

But on a personal level? Ava wasn't sure she wanted to go there. At all.

And would there be harm in letting it be? Really? Her TV special would and could be a success without it. The camera would love Luc, and Sawyer's charm was a welcome boon. Their casual banter, Hollywood smiles, and all-American approachability made them easy to watch.

The feel-good aspect the network was after was there. It was a soft, fuzzy masterpiece.

It just wasn't the full story.

It wasn't the truth. Or at least not the whole truth.

"Avie?" Davis prodded. "The last hour? What do you have in mind?"

"I'm thinking it would be a good time to interview Luc," she said, grasping at straws. "You know, a really in-depth look at America's Hero."

"'Kay." Davis drummed his fingers. "That works if he's got the charisma."

"He does," she said emphatically. "He couldn't be more perfect if we'd hired an actor to play the good ol' boy cop."

"Does he have a girlfriend we can play up?"

"What?" Ava asked, her voice all but a squeak. She heard Mihail snicker.

"You know...a girlfriend. Or boyfriend, I guess we could

work with that. An engagement caught on screen would send our ratings through the roof."

Ava blinked at Davis. "What is this, a tabloid talk show? You want me to bring his illegitimate children out of the audience too?"

Her boss's eyes lit up. "Does he have them?"

"No, jeez! He's a good guy!"

"So? Good guys have nice girlfriends whom they propose to on TV. Tell him we'll buy the ring."

"Gross, Davis," Ava said in disgust. "And he's not even dating anyone."

"Huh. Why not? He's a good-looking dude with a million fans. Should we set him up with someone?"

The thought of Luc's being set up with some young, cute groupie made Ava slightly nauseated. Although it was a hell of a lot better than the thought of him proposing. *That* thought made her downright stabby.

Not that she had to worry about the last one. Luc was solidly anti-marriage. Just like she was. So there would be no presenting of rings, on camera, or off.

Ava let that thought sink in for a second and was annoyed to realize that she felt a sting of disappointment.

"Well whatever. I trust your judgment," Davis said. "Just make sure you get us all the happy feels. The one that has the housewives sending letters of adoration."

Ava nodded, feeling increasingly ambivalent about the plastic, posed story she was going to present the more Davis talked. Not that Luc was plastic or poised, but now that she knew he had a complicated past, it felt wrong to not even mention it.

But she couldn't do that to Luc.

Not to mention, it would be torpedoing her career.

"Oh, before I forget," Davis said, taking another sip of her drink. Ugh. Backwash city. "I wanted you to hear it from me...rumor from upstairs is that Holly Granger is interested."

"Interested?" Ava asked, pulling her thoughts away from Luc. Holly Granger was the prime-time superstar over at BNC; what did she have to do with anything?

He leaned down as though he had a secret to share, even though there was no such thing as secrets in the news media. "You know all that chemistry she has with Bill?"

"Yeah?" Bill Terry was Holly's co-anchor; their chemistry was legendary. It was hard to imagine one without the other.

"Apparently they decided to mix some on-screen chemistry with off-screen biology," he said with a gross little wink.

Ava frowned. "They're both married. Bill has, like, five kids."

Davis lifted a shoulder. "Wouldn't be the first time."

Ava held up a hand. "Okay, who cares? What does their affair have to do with me?"

"Keep up, Avie. Things have gone sour. Or something. She's been talking about taking Gwen's place."

No.

No.

That was *her* spot. But if Holly Granger was interested, Ava was screwed.

Unless...

Mihail shook his head more emphatically this time.

Maybe she was going about this all wrong. Maybe she *did* want to make a name for herself. She couldn't measure up to someone of Holly's experience and polish, but she could deliver a kick-ass story that would get her noticed by other networks.

Say, a story about a cop whose partner had been killed arriving on the scene of a botched kidnapping...

"Hey, Davis," Ava called after her boss, who was already strutting away.

He turned.

"Do you think you could spare a fact-checker or two? I've got a couple things I want to double-check on. Just to be sure."

"Oh, Ava," Mihail said quietly. "Don't."

She didn't look at him. Couldn't bear to see his disappointed face. It's not like she was actually going to act on anything.

But she knew there was something strange about that Shayna Johnson case. And there was a story yet to be told with Mike Jensen too.

And Ava would bet serious money that the occasional shadows that crossed Luc's face had to do with his deceased partner.

"What the hell are you doing?" Mihail grumbled as she pulled her keyboard toward her.

Ava pretended not to hear him as she brought up Google and typed *Mike Jensen New York Police Widow.*

CHAPTER TWENTY-NINE

Despite Nonna's shrill insistence, Luc deliberately did not invite Ava along to the Moretti family dinner on Sunday.

And not because he didn't want her there.

In fact, it alarmed him just how much he *did* want her there. For moral support...and because it felt right.

Like she belonged. With him.

But tonight, there were things he needed to say to his family. Things best *not* said in front of a reporter.

"So you're still giving me the silent treatment?" Anthony asked, coming to join Luc on the back railing of the ferry as they headed toward Staten Island.

Luc stared out at the Statue of Liberty. "I've been talking to you all week."

Anthony snorted. "Sure. If by *talking* you mean grunting and barking one-word answers."

"This coming from the guy who once called conversation *useless bullshit?*"

"Why talk when you can act?"

"That's a solid tattoo option, but makes for shitty relationships, Anth."

It was a low blow, but Anthony, being Anthony, wasn't fazed. He merely turned around so his back was to the water, resting his elbows on the railing as he studied Luc.

"You're mad at me. At Vin. Definitely at Dad."

Luc met his brother's eyes. "You could say that."

"Because we protected you."

"Don't even," Luc said, standing up straight to face his oldest brother. "Don't spin this. If situations were reversed, how would you feel, knowing your father risked his career to make a deal with the media, and then the entire family knew about it and didn't tell you?"

"Not the entire family," Anthony corrected. "Elena has no idea. Not sure about Mom and Nonna."

Luc leveled his oldest brother with a look that said *don't try to distract me with details*.

Anthony sighed and ran a hand over the back of his neck as he stared at the dock. Then, to Luc's surprise, his brother looked up and met his eyes.

"I'd be pissed."

Luc threw his hands in the air. "Thank you."

"I'd be pissed and then I'd get over it," Anthony continued.

"*Really*." Luc drew out the word. "You, who still holds a grudge against the defensive lineman that sacked you in JV football? You'd forgive and forget?"

"We're not talking about some chump fourteen-year-old with shit for brains. We're talking about your *family* who did what they could to protect you."

Luc leaned forward again, running his hands through his hair.

Anthony was right. His dad had been out of line to interfere. His brothers had been out of line to go along with it.

But you couldn't argue their motive. They'd wanted to protect their *bambino*.

Hell, if Luc was completely honest with himself, it wasn't even their interference that was eating at him.

It was the fact that he'd needed protection in the first place.

For nearly two years, Luc had thought it had all been in his head.

He'd thought the battle was isolated to his own messed-up brain as he tried to convince himself that he had to stop blaming himself for Shayna. That it wasn't his fault that Mike was dead.

But if his dad had felt it necessary to "call in a couple favors" to keep the media off the story . . .

It meant there was something to hide.

And so even though Luc wanted to rail at his brother, and his dad . . . hell, he wanted to holler at his entire family for treating him like the baby.

But he couldn't.

Because *they* weren't the problem.

Luc was.

He stared down at his hands and took a deep breath. "What would you have done differently?"

Anthony lifted an eyebrow. "Well, for starters, I would have told you about Dad's master plan if it meant you'd do less sulking."

"No, I mean on that day," Luc clarified. "When Mike died. What would you have done if you were me?"

Anthony sighed. "Luca. Don't. Not this again."

"Tell me," Luc snapped. "I need to know."

Still, his brother resisted, his expression tense and angry. "You think you're the only cop with regrets? You think you're the only cop that hasn't looked at dozens of decisions he's made in his career and wondered what-if?"

"Well not *everybody's* regrets involve two deaths," Luc shot back.

"Yeah, but some of them do, Luca. Some of them involve a hell of a lot *more* deaths. It's the name of the game. It's a shitty reality, but it *is* reality. People die, Luc. Kids die. Cops die. It always happens on somebody's watch, and I hate like hell that it was yours, but it happened. You've got to deal."

"I should have moved in earlier," Luc said, barely hearing his brother's rant. "I knew we'd found our guy. I knew she was in that house. If only I'd gone around the back, trusted my gut..."

His brother's hand found his shoulder, and that somehow made everything more real. Anthony wasn't exactly an affectionate guy.

"We've already been over this," Anthony said quietly. "You trusted the system. You did what you were supposed to do, Luc. And you know as well as I do that it could have just as easily gone the other way. You could have broken orders, gone barging in the back door. *Maybe* Mike would be alive. *Maybe* you'd save the girl...but maybe not."

Luc opened his mouth, but Anthony pressed on. "There's always going to be a what-if, if you let there be. The best any of us can do is learn from the shitty stuff and try to apply it to next time."

Luc knew all of this, of course. He'd heard it before.

He just didn't know how to start believing it.

CHAPTER THIRTY

Luca."

"Ma," Luc said, letting himself be pulled into a long hug by his mother, even as he gave an exasperated sigh. "Were you waiting by the door?"

Her eyes went wide and innocent as she pulled back from the hug. "What? I was just coming down the stairs and saw you and Anthony coming up the walk…"

Luc lifted an eyebrow. "And yet you let Anthony scoot by."

She waved her hand. "That boy's never let me hug him."

Luc waited. "And?"

His mother sighed. "And I wanted to talk to you. See you."

Anthony glanced down the hall in the direction of the kitchen. "Dad told you?"

His mother's warm hand found his arm. "Come talk to me."

Saying no wasn't an option.

Luc knew he was biased, but Maria Moretti was pretty much the gold standard of mothers.

Short and pleasantly plump, with salt and pepper dark hair and generous laugh lines, she looked every bit the part of the "understanding matriarch."

Growing up, she'd been the type of mother who Luc's friends confided in, even when they were at odds with their own parents.

But that was not Maria Moretti's real feat; the real accomplishment was that Luc's mother had always gotten her *own* children to confide in her.

Granted, the *pignoli* she always had on hand at the exact right moment likely helped—if spilling your guts about the C– on your English exam meant getting another of the delicious almond, pine-nut cookie, then you spilled your guts.

Same went for fessing up on who *really* broke that Venetian vase, and whether you and Marisa Perkins were really "studying."

As Luc let his mother lead him into the tiny sitting room off the foyer, he realized not much had changed. She was still the kind of mom you talked to. About the important things.

But the important thing his mother wanted to talk about wasn't what he expected.

"So, where is Ava?" she asked, curling up on the ancient leather love seat, pulling her legs beneath her.

If Luc hadn't already been sitting in what Vincent had once dubbed the "interrogation" chair, he might have stumbled at the unexpected question.

"Ava?"

His mother gave him a knowing smile.

"What the hell does Ava have to do with the shit storm that got unleashed last weekend?" Luc asked, referring to the disastrous Father's Day drinking session that had ended with him storming out of the bar like a sulky child.

"You went to her after, did you not?"

Luc's eyes narrowed. Now, just how the hell did she know that?

"Actually, she came to me," he heard himself say.

Damn.

He was already running his mouth, and she hadn't even offered him a *pignolo* yet.

At least he'd stopped short of telling his mother about the sexy lingerie show. There were some things one did not tell one's mother, no matter how amazing her baking skills.

Maria's smile widened. "I like her."

Luc said nothing.

"And Nonna likes her."

Well. That was...something. Nonna and his mother hadn't agreed on something since...Luc couldn't remember.

"You've only met her once."

"And?"

"And that's not long enough to determine whether or not you like somebody," Luc said.

"Did you know at first meeting that you liked her?"

Luc snorted. "The first time I met Ava Sims was when she was ripping me a new one for writing her a parking ticket."

"But did you *like* her?" Maria pressed.

Luc opened his mouth, but shut it just as quickly.

It didn't matter. His mom read his mind anyway and laughed gustily. "You liked the way she looked."

"Well it certainly wasn't her respect for traffic laws," he muttered.

"Don't discount physical chemistry," his mother said with a smug smile. "When I first saw your father..."

Luc lifted a hand. "Nope. Just...no. We're not doing that. And don't tell me that you were sold on Ava Sims after one meeting because she's gorgeous. That works on a hot-blooded single man, not his married mother."

"No," his mother mused. "I mean, yes, she's very beautiful, but that's not why I liked her."

"Oh, do tell," Luc said half-sarcastically. "Was it the way she totally sucked up to everyone in this house, because I've gotta tell ya—"

"It was the way you looked at her."

Luc broke off at his mother's quiet, matter-of-fact statement. "You like a girl because of the way your son looked at her?"

Her lips twitched. "You'll understand when you have a child someday."

Luc's stomach twisted. "Mom—"

It was her turn to hold up a hand. "I know, I know. You're not currently on the marriage and baby track. But you never know."

He did know. He would never put any woman or child in the position of Mike Jensen's widow and fatherless son.

No matter how he looked at Ava Sims.

Which, come to think of it . . .

"What do you mean, you liked the way I looked at her?" he asked, even though he wasn't entirely sure he wanted to know.

His mom did nothing but smile, and he pointed a suspicious finger at her. "That. What is that?"

"You know what that is."

Luc did know. Her smile stunk of *mother knows best*.

Actually, it was more like mother knows something you don't know, but she's not going to tell you what because you need to learn for yourself.

It was the worst.

But Luc's brain didn't feel big enough to deal with the Ava dilemma *and* the persistent guilt that his dad had risked his own career for Luc's.

He tackled the second one. It seemed easier, somehow.

"Mom, did Dad tell you—"

"That two years ago that he asked Preston Nader not to run a story on the death of Mike and that poor baby girl?"

"Yes."

"And that he also asked Joe Polinski, Anna Courture, and Keith Jobs?"

Luc leaned forward, both baffled and annoyed at his mother's calm tone. "Mom, he bribed them."

"I didn't bribe anyone."

Luc turned to see his father standing in the doorway, looking every bit as authoritative as he had in his police commissioner days.

Luc stood so he was eye level with his father. "You said you called in favors."

"Different than bribery. I didn't cross any ethical lines."

"Bullshit!" Luc exploded.

"I took them to beers!" his dad yelled back. "I asked them to keep your name out of it. They agreed. That's all there is to it. I made it clear that it was a personal request, not a professional one."

"And the 'favors' you called in?"

His dad shrugged. "I helped Joe move. I gave Anna's daughter an exclusive interview for her high school newspaper. I don't remember the others, but I assure you they were every bit as tame."

Luc sat back down. "What about Mike? And Shayna? They deserved a mention."

"Luc." This from his mother. "Do you really think your

father wouldn't have checked with their surviving family members first?"

Luc's mind went blank as he met his father's troubled gaze. "Did you?"

His dad came into the tiny room, lowering himself next to his wife on the love seat.

The scene was familiar. How many times had Luc sat across from his parents in this very room, sitting in this very chair? Through bad news. Lectures. Good news.

When they'd told him about the death of his grandfather.

When they were upset about his report card.

When he'd gotten his college acceptance letter.

"Luca..." His dad's voice was tired. "Beverly Jensen didn't want a spectacle made of Mike's death. She and I spoke about it at length."

Luc lifted his chin. "Mike deserved to be recognized for his service. And his sacrifice."

"And he *was* recognized," Tony said, hitting his knee with his fist. "He damn well was. Hell, you went to the ceremony!"

"Yeah, so a bunch of fellow cops celebrated him. He deserved for the world to know what he did."

"Yeah?" his father asked. "And how's that working out for you, son? You enjoying the world knowing what you're up to? You like being *celebrated*?"

Well . . . shit. Luc walked right into that one.

"It's different," Luc snapped.

"Is it?"

His mother wasn't smiling anymore, but her voice was still calm. Gentle. "You knew Mike as well as anyone, Luc. Would he have wanted his face plastered all over the newspapers? His name bandied about on the evening news by talking heads that didn't even know him?"

Luc rolled his lips inward as he considered. "Mike would have hated that. So would the Johnson family," he said, staring down at his hands. "They were desperate to avoid media attention during the entire ordeal. They only wanted their little girl back."

Tony nodded. "You went to see them after the funeral."

Luc met his father's eyes. "How did you know that?"

"Because I went to see them too. And I'm guessing they told you the same thing they told me. That they only wanted to be left alone to mourn their baby."

"They should have wanted *justice*," Luc said, swallowing a bitter lump in his throat. "They should have wanted the whole world to know that a cop could have saved her and didn't."

"Don't you dare, Luca," his mother said, her voice as sharp as he'd ever heard it. "Your brothers told me you've been subscribing to this nonsense, but I won't tolerate it in my house."

His head shot back a little. "You won't tolerate what? My remorse?"

"Your misplaced shame. You want to bully your brothers with it, that's their problem, but under my roof, you'll leave the pity party at the door."

"Pity party? Two people are dead, Mom!"

"And those two people deserve more than your sulky martyrdom!"

Luc stared flabbergasted at his mother's outburst. For starters, Maria Moretti didn't have outbursts. And second, *sulky martyrdom*? That's what she thought he was about?

Something nagged the back of his neck.

Was his mother right?

Before he could process it, she kept going.

"You think you're honoring people that died, Luca? Wrong. By skulking around like some sort of failure, by thinking you don't deserve credit for the good that you do, you only give power to the baddies."

Luc almost smiled at that. *Baddies* was how the Moretti clan had talked about police business around the dinner table back when the kids were little, and it still was applied to this day to refer to the scum of New York.

"Hold up," Luc said, not quite ready to roll over and play dead just yet. "If I'm supposed to be so proud of myself, why did Dad get pissed about me dating a reporter?"

"Well not because you have anything to hide," his dad grumbled. "I just know how reporters can be. They're more interested in a good story than the truth. If she found out that 'New York's hero's' former partner had died and that he was first on the scene of a kidnapping-turned-murder, you think she wouldn't jump all over that to boost ratings?"

"Tony!" Maria admonished. "Ava's not like that."

"How do you know? We saw her for, like, twenty minutes," Tony grumbled.

"She's not," Luc's mother said firmly. "Luca, tell your father."

Luc ran a hand over his face. "She's not like that."

"Oh, that was convincing," Tony grumbled.

Even Maria's resolve seemed to have wavered. "Luc, she wouldn't. Would she? Your father's being overprotective, she's a good girl. Nonna and I both like her—"

"Which, we get it, you two agreeing is a bit like spotting the Loch Ness Monster," Vincent said from the doorway, "but I'm with Dad on this one."

"What are you doing here?" Maria said, scowling at her middle son. "We're speaking with Luca."

"Which was totally fine back when he was twelve and broke the window of the science building with his baseball—"

"Never happened," Luc interrupted.

"...but this is adult *family* dinner. In case you haven't noticed, there are three other people waiting in the other room."

"Not anymore," Elena said in a singsong voice.

Elena appeared next to Vin, Anthony loomed over both of them, and Nonna...

"What the ridiculous blazes is happening in here?" she asked, shoving her way forward.

New lipstick today. Purple.

Nonna shoved her bony butt into a tiny opening next to Luc's mother, who rolled her eyes and refused to budge.

"Is this a family meeting?" she asked, looking around. "I can Skype Marco in."

"Oh, by all means," Luc said. "Let's get the entire family involved in my personal life."

"Ooh, personal life," Elena said, pushing forward into the tiny room, making it feel even smaller. "What are we dealing with here? Women? No, wait...Woman. Singular. Ava?"

Luc growled. "You all know I brought her over for dinner once, right? And only at Nonna's insistence? I don't understand how you all have us on the verge of our honeymoon."

"Rumor has it she's been at your place most nights this week."

"Wonder where that started," Luc said with a pointed glare at Anthony. His oldest brother had the decency to look slightly apologetic.

"That, and you held her hand like a whipped schoolboy," Vin said, leaning against the doorway with his usual glare.

Luc ground his teeth but didn't really have a response.

The truth was, Ava sometimes *did* make him feel like a schoolboy.

Except when she made him feel very much like a man, like when she made those breathy gasps...

He shifted awkwardly and his brothers gave him a look that said, *our mother is right there, man. Keep your thoughts clean.*

"So, are we done here?" Luc said, standing. "Everyone's said what they need to say about my sex life, and my professional career, and my apparent lack of judgment?"

This last bit he said with a glare at his father, who glared right back, and the mood in the room slipped from jovial to wary in about five seconds.

"More wine," Elena muttered to herself, scooting out of the room. "Always more wine."

"What about my homemade limoncello?" Nonna said, half chasing after her. "You said you'd try it."

"She only said she'd try it because you wouldn't shut up," Luc's mother said, following the other two women out of the room. "If she wanted limoncello, she'd have *my* limoncello."

Anth and Vin exchanged a glance. "Scotch?"

"Me too!" Luc called after them. "Make it a double."

This conversation was over.

He started to follow his brothers, but his father's hand found his shoulder. "Luca."

Luc stiffened.

"I..." His father cleared his throat. "I did what I did...I say what I say...I want to protect you."

"Because I'm the *bambino*," Luc said, unable to keep the frustrated hostility out of his voice.

Tony met his eyes unflinchingly. "Because you're my

son. You think I haven't kept an eye on all my boys? You think it was easy to be police commissioner *and* father to four cops? You think it's not a daily struggle, even now, to let you live your lives without wanting to fight for you?"

No, Luc thought, searching his father's face.

It wouldn't be easy.

Not for a man who was even more dedicated to being a good dad than he had been to being a world-class cop.

Slowly, Luc nodded. "I get it."

I forgive you.

Not that his father was expecting, or even wanting forgiveness.

His father nodded back.

As far as communication went, it left a lot to be desired. But for now, it was enough.

Or so Luc thought.

"Luca," his father said when Luc was about to step into the hallway to seek out a much needed drink.

"Yeah."

"I like Ava," his father said after a brief pause. "She's smart."

Luc said nothing, bracing for the *but*.

"Just…be careful. If you're as confident as you seem that there's nothing but a short-term fling between you two, there's also nothing to stop her from prioritizing her career over your non-relationship."

The tension that had just started to dissipate increased tenfold as Luc took in the truth of what his father was trying to tell him.

He and Ava had made damn sure they both understood their zero-commitment situation.

And his father was right.

Ava wanted to be anchorwoman more than anything.

Hell, he *liked* that about her.

But if Luc was little more than a fuck-buddy…

What was to stop her from using him as a stepping-stone to her ultimate goal?

CHAPTER THIRTY-ONE

I swear to God, Sims, if you're going to try to put makeup on me again for this interview..."

"Nope," she said, topping off both of their wineglasses at her tiny kitchen table. "I've already told the crew that you've insisted on looking blotchy and tired on national television."

"Blotchy and tired, huh?" Luc asked as he took their Thai food out of the delivery bag. "You didn't seem to think I was blotchy and tired when you jumped my bones as soon as I entered the door."

She took a sip of wine. "What can I say? I *may* be changing my mind about that whole man-in-uniform thing."

He wiggled his eyebrows. "Told you. Chicks dig it."

Ava frowned before she could catch herself.

Chicks dig it.

As in, other women liked Luc in uniform.

Other women probably liked Luc *out* of uniform too.

Ava's frown became a full-on scowl, and she moved to

the fridge to put the wine away before he could catch her expression.

She had no claim on him. She knew that. Ava didn't *want* a claim on Luc Moretti or any other man. Fidelity for as long as they were sleeping together, sure. But they both knew the name of the game:

They'd part ways before things got serious.

He'd see other women. She'd...

Well...

Crap. The thought of other men didn't appeal.

And the thought of Luc's hands on another woman...that didn't appeal either. In fact, Ava was feeling downright stabby just thinking about it.

She slammed the fridge door with more force than necessary. What was going on here?

"Sims, how much pad Thai do you want?" he asked, oblivious to her unfamiliar feelings of possessiveness.

"Surprise me," she said, pasting a smile on her face and returning to the table.

He gave her a look. "Are you still sulking because I wouldn't let you order sushi again?"

She plucked a peanut from the top of the pad Thai container. "Considering the fact that you've been occasionally throwing Spicy Tuna at me as a nickname, I decided it was time to branch out."

"Well, as someone that grew up on steadily Italian fare, I'm not one to talk about variety, but I've seen you every night this week, and we've had sushi for four of them. Is that even healthy?"

"Probably not," she said as he placed a plate in front of her. "But these spring rolls aren't exactly a salad with dressing on the side now either, are they?"

In response, he picked up one of the deep-fried rolls, bit it neatly in half, and then turned it to show her the exposed filling. "You seeing what I'm seeing, Sims?"

"Steam?"

"Carrot," he said before popping the second half in his mouth.

"Three whole tiny shreds of a carrot? Pump the brakes on the health kick there, Moretti. Who says police officers have bad diets?"

Luc paused in his chewing. "Yeah, who does say that?"

She shrugged. "What can I say, the doughnut thing is pervasive."

"You're not putting any doughnut references in your story, are you?" he asked skeptically.

Ava fiddled with her fork. Talking with Luc about the news special was unavoidable. It was the entire reason they were even together.

But lately, she tensed whenever it came up "after hours."

She was too afraid that he'd ask the wrong question—or the right question, depending how you looked at it—and she'd be forced to

(a) lie to him

(b) tell him about her suspicions of a two-year-old cover-up

Either option would mean losing him. Hell, her current path of lying by omission would mean losing him.

She just wanted to put it off for as long as she could.

"Of course I'm mentioning doughnuts," she said, reaching over to pat his cheek. "It's part of my intro."

He wiped his mouth with his napkin and studied her. "You know, despite the fact that I'm the star of this thing, how is it that I don't even have the faintest inkling of what the final product will look like?"

Her eyes dropped to her plate. There he went with the questions again. There was nothing suspicious in his tone, but he was right…she'd been very deliberate about not bringing him into the production of the series.

She still dropped by the precinct from time to time, still followed him and Sawyer around once or twice a week in hopes that they'd get some sort of thrilling footage…

But for the most part she tried to separate *Officer Moretti, America's Hero* from Luc.

Her Luc.

Ava caught movement out of the corner of her eye and leaned down to see her cat accepting a piece of chicken from Luc's fingers.

Her mouth dropped open and she used her fork to point at the cat. "What is happening there?"

Luc gave her a guilty expression. "Is he not allowed table scraps?"

"No, that's not a big deal, but what is he doing out from under the couch?"

Luc reached down to scratch the cat under the chin. "What do you mean? We're buds."

"No," she said shaking her head. "Honky Tonky doesn't have *buds*. He doesn't like people."

The fat cat leaped into Luc's lap, making a liar out of her. *Traitor* she mouthed.

The cat yawned.

"Your kitty likes men in uniform too." He set the cat back on the floor so he could continue eating, and the cat mewled in protest.

"You're not even in uniform," she said, waving a hand over him.

He was wearing a white undershirt and some blue pajama

pants left by her brother on the one and only time he'd come to visit her in New York and stayed at her apartment.

Luc sat back in his chair, eating another spring roll, and Ava narrowed her eyes at the speculative way he was watching her.

"What?" she asked.

He shrugged. "Just trying to figure out what causes that look."

"I have a look?"

"Babe, you've got dozens. But there's one in particular I don't like. As though a rancid memory is stuck in your throat."

"So what, you're a poet now?" she muttered, grabbing at her wineglass.

Luc shrugged affably. "Fine. Don't talk about it."

He reached for a box of some beef dish she'd forgotten the name of, and dumped more onto his plate, the topic apparently forgotten.

He didn't push.

And unfortunately for both of them, his quiet understanding and no-pressure attitude are *exactly* what she needed to *want* to spill her guts.

So she did.

"My family is a bunch of shallow, glory-seeking jerks."

Luc's chewing slowed and he got up to fetch the wine bottle. "Okay. I knew they weren't exactly family of the year, but... what's that have to do with you?"

Ava shrugged moodily as he topped off her wineglass. "You won't get this because your family is great. But sometimes I get this feeling that mine has totally messed me up."

He sat across from her, his expression patient.

She forged on.

"It's like..." She swirled her glass but didn't take a sip. "Luc?"

"Sweetie?"

The endearment nearly broke her, but she forged on. "Am I bitchy? You know...cynical, shallow, ambitious, unlikable... you know...a bitch?"

Wordlessly he stood, picking up their wineglasses and jerking her head toward the couch. "We are not having this conversation with cold pad Thai between us."

Honky Tonky followed at his heels, leaping up to his lap the second he sat down. Ava shook her head at the sight of the broad police officer and spoiled cat lounging on her couch as though they belonged there.

She hesitantly followed after them, sitting beside Luc. It was oddly vulnerable. The cold pad Thai he mentioned may be increasingly unappealing, but it had provided a buffer.

A buffer that was nowhere to be found when he gently pulled her toward him. Ava sighed in contentment as she settled against his chest, earning a glare from her cat, who refused to budge.

His hand found a strand that had escaped her ponytail, and Ava frowned at the confusion rippling through her.

Confusion at the complexity of a hero cop who was long on charm, short on pretense, with a hidden sweet side.

How was a girl supposed to resist a combo like that?

"So," he said softly. "Who put it in your head that you're...what word did you use? Bitchy? Do I need to beat someone up?"

She shifted her cheek against his chest, adjusting her glasses slightly. "Don't you dare. You'll ruin my whole story if you go vigilante on me."

"Nah, people love that shit," he said. "But seriously... talk to me, Sims."

She shifted her cheek again, this time just for the sheer pleasure of feeling the soft warmth of his shirt.

"I talked to my dad today," she said, petting the cat, who all but rolled his eyes at her.

"The mayor himself, huh?"

She smiled at that. "Seems he found time in his busy schedule of serving Darrington, Oklahoma, to pep-talk his eldest."

"Ah, so it was one of *those* conversations."

"It's always one of those conversations," Ava said.

She heard the bitterness in her voice and hated it. Why couldn't she be one of those people who could shake off the opinions of those around her? Why couldn't she be like Beth, who could cheerfully laugh off her mother's chronic interference on all things wedding, or gently ignore her mother-in-law's demands to sing at the ceremony?

Why did Ava have to let her family and all of their relentless ambition get under her skin?

"If you hold it all in, you'll get constipated, Sims," Luc said, still playing with her hair.

She smiled, in spite of herself. "Is that what they teach you at the police academy?"

"More like street smarts learned from being the youngest in a family of five. You've got lots of opportunities to watch your older siblings sulk their way through high school. Also, Sims? You're stalling."

"Fine, okay," she said on a huff, pushing back from his chest to sit up. She reached for her wine. Took a sip, took a breath.

"I told my dad all about my story. About how it had been

approved for the prime-time spot. And he was thrilled, of
course, and then because I fed off his praise like I'm a pathetic seven-year-old, I kept going. I told him about all the
praise I've been getting from the boss, and the boss's boss,
and how I think I'm going to get a promotion out of it…"

"Okay," Luc said, tucking her hair behind her ear.

"And then I realized…I don't even know if I want it. I
don't know why I'm doing it."

He frowned. "Don't know why you're doing what?"

She forced herself to meet his eyes. "*Any* of it."

"You mean, like…this story?"

"That. And all the other crap stories CBC gives me. No
offense."

He grinned. "None taken."

"It's just…" She nibbled her fingernail. "I don't want to
just recite facts that are handed to me, I want to *find* the facts.
I want…I want to tell the stories that matter. Not the ones
that everyone else is telling because they're popular. Is this
crazy talk?"

Luc's smile was gentle. "I'm going to ask you something,
and promise to think on it for a second before you answer,
okay?"

"'Kay," she said warily.

"Why are you in broadcast journalism instead of investigative journalism? Not that the two have to be mutually
exclusive, but I've seen the way you latch on to topics. I
doubt you've *ever* been satisfied with trying to squeeze a
juicy story into two minutes of the evening news."

Ava looked at him. The question sounded so simple
rolling off his lips.

The answer, she realized, was alarmingly simple as well.
She'd pursued this path because it's the path her parents

put her on. Starting when she was sixteen and her father had gotten her an internship with the local nightly news. It had continued to her college essay...her college major...her first job...all driven by her parents.

Ava groaned and rested her head on Luc's shoulder.

"I'm pathetic."

"You're not," he said, pressing a kiss to her forehead. "Plenty of people get started on the wrong career track for the wrong reason. There's no shame in it. And you have plenty of time to course-correct."

"I know," she said quietly. "I know what I have to do, I guess. It's just...All I've ever wanted is for them to be proud of me, you know? And I know that the good parents are proud of their kids for trying their hardest, or pursuing their dreams, or whatever...my parents really will only be proud of me once I'm anchorwoman. And if they're not proud of me...who will be?"

Luc said nothing, his blue eyes steady. *I will.*

"Sims, do you *want* to be anchorwoman?"

"Of course," was on the tip of her tongue. Even now. As though her brain had just programmed itself to perk up at the word.

She waited for the old burst of anticipation to rush through her. She used to be able to picture her future so clearly. The gorgeous clothes, the cushy chair, the easy banter she'd have with her co-anchor during light stories, and the quiet intensity she'd convey during the heavier stories.

But for the first time since she'd loaded up her used Toyota Corolla and taken a one-way trip from Oklahoma to New York, Ava had a seed of doubt:

What if it wasn't enough?

What if there was more?

"I think the thing is," she said, forcing herself to meet Luc's eyes, "I'm afraid I'm sort of like that villainous career woman you see in the movies. The one that has no husband, no serious boyfriend, no baby, few friends...the one who's got the good clothes and the perfect hair but is completely hollow."

He opened his mouth, but she pushed on.

"Luc, if I died tomorrow...if I got hit by one of those annoying tour buses in midtown, what would people say at my funeral?"

He looked at her. "You're messed up."

"I'm serious!" she said, scooting closer, her fingers finding the fabric of his shirt and clinging. "Would anyone have anything to say about me that wasn't related to my career?"

"Yes. They'd also mention your unpaid parking ticket."

"Luc," she said on a little laugh, shaking him.

"Okay, okay...you want to play this creepy, morbid game, let's play it. Are you driven? Yes. Ambitious? Sure. Have you maybe let your parents push you in a direction that isn't *you*? Maybe. But Sims, none of that makes you a bad person. Not even close."

"But—"

"Your dad is an ass," he interrupted. "Frankly, your whole family sounds like a bunch of smug jerks. Family is meant to boost you up, not tear you down, and you got the short end of the stick on that front."

"But my eulogy..."

Luc groaned. "You're such a weirdo. Okay, you want to know what I'd say if someone asked me to sum up Ava Sims?"

She nodded and started to reach for her wine, but his hand grabbed her wrist. He tugged her forward until she was almost on top of him, leaving her no choice but to lift up and straddle him on the couch.

The cat, in turn, had no choice but to hop to the ground, and Ava was pretty sure she was just on the receiving end of the feline equivalent of the stink eye.

Ava refocused on Luc, assuming he was trying to distract her with sex, and she was all for it, but then she saw his face and froze.

He looked...tender.

His eyes were warm in a way she hadn't seen before, and he gently reached up to straighten her glasses before his big hand rested against her cheek, before stroking along her messy ponytail with a gentle smile.

"Sims," he said quietly. "I haven't known you long. I don't even know that I know you *well*. I don't know your favorite ice cream, or whether you love or hate scary movies. I don't know if your first kiss was a total dud, or whether you prefer lazy beach days or checking out prissy museums while on vacation. And while I *do* know that you love sushi and hate high heels and tend to be bossy, none of that's what I'll remember about you when we've parted ways."

Ava's eyes were glued to his, mesmerized by his quiet words.

"What will you remember?" she asked, her voice husky.

His hands slid up to her face, cupping her cheeks. "I'll remember the way your lips feel against mine. I'll remember the way you trust me enough to take off your high heels around me. I'll remember the way my chest squeezed when I first saw the *real* you, in the sexy glasses and messy hair. I'll remember the way you wiggled your way into my family in record time, managing to make Vincent smile, Anthony laugh, and remind Elena all the reasons she's always wanted a sister. Mostly, I'll remember the way that I haven't been able to stop thinking about you since the moment I saw you in Brinker's office."

"Liar," she said with a smile, trying to lighten the moment.

He narrowed his eyes before wrapping an arm around her waist, shifting forward so his other hand could pull his wallet out of his back pocket.

Ava frowned in confusion as he fished out a piece of paper, holding it out to her.

She took it, her fingers faltering just slightly as she recognized it.

"The parking ticket."

This time he refused to meet her eyes, looking adorably embarrassed as his eyes locked on the stained ticket in her hands.

"I told myself I was holding on to it for the exact right moment to make you pay it. Which you should, by the way...But then I just...I kept it."

His eyes lifted to hers then. "I know this is a short-term thing. For both of us. But don't ever think you're just a meaningless fling to me, Sims. You're not cold. You're...lovely."

Sims. She was always *Sims.* What was with that? Some weird way of keeping his distance?

Yet Ava's heart still melted at his awkward admission. "Lovely, huh?"

He shrugged. "Or whatever."

"Or whatever," she agreed with a smile, leaning forward to place her lips gently against his.

He kissed her back. Softly at first, although the kiss quickly heated as it seemed to every damned time they were together.

"Thank you," she said against his mouth.

"You're welcome," he said in response. "And Sims..."

He pulled back to look at her, his expression serious as his hand cupped her face. "Promise me something. Promise me that you'll stop living your life for your parents, or some outdated dream that isn't yours anymore. Promise me you'll follow your heart. Go with your gut. Whatever."

Her eyes watered at the earnestness in his expression. "You don't know what you're asking," she whispered.

You're asking me to betray you.

"I do know what I'm asking," he said, leaning forward so that his forehead rested on hers. "I'm asking you to do what's right. Because I know you're the type of woman who can do great things. Amazing things. You just have to give yourself permission."

Ava closed her eyes in agony. It was everything she wanted to hear. And it was from precisely the person she needed to hear it from. But doing as he asked...doing what was *right*, would mean losing him forever.

"Hey," he said softly, his thumbs rubbing gently across her cheeks. "What's wrong?"

I'm going to lose you.

But not yet. She didn't have to lose him yet. They still had tonight.

She tipped forward, finding his mouth with hers. In response, his hand slipped around to the back of her neck, tilting both of their heads to deepen the kiss.

Ava's fingers tangled into the soft fabric of his shirt in an effort to pull him closer. His kiss was hot and possessive, and she responded in kind, reaching her tongue for his.

It was their most intense kiss yet, made all the more intoxicating by the fact that neither seemed in a hurry to take it to the next stage. In the back of her buzzing brain, Ava registered that somehow, this kiss wasn't about sex—at least not just that—it was about something deeper and infinitely more alarming.

Luc must have felt it too, because he pulled back just slightly, resting his forehead to hers with a slightly puzzled frown, and when his eyes met hers, she saw her own unspoken question:

What is this?

She shook her head just the tiniest bit.

I don't know.

And then she crushed her mouth against his once more, the force of her body pushing him back against the couch cushions.

His came to rest lightly on her back, and although he returned her kiss, he also let her take control, as though sensing her need to make him hers, if only for one night.

When Ava finally pulled back to breathe, Luc gently tugged at the bottom of her shirt and obediently lifted her arms so he could pull the shirt over her head, letting it drop to the floor.

She was wearing one of her new bras. Nothing as outlandishly sexy as the black number of her semi-striptease, but it was white and aqua lace that she'd picked simply because she'd thought it was pretty.

Luc apparently agreed. His fingers traced softly over the top of the cup before he leaned forward and planted a sweet kiss on her breastbone.

"Lovely," he said, echoing his earlier statement. "You are lovely."

Then his fingers flicked against her back, and the bra went the way of the shirt, and in silent agreement, she lifted up to remove the rest of her clothes while he did the same.

"Bedroom?" he asked, standing above her.

In response, she placed a hand on his chest, pushing him back to the couch before launching herself on him once more.

If their kiss had been slow and purposeful, the pace now was frantic, as hands and lips grew greedy and restless. And when she reached between their bodies to stroke him he groaned and lifted his hips to hers.

"Damn it, Sims. Now."

She pulled back with a frustrated moan, tapping a finger against his chest. "Don't. Move."

She disappeared into the bedroom, coming back seconds later with a condom that he tore open and rolled on in record time before pulling her down once more to straddle him.

Her hands found his face, pulling him into a hot kiss as his hands found her hips, guiding her until she was poised above him. He paused for a heartbeat before pulling her down, sliding in inch by inch until they were as close as two people could be.

Luc pulled back from the kiss just enough to meet her eyes. He lifted a questioning eyebrow, and somehow she knew exactly what he was asking.

Me or you?

In response she lifted up slowly before sinking down on him again. She repeated the motion, even slower this time, and she gave him a silent response. *Me. I'm in control.*

Ava alternated between fast and hard and slow and torturous, Luc's hands on her hips as he let her ride him.

And when she leaned over him resting her face against his shoulder, asking him to touch her, he did, his hand sliding down to press her clit in a perfect rhythm as he rocked up into her.

Ava came first—how could she not with a guy like Luc Moretti beneath her?—and when she collapsed against his chest, he let her, stroking her back and letting her savor the sweet aftermath of her orgasm instead of immediately seeking his own.

When she finally caught her breath, she put her hands on his shoulders to sit upright, the contact slightly slippery from their sweat, and narrowed her eyes at him.

"You really are a good guy, aren't you?"

He grinned, quick and easy, before sitting up and catching her lip gently between his teeth. "Am I?"

Then his arms went around her as he thrust up once into her, hard, so her arms went around his neck and held on as he plunged in and out of her, his pace quickening until he came with a groan, and she could have sworn she heard him whisper one word. *Ava.*

CHAPTER THIRTY-TWO

Three days before Luc had to sit in a leather chair and spill his guts on national television as the grand finale of this *America's Hero* bullshit, he had a revelation:

He needed closure.

Actually, that wasn't the revelation.

He'd always known he needed closure; it was the *how* that had been eluding him for two years.

Therapy hadn't worked.

Neither had ignoring the memories.

Exercise hadn't been the answer, nor had losing himself in work. It wasn't losing himself in sex with nameless women.

It hadn't even been the support of his family, which had gone deeper than he'd even realized.

But he hoped closure was *here*, in a homey Brooklyn walk-up with a tiny patch of grass doubling as the yard and a blue bike in the front.

Joey's bike. Who'd taught him to ride it? Not his dad. His dad was dead.

Luc shook his head.

That's not what this was about.

Taking a deep breath, he headed up the steps, his hand hesitating only briefly before he forced himself to knock.

The door opened almost immediately, and a dark-haired boy with hazel eyes stood before him.

Joey.

He looked so much like Mike, it physically hurt.

But as much as Luc wanted to sink to one knee and simply stare at the boy, he knew better.

"Hey, bud. You remember me?"

"Sure," the eight-year-old said with a shrug. "Uncle Luc."

The old nickname was like a vise on Luc's heart. "Yeah. Yeah, it's Uncle Luc."

The boy stepped aside. "Where's your gun?"

"Off duty today, bud."

Actually, off-duty cops were allowed to carry, and Luc often did, but not today. Not for this.

A woman came out of the kitchen drying her hands on a blue and white towel. Luc looked up and met her familiar brown gaze.

"Hey, Bev."

"Luca."

To his surprise, she was in front of him in five steps, wrapping him in a warm hug he surely didn't deserve.

When she stepped back, there were tears in her eyes, but she was still smiling. "I'm glad you've come."

She was?

The way Luc figured, she'd only agreed to this meeting out of pity, but it wasn't pity he saw in her welcoming gaze.

"Mom, can I go play Mario?"

"Honey, you haven't seen Uncle Luc in two years. Don't you want to talk to him?"

Luc and Joey exchanged a man-to-man gaze. Eight-year-old boys didn't want to talk when there was a decent shot at playing video games on the table.

"Nah, let him go, Bev. I'll swing by another time; maybe we can throw a ball or something."

The boy's face scrunched, and Luc backtracked. "Or I can kick your butt at Mario."

"Get real," the kid said, good humor restored. "I know *all* the shortcuts."

Joey started to bound away with a cheeky grin, but drew up short when his mother cleared her throat.

"Nice to see you again, Uncle Luc," the boy said dutifully.

The boy's eyes crinkled a little like his dad's when he smiled, and Luc's chest tightened again.

"See ya, bud."

Both he and Beverly watched as Joey headed to video game heaven, and Luc gave a rueful shake of his head. "I shouldn't have stayed away."

Bev's hand touched his arm briefly. "I know why you did. No judgment here. Come on in; I've got coffee and I've got beer."

"Coffee's great," he said, following Beverly into the small but cheerful kitchen. She'd redecorated since Luc had last been here after Mike's memorial.

The former blue walls had been repainted a bright yellow, and she seemed to have some sort of citrus theme going on, with lemon and lime decorations all over the place.

He was glad it was different. Though it was still too easy to remember what it had been like before.

Luc sat at a tiny white table as she pulled a mug out of the cupboard, also with lemons on it.

He studied her, looking for signs of a broken woman, but there were none. She was simply the curvy, warm woman he remembered.

A little sadder maybe. How could she not be?

But this was not a woman who'd let herself be destroyed by the loss of a spouse.

She was a survivor.

Just as Mike would have wanted.

"You're looking good, Bev."

She laughed as she handed him the coffee, black, the way he liked it. "Good of you to say. Mid-forties aren't agreeing with me. The hair is easy enough to fix, thank you, Clairol. The lower metabolism…" She patted a rounded hip. "Not so much."

She smiled, poured herself coffee, and sat across from him, studying his face.

"You're looking happy, Luc."

The word surprised him.

Happy? Was he?

If he was, he didn't deserve to be.

Bev smiled into her coffee. "I know that look."

Luc groaned. How was it that all females thought he had a *look* lately. "Do I even want to hear this?"

"Probably not, but what kind of friend would I be if I didn't tell you that you have the mark of a woman all over you?"

He glanced down at his light gray polo and jeans.

"No, not like that," Bev said, waving her hand. "It's on your face. Someone's got you feeling happy and you don't know how to react."

An image of Ava with crooked glasses, messy hair, and a

sassy smile flitted through his mind. He pushed the thought away.

Luc wasn't going to go there. Not now. Maybe not ever.

Instead, he reached across the table for Beverly's hand. "What about you, Bev? Are *you* the woman making some guy happy?"

It was a bold question, and he hoped she wouldn't take it as an affront to Mike's memory.

But it had been two years. And if anyone deserved to be happy, it was this woman.

To his relief, a shy smile crept across her face and she glanced down at the table.

"Maybe. It's early yet, but there's this single dad at Joey's school. We've done coffee a couple times, and have dinner plans on Friday."

Luc squeezed her hand. "Can I watch Joey for you?"

She glanced up in surprise, and he regretted her astonishment. He should have been here all along, helping out.

"I should have been around," he said gruffly. "I'm hoping better late than never..."

She squeezed his hand back. "Luc. You don't owe us anything. And his grandparents are watching him this weekend. But thank you."

Luc cleared his throat. "Beverly, we never really talked about what happened that day."

"The day when Mike died."

Luc flinched at her candor. "Yes."

Bev stood and retrieved the coffeepot even though they'd both barely touched their mugs.

"Luc, have you ever talked to your mom about what it's like to be married to a cop? To have four sons that are cops?"

He frowned. What did his mother have to do with this?

"Not really," he admitted.

"Growing up, did you ever see the tension on her face when your dad was later than he said he'd be? Or the slight bracing every time he left for work in the morning?"

Luc swallowed. Nodded. Sure, he'd seen it.

Beverly's expression was both sad and kind. "Being married to a cop isn't like being married to a Wall Street broker or a bartender or a marketing manager, Luca. The back of your mind...the back of your heart...always knows that every time you kiss him good-bye in the morning might be the last time you ever see him."

Luc opened his mouth, but she cut him off.

"I know you think there were things you could have done differently, and maybe there were. But Luc, it could have just as easily happened if he'd been called to a domestic dispute case gone wrong, or hostage situation, or just some unstable whacko."

He opened his mouth again, but Bev wasn't done. "It could have just as easily been you that was shot, Luc. You ever think about that?"

Her quiet statement rolled over Luc like a semi.

He hadn't thought about that.

Not *once* had it ever occurred to him that he and Mike had walked side by side up the walkway to that decrepit house.

It hadn't even really occurred to him that he'd been two feet away from Mike when the bullets ripped through him.

Luc had never stopped to think that when the asshole had opened his front door and taken aim at a cop, he'd done so at random.

It could have just as easily been Luc who died that day.

And it could have been Mike who was beating himself up over his partner's death.

Bev nodded as she saw that he understood. "I don't blame you for feeling what you feel, Luc. I know you feel guilty, just as I know in my heart that Mike would have the same struggles, the same survivor's guilt if things had ended differently. And I would have told him what I'm telling you now: don't let a terrible twist of fate destroy your life. It's done, Luc. It's *done*. And the best any of us can do is put our best foot toward tomorrow."

Luc started to take a sip of coffee before realizing that he didn't even want it.

"Bev, there's something I need to tell you about that day. Something I should have talked to you about a long time ago."

She nodded once, telling him to continue.

Luc took a deep breath. "So you know that Mike and I were first on the scene the day Shayna Johnson didn't come home from school. We were in the area when the call came through, so we took the statement from the parents, talked to the neighbors...the whole bit. Later, of course, the case became much bigger, but by then, Mike and I were both invested...obsessed, even, with the case."

Bev cupped her coffee mug with both hands. "I remember. It was all he could talk about at dinner. He wanted so badly to find that little girl."

Me too.

Luc was quiet, remembering, before he forced himself to continue. "That day when we got the call that a witness a few streets over kept hearing a little kid cry for help from a second-story window..."

He forced himself to meet Beverly's eyes. "I *knew*, Bev. I knew the kid was Shayna, knew that Jonas Black was our guy. We'd interviewed that bastard twice. I *knew* something wasn't right. Wrote it in all my reports, but didn't have a lick of evidence beyond my hunch..."

He swallowed. Continued.

"I wanted to park up the street, go in the back, but the orders were to stay put. We had to play it by the book. The woman that had called in the tip was something of a crank. Lots of false reports, shit like that, so we were supposed to sit and wait for the damned search warrant, wait for the green light to go in."

Luc took a sip of coffee. It was cold now, and Bev just looked at him with her steady, quiet gaze as he continued.

"Finally it came over the radio that the judge wouldn't authorize the warrant. Best we could do was knock and see if anything was amiss. It was bullshit. *Total bullshit*. Mike said he'd back me up if I wanted to trust my gut. Said *he* trusted my gut. But I didn't want to get him in trouble."

Luc put his elbows on the table, head in his hands. "Black saw our car, Bev. He saw us, panicked, and strangled that little girl. Then he opened the front door, firing his gun before Mike or I could even think to draw ours."

He fell silent again, before ending his story in a husky voice. "You know the rest. He fired three shots. One went wild, two hit Mike. Then the bastard dropped the gun and ran."

Beverly spoke for the first time. "And you ran after him. Caught him."

"Yeah," Luc said, his voice rough. "While Mike lay there dying."

"Don't," she said, shaking her head. "Mike died instantly. You know that."

Luc did know that. At least, he knew that's what they'd told him. The first bullet that hit Mike had literally exploded his heart.

"Luc," she said, her hand once again reaching across the table. "I'm glad you're telling me this for your sake. But you didn't need to. There's nothing you did that requires my forgiveness."

"I could have done something differently, Bev. I could have made a different choice, and Mike and that little girl would still be alive."

She studied him for a long while, and finally she nodded. "Okay then. If that's the case, I forgive you."

I forgive you.

He let it sink in. Tried to speak, but his throat felt abnormally large and dry.

Wordlessly he pushed awkwardly to his feet and, moving to her side of the table, pulled her into a rough hug, which she returned.

"Thank you," he said against her hair. "Thank you."

She rubbed his back. "Does this mean you won't avoid us anymore?"

He laughed guiltily. "Yeah. This means you're going to be stuck seeing a lot more of me."

She pulled back, her eyes watery as her hands found his face. "I'm glad. Mike would have wanted you to know Joey. Plus, it'll be good to have a cop around if this new guy turns out to be an ass."

"You call me anytime," he said in all seriousness, even though she'd been joking.

She smiled. "I've missed you, Luca."

"I've missed you too. I don't know what I'm more ashamed of, that I waited this long to come by, or that I barge in on your Saturday without a word of warning."

She waved this away as they headed to the door. "Don't even. I'll call Joey down so you can say bye."

Luc shook his head. "Nah. The dude hardly knows me; I'll have a better time winning him over if I let him sneak in a few more minutes of video game time."

"Oh, sure, make me the bad guy when I call him down to help me fold laundry."

"Give him five more minutes, Mom. Let him enjoy the good stuff for a little bit longer."

Her eyes went sad, just for a second, and he knew she understood his silent meaning: *life is short.*

She opened the door and he kissed her cheek before stepping onto the porch. "Thanks again, Bev. For everything."

"Oh gosh, my pleasure. Not every day one gets to see America's Hero in the flesh."

Luc groaned. "You've seen the YouTube videos?"

She laughed. "Of course! Joey and I watched them half a dozen times when they came on the local news. And I bet your family's over the moon that you're about to become a national sensation."

Luc frowned. "How did you know about that?"

Bev looked puzzled. "Well, the reporter told me, obviously."

Luc went cold. "Reporter?"

"Sure, the one from CBC? She was here a couple days ago, saying they were doing a small segment on Mike as part of the special."

The entire world around Luc seemed to go silent. He didn't hear the cars on the street, the couple fighting next door, or the kids yelling nearby. He only watched Beverly's mouth move as he tried to comprehend what she was saying.

"This reporter, what was her name?"

"Um, Anna? Ava? I can get her card..."

Luc closed his eyes. "No. I know her."

Beverly looked thoroughly confused. "Was I not supposed to talk to her? I thought you knew, assumed that's what prompted you to come by today..."

Luc took a step backward, pasting a smile on his face. "Don't worry about it, you didn't do anything wrong. I should have figured she'd find her way here. That's what reporters do, right? Dig into your past?"

"Okay, but, Luc..."

He gave her a wave before turning and walking toward the street like a zombie.

Ava knew about Mike.

Which meant she knew about Shayna.

Two days ago, Ava had gone to Mike's widow's house.

And last night she hadn't breathed a word about it.

Luc stopped in the middle of the sidewalk and closed his eyes.

His father was right. Ava Sims was going to sell him out for the sake of her own career.

CHAPTER THIRTY-THREE

Ava held up a finger to stop Carly, who was coming at her with yet another makeup brush. Her eyes scanned the studio for the hundredth time.

"Has anyone seen Officer Moretti?" she yelled over the clatter.

A handful of people looked up from their clipboards and shrugged.

"Where the hell is he?" she muttered as the makeup artist motioned for her to close her eyes so she could apply a contouring eye shadow.

Today was it.

The face-to-face interview and the finale of *America's Hero*. The execs had tossed around the idea of filming it on location at Luc's apartment, but Ava pushed to have it on set in the studio.

She hadn't wanted to invade his home. At least, not more than she already had.

Ava opened one eye so she could see her cell phone and sent Luc a text. Another one:

Where are you?

Her thumb scrolled up so she could see their entire text conversation. Her latest message meant that it had been one, two...eight texts from her since the last one from Luc.

Three days ago.

She tapped the corner of her phone against her knee and tried not to freak out.

Then Brent Davis came storming up to her with murder on his face, and not freaking out wasn't really an option.

"Avie, where's your interview subject? We're supposed to start in fifteen minutes, he hasn't been through makeup, hasn't got his mic on..."

"Relax, Davis," she said with calm she didn't feel. "It's not like this is live."

The show would be taped today but wouldn't be aired for a couple of months. By which time, Officer Moretti would have nothing to do with her.

The script she'd been practicing all morning assured that.

A script that ensured there was a very real possibility that he might walk off camera when she blindsided him with questions about November 12, two years ago.

Her bosses wouldn't be happy at the unexpected drama on a feel-good piece, but that's not what Ava was worried about. They might get pissed...might even cut the story, go with something lighter, but that's okay...because this story was big enough that someone else would pick it up. One of the other networks. Or the *Times*, *Wall Street Journal*.

There was a story here. A career-making one. She was positive of it.

She should be thrilled.

But *thrilled* was hardly the emotion lodged in Ava's heart. It felt a lot more like dread.

Because there would be drama, yes. There would also be hurt.

Luc's hurt.

She pushed the thought away as she pep-talked herself. "This is what you've been working toward, Ava."

"What's that, babe?" Carly asked.

"Nothing," she muttered.

"Well he'd better be here," Davis said, hands on hips.

"I'm sure he's just running late," she said.

"And he knows to come in uniform?"

"Yes."

"And he—"

"Davis. I've handled it."

He made a grumbling noise before heading back to the set to yell at the lighting guys.

"Handled it, have you?"

Ava shifted the eye not currently being mascaraed to the right, where Mihail stood, arms crossed, for once free of his usual gummy worms.

"Talking to me again?" she asked.

He shrugged moodily. "Davis brought me in to man one of the cameras."

"And you agreed?" Ava asked, surprised. Mihail hated studio camera work. He always claimed that a monkey could hold a camera still. He preferred to be on the move, camera on his shoulder.

Mihail shrugged again. "Figured someone should be here to buy Moretti a drink after his girlfriend screws him over."

Ava's temper flashed. As did her guilt.

She shifted her gaze to the makeup artist with a sympathetic smile. "Can I have a minute?"

"Actually, I think I'm done," Carly said, standing back to admire her handiwork. "Let me powder you and I'll be gone."

Thirty seconds later, it was just Mihail and Ava.

"First of all," she said, keeping her voice cool, "I'm not Luc's girlfriend."

"Got it, so you're just using him for his body *and* to further his career. Classy."

That stung. "Mihail!"

He didn't bother to look contrite. "When you guys are cuddled up in bed, did you tell him that you went to see his dead partner's wife?"

She looked away.

"No? How about when you barged in on that little girl's family, bringing up the worst point of their lives."

"I didn't barge in," she said quietly.

That much, at least, was true. Both Beverly Jensen and the Johnsons had been more than willing to talk to her.

Mrs. Jensen, because she was eager to share her support of Luc. The woman bore no ill feelings that Luc had survived while her husband had died.

Shayna Johnson's parents had been more guarded.

They'd agreed to talk to her, only in hopes that it would shed more light on the need to act swiftly in kidnapping cases.

Terrence and Jasmine Johnson held sorrow, but no bitterness.

Darius Johnson, on the other hand . . .

Well, Shayna's older brother hadn't been nearly so forgiving of the NYPD's treatment of his sister's kidnapping and death.

Nor the media cover-up that followed.

And it was Darius Johnson's statements that would have Ava's bosses practically bouncing out of their seats with excitement.

It didn't get much juicier than law enforcement covering up the death of two people. One of them a young girl.

And Luc wouldn't see it coming.

Because she hadn't told him.

Mihail's finger jabbed toward her face. "Right there. Guilt."

She slapped his hand away. "Luc's not going to take it personally."

He told me to follow my gut.

Of course, he didn't know just where her gut would lead her.

"So he told you all about it himself, did he? Maybe over dinner, drinks, he told you about watching his partner die and finding a dead little girl?"

Ava's heart twisted.

No. He hadn't told her. And she hated how much it bothered her that he hadn't.

But there was something else bothering her too... something darker that she couldn't shake.

It was that Darius Johnson's account of what happened that day, and the following days, proved Ava had been right all along.

That there really was no such thing as a *true* hero.

Luc Moretti's record wasn't all saving babies and taking care of the homeless.

There was death there too.

Possibly even mistakes, if Darius's versions were correct.

And yet none of that was bothering her as much as the fact that she hadn't heard from Luc in three days.

She'd told herself he was busy, and that they weren't in a relationship, and that she shouldn't expect they'd hang out every day, but...

She missed him.

Officer Moretti might not be who she'd thought—secretly hoped—he was.

But Luc?

Luc was important to her.

And she was about to throw him under the bus.

"Finally!" Davis shouted from the other side of the studio as he strode toward the door. "What the hell took you so long?"

Ava's shoulders straightened.

Luc.

Her eyes sought and found him immediately. As instructed, he was wearing his uniform, and her heart caught in her throat, even though she'd seen him in uniform dozens of times over the past two months.

Today, she let herself see Officer Moretti with fresh eyes. Saw the way his arms filled out the crisp blue of his shirt, the way his pants fit his lean figure perfectly.

But it was more than the dead-sexiness of an alpha man in uniform.

It was the pride with which he wore it.

And that's when it hit her. It didn't matter that Luc Moretti wasn't a perfect cop, because there was no such thing as a perfect cop. No such thing as a perfect *anything*, really.

But she didn't care about that.

Because Luc was a good man.

A *great* man.

A man who put on that uniform every day, not for the prestige, not for the television, not even for his own career advancement, but because he was purely *good*.

He was Ava's opposite in every way.

Ava, whose only goal in life thus far was to get ahead in her career, helping no one.

Why the hell was she letting her life be dictated by people she didn't like, rather than people she *did*?

"Something's wrong," she said quietly.

"Ya think?" Mihail grumbled darkly.

"No, with Luc. He hasn't looked at me."

He'd been in the studio for several minutes now, but not once had his eyes moved around the room to search for her.

This wasn't the man who'd held her just a few nights ago and made passionate love to her on her couch.

It wasn't the man who'd befriended her heinous cat, or ate sushi four days in a row just because she loved it.

Ava had never really let herself acknowledge it before, but there had always been this humming presence between her and Luc.

Whenever they were in the same room, even on the same street, there was a connection.

They *felt* each other. She knew where he was at all times, and he always seemed to have an eye on her, even when he wasn't actually looking at her.

That connection was gone.

She couldn't feel him anymore. And she was afraid she knew why.

He knew.

Somehow he'd found out that she'd gone behind his back, researching his past.

And he *knew* she was going to use it to her advantage. To launch her career in investigative journalism even as she gave up her chance at anchorwoman.

"He's going to walk," she said, her eyes never leaving Luc's stony profile. "He's going to refuse to do the interview."

"Then why's he letting someone put on his mic?" Mihail asked.

Ava frowned. Mihail was right. Luc was standing there, letting the sound guys hook him up. He even let the makeup girl near him, although not without a glare.

He was going to go through with it. He knew what was coming; she knew he knew—she could sense it. But he was going to do it anyway.

But why?

Ava should be thrilled. She was getting exactly what she wanted, but it felt...hollow. Rotten, almost.

"Okay, people, let's get in places," Haley, the production manager, said. "Ava, what's with your shoes?"

She glanced down at her flip-flops. Right.

Mihail handed over her bag and she muttered a terse thanks, ignoring the challenge in his expression.

What did he expect her to do? Inform them that she hated wearing high heels?

Or better yet, tell them that she wasn't going to dig into the messy part of Luc's past just because it would make for a juicier story?

This is how it's done, she wanted to tell Mihail.

Or maybe she was telling herself.

She'd splurged on the shoes. Black Louboutins with their trademark red soles. Ava had been longing for the classic shoes since she stepped foot in New York six years ago.

Now they felt tight, somehow.

She put them on anyway.

The interview stage was designed to look like a comfortable, classy living room. Big brown leather chairs, navy carpet, a coffee table that was already outfitted with water glasses and mugs and a carafe. Rarely did anyone actually drink from the mugs during the interviews, but having the option made it seem like it was just a couple of friends sitting down to chat over coffee.

Luc was already on stage, but had yet to look at her.

Definitely not two friends sitting down to coffee.

Every instinct in Ava's body demanded that she go to him. Talk to him Ava to Luc, not maintain chilly Ava Sims to Officer Moretti silence.

But something stopped her.

Terror.

Though she didn't know if it was terror about losing the story, or fear of losing him.

And the fact that the latter fear was the scariest thing of all.

It wasn't supposed to be like this, she thought as Haley impatiently sat Ava in the chair, motioning for her to cross her legs to the left so she wouldn't flash the camera, before positioning Luc.

He didn't need much help; he'd look good no matter what. A gorgeous, good-guy cop.

America's Hero.

She watched him as he listened to last-minute instructions from Haley. His face was tense, his eyes wary.

She'd done that to him. Ava had made him America's Hero.

As though his being *Luc* wasn't enough.

She knew now. Luc Moretti was more than enough, just as he was.

The lights in the studio went out except for the stage, and Ava heard Haley holler for quiet.

A glance at the prompter told her they were ready.

Three, two, one...

It was go time.

Only then did Luc meet her eyes.

And what she saw nearly broke her heart.

CHAPTER THIRTY-FOUR

Luc made it through the first half of the interview as if he were in a trance, his responses on autopilot as he answered the innocuous questions.

Ava: So you're a born and bred New Yorker. Ever thought about moving somewhere else?

Luc: Never.

Ava: You live with your brother and grandmother. What's that like?

Luc: About like you'd expect; the food is excellent, the privacy nonexistent.

Ava: When did you know you wanted to be a police officer?

Luc: I'm not sure there was ever a choice. It's who I am.

Ava: You come from a pretty impressive cop legacy. What's it like being the son of the former NYPD Commissioner?

Luc: Let's just say it brings a whole different meaning to *father knows best*.

Ava: Tell us about that day in Battery Park. What were you thinking when that little girl went over?

Luc: You don't think in a situation like that. You react.

Ava: You gave your coat away on one of the coldest winters in New York history. Did you get another one?

Luc: I bought a new one the day after, although I continue to receive replacements from generous people who saw the video... I appreciate the sentiment, although I donate those to a homeless shelter and encourage viewers to do the same.

The questions went on and on, and Luc forced himself not to snap at Ava that she already knew all of this stuff.

Because he wasn't talking to Ava, friend and lover.

He was talking to Ava Sims, reporter. She looked the part too. She had on some expensive, sexy heels. Her hair was shiny and perfect and sort of hard looking, molded into big waves. Her glasses were nowhere in sight, nor were her yoga pants. She wore an emerald green blouse and black slacks. She looked pretty. Perfect.

He hated it. Hated her.

He wanted *messy* Ava back.

But messy, approachable Ava had been a fake, hadn't she?

Because although he knew he'd seen glimpses of the *real* Ava—sweet, funny, and vulnerable—the aspiring anchorwoman part of her was bigger. Bolder.

It was this cold, calculating Ava that had ruthlessly dug into his past and then instead of talking to him about it, gone behind his back to talk to Beverly Jensen and the Johnson family.

His family had begged him not to come today, and up until an hour before, Luc had fully intended to skip this farce of an interview. He couldn't stop them from running the footage and info they already had, but that didn't mean he had to be a willing participant.

But his family hadn't known the whole truth. Hadn't known that it was Luc himself who had pushed her to this. Luc who'd insisted she follow her gut, tell the big stories, blow off the superficial BS and dig for *truth*.

She was dedicating her whole heart to her career, and really, was Luc any different?

Were *any* of the Morettis different? Cops got credited with being a lot more noble than reporters, but at the end of the day, they were both jobs. And more important, they could both be dreams.

Being a journalist was Ava's dream, and he couldn't bring himself to take that away from her.

Even if he destroyed his own dreams in the process.

And so he made two phone calls. One to Bev, the other to the Johnsons. He wanted their blessing before talking about their loss on national television, and he'd gotten it.

They'd all agreed that it was time—that some publicity would do more good than harm.

And so Luc had come to the studio. For Shayna. For Mike. For himself.

But mostly for Ava.

He'd done it for her, even though she'd betrayed him.

Luc refused to let himself acknowledge what that might mean, but some part of him already knew. Knew that his feelings for this woman went deeper than he'd realized.

Her questions continued, alternating between cheeky and somber.

Is it true what they say about cops and doughnuts?

How do you think 9/11 changed the perception of first responders, especially in New York?

Then she asked him one that caused him to stumble for the first time since he'd sat in the overstuffed chair.

All the ladies out there are wondering, so I have to ask… are you single?

Previously, Luc had been looking at Ava without really seeing her…not wanting to connect with her now that he knew what was coming.

But with that last question, his eyes zeroed in on hers, and she lifted an eyebrow. A challenge.

Challenge accepted, Sims.

"Yes, I'm definitely single," he said, his eyes never leaving hers.

Ava was a professional, and the only sign that his response hit close to home was a slight, almost imperceptible, shifting in her chair.

"I'm sure the single women of New York will be glad to hear it," she said with an easy smile, giving away nothing. "Are you looking to settle down someday?"

He knew that she was asking for the benefit of the viewers.

All day, she'd been asking questions that she already knew the answer to, and this one was no different.

Except it *was* different, somehow. They both knew it.

There was a too-long silence, and out of the corner of his eye, he saw that Haley woman exchange a puzzled glance with her assistant.

Then he cleared his throat. "You know, being married to a cop is hard. Really hard. I don't want to put any woman through that."

"What if she decided it was worth the risk?" Ava said.

Her easy smile never wavered, but Luc found himself searching her face all the time.

Was this just another generic interview question?

Or something more?

Luc intentionally let a wide grin spread over his face. "Well then I guess I'd have to decide if *she* were worth the risk."

There was a beat of silence. Everyone watching would assume his response was a guy response, just a twenty-something dude trying to maintain his bachelor status for as long as possible.

But the slight flinch in Ava's features told him she heard it for what it was.

He was telling her that *she* was a risk.

One he wasn't willing to take.

Ava recovered. "A dedicated bachelor then," she said with an answering smile.

"I think so." He fake-smiled right back and their gazes clashed for a second too long before she leaned forward to take a sip of water.

Her hand shook just the tiniest bit, and Luc instinctively tensed before forcing himself to relax his shoulders.

It was coming.

She sat back in her chair and Luc waited for her to triumphantly throw down her trump card.

But to his surprise, there was hesitation there.

No, more than hesitation. Agony.

She didn't want to do this.

She didn't want to sell him out.

For a second, Luc felt like he could fly.

Until he remembered that it didn't have to come to this. She could have told Luc earlier what she was planning.

Every step of the way, Ava had made it clear *this* was what she'd wanted more than anything. It was time to see it through.

He patiently waited for her gaze to come back to his. The entire hesitation had probably lasted only a couple of seconds; likely the audience would see it as nothing more than a slight gathering of thoughts, but it felt much longer.

And when her eyes finally found his, she looked so bewildered and lost that he wanted to rip off both of their mics, hold out his hand to her, and lead them both away from this circus.

Instead, he nodded at her. Nothing obvious. Just the slightest tip of his head.

Permission.

Do it, Sims.

And so she did.

"Officer Moretti, as I was researching your impressive history as a police officer, I couldn't help but notice there was a bit of a, shall we say, blip on your record…"

Luc refused to acknowledge the pain that ripped through him.

You can do this.

It was time to put everything behind him. It was time to move on.

And Ava had just made it really easy to move on from *her*.

CHAPTER THIRTY-FIVE

It had taken a serious amount of groveling, but Luc had eventually convinced Nonna and Anthony to give him his space.

Actually, Anthony had agreed almost immediately. After making sure that Luc wasn't inclined to do anything stupid, Anth had quietly packed an overnight bag. His brother understood that sometimes being alone with whiskey and dark thoughts was exactly what a situation called for.

Nonna, on the other hand, had only been coaxed out of the apartment when Anthony held a lighter under her precious yoga mat and threatened to toss all her lacy push-up bras in exchange for bulk cotton bras from the local drugstore.

Luc had thought his grandmother was going to faint at the notion, and she'd finally agreed to leave, only after making Luc homemade macaroni and cheese. It wasn't classic Italian in the least, but it *was* bona fide comfort food.

Luc hadn't touched it.

Neither had he gone for the whiskey, although he figured that would be on the agenda at some point tonight. For now, it was him, a beer, ancient flannel pants, and hopes of losing himself in TV, or a book, or anything that would save him from thoughts of Ava.

It was strange how one could carry around two years of emotional baggage, finally heal, only to be ripped wide open by a woman.

Even more ironic was that it was the same woman who'd helped him come to grips with the first issue.

Without Ava and her CBC vultures shining a light on every dark corner of Luc's past, he'd never have gotten the courage to talk to his brothers about his nightmares.

His father never would have come clean about his interference with the media two years ago.

Luc wouldn't have gone to see Mike's widow, wouldn't have called to check in on the Johnsons...

He certainly wouldn't have talked about it on national television. Wouldn't have spoken about his feelings of guilt that often came with the sometimes no-win world of law enforcement.

Luc couldn't quite say he was over what happened that day. He probably wouldn't ever be over it, and that was okay.

But for the first time, he felt like he could move on. Each breath was just a little bit easier.

Luc tipped his beer back. Not that he'd be sending Ava and her people a thank-you note. Any good that had come out of her manipulation was a happy coincidence.

It certainly wasn't from good intentions.

Luc wasn't sure that Ava Sims had any.

He swore softly and stood to get another beer as he

remembered what an ass he'd made of himself at her apartment a week ago. When she'd asked if she was a cold, calculating bitch, he should have said *yes*.

Instead he'd looked into those lying gold eyes and let himself be totally fooled by a truly beautiful face.

And the hell of it was?

He didn't hate her. Not even now, when he knew he'd been thoroughly used.

What he felt for Ava wasn't hate, or dislike, or antipathy.

It felt alarmingly the *opposite* of that. A word Luc wasn't ready to put a name to under the best of circumstances, and certainly not when the circumstances were what they were:

Completely shitty.

He popped the top off his beer, but set it on the counter instead of taking a drink. He couldn't seem to help but torture himself, wondering what she was doing now.

Popping the champagne with her skeevy co-workers?

Laughing with Mihail as they planned their next story?

Would she still work for CBC? He had no idea how that worked. He knew she wouldn't deliver the story she wanted, but it was a headlines grabbing story all the same. That had to count for something.

He hoped so. In spite of everything, he still wanted that for her, because *she* wanted that.

In spite of it all, he cared enough about her to want her happiness. Desperately.

He was an idiot.

"This sucks," he muttered to nobody.

He was halfway back to the couch to resume his brooding when there was a knock at the door.

A strange sense of calm came over him as he moved to open it.

He knew it wouldn't be his brothers.

Nor would it be Nonna or his interfering parents.

It wouldn't be Lopez or any of his other guy friends.

He opened the door.

Ava.

While he wasn't surprised to see her standing there, he *was* surprised to see this version of Ava.

Gone was the smart-looking blouse and pressed pants and perfect makeup.

Her brown hair was pulled back in a messy knot and her lipstick was long gone. Her feet were in flip-flops, her glasses just slightly askew on her nose. Seriously, why didn't she get ones that fit better?

"Sims," he said, leaning against the doorjamb.

"Moretti." She pushed past him.

"Come on in," he muttered.

He'd barely closed the door before she threw a crumpled-up ball of paper at his head. He dodged it. "What the hell?"

"I'm not paying that damn ticket."

In spite of everything, he nearly smiled as he played dumb. "What ticket?"

"The one you left on my desk at the station!" she snapped. "You can shove it up your *ass*, Moretti."

He lifted an eyebrow, mockingly.

She got in his face, shoving at his shoulders, and he was surprised to see anger in her eyes. Why the hell was *she* angry?

A tear ran down her cheek and Luc felt real alarm, even though he was supposed to be mad at her. "Sims?"

"Why'd you do it?" she asked.

"Honestly, if I knew you were going to be such a pain in the ass, I probably wouldn't have bothered with the ticket," he muttered. "I'd have let you be some other cop's problem."

She shoved at his shoulders again. "No, I mean why'd you get up there and let me ask you those questions?"

Ah. *That.*

He swallowed. Lied. "I didn't know you were going to ask them."

"You knew. You *knew.*"

"Yeah, I knew, though not because you told me!" he exploded, temper snapping. "What the hell, Sims?"

Her eyes darted away, guilty, as she should be. "When we were feeding each other spicy tuna rolls you couldn't find two seconds to say, by the way, I know about Shayna and Mike and the cover-up?"

"It's not a cover-up, not officially," she said quietly. "We did our homework. There's no way anyone can press charges against you or your father, or your brothers for colluding."

"Oh, well, that's nice, Sims, thanks for that," he said sarcastically. "That makes me feel so much better about the fact that I fucked up and people *died.*"

"You didn't fuck up," she said quickly. "I tried to make that clear by the end of the interview that there was nothing you did wrong."

"But you certainly planted the seed, didn't you? Had to make sure everyone knows a little girl and another cop *died* on America's Hero's watch."

"You're twisting my words."

"Yeah, Sims, *you're* the victim here," he said, swearing and moving toward the kitchen, needing space from her.

"Luca—"

The sound of his name on her lips ripped at him, and he closed his eyes. She moved up behind him.

"Why did you let me?" she asked, her voice small. "I need to know."

He turned around, prepared to lay into her about how she didn't have the right to ask anything of him. He'd already given her everything.

But then he saw the vulnerability on her face, and all he could see was a woman who'd never been loved, not really. A woman who had everything she'd ever wanted within her grasp but who wasn't really sure it was what she wanted after all.

He knew the feeling.

And though he knew it was the worst kind of mistake, he did what he hadn't done that day two years ago. He acted on his instincts.

He pulled her toward him.

The kiss was hard at first. He meant it to be hard, punishing and fast, just to give them both a taste of what could have been, but when she made a soft noise against him, he couldn't bring himself to push her away.

The kiss gentled, their lips brushing softly, their tongues teasing. Her hands slipped up his back and his found her face. The kiss went on endlessly, a quiet declaration of something neither would say out loud.

When he took her hand and led her to the bedroom, she let him lead her.

And when he roughly pulled her shirt over her head, pushing her pants down her hips, she let him do that too.

She wasn't wearing a bra, and he didn't bother with preliminaries as he took her the way he wanted. His knees bent, his head dipped, and he wrapped her nipple in his mouth, suckling her as she clutched at his head.

He moved to the other breast as her fingers fumbled with his belt, and he stepped back just long enough to take off his own clothes before wrapping an arm around her slim waist and pulling her back to the bed.

His eyes held hers as his fingers hooked into her panties, tossing them aside as he spread her thighs. His gaze held hers as he lowered until his shoulders were behind her legs and his mouth was inches from where she was already damp and ready for him.

She started to remove her glasses, but he stopped her with a curt, *don't.*

Then he licked her, his gaze held hers until she cried out and arched her back, breaking the eye contact. He licked and suckled and teased, his assault rapid and relentless, only to stop when she was seconds away from release.

Her eyes were glazed with unfulfilled passion as he moved up her body, and when he kissed her, she returned his kiss sweetly and urgently.

He couldn't remember ever wanting a woman so badly, and yet once again, the kiss gentled in a way he hadn't experienced before.

There was heat and urgency, and there was something else there as well, and instinctively he knew what it was...

Their bodies knew what their minds struggled to accept. This was the end.

Her legs parted and he settled between them.

He pushed into her slowly, their breathing shallow and rough as they each tried to make it last.

When he was buried all the way inside, he pressed his face to her neck and stayed perfectly still.

Ava.

They moved slowly, the mating slow and hedonistic as though they were in some sort of trance.

Her hands found his face, forcing him to look at her as their pace quickened. "Say my name, Luc."

He tried to look away, but she wouldn't let him. "Please."

Luc let out a sound of outrage as he understood what she was really asking for. Forgiveness. A chance.

And he cared about her.

But he wouldn't take the risk.

Instead of saying anything, he buried his face against her neck, exploding with a gasp.

He felt her convulse around him seconds later, their bodies shuddering together in a harmony that their hearts would never find.

Luc wanted to linger, and it was *because* he wanted to, he forced himself to move the second the aftershocks came to a stop.

He stood, pulling his pants back on without looking at her, quietly picking up her clothes, handing them to her without making eye contact.

"Luc?" Her voice was questioning.

"You should go, Sims."

She sucked in a breath. "Seriously? What was this, a booty call?"

He shrugged. "I didn't ask you here; you just showed up."

Pain flashed across her face, but he refused to relent. "Sims, we knew what this was coming to. No relationship, remember? I'm not going to put any woman through being married to a cop, not knowing if he's coming home each night. Especially not you."

Her eyes narrowed as she stood, pulling on her panties and bra as she continued to glare at him. "Why *especially not me*, Luc? Is it the same reason why you showed up today, sacrificing your own reputation for the sake of my career."

She was trying to coax him into an admission, and he sidestepped.

He gritted his teeth. "You got what you wanted, Sims. Did they offer you the anchorwoman position, or did you take your ammunition and go to a competitor?"

"They offered it," she said quietly. "They were a little shocked at first, but they said it was too big of an exclusive to pass up, even if it's not their original vision."

His heart soared on her behalf just for a minute, but her next words shut him down.

"But I'm not going back to CBC."

Huh? "Why, you get a sweeter offer somewhere else?"

"Nope. I quit."

"You what?"

What the hell?

She lifted a shoulder. "Well I guess *technically* I haven't quit yet, but I plan on it."

"What the *fuck*, Sims. Journalism is your life. You were born to tell stories."

She lifted her chin, met his eyes. "Maybe there's something I want more."

Something hot and hopeful surged through him, but he stifled it before he could identify it.

Luc turned away. "You betrayed me, Sims. Let's just leave it at that."

"No way, it's too late for that, Luc. Don't play this game. You don't get to invite me in, make love to me like a man *in love*, and then decide you're still mad at me after all."

He left the room, but she followed.

"You want me to grovel, I will," she said. "I should."

"Yeah, you should, Sims." He retrieved his beer, taking a reluctant sip.

She spread her arms. "Okay. Let's go. I was wrong, Luc. So, *so* wrong. I knew something was weird about the Shayna

Johnson incident weeks ago, and I should have asked you about it."

He turned away.

She kept going. "And when I talked to Beverly Jensen and learned about what happened with Mike, I should have told you that too. And when I put the pieces together that your dad had called in favors—"

"Leave my dad out of it," he snapped.

"I *did* leave him out of it," she shot back. "Did you miss the fact that I never *once* mentioned your family's involvement? CBC is pissed that I 'forgot' that part, but I would never do that to you."

He snorted. "Right. Because you *clearly* have a moral compass."

Her hand found his arm. "Luc, you're the one that's been telling me all along that you weren't a saint. I'm not saying that I didn't act selfishly. I did, and I'll spend the rest of my life hating myself for it, but we set out to show the full picture of being a cop, and we did."

"I can't wait to get my gold star in the mail," he muttered, shaking off her hand.

Her fingers came right back, wrapping firmly around his wrist and pulling him around. He let her.

"You're a good cop, Luc. You didn't do anything wrong. You know it, I know it, and the people that matter know it."

She released him long enough to go to her purse, which she'd left by the door, and came back with a small recorder. She handed it to him.

"What's this?"

"It's the audio of the video Mihail helped me record before I came here."

He looked at her. "Sum it up for me."

Ava licked her lips. "It'll be the follow-up to the interview, in case CBC…twists things. In it, I explain everything I just told you. That neither Beverly Jensen, nor Shayna Johnson's parents, nor any law enforcement officers find fault with anything that you do."

He rolled his eyes, tossing the recorder aside, but she pressed on, her voice louder, stronger.

"I've already called contacts at competing networks that will air it, Luc. It'll set the record straight. It'll show the viewers what took me way too long to understand. That you're America's Hero not because of your acts, but because of your *heart*. That you'd be less of a hero if you didn't beat yourself up every day for the death of a friend and a little girl. I tell them that—"

He closed his eyes. "Get out, Ava."

"But—"

"Out!"

"Don't you understand what I'm trying to tell you?" she asked. "I'm trying to tell you I—"

"It doesn't matter!" he yelled with a wild wave of his arm. "What did you think was going to happen, that you'd apologize and in a few months we'll be curled up on the couch, watching your stupid TV series while planning our wedding? Fat fucking chance."

Her eyes filled with tears, and he fisted his hand so he didn't reach for her.

"There's no future for us, Ava. I showed up today for you, yes. I care about you and wanted you to get what you'd sought so desperately to achieve. But that's as far as we go."

"But I said I was wrong—"

He held up a hand. "Don't. We're both getting what we

want. You can still go be a superstar journalist. Go get your damned Pulitzer Prize, or whatever."

"And you? What will *you* get?"

Luc moved toward his front door, opening it as he picked up her purse and held it out to her.

"Solitude."

Ava gracefully took her purse out of his hand, chin held high as she accepted her banishment. "You're being an ass, you know that, right?"

Luc shrugged. *Don't care.*

Her eyes continued to hold his. "I love you. You know that too, right?"

Her soft-spoken words did something dangerous in the vicinity of his heart, and once again, he almost reached for her. Almost.

"I can't, Sims. I can't."

She pressed her lips together and nodded once.

Then she walked away.

CHAPTER THIRTY-SIX

I look horrible in coral," Ava said, staring at her reflection.

Beth came up beside her, radiant in her wedding dress. She wrapped an arm around Ava's waist. "You do, kind of."

Ava gave her friend an exasperated look. "But you picked it out."

Beth shrugged and took a sip of her champagne. "You know how some of those brides claim they don't care about their gorgeous maid of honor upstaging them on their wedding day? Yeah, I'm so not one of them. Just be thankful I let your size two, shiny-haired ass stand next to me at all."

Ava sighed and held out her glass for a refill. "It's the least you can do."

Beth waggled a finger. "Pour it yourself. Spilling champagne on my wedding gown at my wedding is acceptable. Charming, even. Spilling it on my dress a week before the ceremony? Trashy."

"How does everything feel?" the tailor asked, coming

over to where she'd been arguing with Beth's cousin over how low the neckline of the dress could go without risking a wardrobe malfunction.

"It feels like I won't be able to eat for a week," Beth said, resting her hand lightly against the bodice of the gown.

The severe-faced tailor nodded. "Excellent."

Beth rolled her eyes. "Yeah. Wonderful."

"And you?" the tailor asked Ava.

"I'm good," she said with a smile.

It might have been the biggest lie she'd ever told in her life. Ava was so far from good it wasn't even funny. She hadn't been good in...twelve days.

Beth's face lost some of its glow as she took in Ava's forced smile. "He still hasn't called, huh?"

Ava shook her head and she refilled her champagne flute. "No call. No text. No courier pigeon. No Twitter, no Facebook."

Beth made an angry noise. "It's his loss."

"Is it?" Ava murmured. "He's right not to trust me."

"Bullshit. You're unemployed because of him."

"No," Ava snapped, using a sharper tone than she ever had with Beth. "That's not what this is."

Beth didn't back down; her hands went to her hips, emphasizing the hourglass outline of her mermaid-style dress. "So you didn't turn down your dream job as a show of faith for your non-boyfriend."

"I turned it down because it wasn't what I wanted."

Beth's mouth dropped open.

Ava understood the sentiment. Half the time her mouth still dropped open when she had the thought. But it was true. She'd been chasing the dream for so long that she'd lost sight of why she wanted the dream. And now that it was in sight...

"I don't want to be a talking head, B," she said.

"Well okay . . . I can't say I'm going to argue. But why the change? It'd better not be because of a guy. We are so not those girls."

"It's not because of Luc," Ava said softly, watching the bubbles sneak up the side of her champagne flute. "He was the catalyst, perhaps, but not the reason."

"Not now," Beth snapped at one of her other bridesmaids before pulling Ava farther toward the corner of the room. "Candice! I said not now!"

"You're such a delicate bride," Ava murmured.

"I'm a hungry bride," Beth grumbled. "I had carrot juice for breakfast. I didn't even know that was a thing. But don't try to distract me. What changed?"

Ava shrugged. "The anchorwoman job just sounds . . . awful. The early morning, the constant need to look perfect. The high heels, all the sitting."

"Okay, I'm with you there," Beth agreed. "I've always thought it sounded like a wretched gig. I mean thousands, no *millions*, of people actually get to watch individual wrinkles develop in high definition. But that's not what I'm asking. Last month you were all about it. This month, you're not?"

Ava took a sip of her drink. Wasn't that just the question of the day?

Year.

Decade.

"I don't know," Ava said finally. "I think I realized that I wanted the prestige of it all."

Beth nodded. "I get it. And you wanted to show your Grade-A asshole of a father that you could do it without all of his string-pulling and mighty influence."

Ava choked out a little laugh. "Shouldn't I be lying on a couch for this sort of analysis, doc?"

"Well, it's true, isn't it? I've always wondered if your career ambitions weren't born out of stubbornness more than actual interest."

"Thanks for telling me," Ava muttered. "You could have saved me a couple years."

"Eh. It's a sunk cost," Beth said with a wave. "Move on."

"From therapist to economist just like that," Ava said with a snap of her fingers. "What's next?"

Beth folded her arms. "Next? Best friend. What caused the epiphany, Ava?"

Ava forced herself to meet her friend's eyes. "*He* did. And no," she said, holding up a hand when Beth's freckled face started to go irate. "I didn't give up my career for a man, so don't go all woman-hear-me-roar on my ass. I'm trying to tell you that for the first time in a long time, something mattered to me more than proving my dad wrong, more than sitting behind that desk."

"And that thing is . . . Luc Moretti."

"Yeah," Ava replied quietly. "I want Luc more than I wanted the job. Which in turn got me thinking about why I wanted the job in the first place, and I realized . . . I didn't."

Beth's shoulders slumped. "Love. It's a bitch, huh?"

"Totally."

"Do you need money?"

"No," Ava said, grabbing her friend's hands. "No, I actually got another job. Actually, it was Luc's sister who provided the introduction. Starting in two weeks I'll be employed by the *Times*."

"As in the *New York Times*?" Beth asked, face confused.

"Yup."

"Newspaper? Print journalism? Isn't that…a change?"

Ava shrugged. "Yep. But it'll allow me to do what I've always done best. Tell stories. And if I want to tell them while wearing no bra and yoga pants, they won't care."

"Can you even write?"

"Ye have little faith, *friend*. Yes, I can write. I've always written all my stories out before I turn them in to be truncated for TV media. I gave them some samples, and…they hired me."

"Does this mean your and Mihail's weird relationship is on the skids?"

Ava felt a little wave of sadness. "Yeah. He's happy for me, but he belongs behind the camera. And not the point-and-shoot kind. We'll still be friends, though."

The tailor hovered, and Beth held up a commanding bridal finger. *One more minute.*

"Ava." Beth's voice went uncharacteristically soft, quiet. "Are you going to fight for him?"

Abruptly Ava felt the now familiar lump in her throat. "I don't know how, Beth. I told him I love him and he all but kicked me out. Is it possible to get much more vulnerable?"

"Maybe he'll come to you. Maybe he just needs time."

"Yeah," Ava said, forcing a smile. "Maybe."

But she didn't believe it for a second.

CHAPTER THIRTY-SEVEN

Luc, you're being an ass, you know."

Yeah, I've been hearing that a lot lately.

Luc rolled his shoulders restlessly against the way his uniform chafed uncomfortably against his skin in the hot, crowded diner. "This coming from *you*?"

Vincent shrugged, looking perfectly comfortable in his white linen shirt. Most of the time Luc wasn't jealous that as a detective, Vincent had the option of wearing plainclothes while the rest of the family had the standard-issue uniform.

Hell, for occasions such as this, Vincent probably would have done well to wear his dress-up uniform too.

But...this was Vincent. Doing the expected was not really his thing.

Vin nodded in the direction of Anthony who was currently locked in conversation with some of the other NYPD captains. "How long until you think he starts asking us to call him 'Captain' at family dinner."

Luc snorted. "I think that's already started. I asked him if he'd used the last of the milk this morning and he refused to answer me until I used his title."

Anthony had finally gotten that damned promotion, and Luc couldn't be happier for his big brother. In true Moretti fashion, they'd opted to skip all of the fancy banquet halls for the celebratory party and opted with the place they all felt most comfortable: the Darby Diner.

Although, the evening was emotional in another way too. In addition to celebrating Anthony's promotion, they were also bidding farewell to Helen. The elderly waitress had told them last Sunday that she wanted to spend the rest of her days with her grandchildren in Houston, and the Morettis had insisted that she come to Anthony's party...as a guest. It made for a bittersweet evening. The start of one person's career. The end of another's.

A petite, angel-faced blonde appeared between Luc and Vincent, linking arms with both of them and pretending to use their body weight to "swing" like a little kid.

Luc happily complied while Vincent jerked his arm away with an irritable growl. The pretty blonde blew Luc's pissy brother a kiss, which he patently ignored.

Luc grinned, in spite of his bad mood.

Jill Henley was the darling of the NYPD. With her light blond hair, huge blue eyes, and heart-shaped face with matching dimples in each cheek, she had definitely hit the genetics jackpot. Her personality was equally compelling. She had the sort of friendly charm that had been known to coax even the roughest of suspects to start talking.

In other words, she was the perfect good cop, to Vin's bad cop.

Which was damned convenient considering they were partners.

Jill ignored Vincent as she stood there, arms linked with Luc. "What's up with your brother? Constipated again?"

Luc grinned down at her. "Which one?"

"Good point. Your big brothers must have left all the friendly genes in the womb for you to soak up."

"Disgusting," Vincent muttered.

Luc kind of agreed.

Jill's eyes sought and found Anthony. "The captain's dress uniform looks good on Anth. *Really* good."

Vincent gave her a dark look. "You hitting on my brother?"

Jill batted her eyelashes. "You jealous?"

Vincent snarled, which Jill ignored. "Hey, did you guys meet Helen's replacement?"

"Yeah," Luc said distractedly. "Megan."

"Maggie," Jill corrected. "Poor thing dropped a pitcher of iced tea. Splattered all over Anth's shoes. As you can imagine, he did that pissy, glaring thing, and she looked about ready to cry. Still, she's cute, don't you think?"

Luc searched the room until his eyes landed on the brunette woman who would be taking Helen's place at the diner. She was a far cry from the hunched, motherly figure of her predecessor. The waitress looked to be around thirty, curvy in all the right places, with a wide friendly smile. Jill was right. She was cute, in the friendly, girl-next-door kind of way. Something that had appealed to him back before his tastes had idiotically shifted from soft and sweet to sharp and ambitious.

Maggie stopped to talk to Luc's father, and Luc's eyebrows lifted at the ease in which she drew his often-crusty father into laughing conversation. Impressive.

"Right?" Jill jabbed his side. "Cute."

Luc shrugged.

"Drop it, Henley," Vincent told Jill. "*Bambino* here no

longer recognizes women whose names aren't palindromes," Vincent said.

Luc shot him the finger as Jill shifted her attention to Vincent. "What about you? Do you think she's cute?"

Vincent merely glared at Jill and walked away.

Luc shook his head as he took a sip of his rapidly warming iced tea. "I don't know how you two survive each other."

"Right?" she said, her voice unperturbed. "I'm thinking we should totally have a TV show based on us. The dark, dickwad cop and his perfect, darling partner."

Luc smiled. "The latter who is of course, unaware of her charm."

"Naturally."

"You have seen most male/female partner cop shows, right? You know how those generally end up." Luc glanced down and wiggled his eyebrows.

Jill rolled her eyes. "Yeah, trust me. That's *not* happening with your dearest brother."

"No? How about with me?"

She arched an eyebrow, knowing he was joking. "Rumor has it you're taken."

Just like that, all the mirth, all the elation about his brother's promotion, seeped out of him.

Ava. He hated that he knew exactly how many days it had been since he'd last seen her. Twelve.

Twelve of the shittiest days of his life.

Jill pointed across the diner to where his mom and sister stood talking to Nonna. "Does this have anything to do with why the women in your family aren't speaking to you?"

"Oh, Nonna speaks to me," Luc said. "This morning, in fact, I woke up to see her sitting on my bed where she sang the entire lyrics to 'I Will Always Love You.'"

Jill glanced up at him. "Dolly Parton style or Whitney style?"

He gave her a look. "Really?"

She shrugged. "There's a distinct difference. But I suppose that's not the most important question, is it?"

He remained silent, but Jill didn't take the *back off* hint.

"The more important question is how are you going to get them to start talking to you again," she said, tapping a finger against her pouty mouth.

"They'll get over it." He took a sip of iced tea, crunching moodily on one of the last remaining ice cubes.

"Maybe. But will you?"

"Don't, Jill."

She ignored him. She might as well be his sister for all she listened to him. "*Or*, you can see that maybe they're right. That maybe you're punishing this Ava woman and yourself for nothing."

"You are aware that a couple weeks from now, there's going to be a three-hour special on my life, right?"

She shrugged. "Not Ava's fault you leaped into the East River to save a Barbie."

"I didn't—"

"I know, I know, joking. But seriously, Luc...aren't you being hypocritical? You can't on one hand keep telling yourself that you've forgiven her, for what was, admittedly, a shitty move on her part, while also refusing to let her into your life."

"Cops don't make good husbands, Jill."

She patted his arm as she eased away. "Now now...who said anything about husbands?"

Shit.

Jill grinned. "Aw, *bambino*. You're worse off than I thought."

"How's my son worse off?"

Luc and Jill turned around to see Luc's father standing behind him. Tony was all smiles for Jill, although his gaze never really left Luc.

"Hey, Big T," Jill said, standing on her toes and waiting until Luc's father leaned down so she could kiss his cheek. "I was just telling your son here that he's being an idiot."

"Something you typically reserve for my other son," Tony said with a smile. "Not that I disagree. Vincent can be... difficult."

"Yeah, okay," Jill said. "We're just going to pretend that's not a *massive* understatement. But don't think you can distract me from the fact that Luc let a very good woman walk away."

Luc glared at her. "You've never even met Ava."

"Oh, and whose fault is that?"

Luc's jaw worked for several seconds as he glanced around the room, looking for someone, or something, on which to fix his gaze. But his eyes couldn't seem to focus on anything. Because the one person he wanted to be looking at was nowhere around. Because he hadn't invited her. Because she didn't *belong*.

"Jill, can we have a minute?" Tony murmured quietly.

"Sure," Jill said. She grabbed Luc's hand as she passed. Squeezed. He squeezed back.

Luc stood shoulder to shoulder with his father for several minutes in silence.

"Is she right?" Tony said finally. "About Ava? You let her walk away?"

Luc glanced at his father. "I'd have thought you'd be thrilled."

His father turned to face him. "Why the hell would you think that?"

"Maybe the fact that you were trying to warn me off of her every time we talked? I thought you'd be elated that she's out of the picture."

His father held his gaze before looking away. "I think maybe I was wrong about that."

Luc's head jerked back in surprise. His father had always been a fair, if not sometimes stubborn, man, but admitting he was wrong had never been one of his strong points.

"How so?" Luc asked warily.

His father rubbed a hand over his face. "Well, I don't know that this will translate until you have kids of your own, but when you're a parent, you can get... crazy. And you can do things you wouldn't normally, say things you shouldn't... whatever it takes to protect your own."

"I know, Dad," Luc said huskily. "You did what you did about Mike and Shayna because you thought it was *right*."

"I'm not talking about that," Tony said. "I mean, yes, I'd do that all over again, although I wouldn't have kept it a secret from you. But what I'm trying to say, Luca... being a cop's important. It's damned well defined me and this family for decades. But it's not the *most* important thing."

"Dad—"

"I take it for granted," Tony said, his voice sad. "I have your mother. And you kids. And I forget... I forget that you need space to find yours."

"Find my what?" Luc asked, even though he already knew the answer.

His father met his eyes. "Your heart. The one who makes you a better cop because she makes you a better man."

Luc swallowed, and he stared blindly at the crowd. "I think I already found her."

His father's hand landed on his shoulder. "That's what I've been trying to tell you."

CHAPTER THIRTY-EIGHT

There were flowers on the grave.

They looked less than a week old, which struck Luc as odd considering he knew Shayna's parents only came on the anniversary of her death.

He didn't blame them for it.

Jasmine Johnson had said that they didn't like the reminder that their vibrant little girl lay still and buried.

They preferred to let her live alive, laughing in their memory.

Coming to the cemetery ripped their wound wide open again, Jasmine had said.

Luc knew the feeling. He hated it.

But he also needed it.

He'd been coming the first Friday of every month since the funeral, and each time he felt like he was discovering her tiny body all over again.

Curiously, not today though.

Today he felt...at peace.

There was sadness, certainly. It was impossible to look at a gravestone celebrating a life of only seven years without feeling a pinch of remorse.

But there was something different today. The sorrow was gentler, not quite so eager to choke him in a vise.

"Hey, sweetie," he said, kneeling in front of Shayna's grave and putting a hand on the cold stone as he always did. "Looks like you've got some pretty tulips here. I always get you roses. Do you like the tulips better?"

He set the bouquet he'd bought against the slowly dying tulips.

"I bet you like both, huh? They're pink. Your mom told me it was your favorite color."

Luc stared at the flowers for a long minute. "It seems like forever since I've last been here. I know it's been a month, but...a lot's happened." Luc let out a rough laugh. "A lot."

He'd long ago stopped feeling foolish talking to a gravestone, and a little girl who had never known him.

He kept talking anyway.

"Remember how I told you last time that I was kind of famous? Well, now I'm really famous. Like, national TV famous."

His finger traced the S of her first name. "You're a little bit famous too. I talked about you. How I couldn't save you. How I wanted to more than anything."

He inhaled.

"Your brother blames me, you know. That's probably fair. I blamed me for a long time too." Luc clasped his hands in front of him as he stared at the ground. "But you know what, Shayna? The only person to blame is the guy behind bars.

And I helped put him there so he can't hurt anyone else, okay, honey?"

He pinched the bridge of his nose. "I did my best. You know that, don't you? I did my best, I swear to God."

His voice clogged. It always did when he was here.

"She knows."

Luc's head snapped around, his eyes taking in the rubber flip-flops through the haze of unshed tears, his gaze moving up long, slim legs to short-shorts, a fitted yellow tank, and...

Ava.

Slowly, he stood, his eyes looking beyond the casual clothes, beyond the fresh-faced girl-next-door look, with her ponytail and flip-flops.

His brain registered that this was a far cry from the polished, plastic Ava Sims she'd chased so desperately, but his heart registered that she was happy.

Which made *him* happy.

Luc didn't even try to fight the realization that swept over him.

There was no fanfare, no blaring horn. Just quiet understanding and acceptance that his family was right.

He was so far gone over this woman it wasn't even funny.

"Shayna knows you did your best," Ava said again, her voice quiet but not condescending.

Luc's eyes dropped to the flowers in her hands. Tulips.

"You brought the flowers," he said.

"Last week," she said, her eyes going beyond him to the small gravestone. "I wondered who the other were from. I assumed her parents."

Luc shook his head, moving aside slightly so she could move past him, setting her flowers next to his. "They...it's too hard. They carry her with them, always, but being here, her final resting place...I think it's too raw for them."

"But *you* come." She laid her tulips next to his roses, then stood so they were standing shoulder to shoulder.

"As do you." There was an unspoken question in his words. *Why? You didn't even know her.*

"I probably don't belong here." Her voice wobbled. "I used those people's pain for my own gain, Luc. And I hate myself for it. But even that's not why I'm here. It's just, a little girl died, you know? I couldn't *not* come."

He knew the feeling.

They were silent for a long while, lost in thoughts in a quiet, deserted cemetery in the Bronx.

"Mike was cremated," Luc said eventually, breaking the silence.

Ava nodded.

"Bev scattered his ashes a ways off the coast of Maine. They used to go there every summer. It was his favorite place."

At first he thought he imagined it. The soft brush of her pinkie against his. He glanced down to see her little finger reach for his, just briefly. In solidarity. In kindness.

Because despite what she thought about herself, Ava Sims was a kind woman. A *good* woman.

He saw his own pinkie brush back. Followed by his ring finger, then his third, until they were standing palm to palm, not quite holding hands, but almost. It was more intimate than holding hands, somehow. More intimate even than kissing.

"I've missed you," he heard himself say.

Her hand twitched as her breath quickened a little, then it slowed, as though she forced herself not to react.

She said nothing.

Why should she? He'd all but planted his boot on her ass and kicked her out the door when she'd told him that she loved him.

Luc closed his eyes.

This woman loved him. And he'd thrown it back at her like a fucking grenade.

And not because he didn't love her back.

He did.

Desperately.

It was strange, how one could spend months…years… believing one thing with every fiber of one's being, only to have your entire paradigm changed in a moment.

This was that moment.

Luc was still more aware than ever that this could be *his* grave that Ava would one day be bringing flowers to. Although hopefully not pink tulips.

But on the other hand…

He loved her. He loved her too much to let her go.

"Sims."

Her fingers flinched as though she wanted to jerk her hand away, but his fingers grasped at hers, clenching them, maybe just a little bit desperately. Okay, a *lot* desperately.

He pulled her around to face him. "Is it creepy that I'm about to do this in a cemetery?"

Ava licked her lips. "Do what?"

Luc swallowed and reached slowly for her other hand. "Not so long ago, the two of us were on the same page about relationships. They weren't for us."

"Right." The word was bland, calm, betraying nothing.

"That night, at my house…you…" Luc cleared his throat. In all of his family's constant interfering over the past couple of weeks, how had nobody told him how hard this was going to be?

"That night at my house," he continued, "you made it seem, like maybe…maybe you'd changed your mind about wanting a relationship."

Ava gave a soft, sad laugh. "I wasn't looking for a diamond ring and babies, Luc."

Luc lifted his chin to meet her eyes. "What if I told you I was?"

She blinked but said nothing, and Luc's hands squeezed on hers, nervous as hell as he moved even closer.

"Look, Sims, I'm not proposing. I don't want to freak you out, and I know you're probably having second thoughts about wanting anything to do with me after the way I let you leave that day, but Sims…Sims…letting you leave was the dumbest thing I've ever done. Pushing you away because of what happened to Mike, well that was the most cowardly thing I've ever done."

God he was bad at this.

He drew her even closer, slowly lifting a hand to her face. "See, the thing is, Sims, you *know* me. You know me like nobody else does. I've never been America's Hero to you. I haven't even been *Officer Moretti* to you, and that used to make me crazy, because I thought that being a cop is who I was."

Her eyes watered, and he pressed on, his other hand moving up so he was cradling her head in his hands. "I love being a cop, but I love you more. I'd give up being everybody else's hero, if you'll just let me be yours. Please, Sims."

He searched her face, his heart kicking into overdrive when he saw the doubt and fear there. She was going to say no. He was too late.

So Luc did the last thing he could think of. He begged the only way he knew how.

He rested his forehead against hers, his thumbs brushing lightly over her cheeks as he closed his eyes and pleaded. "*Ava.*"

The touch was so light that he thought he imagined it at first, but then there was no mistaking her hands coming up to his arms, her fingers encircling his wrists.

Scared to hope, he opened his eyes.

She was smiling.

"You called me Ava." Her voice was husky.

"I've called you Ava before."

She shook her head. "No."

He hadn't?

"I'm saying it now," he said, dipping his knees just slightly so they were at eye level. "I love you, Ava. And I'm not saying things are going to be easy, but I'd rather go hard with you than easy alone."

She brushed her fingers gently over his mouth and he kissed them.

"So," he said, voice rough. "I'm assuming based on the fact that you're not slapping me or walking away that I've at least got a chance, but help a guy out here."

His hands moved down to her back, clutching at her, maybe just a little desperately. He couldn't help it. She mattered too much. *Please love me back.*

Slowly, she leaned in, pressing her mouth to his. "I love you too. And I don't want you to be my hero. I just want you to be *mine.*"

"Thank God," he muttered, yanking her closer and crushing his mouth to hers.

Her fingers tangled in his hair, and she kissed him back,

hot and hungry for several seconds before yanking her head away.

"Okay, the *tender* scene in the cemetery is one thing, but this..."

"Yeah, this is...let's not tell anyone."

"Definitely not," she agreed.

He turned his head slightly, looking down at the pink flowers. "Do you think she's looking down on us?"

"Nah," Ava said, resting her cheek against his chest. "I'm one hundred percent sure that Shayna is somewhere enjoying an endless summer, eating strawberry ice cream, and playing with the biggest dollhouse she's ever seen."

"I hope so," he said quietly.

Ava took his hand, pulled him gently away. "Buy me breakfast?"

"That's right, you're unemployed now," he said as he followed her down the hill toward the subway. "I'll probably be buying everything. Hope you like street meat."

"Oh, about the job thing—"

Ava linked her fingers in his and started to tell him all about her new job offer with the *New York Times*. Luc mostly listened, but he couldn't resist sneaking a glance over his shoulder.

He wasn't the sentimental type to imagine he saw the fluttering of angel wings or anything.

But he could have sworn he heard the sound of a little girl's laughter...

It takes a sweet waitress named Maggie to catch a crook—and capture the heart of Luc's brother, Captain Anthony Morretti—in the next sizzling novel of New York's Finest...

Please see the next page for a preview of

STEAL ME.

CHAPTER ONE

For Captain Anthony Moretti, three things in life were sacred:

(1) Family.

(2) The NYPD.

(3) The New York Yankees.

And on this breezy, September Sunday morning, two out of these three things were making him crazy. Not in the good way.

"What do you mean, you don't want to talk about it?" his father barked, leaning across the table to help himself to one of Anthony's pieces of bacon.

Maria Moretti's hand was deft and practiced—the mark of a mother of five—as she swiftly swatted the bacon out of her husband's fingers. "The doctor said you were supposed to take it easy on the bacon!"

"I *am* taking it easy. This is Anthony's bacon," Tony clarified, rubbing the back of his hand.

"Is it?" Anthony muttered, glancing at the now empty plate. "I don't seem to remember actually getting to eat any of it."

His youngest brother stabbed a piece of fruit with his fork and waved it in Anthony's face. "Cantaloupe?"

Anthony gave Luc a withering look. He could appreciate that his baby brother felt man enough to get a side of fruit with his Sunday brunch, but Anth would stick to potatoes and fatty pig products, thanks very much.

"I think I'm going to hurl," his other brother, Vincent, said to no one. "Shouldn't have gotten the side of pancakes. Too old for this shit."

Anthony felt the beginnings of a headache.

Item number one on his priority list (family) was also his number one cause of his frequent *please, God, take me away to a deserted tropical island* prayer.

But there was no tropical island. Just the same old shit.

For every one of Anthony's thirty-six years, Sundays had looked exactly the same. All the Morettis filed obediently into their pew at St. Ignatius Loyola Church on the Upper East Side of Manhattan for ten o'clock Mass.

Breakfast always followed, always at the same diner, although the name had changed a handful of times over the year.

The sign out front currently read *The Darby Diner*, named after... nobody knew.

But the Morettis had never cared what it was called. Or why it was called that. As long as the coffee was hot, the hash browns crispy, and the breakfast meats plentiful, they were happy.

Granted, the greasy-spoon food of the Darby Diner was a far cry from the Morettis' usual fare of home-cooked Italian meals, but Anthony was pretty sure they all secretly loved the weekly foray into pure Americana cuisine. Even his mother didn't seem to mind (much) so long as her family was all together.

"So what did you mean, you don't want to talk about it?" Tony Moretti repeated, glancing down at Anthony's plate and scowling to see the bacon supply completely depleted.

Anthony scooped a mouthful of Swiss cheese omelet into his mouth before sitting back and reaching for his coffee. "It means that Ma doesn't like cop talk at the table."

"*Riiiiight*," Elena Moretti said from Anthony's left side. "Because you guys *always* respect Mom's no-cop-talk rule."

Anth took another sip of coffee and exchanged a look and a shrug with Luc across the table.

Their sister made a good point.

In a family where four out of five siblings were living in New York, and three out of *those* four were with the NYPD, cop talk was likely.

And when the family patriarch was the recently retired police commissioner?

Cop talk wasn't just probable, it was *inevitable*.

Still, it was worth a shot to throw up his mother's token rule of "no cop talk." Especially when he didn't want to talk.

About any of it.

It had been a long time since he'd been the one in the hot seat, and he wasn't at all sure that he cared for it.

Scratch that. He was sure.

He *hated* it.

But his father could be like a dog with a bone when it came to his sons' careers. And today, like it or not, it was Anthony under the microscope.

He surrendered to the inevitable.

"Dad, I told you. It'll get handled." He went for another sip of coffee, only to find his cup was empty. Diner *fail*.

He scanned the dining room for the waitress, partially because he wanted more coffee, partially because he wanted a distraction. Partially because—

"You've been saying it'll get *handled* for weeks," Tony said, refusing to let the matter drop.

"Yeah, *Captain*. You've been saying that for weeks." This from Anthony's other brother, Vincent. Two years younger than Anth, Vin was a homicide detective and the most irritable and irreverent member of the family. And the one least likely to kiss Anth's ass.

If Anthony was totally honest, he was pretty sure that most of his younger siblings respected him, not only because he was the highest ranking active family member, but simply because he was the oldest. He was the one they'd come to when they needed to hide that broken vase from Mom, or when they were scared to death to tell Dad about that D in chemistry, or in the case of his brothers, when it was time to learn their way around the female anatomy.

But Vincent didn't respect anyone. Not even big brother. Vin was always the first to jump at the chance to gently mock Anthony's status as captain.

A title that had been hard-earned, and still felt new. As though it could be ripped away at any time.

Which was *exactly* the reason his father was on his ass right now. Anthony had passed his captain's test three months ago and had every intention of climbing the ladder all the way to the top. The *very* top.

It was a path Anth had never questioned. A path that up until recently, had been remarkably smooth.

And then...

And then *Smiley* had happened.

"Well surely you've got a couple leads to go on," Tony said, leaning forward and fixing Anthony with a steady look.

Anthony looked right back, hoping the bold gaze would counteract the hard truth. *That Anth didn't have a damn clue who or where Smiley was.*

For the past two months—the majority of Anthony's tenure as captain of the twentieth precinct—the Upper West Side had been plagued by a smug and relentless burglar.

Nickname? *Smiley.* Courtesy of the idiotic yellow smiley-face sticker he left at each of his hits.

The plus side, if there was one, was that Smiley hadn't proven dangerous. If it had been a *violent* criminal on the loose, Anth's ass would have been on the line weeks ago.

But still. It had been eight weeks since Smiley first hit, and the man was getting bolder, hitting three brownstones last week alone.

And Anth wasn't even close to catching him. Neither was anyone else in the department. Hence why number two on his life priorities—the NYPD—was making him crazy recently.

"We'll get him," Anthony said curtly, referring to Smiley.

"You'd better," Tony said. "The press has gotten a hold of it. It'll only get bigger from here."

"Yeah, thanks for the reminder," Anthony muttered. He picked up his coffee cup again. Still empty. "Damn it. Where the *hell* is what's-her-name? Is it too much to ask to get some damned coffee around here?"

"Now there's a good plan," his sister mused. "Blame poor Maggie because you can't catch a pip-squeak cat burglar."

As if on cue, *poor Maggie* appeared at their table, coffee-pot in hand.

"I'm so sorry," the pretty waitress said, a little breathless. "You all must have been waiting ages for more coffee."

Anthony rolled his eyes, even as he snuck a glance at her. Her friendly smile was meant to hide the fact that she was frazzled, and for most of her customers, that apologetic, dimpled smile probably worked.

It was a damned good look on any woman, but especially her.

Maggie Walker had become their default waitress at the diner back when their old waitress Helen had retired. And while he missed Helen and her too-strong floral perfume, he had to admit that Maggie was better to look at.

She had a wholesome, girl-next-door look that appealed to him mightily. Brown hair that was always on the verge of slipping out of its ponytail, wide, compelling green eyes that made you want to unload all your darkest secrets.

Curvy. Hips that were exactly right, breasts that were even better.

And then there was that smile. It managed to be both shy and friendly, which was handy because he was betting it was very hard for even the most impatient customers to get annoyed at her.

But Anth didn't buy the exhausted, doing-my-best routine, and seeing as she was dealing with an entire table of observant cops, he was betting the rest of his family wouldn't buy it either.

Then Luc leaned forward and gave Maggie an easy grin. "Don't even worry about it, Mags. Didn't even notice I was running low!"

He stared at his brother. Okay. So maybe the family *bambino* could be fooled by pretty Maggie.

He rolled his eyes as Luc shoved his mug toward the edge of the table so Maggie wouldn't have to reach as far.

Then he watched in utter dismay as Vincent did the same. Vincent, who'd practically devoted his life to being perverse, was trying to make life easier for their inept waitress.

Un-fucking-believable.

Anthony was so busy trying to figure out what about the frazzled waitress turned his brothers into a bunch of softies that he didn't think to move his own mug to be more convenient, and Maggie had to lean all the way in to top off his cup.

It was a feat that their *old* waitress could have handled readily, but Helen had retired months ago and for reasons that Luc didn't understand, the rest of the Moretti family had embraced Maggie as Helen's replacement.

Anthony didn't realize that his mug had overflowed until scalding coffee dripped onto his thigh.

"Son of a—"

He caught himself before he could finish the expletive, grabbing a large handful of napkins from the silver dispenser and trying to soak up the puddle of coffee on his jeans before it burned his skin.

"Nice, Anth," Elena said, tossing another bunch of napkins at him. Like this was *his* fault.

"Oh my god," Maggie said, her voice horrified. "I'm *so* sorry, Officer…"

"It's Captain," he snapped, his eyes flicking up and meeting hers.

Silence descended over the table until Vincent muttered *douche bag* around a coughing fit.

But Anthony refused to feel chagrined. The woman had waited on the family every Sunday for weeks; one would think she could get his title right. To say nothing of mastering the art of pouring coffee.

Her green eyes flicked downward before she turned away with promises to bring back a rag.

He watched her trim figure for only a second before glancing down at his lap. A rag wouldn't do shit. He now had a huge brown stain on his jeans.

And this wasn't the first time.

Last week, it had been ketchup on his shirt. Maggie had been clearing plates, and a chunk of ketchup-covered hash browns from Vin's plate had found its way onto Anth.

The week before *that*, it was a grease stain from a rogue piece of bacon that his father had somehow missed.

And it was always the same, oh-my-gosh-I'm-so-sorry routine, and his family would lament the unfortunate "accident" and tell Maggie not to worry about it, even though none of them had basically tripled their laundry efforts since Maggie had taken over their Sunday brunch routine.

"I don't know why you always have to do that," Elena snapped at him.

He gave his little sister a dark look. Elena was basically a female version of Luc. Dark brown hair, perfectly proportioned features, and bright blue eyes. His siblings' good looks had worked very well for them with the opposite sex, but with their brother? Not so much.

"I didn't do anything," he snapped.

His mother—his own *mother*—gave him a scolding look. "You make Maggie nervous, dear. All that glowering."

"Wait, sorry, hold up," Anth said, abandoning the futile

effort of blotting coffee from his crotch. "It's *my* fault that the incompetent woman can't do even the most basic requirements of her job?"

A startled gasp came from the head of the table, and too late—*way* too late—Anth realized that Maggie had reappeared with a clean white rag and what seemed to be a full cup of ice.

"I thought...I wanted to make sure it didn't burn your skin," she told him brightly.

To her credit, her voice didn't wobble, and her eyes didn't water, but damned if she didn't look like she wanted to cry, just a little.

Shit.

"I'm fine," he muttered.

"Thank you, sweetie," Tony said kindly, taking the rag and ice from Maggie. "Maybe just the check when you get a chance."

"Of course. And really, I'm so sorry," she said, not quite glancing at Anthony. "You'll send me the dry-cleaning bill, right?"

"He'll do no such thing," his mother said firmly, reaching across her husband to grab Maggie's hand. "I can get any stain out of any fabric. I'll take care of it."

"You hear that, Anth?" Luc said. "Mommy's going to wash your pants for you!"

Anth shot his brother the bird, wishing his brother's girlfriend had tagged along for breakfast today. Luc was always much more pleasant when Ava Sims was around. He devoted most of his time figuring out ways to feel up the pretty journalist rather than giving Anthony grief.

"I just can't believe Mags called you *Officer*," Vincent said in a sham reverent tone. "I don't know how she missed the nine hundred and forty two reminders that you're a captain now."

"Well she damn well should remember," he muttered. "Is anyone else remembering that she spilled iced tea all over me at my coronation party?"

"She spilled it on your *shoes*," Elena said. "Which were black."

"Still," Anth said, glancing around the room this time to make sure she wasn't within earshot. "I don't know why we have to act like she's a new member of the family when she can't seem to go a single Sunday without spilling somebody's breakfast on me. It can't be an accident *every* time."

"Maybe she wants to get your attention. Your humble, enchanting personality is *so* charming," Maria Moretti muttered into her coffee cup.

Anth looked at his mother. "Et tu, Brute?"

His mom winked.

And then his dad leaned back in the booth, folded his arms, and glared at his oldest son. "So tell me again what you're doing to close in on this Smiley character."

"Oh my God, he's like a dog with a bone!" Elena said, throwing her arms up in exasperation before turning her attention back to her cell phone. "Also, is Nonna texting anyone else? I've been getting mucus reports every five minutes."

"Yes," everyone replied at once.

"She just sent me a Wikipedia link on phlegm," Vincent grumbled.

To say that his grandmother had been upset to miss brunch because of a lingering head cold was an understatement. She'd been punishing them all with updates on her illness.

Anthony glanced at his watch and mentally counted the minutes until he could relax with a beer and watch the Yankees game.

Of the three sacred things in his life, the New York Yankees had always been a *very* distant third to family and the Department.

But lately? It was a rather close call.

Fall in Love with Forever Romance

DRAGON FALL
by Katie MacAlister

New York Times bestseller Katie MacAlister returns to her fan-favorite paranormal series. To ensure the survival of his fellow dragons, Kostya needs a mate of true heart and soul before it's too late.

FRISK ME
by Lauren Layne

USA Today bestselling author Lauren Layne brings us the first book in her New York's Finest series. Journalist Ava Sims may be the only woman in NYC who isn't in love with the city's newly minted hero Officer Luc Moretti. That's why she's going after the real story—to find out about the man behind the badge. But the more time she spends around Luc, the more she has to admit there's something about a man in uniform…and she can't wait to get him out of his.

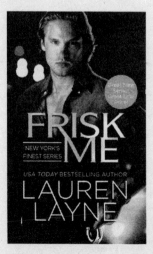

Fall in Love with Forever Romance

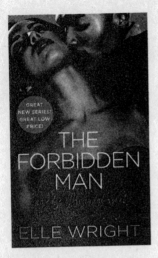

THE FORBIDDEN MAN
by Elle Wright

Sydney Williams has forgiven her fiancé, Den, more times than she can count. But his latest betrayal just days before their wedding is too big to ignore. Shocking her friends and family, she walks out on her fiancé... and into the arms of his brother, Morgan. But is their love only a fling or built to last?

THE BLIND
by Shelley Coriell

When art imitates death... As part of the FBI's elite Apostles team, bomb and weapons specialist Evie Jimenez knows playing it safe is *not* an option. Especially when tracking a serial killer. Billionaire philanthropist and art expert Jack Elliott never imagined the instant heat for the fiery Evie would explode his cool and cautious world. But as Evie and Jack get closer to the killer's endgame, they will learn that safety and control are all illusions. For their quarry has set his sight on *Evie* for his final masterpiece...

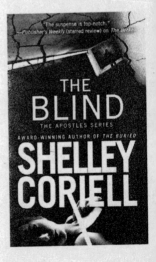

Fall in Love with Forever Romance

THE LEGACY OF COPPER CREEK
by R. C. Ryan

In the *New York Times* best-selling tradition of Linda Lael Miller and Diana Palmer comes the final book in R. C. Ryan's Copper Creek series. When a snowstorm forces together the sexy Whit Mackenzie and the heartbroken Cara Walton, sparks fly. But can Whit show Cara how to love again?

AND THEN HE KISSED ME
by Kim Amos

Bad-boy biker Kieran Callaghan already broke Audrey Tanner's heart once. So what's she supposed to do when she finds out he's her boss—and that he's sexier than ever? Fans of Kristan Higgins, Jill Shalvis, and Lori Wilde will love this second book in the White Pine, Minnesota series.

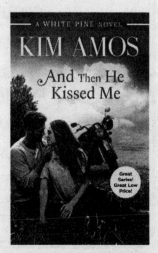

VISIT US ONLINE AT

WWW.HACHETTEBOOKGROUP.COM

FEATURES:

OPENBOOK BROWSE AND
SEARCH EXCERPTS
•
AUDIOBOOK EXCERPTS AND PODCASTS
•
AUTHOR ARTICLES AND INTERVIEWS
•
BESTSELLER AND PUBLISHING
GROUP NEWS
•
SIGN UP FOR E-NEWSLETTERS
•
AUTHOR APPEARANCES AND TOUR
INFORMATION
•
SOCIAL MEDIA FEEDS AND WIDGETS
•
DOWNLOAD FREE APPS

BOOKMARK HACHETTE BOOK GROUP
@ WWW.HACHETTEBOOKGROUP.COM